A Thought of Honour

Rape of the Fair Country

Robe of Honour

THE RACE OF THE TIGER

THE
Race of the Tiger

A NOVEL BY
Alexander Cordell

1963

Doubleday & Company, Inc.

Garden City, New York

With the exception of actual historical personages, the characters are entirely the product of the author's imagination and have no relation to any person in real life.

LIBRARY OF CONGRESS CATALOG CARD NUMBER 63–12169
COPYRIGHT © 1963 BY G. A. GRABER
ALL RIGHTS RESERVED
PRINTED IN THE UNITED STATES OF AMERICA
FIRST EDITION

For Clifford Tucker

Bring not grey Europe's silk or gems—
A candid soul is ample dowry,
Where Freedom laughs at diadems
Beside the thunder-toned Missouri.
Come! Let us fly to Freedom's sky,
Where love alone has power to bind us.
There honoured live, lamented die,
And leave a spotless name behind us.

THE RACE OF THE TIGER

Connemara

It was on my fifteenth birthday, I remember, when Ma started her pains with Melody, the next child, which put the place upside down and me especially. I knew the date of the Beast Cromwell's landing, I could recite part of the Act of Union with the best Irish historian, but I didn't know much about the delivering.

"She shouldn't be producing yet," I said to Karen, my big sister. "She said she was due in June and this is the middle of April."

"She'll produce when she pleases," said Karen. "Go and fetch water."

I picked up the bucket. "D'you think she's got the date wrong?" I asked.

"You are talking of things you don't understand," said Karen. "Away with that bucket and set it on the fire."

"It could be the gripe," I said. "It was a pretty strong rabbit she had last night and she did herself well on it. Is the pain bad with her?"

"I'll tell you one day," said Karen. "Where's Hosea?"

"Down in Galway with the cans and pegs," I replied. "And I'm away up the hill for a hare, for a labouring woman needs feeding."

"Ach, you sweet thing," said Karen, and kissed me. "I'm worried to death, you see. For your mother's inclined to the breech-birth. We should be setting the caravan towards home, for Patsy O'Toole's the best turning woman in Connemara."

This set me faster across the meadow to the well, for I knew even less about the breech-birth. Half-way across it I saw the Turvey caravan and Barney, our gipsy neighbour, sitting in the ditch nearby with his feet up. Back teeth awash, poaching cap over his eyes, he was snoring in fumbles, dreaming of the inns of Galway, so I lowered the bucket and fished out my spoon. Mind, I've spooned out easier ones than Barney Turvey, for he was a man most sensitive

1

to heat and cold, and a cold spoon on the thigh could bring him wide awake and roaring. Sitting in the ditch beside him I lightened him by twopence. With the spoon well down into his pocket I was fishing for a sixpence when Karen howled like a dog on the other side of the meadow.

"Jess O'Hara!"

She was standing by our caravan with her red hair flying out in a wind from the sea, and the language she gave me was enough to singe Satan.

"Bless me soul to hell!" she cried, at last. "Is there any justice? There's me relieving yer mother and not a pint of hot water between here and County Clare. Where the devil have you been?"

"Spooning out the Turveys."

She threw up her hands. "Och, the O'Haras are plagued with thieves and pugilists. And I'll be breaking the back of that big oaf Hosea when he lands home. There's me been working since cockcrow while he's leaping beds with the trollops of Galway."

"He is not," I answered sharp. "He's fist-fighting, for money."

"Then where's Michael?"

"Away somewhere with the Fighting Irishmen."

Hands on hips, she surveyed me, foot tapping. "And this is what I'm landed with—three useless gunks of brothers."

"How's Ma?" I asked, to sweeten her.

"The poor soul's wracked. Fetch that water this minute or I'll damned fry you, big as you are." She kicked the bonfire into a blaze and just then the window of our caravan went back and Ma's head appeared.

"Karen, is that water coming to the boil?" she shouted.

"It'll need a couple of minutes, Ma," I shouted back.

"Right," she cried. "Come in here, Karen, and help me strip the beds for I'm starting the monthly wash."

"What about your labouring?"

"Changed me mind," said Ma. "Dear God, I'd give me soul to lay hands on himself yer father."

The hills above the caravan field were bright in sunlight that April evening, the grasses spear-tipped with diamonds of rain below the gallows where Tim Rooney was dangling, the first of the grain-raiders to hang in 1875, poor soul.

There is a loneliness about a hanging man; swinging black against stars in the music of chains; fluttering his rags in the breeze of morning, dew dropping cold on a gaunt, tarred face. Rosa Turvey, Barney's daughter, was sitting with her back to the gallows, a queer old place for a girl. I knocked up my cap.

" 'Evening, Rosa Turvey."

" 'Evenin', Jess O'Hara."

Her knees, I remember, were brown against the ragged hem of her dress. Never seen knees like Rosa Turvey's before—like wrinkled crab-apples in winter and as smooth as brown ivory in summer, and there was a dark sweetness in her gipsy glance that butterflied the stomach. She said:

"You come up to meet me?"

"Got enough women back home."

"Is it true you're walking out a girl from Galway, Jess O'Hara?"

"If I answer that you'll be as wise as me," I replied.

"Not even a whistle for me, then? Your big brother Hosea whistles my big sister Rachel."

"I'm whistling for a hare," I said, and jerked my thumb. "Try giving the eye to Tim Rooney up there, girl, you'll get more from him than me."

"Pig."

"You're welcome," and I went over the hill to the glade.

There was a hum of honey-bees here and a shine of blackbirds where the sun shafted beams. Five hares were kicking up their legs and nudging each other as I came, for there's nothing so daft as a March hare in April. Ears rose behind hillocks, the long grass waved to cloven feet. Taking off my coat I put it in the middle of the glade, not the least interested in hares, then walked round it in circles, every circle bringing me nearer to the hillocks. Petrified by curiosity, they sat. Wandering up I took my pick of a big fella, belted his ear, and took him up the hill to the gallows.

"Can I see the hare, Jess O'Hara?" asked Rosa.

"Unless you're blind," I answered. "I'm away home to cook me

3

mother's supper—would you have me tarry with you, and her comin' to labour?"

"Then go to hell," she whispered, fuming.

"Pull your dress down, woman. D'you think you're the only decent legs in Galway?"

The Turveys, like us, were a tinkering family, and wherever we O'Haras went they followed, though the quality of their cans didn't match ours. They were the spawn of the devil, said Karen, with Rachel fishing for Hosea, Rosa winking at me, and Barney, their Pa giving our mother the eye from the other side of the meadow.

"Trash gipsies," said Karen now, when I got back to the bonfire. "Didn't I see that Rosa going up Rooney's Hill just now?"

I threw down the hare. "You did. And is there a law against it?"

"There's not, but d'you mind explaining where you've been for the last ten minutes?"

"Hunting this hare," I said.

"Are you sure you haven't been rolling that Rosa?"

I stared at her. "Has your brain gone soft? It'd take me ten minutes to get her horizontal—do I work like bloody lightning?"

"No bad language," said Karen, her finger up. "You keep that nose off Rosa's or I'm nipping off the end of it. It's bad enough to have that fool Hosea moonlighting with Rachel Turvey—I'm not having two in the family." She flung more wood on the fire and shot me daggers from her dark, slanted eyes.

Ma came squeezing through the door then, barged about with washing, stripped it over the hedges, and pegged it on the lines and then set herself down beside the fire in grunts and wheezes.

"There's me sweet wee Jess," said she, patting me. "It's a fine big hare indeed for me supper."

"And eat it easy," I said, "the last one fetched the wind."

"Did you cross yourself when you passed Tim Rooney, boy?"

I nodded, and she sighed. "Ach, there's no justice. There's better man on ropes than on the soles of their feet these days. Where's my big son, Hosea?"

Karen was shaving at pegs. I glanced at her and she looked away.

Sweat was on my mother's face as she peeled the hare. Her black hair was tousled, her face as a hatchet of ugliness, but there was a

4

softness in her for sons. Now she was great in the chest and stomach and carrying enough milk for the famines of Connemara. I watched, loving her.

"Will nobody answer me? Where's me darlin' son?"

"Down in Galway with the cans," I replied, and Karen looked at the stars.

"For the brawling and drinking, eh?" said Ma, and sighed deep in her throat. "Ah, Jess, listen. The drink is the leaven of malice and wickedness. There's some pretty long gullets hanging in taprooms in our family, and Hosea's got his share—taking after himself your father. D'you see the spite it brings to women?" She flung the entrails on the fire. "So I mated for a girl this time, for I'm tired of hairy chests and fists." She smiled. "Though he's a fine big boy, my Hosea, save for the drinking and women."

Karen said, "Rachel Turvey will settle him, Ma."

"He wouldn't give that bitch a second look!"

"Would he not? Haven't you heard him say that any woman's worth a fumble after a quart of Galway porter, and he's winking at Rachel dead sober."

"It's a lie!" I said.

"So it's a lie, is it? Haven't you seen the flouncy swing to her lately? The fella's off his food, too, haven't you noticed?"

I hadn't. He was sinking enough these days to drop twin elephants.

Ma whispered at the fire, "God save us. I'd rather see him filling a house with screechin' children than hunting the taverns for winsome witches like Rachel Turvey." She glanced up. Karen had a leg in the air, drawing on a long black stocking and tying it at the thigh with a bright, red garter.

"Are you away, then?" asked Ma.

"Aye, for the dancing," replied Karen.

I said, "We can't leave Ma—not till Hosea gets back, or Michael."

"If we wait for Hosea or Michael we'll be waiting a fortnight."

"We're not leavin' Ma," I repeated.

"Ach, away to your dancing," said my mother. "The Connemara dancers haven't missed an evening market from Bantry to Wicklow

—there's good money to be earned, and we need it. If you see either of your brothers tell them I'm waiting for them."

"Mike's down with the Fighting Irishmen," said Karen, "he'll not be back till the dawn." She went to the caravan and came back in the scarlet dress she wore for her dancing, and I sensed the itch in her as she tossed me my fiddle. Ma drew me aside, whispering:

"It's a big hunting moon tonight, Jess, so keep her off the fellas, remember," and she kissed me. "Children, children," she mumbled to herself, "it's enough to kill a labouring woman."

Barney Turvey was squatting outside his caravan, jaws champing on his clay; behind him, in a gleam of caravan brass, stood Rachel and Rosa, watchful as ever.

"Don't spare them a glance," hissed Karen as we passed. Down the field we went and through the bulging, dusky streets of Galway and the Spanish Arch to the sea.

CHAPTER 2

Here, beyond the quay, the pennants of the transportation hulks were as stiff as bars in the wind and the coffin-ships bound for America rolled and heaved at their moorings in the thump of the Atlantic breakers. Fine ladies and gentlemen were gathered here for the evening market, treading daintily among the clogs of herring-wives, whose hands were flashing among circling knives and flinging bright bodies into baskets. The wind was sweet with the smells of Galway, of sweat and perfume, brine and entrails, and the reddened belly of the sea heaved at blood-stained gulls wheeling in flight. Urchins, rags fluttering, barged among the crowd; dandies doffed their hats to stately ladies. Shawled peasants drooped by, scarecrowed by hunger, chesty sailors strutted by, black-jerseyed and pigtailed. Bow-legged and glassy-eyed, the riff-raff of the taverns lurched from one quart to another in their porter-sweating dreams of naked barmaids. And the rumbling bellies of the over-fed pressed the bulging bellies of the starving, silk rubbing rags in a bedlam of life.

"It's a fine big crowd," said Karen, "it'll be worth half a sovereign."

Lorgnettes went up, shawls were pulled aside as we went into the crowd. With my fiddle under my arm I followed Karen, watching the bed-stares of the dandies and the old men craning their necks as animals scenting a mate. For the wind had got her red hair now and was flinging it about her naked shoulders. She winked at me and I chinned my fiddle. Laughing, chattering, the people formed a circle about us. Head bowed, Karen stood in the middle of it, slowly raising her skirt; higher, higher, and showed her red garters. I took a swing at the fiddle and she linked her hands above her head, slowly pirouetting; now spinning, flaring her skirt. I scraped out the lilt of the reel and she began to dance. Roars of joy from the people now as a beefy sailor leaped in beside her,

fisting the air, his clogs clattering. Next came a buxom herring-wife
with a fish in each hand, shrieking with delight, her great breasts
shaking. And soon the quay was alive with dancers. Other fiddlers
got the tune now, pennies were rolling and chinking and the
urchins scrambling after them, and I worked like a black booting
them out of it. With my hands full of coins I rose and came face to
face with my brother Michael. Gripping me, he pulled me out of
the crowd.

"Did you have to choose tonight?" he whispered. There was a
trembling in him as he looked towards the Spanish Arch.

"Ma sent us dancing," I said.

"Quick, Jess, take Karen home, there's going to be trouble."

"If there's trouble coming I'm going to be in it, man."

Fine and arrogant he looked standing there watching the Arch;
two years older than me, but a man. "Right," he whispered, "she
takes her chance, and you do, too, you brat. Where's Hosea?"

"He's fist-fighting in Ennis," I said, and his eyes glowed in his
face.

"There's a fine patriot," he breathed, and left me, shouldering
his way through the crowd. Not all the men were dancing, I noticed: some were standing stiff-legged, as men with cudgels down
their trousers, and all were turned to the Spanish Arch. Then a
woman screamed faintly from the town, and the dancers faltered.
Again she screamed, louder, and the fiddles scraped into discord,
and stopped. The crowd froze into immobility as from the Spanish
Arch came the clank of manacles and the slither of naked feet.
Then Redcoats spilled on to the quay in a gush of colour and
brass, and between their ranks came the prisoners.

The felons came four abreast, and all were women. With their
arms crossed before them, some chained, some roped, they walked
barefooted to the transportation ship. Nearer, nearer they came,
and the crowd was muttering. Sailors were spitting on their hands,
fish-wives rolling up their sleeves. And suddenly the people near
the Arch went down on their knees, forming a block between the
prisoners and the ship. Uncertain, the Redcoats hesitated, staring
down, and the people stared back; like tomcats meeting on a wall.

It was then that I saw Beth O'Shea.

8

Roped by the wrists she was drooping beside a tattered matron. The shadows were deep in her cheeks, I remember, her shoulders were bare and wealed with beatings. Then a command rang out and the soldiers began to force a path, callously thumping with their muskets, but their slanting eyes betrayed their fear as they neared me, for the herring-women were around them now and knives were appearing. I saw Michael's dark head among the crowd and the Redcoat beside him suddenly upended. Bedlam! One moment market-day, next a riot. Helmets were coming off and cudgels coming down, muskets waving, knives flashing, a mêlée of commands and shrieks, a fine old Irish brawl. Outnumbered ten to one the soldiers panicked, sinking in a scramble of arms and legs, with Karen quickly in the thick of it with a clog in her hand, tipping off helmets and cracking English skulls. I was after her in an instant.

"Come out of it, woman!"

"Ach, away!" she cried. "It's the best fight I've seen since the Tipperary riots," and she went round stamping on fingers and filling the air with shrieks.

I ducked a swing from a soldier, flattened him into the crowd and gripped Karen, but she fought me off. Over my shoulder I saw the gang-plank of the prison ship rear up and crash and the great square rig above it heel against the sky. Hawsers were splashing into the sea, halyards and strainers snapping as the ship came loose from her bollards. Lurching before the wind she was sweeping fishing-boats from their moorings and crashing against the jetties. Sensing victory, the crowd bit deeper into the soldiers in cries of victory and forced them to the edge of the quay. Arms flailing, shouting, the Redcoats floundered into the sea as Michael and his comrades got among them.

"Right," I shouted, "now run!" and I dragged Karen to the shelter of a wall.

"And I'm ready," she gasped, "for I've just caught a fella's boot. Have we won, Jess?"

"Run!" I shrieked, and watched her gallop for the Spanish Arch, skirts up, hair streaming. Flattened against the wall I looked for Beth O'Shea.

Men and women were dashing past me towing freed prisoners. A priest checked his headlong flight to snatch at a child, and ran with her, his gown billowing. Fish-wives had their thick arms around girls, sailors were dragging at grandmas. Diving among them I scrambled through a tangle of ropes to the edge of the quay where Beth O'Shea was kneeling, gripping a capstan.

"Come on!" I shouted, and seized her wrist, but she arched her back, feet skidding.

"Run, girl, run!" called the priest, dashing past us, and she came instantly. And the last thing I saw of the quay was the Fighting Irishmen flooding through the Arch with the crowd helter-skelter behind them. Arms and cudgels littered the flag-stones, baskets were overturned and herrings flapping to the thieving descent of the gulls.

"Quick," I whispered, and we ran on, snatching at breath till the cottages of Galway thinned and the fields rose up through the night mist. On the track that led to the caravans we rested. Panting, Beth turned on her elbow.

"Where are you taking me? You've got the stink of the bogs on you, man—are you decent?"

"You're a fine one to talk," I gasped. "With you being transported and me as free as a lark?"

She wept then, tearing at the grass, and said, "They got me for thieving in Clare. I stole bread, and the dragoons came . . ."

"So you're a thief, is it?"

This sat her up. "If stealing for hunger is thieving. Have you heard of them dying in County Clare? And you fat and well fed. To the devil and back with you!"

The wind whispered, the grasses sighed, the clouds dropped a drape over the bright April moon. She wept again, and I pitied her.

"What's your name?" I asked.

"No business of yours, fella. I wouldn't have come at all if it hadn't been for the priest. What's yours, for a start?"

"Jess O'Hara."

"Sure, that sounds like a woman. Mine's Beth O'Shea, and if you think you're having sport with me you've another think comin'."

"I've no such intention, dear God."

"Then where are you takin' me?"

"Back home to Ma."

"So you've a mother?" She wiped back her hair. "Whee, jakes! I thought you were a vagrant."

"There's a cheek. A vagrant, is it? Have you never heard tell of the fighting O'Haras?"

She peered at me, kneeling.

"That's us," I said. "We were around Clare in snow-time selling the kettles. So if you've never heard of the Big O'Hara there's no holes in your ears. Didn't he finish your Bull Macalteer in sixteen rounds last January, and him the champion of your county?" I waved in disgust and lay back on the grass. "And me sister Karen's the finest dancer in the whole of Ireland."

"Is that right, Jess O'Hara?"

"It couldn't be truer. She's a riot. And my second eldest brother's the biggest revolutionary since the dear, dead Daniel O'Connell himself."

"Who's that fella?"

I sat up. "D'you mean to tell me you've never heard of the fine Dan O'Connell? Even the beasts of the fields still talk of him. And I've another brother over in Americay working the Pittsburgh iron and I wouldn't be surprised if he ends up governor of the State of Texas."

"God bless the Pope," said she, all eyes. "Have you a relative in America?"

"I have. The name of O'Hara is ringing from Wexford to Clifden, and we're the finest people in Connemara, that's agreed. And I'll tell you something free that you'd better remember. If you're comin' home with me you'd best keep clear of me brother Hosea for he's a holy devil with the women when he smells of the poitheen." I got up. "Are you coming?"

"If he keeps clear of me," she said, "for I'm sick of the sight of men, you included, for telling me a pack of bloody lies."

"Rest your soul, woman, you must be in the arms of Satan," I replied. "Sure, you wouldn't believe the truth if I was smitten with the tongues of angels. Are you coming or staying?"

Bats and blackness were dropping over the land as we went up the crest to the caravans. Ma's bonfire was winking red as we crept past the Turvey caravan where Barney was ripping up the night with snores. And I thought, as I led her into the glow of the fire, that I'd rather be called a liar by this new one than a saint by Rosa Turvey, for there was a bit more to it than crab-apple knees.

CHAPTER 3

I sat by the embers of the bonfire long after the women were abed and peered through the mist, waiting for Hosea and Michael. The buzzards were mewing as cats for cream, the hoar-frost pin-sparkling the grass, but the beauty of that night was sullied for me, despite the pages of my beloved Plato which a wayside priest had given me to read. For Hosea was spilling his manhood in the claws of a cat, and I loved Hosea.

I hated Rachel Turvey and her dark, slanting eyes; the wreath of black hair over her shoulders, the shadows deep in her breast when she washed in the morning to give us a treat. Hating, I nodded over the fire, dreaming of cats and purrs and sweeping hands, and awoke to the whisper of feet in grass, and straightened.

"Where you been?" I asked.

Hosea stood on the other side of the fire, his brown face waving as disembodied in the glow.

"Where you been?" I repeated, and he showed his white teeth in a grin, and bowed.

"I've been going about me lawful business. Do I have to account to a nip of a boy for every minute?"

"You been lovin' that Turvey woman!"

"Bless me soul, hark at that," he answered, double bass. "Shall I tell you me movements? First I went to Ennis and took their Will Murphy in five rounds for a sovereign, and then I came back to Galway to watch me brother and friends cracking the chins of the bloody English. But I wasn't in a state for much fighting myself then, for I was full to the ears with porter."

"And then you had that woman, Rachel Turvey."

He grinned wider, and came round to me, hands on hips, his great bulk blotting out the stars. "Dear God, Jess, did you see those fighting Irish? Did you see that fisherwoman stripped to the waist. D'you know something? If you could put the spunk of Galway into the rest of the towns of Ireland you'd have the country booting Victoria instead of spouting the odds about the Repeal."

"Why do you fither with that Rachel Turvey?"

"D'you think we'll get the Repeal of the Union, Jess? I think we're wasting our time, for we'd be having fat pensions and titles all over again if we gained it. The English Parliament's graft to the eyes but it isn't a patch on the old Irish one—God, what a country."

"Ma will have her in strips," I whispered. "She's trash Irish."

It angered him. "And aren't we all trash Irish—you included? Living like pigs with no settled home."

"We're O'Haras!" I said.

"Christ, that's a fine one! With Karen a pickpocket and you a poacher?" He spat. "Ach, away to hell with your great ideas—your nose is so high you'd drown in a rainstorm." He jerked his thumb at the caravan. "You're raking at me because I chase a decent skirt —haven't you a woman in there or did I see double?"

"A prisoner," I said.

"And did you save her for the love of humanity or the love of Jess O'Hara?" Watching me, he chuckled. "Is she a pretty wee thing? Ah, she couldn't be otherwise for me favourite brother. How's Ma?"

"She had a turn today but she's steadier now."

"Thanks be to God. We're on the road at first light tomorrow. She's not birthing in a ditch, the sweet thing. Is Mike back yet?"

I shook my head, and he whispered:

"Is there any sense in it? He can keep his Irish revolutions—I'm planning to work the roads with the cans, not march for the honour and glory of Ireland."

"You'll march one day," said Michael, wandering up.

"Eavesdropping," said Hosea. "We leave that to women."

Michael sat on a log and stretched his long legs. "Ach, you fool, you can be heard for miles."

There was an inborn dignity in Michael that claimed respect. Hosea was as a crag, drunk with strength, hateful of arrogance. In height they were equal. One day, I thought, they might try each other for weight. Michael said:

14

"They tell me you took Murphy in Ennis today."

Hosea waved and turned. "Murphy couldn't lay a swing on a two-month baby."

"Joe McManus?" Michael glanced up, smiling.

"McManus ducked out of Galway the day we came in."

"D'you blame him? Would the champion of Ireland break his hands on your thick head when he can pick up real money against people like Milligan? You might land him a lucky one, but it would take you a week to do it."

"Aye? Then would you like me to land one on you this minute?"

I rose, gripping a log, but Michael only grinned, and crossed his legs, saying, "Anyone can thump, Ho. And when we're ringing the bells of freedom we won't have the likes of you to thank. Will you spin me for a bed in the van? I'm sick of being under the thing."

"There's no spare bed," answered Hosea. "This Plato fella's got a woman in it."

"What woman?" Michael swung to me.

I told him.

"And you're the one with the brains," he whispered. "You damned fool, Jess—would you have us all swinging up there with Rooney?"

"So you can free them but you can't house them, is it?" laughed Hosea.

"I'm raking her out and kicking her back to Galway," whispered Michael.

"Then try your raking and kicking at me first," said Hosea, and barred his way.

"Ma!" I wailed, and the caravan window went back and Karen's head came out.

"What the hell's happening?"

"Mike's going to kick out Beth O'Shea," I cried.

"Is he? If men come in here we're clouting with the nearest thing handy. Under the van with the three of you or I'll be out there shedding blood. Your ma's dog-tired."

At dawn, with the attics of Galway looped in sunlight, we harnessed the mare and jingled west for Connemara with the Turveys following, as usual. Hosea was at the mare's bridle, his steel-tipped boots ringing on the road. Drooping against Michael on the footboard with the reins in my hand I looked at the sky. Thunder clouds were gathering in the peaks of the mountains, shouldering across the canyons of the sky with a threat to flay us alive. I remembered again the famines of the granite land, the billowing smoke of the Quaker field boilers, the hiss and spit of the Indian meal on my hands, and the bottomless coffins of the famine dead. The wind comes briny along the road to Connemara, the granite slabs glower at the Bay of Kilkieran, the fishing-boats curtsy along the rotting quays. Sitting there, I dreamed in the clanking hooves of the mare; felt again the swinging tugs of the herring on the lines; heard the curlews crying on wet, misty mornings when Hosea and me turned our boat through the foaming troughs; smelled the tar and seaweed, the fly-blown ribs of the wrecked schooners whose sailors were moulded in the sands of Rossaveal. I loved and hated this savage land that made me a part of its scream of freedom.

CHAPTER 4

Two days later we arrived at our two-acre plot of ground set high above the shores of the Bay of Kilkieran, unharnessed the mare, and set up home for part of the summer.

Most summers we came back to the Kilkieran plot to tend our crop of potatoes on Squire Rochford's estate, for you could never tell when the selling of kettles and cans might dry up and put you in the workhouse. The sun exploded over the mountains a day after we got settled in, dripping its liquid fire over the bay, and in its incinerating heat the famine people of Mayo straggled in thin, black lines along the road to Galway, their land of promise. It rained at night, as if in recompense for the sultry days; the red clouds of evening splitting themselves apart in vivid flashes. The rivers heaved, the brooks spewed up in the blood-red soil, cascading over the plains to the blue, mother sea. I was stripped to the waist and hoeing up the spuds when Hosea wandered over from the caravan and sat on a boulder, watching.

"I've been doing some thinking, Jess," he said. "She's a sweet wee thing, that Beth O'Shea. If I hadn't a woman in tow already I'd be walking her down the road to Screeb for a look at the scenery."

"You can give her five years," I said, "she's too young for you."

He chewed on a straw. "Ach, there's nothing like catching 'em young, and she's as clean as a new pin around the place. D'you know she bathes naked in the spring water every morning over in the Hollow? It's a fair sight to see, I'm telling yer. The last time I saw it done was Liza Gallagher, and she was beef to the heels."

"You shouldn't be watching," I said. "How's Ma?"

"The sickness is on her again this morning, and the child's kicking with boots, she says, but I wasn't discussing Ma. Are you gone on Beth O'Shea?"

"My business," I answered, hoeing away.

17

"Sure, and it's mine, too. Put that thing down and listen to me. Was it wise to bring a winsome girl like that out of the Galway trouble, Jess? She's enough to rise a man's blood with her skirts above her knees and a bedding eye on her."

"You're the same with all the women," I said, sighing. "You're like a stallion with his tail up in a thunder-clap—you stick to Rachel."

"But she's enough to tempt the Angel Gabriel himself, Jess. Even Mike's giving her the eye and forgetting about his Irish revolution, and I'm not having murder in the family. Are you sweet on her, tell me?"

I said, looking at the sea, "Keen enough, for I'm having her before the priest in the year I'm sixteen."

He shook his head. "That's a pity, Jess, for I was hoping to lose her. If the Military get on to her we'll be lucky to be transported, and if we start the grain-raiding again this summer she'll likely prove a drag."

"Meet that when it comes, Ho. With Ma coming to her time she's another pair of hands for Karen." I changed the subject. "When are we raiding?"

"Mike says in a fortnight. There's a grain convoy going through Twelve Pins in the middle of the month, and he's after some of that." He nodded towards the road where the famine people were lurching under their bundles. "God, it breaks my heart to see those people. There's not a clam or periwinkle to be found between here and Belmulle—they were after the fishermen's bait down in Rossaveal last night, and one got hooked like a fish, God help him."

"Is the convoy armed?" I asked.

"Mike reckons it's got an escort of six, but there's likely to be more, for they're starving them to death in Clifden."

"There's talk of the food depots opening," I said, "is it true?"

He wiped the sun from his face, and rose. "There's always that talk, but they never bloody open. It's the Relief Committee—they can't get a permit from Squire, and he can't get one from the Queen of England, God, what people! Can you imagine the old priests of Wexford standing for it?" His voice rose. "There's beefy

Irishmen standing watching the convoys and not lifting a finger. And what's the Church doin'? Nothing! While it's singing the praises of God Almighty there's Irish children spitting on the Virgin for a bowl of stirrabout meal and the Protestants collecting good Catholics for a hunk of black bread." He spat. "And there's Fighting Irishmen and Molly Maguires stretching their necks over the length and breadth of the country—the priests turn out for that, right enough."

"Steady," I said.

"Steady, me eye! I'm sick to me stomach. And I'm shaking the dust of this land off my feet the moment I hear from me brother Shaun in Pittsburgh."

"And would you be happier there?" asked Karen gaily, coming up. Beautiful, she looked, with her red hair flowing out and her ragged dress pulled in at the waist the size of a dog collar. Cross-legged, she squatted on the grass. "America's the land of the Red-skin heathen, d'you know that? And you a Church man!"

"I *was* a Church man," Ho grumbled.

"Then you can't change your God overnight, boy."

"And I'm not changing me God!" he bellowed. "If the Lord Jesus could light down among this lot he'd cauterise the Church with brimstone and fire. Didn't He feed the people with bread and fishes? I'm doing likewise for a Christian country."

She swept back her hair. "Then you'd best stay in old Ireland, Ho, me boy. Didn't Shaun write and tell of the American women uncovered in the breast and dancing naked with the virtue fans? And there's rye whiskey going down their gullets like the Irish sink porter."

"Not true," I said, "I've read about the fine America."

"So you say Shaun's lying, is it?" she flashed.

"I'm saying Shaun's mistaken," I replied. "It might be like that in Pittsburgh, but he can't speak for the whole of America. It's been a Christian country since the Pilgrim Fathers and there's a thousand good Catholics to the mile today."

Up on her feet now, blazing. "Are you the be-all and end-all of it, then? Are you believing the lies you read in your books? If you know so much about it d'you mind telling me who discovered the place?"

"Christopher Columbus," I said.

"And didn't he write a book on it, then?"

"Not that I know of."

"Well, I'm telling you he did. He was as Irish as Shaun and I'd rather believe Columbus than that fella Plato."

"Was Christopher Columbus Irish?" asked Hosea uneasily.

"As Irish as me," said Karen. "His ma was born in Derry and his father came from Cork."

"Good God," I said. "Who told you that?"

"Old Peg Doherty. Isn't he the historian around here? He was on the quay at Wicklow when the man set sail."

"I give you best," I said. "Where's Mike?"

"He's out gathering watercress with Beth O'Shea—I've just seen them down in the Hollow."

"If there's cress down there it's the first I've heard of it," muttered Hosea.

Karen walked off with a wave of disgust. "Ach, leave them be. It's the first girl Mike's taken walking and as good an excuse as any, leave him be, I say—you stick to Rachel Turvey, Ho—she's more your sort."

I looked at Hosea after Karen had gone and he lowered his eyes.

"You didn't mention that," I said. "Is it Michael keen on Beth O'Shea, or you?"

"I've got me own girl, Jess. But I'm not having trouble—not between you and Mike, remember it."

"Not unless he asks for it, Ho, she's my woman."

"Listen," he said softly, "she belongs to the one she turns to, no other."

"We'll see," I said.

"Aye, indeed, and I'm telling you this. The first fist raised between you and Mike brings me in with mine and hammering—the pair of you. We've got enough trouble on our plate with the grain-raiding and Ma. Mike's eighteen, Jess. You've got years in you yet before you need think of women."

He left me, going down to the strand, and I flung down the hoe and walked over the heath to the Hollow. It was empty; the great, stone slabs standing as gravestones in the still air. Away beyond it the sea lay flat calm and hazed, the islands of Lettermore thin gleams of yellow in a sea of burnished sun. Black the promontory, spreading west in the blue expanse as the giant jaws of a lizard, and above it the gulls were wheeling as a handful of wood shavings flung into wind. Anger and loneliness came to me, then bitterness as I turned inland and looked towards our little red caravan where Karen's coloured washing drooped on the lines. For beyond it, high on the hill, Michael and Beth O'Shea were coming hand in hand. The wind moved on the sweat of my face, bringing the sound of their laughter. Fine and handsome they looked together, steeped in sun and loving. Seeing me there, they waved, but I did not wave back. Turning, I went over to the caravan and threw myself down on the hot, damp grass and thought of my brother Shaun, and America. Karen was down on the road, handing out meal to the Galway travellers—the meal we had taken in the grain-raids last summer. She turned, calling me, but I did not go.

We ate our dinner of boiled maize and pepper in the caravan that evening, for the sun outside was too hot for Ma, who was being taken short with the child again, said Karen. So silent my mother lay on the bed by our little square table, her eyes closed, the Bantry blanket heaped high on her stomach and her hair wet strands on the pillow. We spoke in whispers, for fear of disturbing her, and I saw the fear leap to Karen's face every time my mother groaned or shifted to the pain of the child. And, after the meal, we still sat together; Michael and Beth sitting side by side staring at the sea, longing for the loneliness of lovers. Ho was smoking his clay, Karen staring at my mother, and I was sewing. I had the arse out of my trews and if you left it to the women in our place you'd be falling through them.

"Dear God, I'm fearful," whispered Hosea. "Isn't there a doctor in the whole, wide county?"

"Not for gipsies," said Karen. "With the priest charging ten shillings a time for last rites on the famine people there's no hope for a doctor at under five pounds."

"Have you found that Patsy O'Toole yet?" asked Michael.

"You're late in asking that," I retorted. "Didn't you hear us say last night she's away up north with her relations?"

"Then can we help Ma sitting here?" he replied. "I was thinking of taking Beth for a row in the currach—she's a mind to see Lettermore."

I watched them. Hand in hand, they sat, with their eyes full of promised sweetings and down from feather mattresses blowing up between them, and they sickened me. Their very presence was a stain on my mother's pain, it seemed. They were aware of nothing but the growing bond between them. Karen said:

"Away with you, then, but don't be late back in case you're needed," and they were up off their seats and through the door like ferrets. I said:

"And is he the fella who is planning the march on London, God save us."

Hosea turned and looked at me, his face expressionless.

"Do they care if Ma lives or dies?" I said.

Karen glanced up. "Leave him! No harm in a bit of a row, Jess, Ma can only hold one hand at a time," and she raised my mother's hand and pressed it to her lips.

"Are we just sitting and waiting, then?" I asked. "Shouldn't we be out looking for a labour woman?"

"There's one in the Turvey caravan," mumbled Hosea. "Won't you give a thought to Rachel, Karen? She's fine strong hands for the child-birthing—there's women down in Rossaveal who'll swear on that."

"Would you have me pollute me own mother?" whispered Karen, eyes glowing.

"Hush," I whispered back.

"And hush yourself! Would you throw a Christian woman to the hands of a savage—all beads and bangles, she is, and showing enough breast to murder a bishop. Can you imagine the palaver when Ma opens and sees that Rachel Turvey serving her?"

"She's a sweet, gentle creature, that Rachel," said Hosea.

22

"Ah, with the men—and man-huntin's all she's fit for, so don't mention her again."

I said, to smooth things, "Isn't there a midwife down in Rossaveal now?"

"I'm away down there to see," said Karen, rising. "Here, you sit with Ma." She tied back her hair with red ribbon. "And you get down to Cashel, Ho—there's new women come in east on the estate, you might find a helper there."

"Aye," said he, and rose, grunting.

"You take the mare, Karen," I said. "You'll be back that much quicker."

Now, outside the van I waved to Hosea and watched Karen bareback on the mare going like a mad thing down the road to the village. And in the red sunset I saw Michael's currach out in the bay, rowing for Lettermore. There, on the islands, were the deep, sandy inlets, the little caverns where we had stored the grain stolen in the raidings. Deep-sea mariners had rowed there among the barbs of night, cut-throats had duelled there, hostages spilled blood. Carved into fury by night, the sand dunes glowered at the bay, their vetch grass standing on end, a fine, fierce place for loving. All this I had planned for Beth O'Shea, and now she was Michael's. Weary, I went back into the van and sat by Ma. Somewhere in the sunset a blackbird was singing, his notes liquid and pure, and the barn owls were ripping up the night for prey. My mother groaned deep, shifted, and opened her eyes.

"Jess," she said, and smiled.

"I'm with you," I whispered.

The sun was staining the window and she turned her head to its redness, sighed, and said, "Jess, fetch Karen."

"I will, Ma. She won't be long. She's away down to the village to fetch a woman who knows about the child-birth, give her an hour."

"Fetch her now," said my mother.

I stiffened in the chair. Her face, in that red light, was suddenly haggard with the gauntness of pain, her eyes coming alive and moving brightly in the sunken shadows of her cheeks. And even as I watched my mother made a fist of her hand and pressed it into her mouth and bit at it, whimpering, "By the holy Jesus . . . Karen, Karen!" and she pressed herself back on the bed and cried aloud, thumping it.

In sudden terror I bent to her and she gripped me and pulled down my face to hers, and as the labour bloomed within her she gripped me harder, forbidding breath, then flung me off and rose in the bed, her eyes wild, smiling in pain, which is a woman's courage.

"Ah, Alannah!" she said, "Oh, me sweet Jess, curse your father, curse him! For the love of God fetch Karen!"

"Ma, she's away. She'll be back . . ."

"Then shut the door and leave me!" She wept. "Och, it's a murderin' labour is this one, dear God!"

In horror I raced through the van door and across the fields, shouting down the road to Cashel. Scrambling up the hill, weeping now, I shielded my eyes from the sun, but the road to Rossaveal was empty. And then my mother screamed once, loud and clear, and I ran in panic back to the van. Bursting in, I stared down at her. Ma was lying still and white on the pillow, eyes closed, and I put my hands to my cheeks and sobbed down at her.

"Is there somethin' up?" asked a voice, and I swung towards the door. Rosa Turvey was standing there with a face of innocence, all dirt smudges, black curls and gipsy bangles.

"It's me mother," I gasped, "she's comin' to child."

"Then accept me congratulations," said Rosa. "To be sure that's a fine event for the family. Is it a boy or a girl you're after, Jess O'Hara?"

"And Karen's away to Rossaveal and Hosea's five miles down the road to Cashel!"

"Why, there's a useless set of gunks. And where's that Beth O'Shea at a time like this?"

"She's away for a row with Michael, to Lettermore."

"God save us," exclaimed Rosa. "I told you she's no good to yer. Have you brought out a child before, Jess O'Hara?"

"Be gad, no, I've never attempted it."

"Then you're attemptin' it now, man, for me sister Rachel's over in Screeb, so it's you or nothing," and she pulled her dress over her head and tied back her hair.

"Rosa, the child needs turning," I whispered, and she opened large, rebellious eyes.

Just then my mother wakened, and seeing a woman before her she put out her hand to her, and Rosa gripped it and narrowed her eyes. She said to me:

"You leave the turnin' to me, O'Hara—outside and fetch water."

I sat on the patch gripping myself, watching the sun sink down into the sea red and hot with him in hissing and steaming. And the two women in the caravan made no sound till a third wailed thin and plaintive in the moonlight, and they called her Melody.

It was warm and sweet within me for Rosa Turvey then, to hell with Beth O'Shea.

CHAPTER 5

And so, with Michael still loopy over Beth O'Shea, I first made love to Rosa Turvey in June. When I had finished loosening the patch I went down to the strand to fetch a dog-fish for Ma, for there was nothing she liked better than one roasted on tongs. I was sitting on the prow of Michael's currach baiting a hook when Rosa came down. Cleaned up a bit these days, was Rosa Turvey, with a red shawl over her shoulders, a black skirt well pulled in and enough white trembles above it to raise blood-pressure. Things were different between the O'Haras and Turveys now, the first time for generations, with Ma bowing to Barney Turvey and people dropping curtsys.

"Hallo," said Rosa, looking glorious, bracelets rattling.

"Hallo to you," I said, for the surest way to lose a fish is to prove too keen.

"Are you going out fishin'?"

"I was considering it."

"If you asked me proper I'd consider coming with ye, you know?"

Into the currach with her before she changed her mind, rocking, squealing in a flurry of brown legs. Never been in a boat before, will I be drowned? One shove and I was away with her.

Got her.

I leaned back on the oars and we carved the bay like a China clipper, with the June sun blinding the sky and the currach heaving through the rollers. On, on to Lettermore where the gulls were wheeling, down into the last, green trough, tossed high on the tip of a breaker as the sand came up. Higher, higher, we were turned upside down and landed spread-eagled in six inches of water. Soaked, we held each other, laughing at the sky, and the next roller in hit us full-blooded and carried us high up the beach in a tangle of arms and legs, and we shivered together, but not with cold.

26

"No," said Rosa, pushing.

The gulls screamed above us, sensing the offal of our stillness, the sun beat down.

"Eh, Jess, stop it!"

I saw through a rift in her hair the hill of the island blazing with sun as I turned her to my lips.

"Eh . . ." she whispered in the darkness of kissing.

I do not think a man is alive until he has followed a bare-footed woman and put his feet in her imprints in sand. And it seemed that I knew each swaying step as Rosa broke into a run. Reaching an arbour of rocks she skidded around, her hair flying.

"*Arrah*, that made you gallop!"

I dashed up, gasping. "You save your strength when you're cornering the Turveys." Seizing her, I tripped her, and we fell together in deep, brown sand. The wind hammered secret places, the gulls screamed. Panting, she smiled, closing her eyes. And the loneliness and brine was as a wreath about us, her breath gusty in her wet shawl as I kissed her again. We lay together, listening to the incoming tide.

"And what now?" Rosa whispered. "Have I collected half a man?"

"You'll see," I whispered back.

"Faith, you O'Haras are all the same," said she. "If you saw an inch of a knee you'd be away and throwing stones at it."

"Show me yours, and see," I said.

"Bad cess to you!" Pushing and wriggling now. "D'you take me for a scarlet woman? Would you have me drummed from Chapel and your ma coming after me with clogs? Won't you tell me you love me, before you take the liberties?"

I looked at her. Much of the Karen in this one, I thought; the same curves and slanting eyes of the Spanish Irish. I said, "Sure, I don't know. The women are scarce in these parts and you have to take what's coming."

The waves were swilling into the cove now and the restless birds were flaying the cliff face and shaking down their beds for dusk. I did not reply but kissed her again, and what began in calmness ended in heat and quick breathing. Rising, I drew her to her feet and pulled her towards the nearby cave.

"Ah, no," she said softly, "it isn't as easy as that, Jess, but I'll race you down to the sea for a bathe."

"For bathing? The moon's coming up, woman!"

"Will you catch your death, then?" She swung back her wet hair. "You're soaked now, man—take your things off!" and she dragged at my shirt.

"For the love of heaven," I whispered. "I'd never have believed it!"

"Ach, there's nothing indecent about it, Jess, it's only in your mind. Clothes hold dark secrets—didn't Adam and Eve get up to tricks the moment they put on furs?"

"You first, then!"

And she did no more but strip off her clothes, flinging them about, and run down to the sea as naked as a faun. Hair flying, she dived, and came up streaming.

"Come on in, you loon!"

In panting haste I flung my shirt high, dropped my trews and raced in after her, leaping the breakers as a mad thing, diving for her legs. Crying out, she was away, but I was after her, upending her in the moonlit water, my hands slipping on her smooth, wet body. And we plunged and floundered as demented things till the moon rose high and painted the island silver.

The tide had taken my clothes and flung them high on the sand by the time I came out, so I took them within the cave for warmth, and began to dress, wondering at the beauty of a naked Rosa. The cave mouth was alight with the moon, I remember, the shadows beyond it black to the seaweed fringe. Dressing in gasping haste, I heard a twig snap, and straightened.

Rosa was standing in the entrance of the cave, and the sea-lights were playing in her hands and running in vivid streams over her hair and shoulders. Rigid, I stood, carved into stone by the naked apparition.

It was silent within the cave save for the dripping of unseen springs and rivulets swirling for the tide. Cold, too, the only brazier being Rosa, and her warm enough to heat the pair of us as I turned her into my arms, seeing beyond her the granite crags of Kilkieran gashing a patterned sky. But she moved from my arms into deeper shadows and I stood there listening to her breathing until she whispered from the blackness. I found her in dim moonlight that streamed in from a crevice of the rocks. Smiling, she stood there, as slim as a boy, with her black hair over her shoulders and the upward tilt of her breasts making her into a woman.

"Come," I whispered, and drew her against me.

Instant the fire, kindled by the kiss, with unknown muscles raising the riot of youth, and Rosa's sighs and gasped provocations heightened the tumult as I moulded her in sand. Lithe and quick was she as I cleaved unto her in the heat and strength of it, and we lay together in the dusk of the cave till the sounds of the island crept back, one by one. Her eyes, I remember, were large and glittering in the strange light, moving in secret reproach over my face, and then she smiled. Brilliant that smile as she pushed me away and sat up, smoothing back her wet hair.

"Moses love us," she said. "That was a step in the wrong direction."

I heard the distant thumping of the breakers; the scream of shingle I heard, and the piteous wailing of the gulls, and Rosa giggled.

"Just imagine old Karen arrivin' in the middle of that one," she said.

Rising, I went to the entrance. "Don't remind me of her, for God's sake."

The moon was round and high over an emblazoned sea, the cottage lights winking along the distant shore. Hosea, I thought, would be down in the village with Peg Doherty, sinking his porter; Ma would be rocking Melody the child; Karen would be at her stitching. I did not turn to the warmth of Rosa beside me. Michael and Beth, I remembered, would be out together in the wild places, under the same moon, seeking the same fierce loving, in joy.

"You happy now, Jess?"

I turned to her. "Aye, Rosa." Beautiful she looked in the ragged dress, her hair tangled, her face upturned.

"First time for you, Jess?" and I nodded.

"Not for me," she whispered, looking away. "You think I'm a free girl?"

"No."

"Us Turveys got a terrible name, you heard?" She smiled sadly then, and suddenly she turned me to her and kissed my face. "Oh, Jess, it's a terrible loving. And they should stop it for the rest of the world, and keep it for you and me. Just you and me for ever, Jess, for it weren't the same before—just Jess and Rosa?"

Bending, I kissed her.

Hosea was standing on the shingle as I ran the boat in, hands on hips, glowering.

"'Evening, Ho O'Hara," said Rosa, dimpling.

"You get back home," he replied. "Your pa's out looking for you with a riot cudgel." He took the painter and pulled up the currach. "Where the hell you been?" he whispered to me.

"Sure, I've been out for a dog-fish, is there any harm in that?"

"Was I born yesterday?" He gave me a queer old look and a sigh. "You watch that Rosa, the Turveys are mad for it—she'll be having you before the altar before you rise to a man . . ."

"And you're a fine one to talk!"

"And you're a fine one for promises," he retorted. "D'you realise we're due down to the village with Peg Doherty at moonrise to talk of the raiding—there's Mike down there already eatin' his heart out."

"Where's Beth, then?"

"She's in with Karen and Ma cooing at the baby—you can't get a word of sense out of the three of 'em."

I hated Peg Doherty, the man behind the raiding, but he was a man of quality when it came to feeding the starving, and the best politician in the county since he was buried alive with five dead children during a Mayo famine. He knew the progressive policies of Dan O'Connell and the fortune of the Queen of England; had traced the ancestry of the grave-digger who buried him and proved him a bastard twice removed—because he was digging when he should have been filling and brought down his spade and cut

30

Doherty in two. And he wasn't partial to me either since I took him for the wheelbarrow. "Fetch the muck-shifter," called Hosca, "it's away down the patch." And there was Peg Doherty on the pail at the bottom with his peg legs sticking through the door, and I'd got him half-way up the path in the blackness before I knew it was Doherty, and him fighting with his bags and tucking in his shirt and playing hell with Connemara gipsies between here and Ulster.

"So you've troubled yourself to come, O'Hara," said he now as I entered his shop, and he raised himself another quart of porter and peered with welted eyes. "God help old Ireland indeed, God help her. With the country going to hell and damnation you're ripping the skirts off the trollops of Connaught."

"I'm sorry," I said.

"Then may we begin, your worship?"

"Ach, indeed, sir," I said.

Most severe he looked, then turned to Michael. "D'you mind I told you about the Clifden convoy, man?"

"Aye, six weeks back, and we're still awaiting it," answered Michael, sullen.

"Then you'll keep for another minute while I tell you that I'm the fella in charge of activities and you'll not cast an eye on an English dragoon till I say the word. They were dragging a galloper-gun, and you'd have come in ten pieces before you'd have crested the rise, me son. Now then."

"When's the next one?" asked Hosea.

"Sure, it's due through Maumturk the day after tomorrow."

"Sunday!" exclaimed Michael.

"As God's me judge, O'Hara. And shall I tell you something else? There'll be two tons of the stuff in carts and more than ten fat heifers following on the hoof, and not a dragoon within miles. The only escort with them is six jumper Irishmen from Clifden."

"Protestant Irish," whispered Hosea, and closed his hand.

"Aye, God help 'em! They change their religion as often as they change their shirts, so if they went to their God too soon St. Peter himself would put a tick against you in the name of holy justice, d'you see?"

"No killing," said Hosea.

"Is it killing to step on a louse, O'Hara? Bless me soul, wouldn't it be an act of God to put them out of their misery, for their bodies are fat for the eternal fire."

Michael shook his head.

"Ach, where's the spunk to yer?" whispered Doherty. "In my day they'd be wearing the blazing cap of the Hessians and wishing themselves dead for the evil, stinking things they are. And you'll be hung for grain-raiding as quick as for murder, so you'll have the satisfaction of dying for something decent."

"Who's with us?" asked Michael.

"There's just the three of you and your sister Karen. D'you want a regiment of guards to take six Irish jumpers, boy? I tell yer . . ."

"What time?" asked Hosea.

"They'll be in the Pass at dawn, nearabouts."

"Where do we deliver the cattle and grain, then?"

"Same place as last time—Pat Mulligan will be down on the shore with his boat. He can take the grain to Lettermore and we'll slaughter the cattle here."

"Dangerous," whispered Hosea, and in the light of the lamp I saw the humped shadows of his eyes and the gleam of his teeth.

"And is the belly goin' out of ye, Hosea O'Hara?" whispered Peg.

"Sure, t'is not!" I retorted. "But it's one thing snatching the grain and another thing driving cattle on the hoof, for they'll bellow to wake the vile Lord Clare himself, and that fella's dead."

"Quiet," said Michael, and Doherty arched himself. "Shall I give the job to others, then? There's fighting men up in Clifden who'd lay Victoria at me feet, never mind ten heifers, and not question it." He pointed down to the beach. "D'you know there's a hundred starvers to the hour passing down there with rumbling bellies. They'll pick the bones of those heifers cleaner than vultures, it's no risk. Are you on?"

Strange how we both looked at Michael.

"On," said he.

"And you'll not be needing help, me boys?"

"We do it alone," said Michael.

"That's the fellas!" Doherty rubbed his hands, his little eyes shining in his ravaged face. "And may the Lord attend your efforts for showing the power and glory of decent Irishmen. Bless me soul, O'Haras—if your brother Shaun was here this night instead of scratchin' for money in the heathen Americay, he'd be kneeling at your feet."

Hosea said, glancing up, "Will you bridle your tongue when speaking of me brother?"

"Indeed to God I meant no harm, son," cackled Doherty, patting him. "It's just that we could do with a few more like him, d'you see? He'd serve the country better fighting at home instead of foolin' his time away in foreign parts."

"Isn't he fighting with the Molly Maguires?"

"Aye, but . . ."

"And d'you expect more of him?" Hosea's voice rose. "There's the likes of us padding the bellies of a few famine travellers and him raising an army to fight for Irish freedom, and like as not die for it."

"No offence, lad." Doherty raised his mug. "Shall we drink on the memory of the fella? God alive, I'd not take issue on the fine Shaun O'Hara, for I'd bleed to death for the likes of him and all he stands for, d'you get me?"

"Shaun, me brother," said Michael, and raised high his mug.

We drank, and I watched Peg Doherty. Through the length and breadth of the secret country he was a respected man, but I did not trust him. He sat at night in his shop and organised the raids. He knew the names of every Fighting Irishman, Fenian and Molly Maguire in the west, but sat at home while we took the risks, with more money under his floor boards than a Protestant bishop. Useless talking to Hosea, for he was thick in the head. Dangerous to mention my fears to Michael, it would surely end in a fight. So I sat and watched Peg's little shifty eyes, and feared.

"Are we away, then?" asked Hosea, and stretched to his full height.

Michael slapped down his mug. "Sunday," he said.

"And you bring the cattle here," said Doherty. "Good night."

Bright the moonlight as we walked home, the three of us, unspeaking, till the red bonfire of the van came up from the crags.

And there was Karen sitting beside it mashing up the meal for next day's dinner and Ma on her stool crooning at the baby, but no sign of Beth O'Shea. Hosea said:

"Are we taking that one with us this time, Mike?" He nodded at Karen.

"Why not? She's better than a goose when it comes to danger, and we need a keen look-out."

"Have you forgotten the child?" I asked.

"What's the child to do with it?"

"If the four of us collect it Ma will be left to fend, with no labourer on the land," I said. "Would you take Beth O'Shea instead?"

"I canna risk the danger to her," whispered Michael.

"Is there no danger to Karen, then?" asked Hosea, stopping him.

"Ach, away," I said, pushing. "It's the bloody love-light in him, Ho. He'd see the family strung up and dangling and fight for every hair of her head, am I right?"

"One day I'll clip that tongue," whispered Michael.

"Will you try clipping it now," I said, "for there's no time like the present. You've been going damned looney over the woman the moment she showed her face, and I'm sick to death of you."

He swung me one but I ducked it and Hosea caught my right on his shoulder and it spun him, but he gripped my arm and twisted me behind him, facing Michael.

"Keep off," he whispered.

"Loose him," breathed Michael, white-faced, "or I'll flatten the pair of you."

"Keep your hands off the young 'un or you'll have me to contend with."

Michael said, trembling, "Then tell him to shut his mouth or I'll be shutting it, Ho. He's been shooting that tongue at me for the last three weeks."

"And don't you know why?"

I brought up my elbow into his ribs. "Heisht!" I whispered, and he took another grip on my arm, and said, "Because you've got his girl. You've got the pick of the women in the county and you have to whip his."

34

"God save us! Is the lad moonstruck?" Michael slapped his thigh and bellowed. "Would a decent Irish wench spare a glance for a wee rapscallion the size of that thing when there's six-foot men out roving?"

"He was bigger than six foot when he pulled her out of Galway," said Hosea, "and he's inches bigger than you for all your size." He twisted me before him, and I stood there blazing, hands clenched, hating both of them. "Now listen," he said, his voice bass. "You'll bed your women spare time, but you'll not mix 'em up with the raidin'. We've got enough fighting coming with the six jumper Irishmen without raising fists in the family, d'you hear me?"

"He can have her, and welcome," said Michael.

"D'you mean that?" asked Hosea.

"Sure I mean it. She's not a woman for loving at all, at all, for I've tried her, and if he can billow her skirt in the Sunday heather he's a better man than me. If she said yes in her life it'd be for her dinner, God help us."

The moon was on his face and I saw his handsome eyes, his teeth shining white above the square cut of his chin. Hosea groaned, and said, "Satan spare us. You'll be having it out some time over a pesky bit of a woman, Jess, and more credit to you, or you wouldn't be O'Haras." He tickled Michael under the chin. "D'you see that now? You'll be keeping it clear of Beth O'Shea henceforth, or I'll be bouncing it. Now away, the pair of you, the women are raising supper."

"After Sunday," I whispered at Michael.

"You're welcome," he replied. "I'll tie up me eyes and put one hand in me pocket, lad."

"Come on!" roared Hosea, and we went through the crags and into the light of the fire. Karen was kneeling on the turf mashing the meal for next day's dinner and I lay down beside her with a straw in my mouth and looked at the moon.

"Where the devil you been?" she asked, mashing away.

"I been out to fetch a dog-fish but there's no sign or smell of one."

"Aye, aye? Have you been using Rosa Turvey for bait, then?"

"I just gave the woman a row," I replied. "There's no harm in a bit of a row over the shoals, didn't you say so yourself, girl?"

"As long as you keep rowing," said she, mashing away. Sighing, she wiped back her hair with her arm, gave a glance at Ma and leaned nearer. "D'you know somethin'? If you ruin the girl her pa will be after the lot of us with hatchets."

"Aw, give me strength," I said. "Would I fither with the likes of Rosa when I can get the pick of the village?"

Hosea took Melody from Ma's arms and held her up, sweeting and booing, more like a girl-wife than the terrible Ho O'Hara, and Karen called:

"Will you watch that child, Ma, he'll be squeezing the stomach from her and not know it."

Ma waved her away. "Ah, leave the man, the fella's practising."

"There's one down here needing practice," said she, and rose and took the baby from Ho and gave her to me.

Strange the feel of a child, the noisy sucking, the wriggles. I held my sister Melody for the first time, and Karen whispered:

"Bad boy! D'you see these eyes of mine? They were given by a witch for seeing things on Lettermore." She prodded Melody. "Ma'll skin you alive if you bring home a child, and that's what will come of bathing naked."

I grinned at her.

"Are you hungry?" she asked.

"Fair starved," and she pushed me a bowl of Indian meal.

"Then get across that—I'll take the child. You'll need all your strength to keep up with that Rosa."

CHAPTER 6

They came in single file through the Maumturk Pass, two grain carts and eleven fat heifers behind them. Michael, Ho and me lay side by side among the rocks, peering down.

"The punches in me eyes is dimming them," muttered Hosea, "but I've ears to hear the grass growin', and I'm hearing dragoons."

"Who's the fella on horse-back?" I whispered.

"Captain," whispered Michael, squinting through the moonlight. "Peg Doherty never mentioned that one."

"Is there only one of him," Hosea asked, "for I'm hearing ten."

"One dragoon on horse-back and the six jumpers," I whispered back. "The fella's armed to the teeth and he's clanking for a regiment."

"We'll take him first, then," said Michael, "he'll need some taking."

It was a black witch of a night in the mountains with early fingers of dawn shafting on the peaks and the rain thrashing the heather in windy squalls. The dragoon leading the carts sat his mare with big, easy grace, and the split pennant of the Eighty-eighth he carried was as stiff as a bar in the wind.

"Can you see Karen?" I whispered.

Michael frowned at the other side of the Pass. "She's with her head down now, but she was up a minute back, looking east. She'll be waving like a mad thing if anything moves on the road to Maam."

"Thank God for her," said Hosea. "I'd rather have her than the O'Shea woman, for she's eyes like a cat in the dark. Are we ready?"

"Aye," said Michael, "and listen." He heaved over to us. "You go down to the road block and flatten the dragoon and Jess and me'll take the jumpers driving the carts. And the moment you're free come and aid us for we'll be doin' 'em at three to one, so we'll be needing you."

"It's a joy," replied Hosea. "I've always fancied meself with a full-blown dragoon, the bastards," and he rose.

"Wait," said Michael, and dragged him down. "Now will you watch that fella? You're not stickin' straight lefts on Joe McManus, Ho. He'll be at you with everything in the Galway arms dump and cut your throat for good measure. And listen. When we've got the jumpers you and me will take the carts to Mulligan and Jess'll drive the heifers along the strand to home, then we all meet east of the village. D'you get me?"

"Aye," I answered, "but what about Karen?"

"She's away back home on her own, for I told her. Are you ready?"

We tracked down through the crags to the side of the road, and watched them pass and the dragoon's mare reared up when she met the road block, unseating its rider as Hosea snatched at its bridle.

"Right," whispered Michael, "among 'em!" and we dashed from the cover side by side, booting at the heifers. Scrambling up the back of a grain cart I got the driver with a stone on the nut and dived off among the bellowing cattle. One moment peace, the next a riot, with the jumpers screaming for the dragoon and the grain ponies neighing. The heifers were climbing each other and bellowing, and the pain rose to my elbow as I set my feet and caught a jumper square. Down he went among the milling hooves and I was after the next one, but he was built for Hosea.

"You Papish sack of guts!" he shrieked, and swung me one that would have dropped a heifer, but I ducked and crossed him, shouting for Michael. Like hitting granite, this one, so I scrambled among the heifers and looked for something smaller.

"Jess!"

There was a jumper on Michael's back and I dragged him off and hooked him solid, spinning him against a pony, and a pair of flying hooves did the rest. The cattle were running now, spilled grain sacks were heaping in the road, and I leaped beside Michael and faced my next one. A year younger than me, by the look of him, his face screwed up in terror, so I hauled him out of it and slapped him sideways. Three left, two with cudgels as Hosea came bawling down the road. One dropped as something dead before him and Michael got another, and the last went down the road to Maam with Karen heaving rocks at him. Blood was on Michael's face as he straightened, panting.

"Did you get the captain, Ho?"

"Sure, he's sleeping like a baby, I envy the man." Seeing Karen above us he cupped his hands to his mouth. "Will you get back home, you bitch of a woman?"

"And see a decent fight go by, you loon? I'm coming down," she called back.

Michael leaned on me. "Will you take her, Jess, she's safer along the strand with you."

"Aye," I said. "Are you hurt, man?"

"Ah, it's nothing." He waved at the jumper Irish cowering in the ditch by the carts. "What do we do with these fellas?"

"Ho will watch 'em," I gasped. "Will you help me round up the cattle?"

Karen jumped the last rock to the road. "Is that what you call a raid?" she panted, holding herself. "God alive, I could have done it quicker with six fat fish-wives, what's been holding you?"

"They had a dragoon," whispered Michael.

"Sure, the man's still only got two arms and two legs. Who's blooded you, Mike?"

Michael turned, looking down the deserted Pass. "Away with you, and stop your blatherin', woman, the Rangers will be through here at first light. Help Jess and take the strand, we'll meet you south of the village."

The sea was mad and grey with him along the shore; great white rollers crashing in with the fury of God in them, and the moon was grinning like a witch from a tear in the clouds as Karen and me flicked the cattle along the strand. Ghostly the cattle moved, hooves slipping in the shingle, their eyes rolling white as they bellowed at the clouds for water, making enough noise to wake the graveyards. Stumbling behind the switching tails we did not speak, Karen and me, till the heifers found pure water pools and stumbled in belly deep, and drank.

39

The dawn was coming up now, pouring blood in the sea and painting red the peaks of Twelve Pins in the distance, and there was a wraithy silence over the land save for the thumping breakers and the curlews crying from the mists. Lying back on the shingle Karen whispered:

"Did you say we're taking these beefers to the village?"

I nodded.

"Who for, for God's sake?"

"Peg Doherty's awaiting them," I answered.

"And is Doherty the chap who gives the directions?"

"He's the leader," I said.

"And who says that—Peg Doherty, I suppose? Is there any sense in thrashing the poor beasts all the way to the village for slaughter when we can hand them over to the travellers at the next quay down?"

"We've got to do as Doherty says, Karen."

She rose and tightened her shawl. "Have we? I say different—to the devil with Doherty. There's him flaking the ceiling with snores while we're out collecting dragoons and jumper Irish. Is he taking money off the famine travellers for the food we're delivering, d'you think?"

I grinned. "Wouldn't put it past him, but you try telling that to Mike."

The wind sighed, the thickets moved, and I saw her eyes switch below the tight scrag of her shawl. "Have you thought of the danger to Ma and the child, Jess?"

"The more's the danger while we sit here gassin'," I answered, "for it's coming pretty light."

"It's too bloody light for me this minute," said she, and took the tail of a heifer and twisted him out of the pool. "We're dumping this flock at the first famine crowd, and that's a mile from here, get 'em moving."

"Then you're giving the answers to Mike, remember."

"I'll give the answers to St. Peter himself," said she, and crossed herself thrice, "but I'm not taking the cattle to Doherty," and she waded into the pool and started thumping the heifers. "*Arrah*, come out of it, yer poor beasts, you're as good as in famine bellies."

The dawn was well up when we reached the first quay down, and the famine travellers were squatting along the strand in black, still patches, warming their hands to little rock fires. The flow of the homeless was increasing now, for the landlords were moving in with chain gangs and crow-bars and bringing down the houses over the people's heads. So they wandered south and east, these people, begging on the roads or sleeping on the shores, scratching in the sand when the tides went out for mussels and winkles, and they left their dead behind them when they moved, and the wind held the stink of their rags and hunger. The workhouses were filled, the starvation dead being buried in the bottomless coffins, and up in Sligo the people of the land were grazing in the fields like beasts, and dying, their mouths stuffed with grass.

"Blood of the Divine Saviour, God help them," said Karen, as we drove the cattle up.

"Ah, woman, food, for the love of Jesus," said one, bowing before us.

"Are you the true faith, old man?" I asked, and he answered, trembling on his stick, "That I am, and the two hundred here with me, but the Lord has turned His face from the people, and a vile sufferin' is upon us."

"Are you down from Clifden, old man?" asked Karen.

He opened great eyes in his gaunt face, and the skin was stretched tight over his cheeks and his clothes were rags on his scarecrow bones. "That I am, girl, but there's many from north of Castlebar and a few from Ballina and beyond, God help 'em, ah, dear."

"Where're you away to now, then?"

"We're floggin' the road to Rossaveal, and then on to Galway, for there's beasts rovin' the fields there for the taking and the Quakers lining the roads to feed us with the meal."

"Indian meal," I said, "the food of the savages, and your people will go black in the face."

"We'd as soon turn green as long as we're fed," said he, hands begging, "for there's some here haven't eaten decent in weeks, and some who can go no further. Their spags are troublin' them, d'you

41

see, and the toes of the wee ones are cut and bleeding on the stones, could you not spare a heifer?"

"I can spare you ten," said Karen.

"You'll feed us the animals, woman?"

"You can feed your fill," I said, "and tether the rest by the pure pools for the other starvers coming from Portacloy, and beyond."

"Have you names?" he whispered, "for the people will give you blessing," and he knelt before us, reaching for our feet.

"Up, old man," said Karen, and raised him, and the tears were running on her cheeks. "Stack your bellies and go back home, for there's no more food in Galway."

"There is that!" He straightened, waving to the crowd about him. "Didn't we hear tell of the people feeding on the roads free—beyond the next village? And not even a spit at the Virgin demanded, for they're true Catholics? Would you send us back to Ballina and beyond where they're lifting the gravestones of the dead?"

"There's even food in the next village," said an old crone, coming up. "The man Doherty down there fed me son, and cheap enough, God bless him—a penny for a bowl of Irish meal and a halfpenny a cut for a hunk of black bread, so you're lyin'."

Karen looked at me, then spat on the earth and smoothed it with her foot. "By the holy saints," she whispered, and turned to the woman. "Not lying," she said. "May Satan fry him for the stinkin' thief he is. Eat, woman, the meat is free."

And the people closed round the cattle who bellowed at the knives, and the night was filled with the cries and laughter as we ran, Karen and me, through the swims of the coming tide.

"They're slaughtering the innocent," said she. "It should be Doherty."

A roasting sun was rising in the blue as we neared the village, but there was no sight of Mike and Hosea, so Karen left me to travel to the van, and I sat there looking at the islands, waiting. Till midday I waited, and Beth O'Shea came up.

"Have you seen your brothers?" said she.

"Would I be sitting here on me backside idling if I'd seen me brothers?" I said.

"God preserve us, there's a temper on you!"

"Me temper's fine," I said, "it's saucy people raising it."

"Is it weary with the fishing all night, you are?"

"Where did you get the fishin'?" I asked.

"Haven't the four of you been after the herring shoals, and didn't Karen say so herself just now. Your mother's been worrying to death for you—does it take all of ye to handle the herring?"

"If you'd been a seaman we'd have taken you and all," I said. "For the wind was like bloody mountains and toppling us and the herring so many they were slipping over the gunwale, then some."

"Tell me another," said she, looking glorious. "For you haven't a single tail of one to show for your night's work. Sure, I know the truth—you've been on the raiding, for Ma herself told me, being in tears with the worrying, but I'd be cuttin' off me arms with rusty nails before I'd let on, d'you believe me?"

"No."

"Ah, Jess," said she, and got nearer. "I've been wearying for the sight of you, d'you think I've got spots?"

"If you have then Mike'll be catching 'em."

"Why d'you say that, darlin'?"

"He's been rolling with you."

"He has not!" Red cheeks and tremblings now, fists clenched and up on her feet, staring down. "Did he say that?"

"Away," I said, "I'm sick to death of women!"

She said then, head low, "It was only walking and finding the cress for Ma, and I didn't sit once, though he asked me. I was saving myself for you, Jess O'Hara, and I've been breaking me heart over that Rosa Turvey."

Weeping now, with her hands over her face and rocking herself, and I got a look at her. If Mike had let this one off the hook he'd be wanting his head read, I thought: a fine, slim waist on her, and good strong legs for getting round a patch, and bright waving hair for a weary man's pillow, and there was an itch in me for her, but I fought it down.

"Mike's not for the women," I said. "The man's wedded to Ireland. You've been wasting your time with Mike O'Hara, you should have stuck to me."

43

"Then will you take me?"

"I'll have to consider it," I said. "You're a poor hand at the cooking and at the first sign of Ma's labour you were away with Michael and leaving Rosa to it. D'you know me sister Melody would be down six feet if it hadn't been for her?"

"I'm sorry," she said.

"And you never wash," I said. "There's Rosa out swimming in the bay every morning, and you with the same patches on you that you brought from Galway."

"That's a lie! I'm bathing down in the Hollow every dawn, and the family are telling of it."

"I'll have to have the proof of that," I said. "Give me a whistle tomorrow dawn and I'll come down and look you over, for I've seen nothing so far that turns me eye from Rosa."

Her face brightened then, strangely, and she clasped her hands. "Will you come if I give you a whistle?"

"God love us," I said. "Anything in trews will do, won't it? There's some roaring fellas down in Kilkieran when you've stolen the sleep of me brother Hosea."

She sat, unanswering, staring at a wild flower in her fingers, and her eyes were shining with tears. And I would have gone to her then, I think, but it was no time for loving. I stood up, searching the strand, shielding my eyes from the brilliance as I looked over the plains towards Maumturk. Nothing moved. The great emerald plains lay in spiked silence, the bright peat-water pools flashing as sapphires and shrouded with haze, and beyond lay the tumbling mountains, their peaks spearing at bed-sheet clouds.

"Bad cess to yer," whispered Beth beside me. "There's me been soaking me pillow at nights for the love of you and you sitting there calling me useless and unwashed."

"Hush," I said, staring down the strand.

"It's a cruel devil of a fella you are, Jess O'Hara."

"Look," I whispered, pointing.

Along the sands a man was coming, walking slowly, hands on hips as someone tracking.

"It's your brother Ho," said Beth, up beside me. "See the fine size of him."

44

"It's not Hosea," I said, staring.

I was worried about Hosea and Michael. We had grain-raided before, snatching a few bags at a time, and they had rowed them to Lettermore in Mulligan's boat, but had never been as late as this. I sensed danger now and sank to my knees, pulling Beth down beside me. We watched the man on the sands. Nearer he came, and I caught my breath as the sun struck in vivid light at his heels. Spurs. We crouched lower. Now, as he stood staring about him I recognised a uniform.

"The dragoon," I said.

"God save us," she whispered, and clutched me, but I forced her away, watching.

"Easy," I whispered, "the man's not tracking you."

Her eyes opened wide in her face. "From the raidin', then?"

"Aye, from Maumturk. Quiet!"

No need to measure this one for size, he was nearly as big as Hosea. Hatless, covered with the dust of the fight, he stood motionless, then moved quickly, taking the path that led through the dunes, tracking our foot-prints from the strand.

"Run," whispered Beth. "Down to Kilkieran, you'll lose him in the village."

"And leave Ma and Karen to fend if he lands there."

"Jess, have you seen these fellas? They're mad dogs when it comes to the women! They're out with their whips cursin' and lashin' till you tell 'em the truth, for I've had them." She began to cry and screw at her fingers, with blank stares at my face, and I pitied her terror. She said, shivering, "If you go to the van he'll have the truth of you from Karen, and he'll land me back on the Galway ship if I'm there, too. Oh, Jess, run!"

"You run, Beth."

"Come with me, save yourself!" she gripped me but I shook her off.

"Have sense," I whispered, shaking her, "and hush, or he'll hear you. D'you expect me to dump me own ma and sister? And the van's two miles inland, woman, the fella's more likely to land in Screeb."

"He's turning for the village!" she whispered, pointing.

I nodded, watching, wondering why he was going to the village, for a lonely dragoon in a place like Kilkieran was likely to end on a tree. We watched him until he was nearly out of sight. "Come," I said, and took Beth's hand.

Karen ran to meet us over the heath.

"Have you seen your brothers?" she called.

I shook my head and she put her hands in her hair. "Your mother's near demented—are they rowing that damned grain to the Arrans or Lettermore, for God's sake?"

"And there's a dragoon come in from the raidin'," Beth whispered.

I added, "The one leading the grain convoy. Ho should have done him proper while he was at it."

"Where is he now?" asked Karen.

"Down in Kilkieran."

She said, softly, "He must have tracked us in the sand. If he done that he's found the cattle, what's left of them. Why has he gone to the village, d'you think?"

I looked at her. "Could be to see Doherty."

"Aye, Doherty," she whispered. "I never did trust that half a man . . ."

"Playing with the raiders and the Military, too, d'you think?"

"We'll soon know the truth of it," said she. "We wait for your brothers—come on, back to the van."

Evening came, then night, and Ma, Karen, Beth and me sat as statues in the moonlight of the van, waiting. Down in the village a clock struck eleven, and still Ho and Michael did not come, and near midnight, with the light doused and the wind whispering over the heath, I rose, hearing footsteps.

"T'is the boys," whispered Ma.

"Then only one of 'em," said Karen, and followed me outside.

He was light on his feet for a big man, and he stood no more than ten yards from the van, still hatless, and Beth must have seen him from the window for she began her whimpering again, and Ma hushed her.

" 'Evening to you," I said.

46

Hands on hips he came nearer, his hair as bright gold in that faint moonlight, and I sensed the authority and power in him. He said, grinning:

"There's a fella bested me today, and I'm after him. Have ye men here?"

"Only this one," said Karen, nodding at me.

He nodded. "He could give this one six inches in height and a foot over the shoulders. Have you seen such a man around?"

"If there's such a man round these parts I'd be knowin' him," replied Karen.

"Would he be thinking of the O'Keefe's?" I asked. "They're fine big fellas indeed, and I wouldn't tangle with them."

"I'm thinking of O'Haras," he said, shouldering past me to the van. "Have you a woman in there whimpering?"

"She's a reason to weep," said Karen. "The hunger is upon her like the rest of us, will you see her?"

He turned at the door. "That's strange, for there's no need for hunger round here, woman. Three miles down the strand the Galway travellers are feasting on beef and stuffin' themselves sick with it. There's joints of the stuff draping the rocks sufficient to fill every shop in Ireland, does she know that?"

Ma was standing in the door of the van and he turned to her.

"Are you the woman of the place?" he asked.

My mother nodded.

"Would your name be O'Hara?"

"Me name's O'Toole, and I'll have you leave us in peace, soldier, for we're peaceful people and strong for the Church of God, and the hunger is upon us."

"Have ye sons, woman?"

She looked beyond him; smaller and old she looked standing there with the fine big soldier before her. "Three sons I had," she said, "and now but one."

"And who's in there behind you?"

"Me child, and second daughter."

"I'll be needing a look at them," he said, and twisted my mother away from the door and she staggered against Karen, who held her, whispering. I was after him but Karen pushed me back.

"Wait, Jess," she breathed.

Shivering, I stared through the moonlight for Hosea and Michael, but the heath was empty, with the mist rising vapours. I went to the door and looked in. The dragoon turned from Melody's bed, to Beth.

"And what's your name, girl?"

"Beth O'Toole."

She had slid to her knees before him, her lips forming words that would not come, and the sweat was streaming on her face.

He grinned at her. "Are you sure of your name, for I've never seen a woman more uncertain of it."

Eyes staring, Beth nodded, clasping her hands.

"D'you know something? I'd swear to my God I've seen you in Galway, is that right?"

Sickened, I turned away, and as I did so he kicked the door shut and Beth screamed once, loud and clear.

"Wait," said Karen.

Nothing but the dragoon's harsh demands now, and Beth's sobbing, and Melody awoke, crying. Karen held my mother between me and the door. Minutes passed, and he flung the door open behind her. Red in the face, hands clenched, he stared down at us, and Karen said, over her shoulder:

"You can frighten the belly out of her, soldier, but you'll only get O'Toole, for that's her name, and it's an end to it."

"And you've never heard of the fighting O'Haras, is it?" he whispered, coming down the steps.

"Never in me life," said Karen. "And I'll let you know something else. If I knew the men you were after I'd not be telling you."

"Don't bother yourself," he whispered. "The O'Haras are here, for I just got it out of the O'Shea woman in there. Papish bitch!" He swung his hand and hit Karen sideways, shouting, "Get the mare in the shafts, for we're going down the road. Catholic swines! If I beat you to death here you'd not loosen your tongues on your men. Ho and Mike O'Hara are the men of this van, for I learned of that from a man of Kilkieran. We have ways and means of opening your mouths in the barracks," and he seized Ma and

Karen by the wrists and twisted them into the van, booting at me for good measure. I knew I had to move then, for soon it would be too late. As I ducked the boot I saw the hasp of his knife in his belt. I swung at him, missed him and swung again, catching him on the cheek. And as he staggered I dived at his legs and brought him down. Yelling, we rolled and kicked, and his thick hands were on my throat as I found the knife, dragged it from his belt and struck it to the hilt, in peat. And as we floundered and rolled it was twisted from my fingers. I caught a glimpse of his face as I scrambled clear of him, his wild eyes and bright hair in the second before he rushed me. And I steadied myself as Hosea had taught me, pivotted on my toes and hooked him solid on the chin with all my strength, and he dropped, but seized my ankle and pulled me on top of him. Shouting, clawing, he was on me with enraged strength, his fists thudding the grass as I ducked them; one grazed my face, steadying it and the next caught me full in the mouth. Dazed, with the faint moon swinging over the sky, I twisted sideways, and he fell full length, lying still. So still he lay, arms outstretched, gasping, then all was quiet. Karen was in the mist of the night, slowly making shape. And she rose then and stood above me, staring down.

I wiped the blood from my mouth, kicked myself free of the dragoon, and took the knife from her hands.

"Quick," she said.

On the edge of the mere we put him down deep.

Hosea and Mike came back with the dawn, and they came along the road from Kilkieran. Sick to my stomach, weary, I got up from the rock and went down the hill to meet them.

"Ah, thank God for you," I said.

"Thank God for nothin'," grunted Hosea. "There was a squad of soldiers waiting on the beach and not a sign of Patrick Mulligan—the people in the village say he's been in the barracks for days, thank God for Doherty."

"Running with the raiders and the Military, too," muttered Michael.

"And giving out our grain to the travellers at a shilling a bag, and us risking our lives—did you hear the like of it—Christ, what people! Is it well in the van?"

"Well enough," I said. "The women are sleeping."

"They'd best make the most of it," said Michael, "for they'll soon be waking—we're away out of here at first light."

"We're away down the road this minute," I said, and told them of the soldier, and it stopped their breath.

"Did you have to kill him?" whispered Michael. "Bad cess to you—you have us in real trouble now—and he did no more than loosen your teeth."

"It was Karen who settled him, man—she couldn't do otherwise, he was beating us down to Galway barracks."

Hosea groaned. "Then he'll be on his way to the barracks himself now, that's a fact. Don't the priests tell how dead soldiers rise from their graves and make a report of the crimes against them."

"He'll need to be digging," I said, "for he's ten foot down. And are you believin' all the priests tell you, Ho?"

"I don't," muttered Michael uneasily. "Those fellas are sharper than the parsons, and that's going some, but I'm telling you this, Jess—they'll not rest in Galway till you and Karen are swinging. And you can't roam Ireland for the rest of your life, you'd be safer in England."

I spat. "That's what Karen says. If we can raise the loot we're away to America and me brother Shaun."

Hosea stared. "America, is it? And where will you be raisin' the money?"

I sat down on a rock. "Karen mentioned that, too. It's common knowledge that Doherty's got it stacked under his boards, and we wouldn't be racing from murder now if it wasn't for Doherty—have you thought of that?"

I saw the secret looks flash between them, and the grins, and said, "Is Doherty in a fit state to argue about it?"

"I doubt it," answered Hosea, "for there's daylight under his pegs."

I rose, staring. "So that's what you've been up to in Kilkieran."

Michael whispered, "It is the law, Jess, we couldn't do otherwise. Patrick Mulligan's widow told us of Doherty, so when they hoist Pat aloft in Galway barracks he'll be going to St. Peter with his bloody informer."

"And you lifted the money, too?"

"Eighty sovereigns for Pat's widow and five apiece for us—it's not thieving, it's the hangman's fee. And you're welcome to my five, though I've a hankering meself for a sight of America." Hosea sighed.

"Take mine," said Michael. "I'm not leaving old Ireland."

We walked slowly through the mist till the van loomed up, and Karen came running over the heath with hugs and kisses for them.

"Have you got the Doherty money, Jess?" she swung to me.

"These swabs here have beaten me to it," I said. "It's hard luck on you, girl, but I'm having five sovereigns off Mike for the trip to America."

"And you're leaving me to fend?"

"You can only swing once," said Hosea. "And Jess and me are planning to work with Shaun in Pittsburgh, sure, me heart's bleeding for you."

"You lumbering oaf!"

"Heisht! You'll be having Ma out. D'you think we'd leave you? We'll be flogging the road to Wicklow in minutes, but there's only ten sovereigns between the three of us, so you can pray to God for your ticket."

The door of the van came open then and Ma opened her arms to us. "Holy Mary be praised," she said, "for I've been praying, praying for you. Won't you take me from this God-forsaken place?"

In whispers, we told her, and Hosea said at length, "They tell me there's some hunking fighters in the pagan land, and I aim to meet them, for I've cleaned up this country of anything on two legs."

"Are you forgetting Joe McManus?" asked Michael, grinning.

"And do you realise your brother Shaun's not even expecting you?" whispered Ma.

Hosea smiled. "Is he not? I told him I'd be coming in me last two letters."

"Will you be staying with Ma, Mike?" I asked.

He rubbed his chin, grinning. "I'm taking the van with Ma and

Melody, Jess, for I've visions of a bed with Beth O'Shea, and her willing."

"Are you marrying the wench?" gasped Karen.

"The saints be praised," he answered, "who's talking of marrying."

"It's a heathen family, sure enough," said Karen. "You should be buying a ticket to the pagan land yourself."

And so, in the summer I was sixteen, we left the land where I was born, and I was sad for Connemara.

What is there in a country that leaves its barbs in the heart?

In the red shafts of the coming dawn the mountains rose in glory from the mists, and the sea was blood and tipped with foam in a rolling thunder. Ripped by the rising wind we got the old mare in the shafts, and with Beth standing frightened and tearful we got Ma aboard while Michael leaped up for the reins. I will always remember my mother as I saw her then, standing at the door of the van with Beth O'Shea behind her. We shed no tears, we took no hugged good-byes, but stood in a sudden squall of rain, Karen, Hosea and me, and waved till the van was round the bend of the road on its way up north to Cloghmora, the place where Ma was born. And we stood like statues in that pelting rain, the three of us, watching the van till it was a dot on the road to Derryrusk, and Karen wept. We spoke no word, for Karen never wept, but stood there either side of her till Barney Turvey came up with his van and Rosa and her sister aboard.

"What the hell's happenin'?" he demanded.

"Ma's away," said Karen, head low, "to Cloghmora, and we're off to Wicklow."

"Will you tell me what I'm to do?" he asked. "The Turveys have been following the O'Haras for the last twenty years, and now the O'Haras are splitting."

"We're for America, Barney," I said. A dear little man was Barney Turvey, with his round plum of a face and his clay cocked up, and the water was running streams off his broad, gipsy hat as he turned in his seat. "Did you hear that, women?" And the heads of Rosa and her sister Rachel popped out through the awning. "The

O'Haras are splitting. There's one set going to Cloghmora and another to Wicklow, which way are we taking?"

"Same road as Hosea," said Rachel, and popped in from the rain.

"You can land me with Jess," cried Rosa, "get movin'!"

"Which leaves me with Karen," cried Barney, and winked. "Haul ye aboard, O'Haras, you can travel as guests."

CHAPTER 7

We took it in turns on the footboard, which meant that we didn't have to sleep with the Turveys, said Karen, for sweet though they were, you can't mix gold with dross, which was one in the eye for me and Hosea. And on the second night of travelling the three of us were on the footboard, with the road to Wicklow stretching a silver ribbon over the moors. The wind was coming in from the Atlantic in hostile bellows and the trees were lashing each other in neighbourly hatred, with the bright moon scudding across the heath and flashing on the thatches of wayside cottages above the black gobble of their doors. With the reins in my hand I sat between Karen and Hosea, ears shivering for the jingle of dragoons, but there was no fear in Hosea.

"Did you remember your fiddle, Jess?" he asked.

I nodded, and had to grin. For he had changed from his soaked clothes into a gaily coloured dress he had got from the English charity ladies, and there was nothing to choose between him and Karen save for the black hair sprouting from the neck of his bosom.

"Who are you grinning at?" asked he.

"You're a fine manly sample to be taking to America," I said. "If Joe McManus could see you now he'd be wanting to sleep with ye."

"And a pity it would be for Joe McManus!"

Karen shoved him. "Stop your roaring, the fella might hear you, Ho. He'd take you in three rounds, and you know it."

"D'you think so?"

"Hush, the Turveys," I whispered above the clank of the hooves.

"I will not hush. D'you hear her nettling me? And herself is dependent on me catching the Irish champion to earn her ticket to Americay!"

Karen sniffed. "Then I've a fine wee chance of travelling at all,

54

be God." She made a face. "You've been living it soft for the last six months and you've left your best punches in Rachel back there."

"It's a lie!" Up on his feet now, and I pulled him down. "Heisht!" I whispered.

He said, glowering, "Have you thought I might love the woman and be having her before the priest now she's away from Ma, for she never approved of her."

"Not before time," said Karen.

"Look," he hissed, "d'you see this thing?" and he brought up his fist.

"Hosea!" I said sharply.

"Then bridle her—she's always the same when Ma's back is turned—she's got a tongue on her like the serpent of Babylon."

"Will you let a decent man sleep?" shouted Barney, head out. "Och, you daft O'Haras!"

"Count the money," I whispered, to change the subject.

"I've counted it six times, and it's still only enough for two tickets to Americay."

"And the way this one eats it'll last two days," said Karen. "Jess, shall we take the road to Dublin City, for the Turveys don't know if they're in Ireland or China."

"Why Dublin? The ships leave from Wicklow, too, and the place is quieter from dragoons."

"Can I rake out Joe McManus, ye fool, if you land me in Dublin?" asked Hosea. "The man lives in Wicklow, and there's a chance of finding him in—it's your only hope for Americay, unless you sleep with the Mayor."

"Do you know the street he lives in?" I asked.

"I've branded the place in my mind," said he. "When he opens his door I'll throw five pounds in his face and challenge him."

"What if he lays you cold?" asked Karen.

"Ach, he'll never do that, depend on it, will ye gamble?"

"Sure, I've nothing to lose except me stomach and America," said Karen. "I'm with yer, Ho, you sweet thing."

"D'you hear that, Jess?" he boomed.

I pondered, remembering the terrible McManus, with a chest

on him like a pork butcher's swill cask. If Ho reached America he'd be landing in his coffin.

"I'm doubtful," I said.

"So me big brother doesn't match this McManus fella, is it?" flashed Karen. "Are you tellin' me there's a man alive who can tame the fighting O'Haras? And the thing's got a right to prove he's the best man in Ireland."

I shrugged. "Up to you, Ho, you're fighting him."

"Och, no, it's up to McManus," said he, thumping his fist. "He's a generous man when he's loaded with gold. What's ten times five sovereigns?"

"Fifty."

He slapped his thigh. "We'll be rolling in money. When we met last time he gave ten to one against me, so I'm after the same odds now."

"Have you met before, then, you never mentioned it," whispered Karen.

"We have, but I never saw the going of him, for I left meself open, the man was lucky."

"God help us," said Karen.

The sun was on his ladder of the sky when we got into Wicklow four days later. The three of us left the Turveys feeding and went up the streets of the town. Beggars cried to us for alms, their drum-stick limbs crippled by hunger; wizened girl-mothers, their shawls starvation tight round their sunken faces, clutched at skeleton children, and stared at Karen. With her red hair flowing out in the sunlight she swept through the baskets of the market-place, me beside her, while behind us lumbered Hosea, his big fists clenched in his sullen dreams of Joe McManus. On, on through the town. Doors were coming open, windows going back, and the early street-vendors pierced the clatter of hooves and hobnails with their unearthly cries. For although the sun was scarce from his bed Wicklow had flung off the veil of night. Blankets flapped from dormers, pots poured from attics, chairs scraped flags, and mugs bubbled porter: God and Satan unleashed into a hot, Irish morning. I elbowed Hosea.

56

"Have you remembered the street now, Ho?"

He was squinting into the sun. "Dear heaven. There was a sweet Murphy widow bedding in the inn on the corner, I remember, and her name was Mona."

"She'll kill ye," said Karen. "You'll be safer with McManus," and she gripped a tipsy lout standing on the cobbles. "D'you know the house of Joe McManus, fella?"

"My soul to hell," said he, "are you seeking him?" He shivered. "D'you realise the man might be in?"

"Would she be askin' if she hoped he was out?" bellowed Hosea, his fist under the lout's chin.

"Blood and hounds!" whispered the lout. "You're asking for trouble, the three of you, for you two'll be flattened and your woman carrying if you waken McManus at this time of the morning. It's the third door round the corner, and in the name of decency don't mention Tim Brophy," and away down the street he went beating lightning.

Nuns passed us, their sweetheart Christ smothered in their breasts of virgin blackness; priests strolled by, their eyes holding dreams of coming glory. A haltered wife trod her way to market for sale, drooping on the rope of a tipsy husband. Merchants, gentlemen, and prim little housewives scurried in the reek of tar and seaweed, and below us the masts of the emigration ships swung at a cloudless sky.

"Won't you call this off, Karen," I said as she reached the McManus door, "for I can't abide bloodshed. Can't we fiddle and dance for the ticket money?"

"The fiddling after," said she, "for me blood's up. Are you ready, brother?"

"Ready," shouted Hosea, sparring at nothing, and she battered the door with her fists, shouting, "Out, McManus, you jelly-livered lout, away from your bed for fighting!"

No reply.

"Fetch it one with this," said Hosea, and gave her a boulder and she brought it down on the door enough to shift the roof tiles.

No answer.

"He's peeped through the curtains and died of a heart attack," said she. "Bring your fist to this panel, Ho, and land it in the hall."

By now the little street was filling with people, and a beggar came up with a big black bear on a chain, whistling it into a cocky step, and while Karen was bending at the keyhole it came up and barged her, and her head hit the door like the crack of doom.

"Will you get the bloody animal out of it," said she, clouting it. "D'you see here, Ho—if you poke a stick through this hole you'll blind the fella in the eye, for I swear he's peeping." And there was the pair of them with their backsides up and the bear running wild in the crowd growling booms of thunder. Some bear, this one, for it came to them bounding and its chain caught their legs and took their feet from under them. Hosea yanked Karen up in a tangle of lace and flannel.

"Does this thing want a fight?" he shouted, and cracked it one, and away it went again in the crowd bringing people down like ninepins, and howling.

"It does," said a voice. "Is it a fight you're after, boxer?"

"It is," replied Hosea, hands on hips above the five-foot bear-trainer. "You'll be seeing blood spilled when I fetch out the Irish champion."

"Indeed," said the trainer. "But you're wastin' your time on Mc-Manus—d'you know why that house is empty? It's because Mc-Manus is down in the workhouse hospital after wrestling this very fine creature." He jerked his thumb at the seven-foot bear. A good talker, this one, with a prune for a face and as bandy as a baby, and he turned to the crowd then, bawling, "Isn't it right that this animal chewed up McManus? Isn't it true he's the heavyweight champion of Ireland?"

Shrieks of delight now, with caps and sticks going up in the air, for the people were as tight as herrings in an ice-cask now, and ragged urchins doing cartwheels on the edge of them.

"Is that gospel?" whispered Hosea, eyeing the bear.

"I'll swear by me God," said the trainer. "The animal made mincemeat of Joe McManus, and took his five pounds in the bargain."

I tapped Hosea's shoulder. "Come out of it, Ho."

"Aw, to hell, Jess—didn't you hear mention of five pounds—it's Karen's Americay ticket."

"The thing's a killer," I shouted. "Karen!"

"And so's McManus," she shouted back. "Are you game for the thing, Ho?"

The trainer beamed. "It's a fair match, d'you see? The creature's fangs and teeth are drawn, and it's working on punch alone—the same as McManus."

"Are you giving us odds, trainer?" asked Karen, shoving the bear out of it.

"I am not," said he, indignant. "Would you have me life-blood? Have you noticed the size of this fella of yours? Sure, the pair of you must be working in seven-foot beds."

"Two to one, or it's off."

"On!" said the trainer. "Shall I hold the money?" And he fished out ten sovereigns.

"I'm holding it," said Karen, and dropped it in the bag down the front of her. I closed my eyes, and when I looked again Hosea was rubbing his chin and eyeing the monster and it was slobbering over his head, its belly rumbling to be heard in Connemara.

"D'you think I can handle the brute, Karen," he asked, looking up its throat, "for there's a wee difference between a sixteen-stone McManus and a thirty-stone man-eater from the wilds of Siberia."

"Then shall I strip to the waist and clump the beast myself?" she demanded. "Has the belly gone out of ye, Ho O'Hara—would you be backing from a fight if Mike was here?"

"Sure, I was only wondering," said he.

"Then stop your wondering and start your thumping, for I'm aimin' to get to America," she cried, and swept the people back, forming a ring.

The crowd was screaming in a fever now; women jabbering, silver-knobbed gentry calling odds, and sailors barging in from the ships with hurrahs and porter bottles.

"Hosea!" I yelled, fighting to get back to him.

"Have a heart, Jess," he shouted back. "Can I call myself the champion of Ireland with this beast standing on two legs before me. Och, away! Are you ready, trainer?"

59

"I am," said the trainer, and he slipped the bear's collar chain. And the moment it was free it up and fetched Ho one on the chops that would have killed McManus, then caught him by the shoulders and swung him in circles with his hobnails knocking the locals cold and the porter bottles bouncing and crashing on the cobbles.

I covered my face, and when I peeped through my fingers Karen had a quart bottle of porter up and taking aim.

"Mind Hosea!" I screamed.

"That's what I'm doin'," she cried, and she brought down the bottle on the beast's head and it dropped Ho and walked about dazed.

"So you're running now, is it?" roared Hosea, climbing up, and he brought up his fist on the thing's jaw that made mine sing, but the bear took no notice. It just stood there, hands on hips, so to speak, slavering down at Karen and her smiling up into its face all innocence, the bottle behind her back, and the moment it turned she fetched it another one, knocking it bow-legged.

"Me beast's acting queer," hollered the trainer. "Are you ill, Siberia?"

Bruno going bandier as Hosea was after him with uppercuts and belly-smashes, and the crowd was roaring and dancing with joy. Up bobbed the trainer again as Siberia staggered.

"Sure, the poor, dumb creature's not himself today," he shrieked. "Is someone in there afflicting him?"

"Aye, me brother," shouted Karen, and she swung her bottle and wanged it another one. "Is this fella supposed to be the champion of Ireland?"

"Bets off!" shouted the trainer. "Somebody's bottling him!"

Boos and groans from the crowd at this, for Ho was handing Siberia the lacing of his life, cuffing, hooking, and driving him into the sailors. A left swing, a right swing, and Siberia went sprawling, upending the Navy. Hosea dived on top of him and up went Karen's bottle.

"Mind Hosea!" I bellowed.

And she caught someone a crack they heard in the city of Dublin.

The next thing I saw was Siberia spread-eagled and Ho staggering round streaming Wicklow porter, one eye on Clifden and another on Bantry, and a lump between his ears as big as a duck's egg, and sparking.

"Did the beast strike me, Jess?" he asked, tottering towards me.

"It did," I said.

"Did you see it swing a bottle, for instance, for it felt precious like one?"

"More'n likely," I replied, "for it fights more brutal than Joe McManus. You stay here, I'm going after Karen."

But there was no moving, for the sailors were ringing us and emptying porter bottles over Hosea's head and the maidens of Wicklow were dancing about us. Faintly, above the shouting I heard a woman wailing, and the people pressed back as Karen came through them, skirts up, hair flying, with Siberia on all fours galloping behind her. Down the hill she went with the black beast slavering and swiping and the trainer skidding the cobbles on the end of his chain.

"The poor creature," said Hosea, "that's unfortunate—d'you think she'll be mutilated?"

"She can handle it," I said.

"Has she the money with her, for that's important."

"She has," I replied, "and it'll take more than half a ton of bear to ease it out of her. Do you fancy a quart of porter to settle the dust of the fight?"

"I do," said Ho. "And when I've sunk that I'm away down to the workhouse hospital to settle Joe McManus, if I have to drag him from his bed."

"One bear at a time," I said. "America."

We passed the trainer in the main street with Siberia's nose down on the flags like a gentry bloodhound, and we found Karen on the quay peeping behind a bollard. We bought our ship's provisions and stood in the queue for the emigration tickets among the exiles-to-be standing in tearful groups, singing their songs of home. And I saw beyond the water the bright red of the Turvey caravan and the mare wandering loose beside it. Rosa and her sister Rachel were standing near, staring down at the harbour at the forest of masts and spars, all dominated by the giant *Pennsylvanian*, the three-hundred-ton monster that was sailing that night.

"Have you said good-bye to Rosa?" asked Karen.

"I suppose I'd better do that," I answered. "Are you taking your leave of Rachel, Ho?"

He flapped a hand scornfully, "The woman means nothing to me," he answered.

"Has she faded in a night, then?" asked Karen. "This time yesterday you were going down her throat like a starling feeding young. You should both say farewell to Barney, at least."

"Have we the time, woman?"

"It doesn't need three of us to get the tickets. But don't make a meal of it, you're in sight of a decent town."

Rachel, I noticed, was coming down to the harbour with her peg-basket in her arms. Hosea went to meet her, picking a path through the nets and luggage. Slowly, she approached him, and lowered her basket, waiting.

Rigidly, they stood apart, and Rachel lowered her face. Suddenly Hosea cleared the ground between them, kicked aside her basket, and took her into his arms.

"One thing's sure," whispered Karen. "There'll be just the two of us sailing for America."

"Don't be daft," I said.

"He'll never see the sky of the pagan land while that one lives— ach, that's pretty . . ." for Hosea had kissed Rachel. "Aye, indeed, there's much more to it than beds."

Rosa, I saw, was still up by the caravan, so I ran through the gathering crowd and panted up the hill. So still she stood, head turned away from me.

"Rosa . . ."

"So you're dumping me, O'Hara?"

"I'm not going for a lifetime, girl—I'll be back in no time."

"If you're away to Americay you're away for good, 'cause I've seen 'em."

"I couldn't leave you for years, Rosa, I'd be aching for you," I said, trying to turn her, but she shoved me away and stared at the sea.

62

"That isn't what you told me in the cave on Lettermore," she said. "For all you know I could be comin' to a child, Jess O'Hara, and you'd be the father."

"You're no more coming to a child-bearing than me," I said, "and you know it. I'll be earning my fortune in America, and come back loaded, and I'll set you up in jewels when that happens, and you'll live in a fine square house like Squire Rochford, with servants dancing attention on ye, and galloping horses before your dinner."

"God save us," said she, turning, "and when is all this happening, then?"

"About two years—when I get back."

"I'll be awaiting," she whispered, and walked past me. "I'll be waitin' along the road to Wicklow, two years running, for the best fella for loving I've struck in the county is you. But after two years I'm away travelling."

"I'll be back," I whispered, and took her to me, and kissed her. She waved but once as I went down the hill and said good-bye to Barney.

Hosea was standing alone on the quay when I got back, kicking at stones.

"Are you ready, then?" I asked him, but still he stood there, and screwed at his hands.

"Jess," he said, "you're near six feet up now, you have no need of me."

"But Shaun's expecting you!"

He wiped his stubbled chin. "Ach, away with you to the promised land and leave me in peace, for I've changed me mind. I'd wilt and pine in Americay, sighing for a whiff of the wind of Connemara."

I sighed. "Rachel, isn't it?"

He nodded. "I've known her since she was a wee sprite from the midwife, and now I'm aching for her, will you let me stay?"

I stopped my grin. "I'll make the sacrifice."

"Oh," he whispered, "you're a good and generous brother. I'm having her before the priest, d'you see, and cleaving her for a child, and we'll take the thing home and lie it on Ma's knee, another O'Hara. Will Karen let me stay, d'you think?"

"I'm pleased to be rid of ye," said Karen, coming up, "and I knew you'd dump us at the last minute, so I got only two tickets. Will you kiss me good-bye, Ho?"

"I will not," he replied. "For I'm being faithful to Rachel from now on, but you have me best wishes."

"I'm obliged," said Karen.

"Are you away now, then?"

I looked at him. He dashed the tears away, gripped me, and kissed me. Head low he stumbled across the quay to Rachel. Hand in hand they fled for the fields. Turning, Karen looked me up and down.

"I must be daft," she said softly. "How old are you—sixteen, isn't it?"

"Aye, sixteen," I replied.

"Then it's time your dark soul was showing through your chin," she said, "for if I'm sailing to America I'm going with a man."

"You'll see."

"I'm hoping so," said she, "because I'm expecting it." She waved towards Hosea. "So he's the last fella I expect to see kissing yer."

I waved once to the hill, and followed Karen down to the sea.

CHAPTER 8

With Karen stooping as a beast of burden we dropped our bundles on the deck of the *Pennsylvanian* amid the crammed humanity fleeing from Irelan ook our place in the queue before the First Mate. I glan ound. Fragile grandpas, stricken by years, were there: feeble grandmas pinned on sticks, children, matrons, and bright-faced maidens—all sandwiched in the floating coffin-ship, shrinking to the coarse mouths of pig-tailed sailors. We waited hours.

"Right, ye name," said the Mate, and his blue eyes fixed me from under his gold-braided cap.

"Jess O'Hara."

"Her?" The eyes switched to Karen.

"Karen O'Hara, me sister."

He scribbled away most official. "Where you from?"

I lowered a hand and tapped Karen's thigh. "Dublin."

"Occupation?"

"Dancers," I replied.

He nodded, quilling away. "Have you ever danced in Connaught County, O'Hara?"

Karen said, "If you answer that he'll be as wise as us—just shove it down, sailor."

He sighed, put down his quill, and eyed her. "So we're transporting hostile Irish, is it. I'm asking you, woman—have you ever kicked up your spags in Connaught County?"

"Where's that place?" asked Karen, all eyes.

"So you've never heard of it, even. Have you heard of Clifden?"

I knew what he was after, and said, "We've never roamed far from Dublin, sir, and what would we be doin' in a haunted place like Clifden?"

"Or Kilkieran?"

I shook my head and closed my eyes with relief as he said,

scratching away, "I was just checking, for the Military are hanging the grain-raiders right and left in Connemara, and they're after murderers, too." He dusted his paper. "So I'm wondering what you're doing sailing from Wicklow when there's six ships a month hauling out of Dublin." He reached out. "Can I see your scarf, O'Hara?"

I knew the danger now. They were checking on the Molly Maguires, for they were devils when it came to blackening their faces for the raidings and killings. He eyed the scarf and tossed it back to me. "It's as clean as one can expect for a Dublin dancer, and now shall I tell you somethin'? The woman beside you has a slit in her tongue, but I'll be having six inches off the thing before she hits Philadelphia. I happen to be First Mate on this ship, d'you see, so I'll trouble you to call me sir in the future. Is that clear?"

"Aye, sure, that's different," said Karen gaily.

"Right, then," said he, rising. "And for the cheek of your sister, O'Hara, I'll trouble you to be up the main sheets, out on the topsail and down the main spars in under five minutes to prove yourself a sailor, or you'll be sitting in Wicklow while we're in America."

"Are we sailing the damned thing, too?" demanded Karen.

"You are," said the Mate. "For when we hit the storms of the Atlantic it's the men in the rigging and the women on the pumps."

"You're not pumping me. I've been sailing the sea before you knew port from starboard—can I go aloft with me brother?"

I pushed Karen aside and leaped for the rigging, swinging myself up, seeing above me the floundering boots of a land-lubber emigrant doing the official test, like me. Up, up, swaying in blusters now, with the canvas billowing fifty feet above the deck. The tackle blocks were whistling sea-shanties as I went past the landlubber.

"Oh, God, help me," he breathed, streaming sweat and clinging on.

"If I touch you he'll have you ashore," I panted. "Up, man, up—don't look down."

On the rim of the crow's nest now, swing out into space; up like a monkey to where the pennant was streaming, loving every min-

66

ute of it. And I saw, on a distant hill the red dot of the Turvey caravan trundling in dusty billows along the road to Dublin, and the speck of Hosea leading it. I took one joyful gasp at the wind, came down hand over hand, and dropped the last ten feet. The land-lubber emigrant was being fished out of the sea. Karen faced me, her eyes screwed up with anger.

"Look, d'you mind explaining to the gold braid here that I was up and down bigger masts than that before he got his ticket, and the gunk's insisting I work with the women!"

"Come, come," I dragged at her.

"Then is this oaf running the thing, or has it got a captain?"

"Away, O'Haras!" The Mate brought his fist to the table. "Mark, Mary, and Joseph, will you tell me what I've collected? Away!"

With the bundles in my arms, kneeing Karen before me I got her below decks, and the curses that followed us must have chilled Satan.

Into the curved belly of the ship now, along the coffined bunks that pinned her vitals, each little coffin sixteen inches wide; men on the right, women on the left, a ragged canvas dividing them. Here sat young Irish girls with refuse of the taverns for bedmates amid the champing of crones and screeching of babies. Muscled young men stood idly watching, tipsy drunkards were belching in the scuppers.

"Holy Mother," whispered Karen, and crossed herself.

I said, "You realise you're in this pit for the next nine weeks— d'you still fancy America?"

These were the four-pound-ten bunks that were good enough for Irish, the official single bunks, though many men and women were making double beds. The plusher, married bunks were on a deck above us.

"We're changing our minds on this," I whispered. "Do you think we might marry, and make it official?" I nudged her. "Another ten shillings and we lie together, up in the married bunks."

She smiled wide. "D'you kick?"

"I'm a galloping mule, but you'd better have me than an English tipsy for we're calling at Liverpool, and there's likely to be three of us going ashore in America."

"Not if they land on this O'Hara," said she, and followed me up the ladder to the fo'rard deck. Respectable here, well-dressed couples with sea-chests and a man even bowing.

"Hey, you!" A five-foot steward came running, preceded by his stomach, his pudding face sweating rivers. Out with his notebook, very official. "Names?"

"Mr. and Mrs. O'Hara," I said. "Double bunk."

"Tickets?"

I showed him them, and dropped him a sovereign. "Well," said he, "that's a different story indeed," and he spat on the gold. "It'd be a crime against humanity to send you to the singles with a woman beside you of those proportions. What's the relationship?"

"Brother and sister."

"God help us," said he. "I'm Cupid himself when it comes to romance, O'Hara, but we can't have sin on a respectable ship—shall we say thirty shillings?" and he held out his fat hand.

"Pay him," whispered Karen with a look to kill, and she drifted away.

"Is the woman in child, O'Hara?" he breathed confidentially.

"The woman's single."

"Man," said he, bored, "use your intelligence. The food on this crate isn't worth biting unless you're a milking mother, or suchlike—do you see the connection?" He grinned, evil.

"How much?" I asked, thinking of Karen, for I'd heard talk of people coming down to broomsticks on the nine-week voyage to America.

"Another ten shillings and I'll give you personal service, O'Hara," and he pocketed the two pounds total. "Bless me soul, indeed. Another woman in child—that's the quickest conception I've heard of since me sister caught it running in a lane in Liverpool. I'm the fastest worker on the Atlantic run, they tell me, for I have them breeched, milking, and weaning between the time they leave here and set foot in Philadelphia, do you blame me?"

"I do," whispered Karen, coming back. "I've a mind to report

68

you to the Captain himself for the evil, stinking little thief you are!"

"Ay, ay, ma'am, and you're right," said he, "and I'm about to give you the proof of it. Do you see this little whistle here?" and he fished one out. "If you don't beat it to the bottom bunks within the next ten seconds I'll clamp the pair of you in irons for attempting incest."

I stared at him, disbelieving my ears.

"What does he mean?" whispered Karen.

"Are you going?" he demanded.

I dropped my bundles and approached him and he raised the whistle.

"Wait, Jess!" Karen threw herself between us.

"The thieving, dirty-mouthed swine," I whispered.

Gripping me, Karen swung to him. "Wait, fat thief," she said. "We're two months aboard this coffin ship, and before that time's up you'll wish you'd never set eyes on the sly O'Haras."

"Below," he commanded, cheeks puffing up.

Trembling, we went below to the bottom deck.

By sunset the ship was shivering to the loading and we heard the grunts and squeals of pigs and cattle coming aboard. On deck now, we watched the tearful emigrants, the sobbed good-byes, and listened to the songs of home, though we did not sing. And at midnight, when the tide was running full and the mackerel shoals flashing in the rollers of the harbour, the *Pennsylvanian* heeled and flung off her sweating hawsers, broke loose from the surly grip of earth, and tacked in a blustering wind for the wastes of the sea.

Three weeks out from Wicklow now, and well into the gray Atlantic. Liverpool and the French and German ports were behind us and the ship was a jabber of foreign tongues. Sheep-like in docility, the foreigners had trooped aboard, as we, ragged, half-starved, escaping from Europe's Industrial Revolution to life in the Promised Land of America. For the first seventeen days we made good time, tacking to a fine sou'west haul while below decks, like iced herrings, the coffined Irish lay in spewing agony and chanted their pleas to the Virgin in a shriek of outraged steel and timber. Then, with a change of the wind we became becalmed and they rose from their racks in numb misery and staggered up to the sparkling deck.

For four days we dipped and wallowed in a burnished ocean, the sails drooping as dish-rags on the spars. Swedes, Germans, Dutch, and French were sprawled in the scuppers, eyes shifting at the women, cards flicking, coins chinking. The Welsh were there, rigid in their chains of Non-Conformity, aloof to the songs of the rollicking Irish, watching in open hostility as Karen danced. Elbows on the rail, I watched her, too. Round and round she went, her tambourine held high while Irish fiddles swung out the time for her. When the dance ended she ran to me in a flurry of laughter, fighting off a big, handsome Swede.

"You're making a show of yourself," I said.

"Are you talkin' to me?"

"I am. Away below and straighten yourself. You're showing enough breast to roll the eye of Lucifer, and you're heatin' their blood."

"Are you me bloody keeper, then?"

Up he came, and I turned away, groaning. He was big, blue-eyed, and handsome, with a grin like an orchid. "Is he annoying you, Irish girl?"

"I'm needing no help from you," retorted Karen.

He grinned wider, not understanding. "You dance again, Irish?" He gripped her wrist, turning her, winking at his German companions.

"Will you keep your paws off me!"

One after another they wandered up, grinning. Rough jokes were growing among them, thighs being slapped, and I saw beyond them the young Irish peasants rising from their haunches. The Germans surrounded Karen now and she was pushing them off, eyes blazing at the indignity.

"Jess!"

"Aye?" I half turned.

"Will you shift these fellas!"

"You fetched 'em, you shift 'em," I said, and wandered off. Then a foreigner snatched a fiddle from a hulking Derry man, took one in the chops, and somersaulted for his trouble, and next moment it was a riot. Belts were coming off, fiddles splintering on heads, fists going up and chins going backwards. Jews and Italians, English and Spanish, their tempers brewed up in the fevering sun, dived head first into a mid-Atlantic bruising, with women screaming, children squealing, and the crew getting among them with rope-ends and battens. Too good to miss, this, so I ducked in among them, yanked someone off Karen, and dragged her up from the deck. The big German faced me, and I waited for his rush, but the rush never came. Tapped from behind, he turned, and the blow that dropped him moved six inches. The young man straightened, licking his knuckles.

"Did you learn that in Ireland?" I gasped, snatching Karen away.

"*Diawch*, no, man! They're ten a penny in the mountains of Wales," and he spun and clouted a Spaniard. "Get your wild-cat out of here before they clap her in irons." Seizing Karen's hands we barged head down for the fo'castle deck, went flat behind a hatch, and lay peering. The Welshman grinned.

"Do they know what they're fighting about now, that lot?"

"I know how it started," I said, glaring at Karen.

"With a dance like that she'd start a massacre—is it right she's your sister?"

"Aye," I muttered, "me ma was cursed."

He rubbed his chin, anxious. "Shall we heave her below and get into it again, Irish? It seems indecent to let a good fight go by."

He had a fine handsome face on him, a dent in his nose I'd have given my soul for, and a voice like music. And Karen was staring at him like a woman dazed.

"Thank God for you, sir," she whispered. "May the Lord pour his holy blessings on your head for savin' us, you fine big fella."

"Come on," I said, yanking at her.

The fight was ending, with sailors flailing at Irishmen, and gold braid crowning the foreigners. The corpses of Frenchmen were fingering lumps and a fiery Italian being frog-marched for irons. Towing Karen behind me I raced below deck.

In the bunk that night, where nobody cared if you were married or single, I stared at the ceiling, watching the slow swing of the lanthorn, and gasped for breath in the fetid air as the big ship wallowed in a glassy sea. Karen was asleep in the spare bunk beside me, her hair tangled with sweat. At midnight I rose, stripped to the waist, and tiptoed through the sleepers to the steps. The emigrants lay in grotesque attitudes of exhaustion by heat; naked men and women sprawled across each other in restless sleep. A child whimpered as I passed: an Irish child-wife covered the face of her suckling baby, smiling up as I raised a hand to her. Bearded grandfathers grated at the beams, fat women panted in the grip of their stays. Ragged washing dropped on make-shift lines, pots and pans littered the bunks, rats scuttled over the sleepers, foraging for half-eaten meals. I looked at the faces of the emigrants; young faces, old ones, famine faces, dead; dead, those sleeping faces that nurtured ambitions for the glory of America.

It was cooler on the deck, with the moon an orb of astonishing brilliance above a sea flat calm and misted. Nothing stirred. The halyard lamps were spluttering red in a rhythmic creaking of timbers. Here the emigrants, forced up on deck by the stench of the bunks, were lying around like a battlefield slaughter. I leaned on the rail, wiped away sweat, and stared at the emblazoned sea.

" 'Evenin',' " said the Welshman.

He appeared beside me. I nodded. "Good drinking weather."

"First pint for evaporation," said he, and sighed. "God, the masters are against the winter crossings but they want to lie here frying in Hades. Where are you going?"

"Pittsburgh," I answered.

"Same as me, then. You collecting yourself some land?"

"Going into iron," I said. "Me brother Shaun's foreman in a works there."

He closed his eyes. "God help you," he said.

I glanced at him sharply. "And what's wrong with iron-making? My brother Shaun started from nothing, and now he's a foreman, sure, he's done well for himself in the furnaces."

"Then he's been lucky, for most of them end on fire. I was in iron in the Top Towns back home, and that was bad enough, but they reckon it's a bitch to nothing in Pittsburgh. You're Irish, man, you ought to be on the land."

"Shaun reckons there's a fortune in it if you work."

He chuckled deep. "You'll work, boy—Christ, you'll work—and you'll make a fortune if you live to enjoy it. But there's more immigrants dying in furnaces than sleeping in beds. What's your sister doing?"

I shrugged. "Same as me, I expect—that's up to Shaun."

This turned him. "Do you know what iron does to a woman? If you'd been to Merthyr or Dowlais you'd know the truth of it, but I've seen them. She'll be crawling around with a tram behind her like a chained beast, with a kick in the backside every time she slackens." He wiped his face, and sighed. "God, you Irish, will you never learn?"

"Is that the truth?"

"The place is hostile to the Irish nation, that's the truth of it, man, so you only collect the labouring jobs, the unions see to that. Can you blame them? You're spreading yourself to the corners of the earth and you'll work for a bag of potatoes."

"Don't you like the Irish?"

"Welsh or Irish, they're all the same to me. All God's creatures are entitled to eat." He smiled then. "No offence, man. You know, your sister would earn ten times your wage in the saloons. She's got a fine leg on her and a pretty swing to her hips."

"All the chaps say that," I said.

"Then here's another. So with your permission I'd like to walk the decks with her. I'd be respectable, mind, and keep it decent, for I was brought up Chapel."

"And she's a Catholic, so that's a pity."

"Whee, jakes, man, I'm not after marrying her!"

"And that's another trouble," said I. "I've enough bother getting the woman to Pittsburgh in one piece without trailing followers."

"So she hasn't a word in it, then?"

"Not one, so you keep clear of her."

"Dammo! We'll soon see about that!"

73

"We will," I replied, "for you'll have me fist in your eye at the first move you make or me name's not Jess O'Hara."

"And mine's Will Rees, for your cheek. There's daft Irish. D'you keep your sisters in cages?"

"When the Welsh are about," I said, and walked off, and he stood there as if I'd got his legs with me.

Back in the bunk now, I stretched out beside Karen on the rope coils, and she rose as a ghost in the yellow light, pushing back her hair.

"Where you been."

"Cover yourself decent," I said.

Very beautiful was Karen's breast, smooth and brown, and she wasn't particular about showing it, not knowing the difference between front and back.

"You're me brother," said she, "and you'll be seein' a pair and a hundred of the things before you're finished. Where you been?"

"You'd be killing yourself if I told you," I said. "There's you been snoring the night away down here while I've been taking the air, talking to important folks."

"And who's important on this lousy crate?"

"The big Welsh fella, for one—to say nothing of a wee chat with the Captain."

"The Welshman, did you say?" And she pulled up her dress as if the chap was half-way down it, staring. "D'you mean the fine big man who saved us in the scrap."

"I mean just him," I said.

"God save us," she whispered, vacant. "And me down here wasting me life. Will he still be up there, d'you think?"

"I doubt it, for I shifted him. He was after walking the deck with you tomorrow, so I threatened a hit in his eye. You'll be meeting some strange people in the city of Pittsburgh, but you'll not be including the Non-Conformists, for they're pagans."

"Don't he worship the same God?" Her voice rose, and she was up on her knees.

"Hush, you're raisin' the people," I whispered, and pushed her back.

74

"I'll be raising hell itself if you start your dictating," said she, looking venomous. "For I'd rather have a pagan Welshman beside me this night than a hulking big Irish brother!"

"Ach, go to sleep!"

So still she sat, staring down the bunks, eyes narrowed in her dreams of the Welsh when she should have been dreaming of mating with Irish, and I laid a curse on the land of their fathers.

CHAPTER 9

From the motionless calm, the incandescent brilliance of a mirrored sea, the wind flung off the shroud of her ten-day grave and swept into witchery and madness. Red clouds poured up from the east and exploded in flashes, and in the storms, with the sky rolling thunder, the cholera came, though they called it typhus.

It began in the married bunks above us, found an Irish boy, turned the soles of his feet to the back of his head; blew in the face of a grandmother, and killed her in hours. Next a Dane, three Hungarians, and a milking baby, and the Irish began their keenings and wakes as it got among them. With her top-gallants in tatters, heaving and plunging in a tumultuous sea, the *Pennsylvanian* began her role of a floating coffin.

They died in the married bunks mostly, though a whole family was snatched from the gentry's quarters, and the corpses were hauled up on the streaming decks. Full rites, full respect, this burial at sea; up by the hands and feet, a swing, a splash, and the still white body wallows away to starboard. I stood on the slanting deck and wondered if sharks died of cholera. And in the blustering haul the ship listed dangerously with a shifted iron ballast. The storm rose in ferocity. Decks awash, with her topsails gone and her mainsails in rags, she floundered on. Two sailors overboard one night, two more died of crushing, and we buried again five weeks out, but this time washed clean of the cholera. Under a watery sun we tacked at three knots. Off came the hatches and up came the emigrants, staggering from the agony of the holds: the tattered, gaunt Irish soaked with sickness and bilge-water, the cowed foreigners, the dejected but still rigid Welsh clutching their Bibles —all tamed by the fury of the Atlantic. They huddled together in misted sunlight, and slept.

Karen was sitting on the rail that morning, swinging her bare legs, combing out her hair, and she said:

"Have you seen that Welsh boy lately, Jess?"

I shook my head.

"That's strange. I've never seen two yards of a fella disappear so entirely. That Welsh is a fine way of speaking, and he's hair the colour of a Tipperary crow. D'you think he's got an eye for me?"

"For a gipsy Irish? Have sense."

"And what's wrong with gipsy Irish?" She glared down at me, comb held high.

"Would he give you a second look?" I asked. "He'll be after a Welsh woman the moment he's free of here, for you're the wrong religion."

"And what's the religion to do with it? There's been prayer books sitting on Bibles since the days of Adam and Eve, and you know it."

Disinterested, I jerked my thumb at the sea. "Whale," I said.

She jumped down beside me. "Am I interested in those big black devils frothing their lives away when I'm worried about a friend?"

"Probably dead," I said. "Took by the cholera."

"He was well enough when I saw him last. He was up fo'rard working with the sailors on the jib sheets, and d'you know who I saw up there with him?"

"No." I turned away.

"That thieving steward who stole your money. The man's no sailor, you know. He was hanging over the rail and going greener when the pair of us collided."

I turned back. "Are you telling me he's overboard?" I whispered.

"Now, I couldn't swear to that, for one moment the poor soul was there and the next moment he wasn't, it's unfortunate."

I glanced around. "Karen," I breathed.

"Have a heart, Jess—d'you think I lifted him? I'd not harm a hair of a human head, let alone the sweet, wee steward's, God rest him."

Footsteps sounded as I groaned at the sky. "Hush," I whispered, "here comes your Welshman."

" 'Morning, O'Hara," said he, and fluttered an eye at Karen.

I grunted reply.

"The people are waking from the dead," he said, and turned at the rail.

The ship was clipping along at a merry rate now and Irish bag-pipes were out and the crew yelling sea-shanties. Love-making was among the younger ones, too, with spoonings and sea-promises going on behind deck-coils and God knows what going on below decks, said Karen, and the sun was shining on a bright, forgiving morning.

"Is it right you're travelling to Pittsburgh, too, Mr. Rees?" asked Karen, and she pushed back her shawl and slanted an eye at him.

"Pittsburgh eventually," he answered. "I'm staying with relations in New York for three months."

"What takes you to that muck of a place?" I asked. "Pittsburgh's the city where they're making their fortunes—there's no furnaces in New York."

"I'm studying there," he answered. "My old uncle's got an iron-works in Pittsburgh but I'm learning the tricks of it at a college, before I take it over."

"Take over an iron-works!" exclaimed Karen.

"Helping to build it, at first, Miss O'Hara, it's only a wee place at the moment."

"I thought you were an expert in iron, Rees," I said to cool him.

He smiled at Karen. "One's never too clever to learn. And I've brought some new ideas from Wales these people could do with, so I'm working on experiments."

Karen said, her eyes wide in child-like wonder, "Will you be bringing your wife to America after you've made your fortune, sir?"

"No wife," said he, grinning down at her.

"Then your girl?"

"I've only one girl, and she's my cousin," said he. "She's in New York now and she'll be coming to Pittsburgh to keep house for me, she'd be pleased to receive you when we're settled in."

"The saints be praised, Mr. Rees," said Karen. "Do you fancy a stroll round the deck to stretch yourself?" and she touched his arm.

"Good idea," I said, "I'm stiffening up standing."

The look she shot me should have dropped me dead.

And that night, with the ship's bell tolling drearily above, I woke, put out my hand, and found Karen absent. Pulling on my shirt I went quietly up on deck.

The ship was painted silver in the moonlight, the phosphorous lights flashed in the foaming wake. Karen O'Hara and Will Rees were standing there, mouth against mouth, enwrapped in the age-old tyranny that joins and divides. They stood as ghosts, removed from the secret giggles of lesser lovers, and I knew that they were one when he kissed her again.

"Ah, Will, I must go!"

"Please stay, Karen."

I watched. Very pretty it looked, this kissing in moonlight, the pair of them as black statues against the rolling clouds. Pushing at him now.

"Got to go, Will—Jess'll miss me and there'll be hell to pay."

"And to hell with your brother Jess, I'll handle him."

I grinned.

"Will, he'll be up here and swiping you in a minute—the fella sleeps like a cat . . ."

"Karen!"

"Ach, stop that now, behave yourself . . ."

I stiffened, peering.

"Karen . . ." a whisper. I sat on a bollard and began to sweat.

"Och, no," said she. "Have sense. Cool yourself, fella—are all you Welsh as daft? Down by here, in the middle of the deck? Sure, the Captain himself will be clapping us in irons."

Nothing then but the swish of the sea and the sigh of the halyards.

"Eh, dear," whispered Karen.

"Oh, Will," she said.

I sighed, rose like a mouse, and tiptoed down to the bunk, and laid there, and an hour later she came and undressed in stifled haste beside me.

"Jess," she whispered, but I did not wake.

And in the ninth week out from Wicklow quay, with the emigrants lying weakened and dejected in the scuppers or sitting in apathetic groups on the hatches, the gulls came and the man up in the crow's nest went demented.

"Land ahoy on the starboard bow!"

I rose, disbelieving it, until I saw the gulls, then leaped up the mainmast ladder and stared, shielding my eyes from the sun. As a line of blue thread on the edge of the world, came land.

Philadelphia!

Now the emigrants poured up on deck in screaming joy, dishevelled, emaciated, thrusting boney arms skywards in thanksgiving, sinking on their knees and bowing their heads amid a screeching of bagpipes and fiddles. Aloft still, I searched the milling heads below, but there was no sign of Karen. More gulls came, wailing their welcome from the rocky outcrops of the New World, now circling us in flocks, and the *Pennsylvanian*, garlanded by their beating wings, waddled west into the bright sun, battered, listing, her rigging festooned with broken spars and fluttering sails. Into the Delaware River now, on into the harbour and its bright sheen of water; beset by guiding long-boats and lusty rowers, threading a path through the anchored barques of the Old World and the spice-perfumed schooners of eastern seas—on, on into the commands of the berthing, the splashing cables, the creaking windlasses of the jetty, the flung cables—all the bedlam of a sea-port boiling with throngs of labourers and blue-coated officials who lined the front, openly disdainful of another bloody bunch of foreigners and Irish. But the people aboard were going mad with joy, standing up on the rails and waving, many climbing the sheets for a better view. Seeing them coming up below me I began to swing myself down, and came face to face with Will Rees.

"I'm not saying good-bye to her, Jess," he said.

"Why not."

There was a silence in him, his eyes dreamy. He did not reply.

I said, "You've had a mighty fine time with your loving these past three weeks, and I didn't agree with it, but you're not being decent to drop her flat."

He shook his head. "I'm not saying good-bye. If I try it she'll never see Pittsburgh, or I won't land in New York. Better this way, man, tell her I'll come for her."

"She's sharp for the fellas," I answered. "You'll be lucky if she waits."

"She'll wait," he whispered, and fished in his pocket and

brought out a little wooden spoon. "It's a love token of the Welsh," said he. "I carved it special from the mainmast, will you give it her?"

I took it. "Is it witchcraft?"

"It's pure, O'Hara, and the Welsh way of saying she's my girl till I fetch her. There isn't much God in that."

I shrugged. "Good luck," I said, and went down hand over hand, leaving him up there. I found Karen jammed in the middle of the cheering mob, and she had our bundles on her back.

"Have you seen Will Rees?" she gasped as I took them off her.

"He's packing in the hold, he'll be up in a minute. Come on, the gang-plank's down."

Cases and sea-trunks were being dragged along the deck. Children were heaving at bundles, the ancients sitting in haggard silence. Bright-haired Scandinavians were whooping with joy, some Welsh standing in whispered conspiracies, queer these Welsh.

"I'm not leaving without Will!" said Karen. I took a fresh grip on her wrist but she twisted it away. Lowering the bundles I sighed deep. "Look," I said, "d'you expect me to be interested in a bloody Welsh fella when there's a four-hundred-mile spagging facing us to Pittsburgh."

"I anna leaving 'im." She stood there screwing her fingers and the crowd barged her on their way to the gang-plank, tripping over our bundles, cursing us.

"Have you thought that he might have left you?" I asked.

"He wouldn't do that, not Will. He promised to meet me here, by the fore-mast, and Jess, I'm not shifting."

"You'll wait all your life, then," I said. "Look," and pointed.

Karen gripped the rail, staring down, and the last thing she saw of Will Rees was the back of him going down the gang-plank. Reaching the Immigration Office he pushed through its door without a backward look. And Karen made a fist of her hand and put it against her face. "Right," she whispered, "I'm loosed! For all I give him he gives that. May the curse of the evil Cromwell be upon him, the damned pagan savage!" and she wept.

"That's better," I said. "Now find a fine big Irish lad in Pittsburgh and set your soul to heaven, for if you share a bed with a savage again you'll take the thing to hell. Come on, girl, Pittsburgh."

Now the grip of America beneath our feet, the swimming, slanting steps born of two months tossing and turning. With the palaver of the Immigration Office and cholera checks behind us we went through the prodding officialdom and the crashing stamps of authority into the rutted, dusty streets of Philadelphia, past crazy, leaning houses and the timbered churches of ten denominations, bawdy bars and whiskey saloons, making for the railroad centre. With Karen lumbering under her bundle behind me I became aware of eyes, and turned, lowering mine.

"Did you have to come ashore in a scarlet skirt and with a tambourine?" I asked.

White-faced, she stood, eyes narrowed, thinking of the Welshman.

"You're driving the place demented," I added. "Can't you change into your black dress or at least get a tuck in that neckline?"

"Would you have me naked in the streets?" she flashed.

"You're naked now, the town's undressing you!"

"Oh, go to hell," she said, and wept.

I sighed. "Come on," and took her bundle.

Men on horseback were everywhere; lean men, born to the saddle, with leather breeches and thigh-guns; brown-faced and mean, these men, eyes glittering in their half-breed faces. Drunkards rolled by, their bleary eyes slanting at Karen. Red men, cloaked against the heat, squatted on open verandahs, pipes coming from wrinkled faces, mouths dropping at the scarlet apparition. Groups of toughs iced into astonishment, then slapped their thighs in guffaws of laughter. Swing doors came open and men came out sprawling, and I saw behind them a bright confusion of drinkers and degenerates, and bun-topped harlots in black lace showing enough of the great divide to drop a Roman emperor. Melodeons were wheezing and fiddles shrieking against a crescendo of backchat and quarrelings. So this was Philadelphia, I thought—a garbage of a port that guffawed at its immigrants, its identity stained with the clash of hooves and bottles. Quieter here, away from the docks. Businessmen walked by with a lofty arrogance, their ladies gliding under silk-fringed parasols. Painted whores and sweating Negroes as black as Connemara peat went by, all eyes turned to Karen, and I was sick of it. In the shade of a tree I dropped the bundles.

"Have you a shawl in this thing?" I asked, toeing hers.

She eyed me.

"Fish it out and wear it," I said. "You'll have me battered saving your virginity, for you're dropping the eyes out of every man in the town."

"Am I a scarlet woman because me dress is scarlet?" she cried.

"Black dress and shawl," I said, "or we go no farther."

I waited, back turned to her.

"Does this suit you?" she asked at length.

"That's better," I said, and we squatted under the tree. "Now to count the money," and I fetched it out and rolled it on the ground before us.

"That's funny stuff indeed," said Karen. "How d'you count it?"

I shrugged. "Don't ask me—I just put ten sovereigns over the exchange counter and they gave me ten of these."

"Are they silver?"

"Solid," I replied. "They're dollars—one to a pound. They're a bigger coin—the fella explained it."

Karen nodded at the sense of it. "Have you got the decimal point?"

"What's that, for God's sake?"

"There's a decimal point or somethin' or other that goes with 'em."

"Who said that?"

"Will Rees, the Welshman. The man was educated, not like some I could mention," and she went round tipping up the dollars. "You've got no decimal point here, so you've been fiddled."

"Are you believing all that big oaf told you?" I frowned at her. "He had a lying tongue on him. One day he was an iron expert and the next he was planning for lessons in it. Ach, he had a honeying mouth—if you hadn't been watching he'd have wronged you, for that's what he was after."

"So that's what you call it—wronging, is it?" She fluffed up her hair. "If that's so I'm tryin' it again, for I didn't know what I was missing."

I stared at her, and pointed. "More talk like that and I'm writing home to Ma."

"And welcome," she replied, "for I can write, too, you hypocrite. Sure, before I thought of lying with a man you were doin' the Turveys."

"It's a lie!"

"You had that Rosa on Lettermore, or me name's not Karen O'Hara. Are you writing now?"

I grinned at her. She rose. "No point in gassing about loving for we'll get none round here. Are we eating?"

"One big feed, then Pittsburgh."

"Shaun'll be waiting!" She clapped her hands at the sky, forgetting love.

"Like hell," I said, "for he doesn't know we're coming, but he'll find us a roof."

In a dockside tavern now, we ate till our bellies were as tight as little bass drums, and an hour later bought our tickets to Harrisburg by train, for we couldn't afford to train it beyond, it being cheaper to travel by river, we were told. All that night we waited with the rest of the Pittsburgh travellers, and in the morning, when the giant steamed in, we climbed aboard and slept, awaking at midday to the clatter of the iron wheels, and slept again, and I, for one, was dreaming. I dreamed of the blue peat-water of Galway County and the wind-whipped crags of Connemara: of Ma and Michael, and Beth O'Shea, of Hosea and Rachel. Was Rosa sleeping, I wondered, under the same faint stars that pinned the distant Alleghenies, was Lettermore bright in sunlight? Did the mackerel flash in the rollers and the breakers hiss and thunder on the shore? I awoke to Karen's hair blowing over my face, and held her in the swaying seat, and she opened her eyes and smiled into my face.

"Jess, you're weeping!"

"Weeping me eye," I said, "I've been sitting in a wind."

CHAPTER 10

Pittsburgh!
To Harrisburg, then by flat-boat to Hollidaysburg, over the Allegheny Mountains, to Johnstown, and on to Pittsburgh.

Along the deep swims of the Kiskiminetas River we went, and Vandergrift swept by, gilded in sunlight. The bearded pole-men, carved from the same granite as the great Mike Finch, chanted their dirges against a tumble of brown water. Here were prolific woodlands, once the home of Iroquois and Delawares whose naked feet had knifed the bright, luxuriant country. Wild turkeys roamed the banks, wolves howled at dusk, and the night was pierced with the screams of wildcats. And the great plantations withered and danced in the pole-men's fires as we crouched in the glow, Karen and me, ripping at roast hare while the punky gnats ate us alive. Karen stared up at the full moon, sighing.

"Ach, Jess, it's strange. Can you tell me why God starves our little Connemara and rises to such bounty when handling Pennsylvania?"

"It's the sins of the Irish," said a pole-man, gnawing at cornpone.

"Is that right?" said she. "And what nationality are you, buster?"

"Sure, I'm Irish—me mother's name was Murphy. It was her discovered the chicken flying the Atlantic."

"Did she see the skies over Ireland, or you either?" asked Karen.

"I have no wish to," said he, "for this is God's country."

"Aye? Then you'll not know that this is a barren rock of a place compared with back home—you're base ignorant, man—you're fit for nothin' but poling. For there's wild turkeys patrolling the streets of Dublin and ships on the brooks of Galway that would make this wreck a lifeboat."

Brackenridge floated by at dawn, Sharpsburg was wraithy in the screeching of owls and Etna blossomed smoke. I watched the disbelief grow in Karen's face as the Allegheny River traffic thickened. Paddle steamers hammered past, their funnels shooting sparks; barges and drifters, long-boats and schooners wallowed alongside, their crews yelling insults and getting an earful back. And from the darkness came a murmur that grew into a thunder. Sulphurous smoke quickened in the wind and rolled down the river to meet us. Rounding a bend of the river the rolling slopes of Coal Hill flooded above us, an avalanche of light, and the night suddenly flared red, as if the rim of hell had lifted. I rose in the prow of the boat and drew Karen up beside me.

"Lord God," I whispered.

"Pittsburgh!" she said, and the pole-man stooped and bellowed in her ear.

"Have you changed your tune, woman? Did you ever see the like of that in Ireland?"

We stared at a burning city, at roofs and chimneys aflame with fire-shot smoke that stained the river as with pools of blood. And the night was split with the beat of hammers. Hooves clattered on loading bays, bully voices screamed commands, and the moon was obliterated as we drifted to the jetty at Allegheny. Coughing in Allegheny's smoke we leaped out, buffetted and tripped by other eager immigrants, already under the lash of the industry. Pushed along the jetty in a wave of excited people, I swung our bundles against a wall.

"Jess!"

I knew the voice through the passage of years, flattened myself against the wall, and held Karen against me.

"Jess, Jess!"

"Shaun!" cried Karen, and he fought his way through the milling crowd and reached us, beaming, his arms flung wide.

"So you've come. Ah, God bless you!"

This was Shaun, my brother. He swung Karen up and danced her in a circle, and I watched. Most prosperous, this Shaun O'Hara —a far cry from the ragged urchin who jumped the ship at Galway nine years back with a bag of potatoes, and ended up being a foreman in Pittsburgh. Sunday suit on now, very jaunty, with a dandy's

86

swing to his walk as he led us through the immigration checks handing out money right and left to hasten the process.

"How did you know we were coming?" I asked him when we'd time for a breather.

"I'll tell you later, me boy—where's Hosea and Michael?"

Karen told him as we went along the tangled waterfront.

Shaun said, disgusted, "Do they prefer the starvation of Ireland to the profits of a city like this?"

"Nothing wrong with the Old Country," I said.

"God alive, man," he retorted, "what's right with it? While you've been skinning yourselves to death on praties I'm foreman of an iron-works and likely to go higher." We hurried on with Karen between us, and her shooting fearful glances at the flashing sky.

"Is the bloody place burning up?" she asked.

"It's the furnaces," Shaun replied, and sniffed at the wind. "And that stink's the tanneries where they're burning the hides off dead mules, sure, it smells like a Sunday joint when you get used to it."

On, on, down wretched alleys. "Is the work hard?" asked Karen. "They told us on the flat-boat that you lose a gallon of sweat every shift."

"Sure, it's hard," said Shaun. "If you sit on your backside awaitin' your pay-packet you'll be starving to death, but for every pound of flesh you lose labouring they pay you back in silver. Turn here."

Away from the river now, down dark, dingy alleys, with ragged children hunched against doors and drunks in taverns parting their beards and pouring down whiskey with thirsts like Gargantuas. Mangey dogs nosed garbage piles, Negro women were squeezing their breasts into crinkle-haired babies with white, rolling eyes.

"Have you beds for us?" asked Karen, heaving on her bundle, so I took it off her and landed it on Shaun.

"Would I let me own flesh and blood sleep in the street?" he answered. "I've beds right enough, but you might have had the decency to say you were coming."

"But you met us," I said, in wonder, and he flashed me a wink.

"Sure, I met you. The Society's got its tabs on the immigrants."

"The Society?" I asked, but he ignored me.

"This is us," said he, and thumped a door, and I glanced around, waiting.

Furnace workers were sitting on their hunkers in grimed bandages; painted women were curving in doorways, blowzy faces peered from windows. I raised my eyes. "North Canal Street" was painted on the wall above the door of the house. And the door came open six inches to the face of a haunted ghost, white hair to match and hands for gripping broomsticks.

"'Evenin', Mrs. Kovaks," Shaun knocked up his cap, and the sunken eyes in the doorway opened wide at Karen.

"Well, the blessing of God," said she. "They've come at last, is it?" and her stumpy teeth rolled in her mouth. "Sure, I can smell the peat on the pair of 'em from here, come in, come in!"

"You Irish, too?" I asked, going past her.

"That I am, as the bogs. But for me sins I married a pot-bellied Pole—have you seen the fella, Shaun?"

"He'll be oiling his gullet," cried Shaun.

"Is he with the Society, d'you think?"

"Would the Society sign on the likes of Kovaks, Ma—the man's trash. Will you show us the room, and less talking?"

Up a ladder now, Mrs. Kovaks leading, through a hole in the ceiling into a jail of a room with a double and single bed, straw-blown and rat-nibbled, and awry on the wall was a picture saying "God is Love."

"Who's sleeping with who?" asked Mrs. Kovaks, and shot her rhubarb smile at Karen. "For this is a virgin house and I've had some of his sisters."

"Hark at the woman!" Shaun laughed uneasily.

"Aye, hark," replied Mrs. Kovaks. "Some queer things have flown up and down that ladder in the last six months."

"And not a virgin between them," said Karen.

"When they came down in the morning," said Shaun, entering the fun; going double now and slapping his thigh with laughter, and I remembered a bright, spring morning and an urchin Irish boy, bundle on his back, bound for Galway. Karen said softly:

"But it's changing now I'm here, Shaun."

"Beggin' your pardon, milady," said Mrs. Kovaks.

The night roared on down the streets of Allegheny, and I awoke at dawn amid Shaun's strangled snores and the flames of the furnaces dying on the window. Rising from the bed I looked toward the river, seeing beyond the maze of alleys the broad river spiked with masts and derricks against a red dawn. And from the mists of the cooling-pits and the pulsating glow of the furnaces came the imperious clang of the accident bell. Shaun heard it in sleep, and groaned, turning. Crossing the tiny room I stood above Karen in the single bed. She was breathing in the soft rhythm of a child's dreamless sleep, but stirred as I stood watching, and opened her eyes.

"That you, Jess, boy?"

"Aye."

She gripped my hand. "It's a hell of a place," she whispered. "Hosea was right, for all the stupidity of him—we've swopped a witch for a devil. Be Jesus, this place needs cauterising with brimstone and fire."

"Go back to sleep, you'll need it," I said, and climbed in beside Shaun.

In the stink of the tanneries and his whiskeyed breath I lay, staring at the ceiling, seeing his spread-eagled journeys in his city paramours, and remembered his youth despoiled. And I hated him, and Pittsburgh.

"Mind," said Shaun next day, "it's nothing particular, and you'll have to start at the bottom like the other immigrants."

"As long as it's a job," I replied. "Have you got one for Karen?"

"I could fix her in the iron-works—tub-pulling."

"Not the iron-works," I said.

"And why not? Is she something special? Do you realise that unskilled labour's ten cents a body in this place?"

"It might be," I answered, "but she's not working in iron."

Although not yet six o'clock in the morning the streets of Allegheny were teeming with people; doors coming open, windows going back and slops pouring down the cobbles. We walked on, Shaun and me, leaving Karen back in the house with Mrs. Kovaks and her Pole husband Timko. A slob of a man, this fella, with a ten-gallon belly on him and an evil roll in his eye when he first saw Karen, and I had half a mind about leaving her.

"She's a fine strong woman for the laundry, mind," said Shaun absently.

"And a fine strong fist you'd collect for even suggesting it."

"Then you do the suggesting, for I'm not wet-nursing her, Jess. She takes what she can get—like everyone else in Pittsburgh."

Along the waterfront we went through the debris of the unloadings, with the mules screaming from the tanneries and the red belchings of furnaces; across the bridge with us and into Duquesne. I said, catching Shaun up:

"She's hell-bent on her dancing, d'you know that?"

"She'd be safer scrubbing shirts," he answered gruffly. "There's ten red lamps to the mile here and they dance right enough, but not to Irish bagpipes—forget about Karen, I'll handle her."

We walked on, quickening our pace in the army of workers converging to its labour; to the glass-works, iron-works, ship-yards, and tanneries; all rushing to beat the clock, said Shaun. Shawled women went past us in droves, their faces expressionless, as if the brief respite from labour had dulled them. Hand in hand went the child-labour in tatters for the mills. Over the bridge and into Monongahela we went, and up to some compound gates.

"Wait here," said Shaun, and entered the compound, and I leaned against the wall and watched the iron-workers coming in. A stew-pot of humanity flooded past me, gesticulating, jabbering— Poles, Germans, Scotch-Irish and Hungarians, said Shaun later: Negroes, red men, yellow men, all raked from the earth into the labour of Pittsburgh, the bountiful. And thick-necked foremen were standing in the compound counting the heads, steering them left and right like cattle for the knacker-knife. And I saw through a gap in the crowd three men standing against fire as a furnace belched—Shadrach, Meshach, and my brother Shaun Abed-nego, who was railing them in fury, his voice a scream, his fist raised. Disgusted, he came back to me, pushing men out of his path. "The double-timing bastards," said he. "The Society had a job fixed for you and they've pulled in a Hunky. I've a bloody good mind to see McNamara." White-faced, he spat.

"And who's McNamara when he's home?"

"Boy, you'll damned soon know."

"And what's this Society, for I've heard little else since I landed in this dump."

"Hush your mouth." He glanced at me.

I shrugged. "What happens now?"

"We wait." Grunting, he eased himself down on his hunkers against the wall, and I sat beside him. Other men joined us, squatting in a line, staring moodily across at the Point. From the compound the clamour of the works grew in a flaring of hearths and thudding of drop-hammers. I said:

"D'you call this work, then? I can do this back home on the lazy bed hoeing spuds." Shaun scowled, not replying. The other waiting men were staring anxiously at the gates, and their faces, I noticed, were pale and lined deep with hunger. And then, in a sudden roar of a furnace a man screamed. I leaped up. The man screamed again and again within the works, like a woman being mutilated. Shaun grinned and rose lazily.

"That's us, man. You're in," he said.

"For God's sake what's happened?"

"Aye, the fella was bang on time, Jess—it's a lucky day for the O'Haras," and he went to the gate and pulled men away from it. "Out of it, you bastards, I'm a foreman," he shouted, and turned to me as the gates swung open. "It's a cleaner. We blew Number Six last week, and they're inside it. The slag must have shifted and singed a couple of them. Christ, they're making enough commotion for the grids of hell."

I closed my eyes. Two men now, snatching at breath in the agony of the burning, their shrieks unearthly. Shaun said, inside the compound, "D'you fancy a cleaner's job, mate? The winter's coming on, remember, and it's a bloody sight warmer than pushing the buggies."

I did not reply, for the accident bell was clanging now and the stretchers were coming out. They carried the cleaners past us. They lay in shocked agony on the stretchers, their clothes still steaming from the incinerating slag and the onslaught of the cooling buckets. One raised his head as he went by, his eyes peering from the white scald of his face. Shaun said:

"To hell with it, Jess, I was right. Cleaners. Tell you the truth I was hoping for a top-filler."

"Top-filler?"

"Aye, up on the filling-skip. You're made for the job with those bull-shoulders and you're light on your feet for a big fella—Hosea would fill it a treat, for instance. But there's a difference, mind. If you trip over the skip you're smack into the furnaces, but you only risk a scorching when you're cleaning a furnace hearth."

"A big difference," I said, and he smiled indulgently.

"Sure, man, sure—four dollars a week. Hey, Mannigan!" He waved at the puddling-shed, and a man waved back. "It's me brother from Ireland! He's the next man in."

"Cleaner, Number Six, Shaun," yelled back the foreman. "Is he covered?"

"Would I be bringing him if he wasn't covered, you ape? I'm seeing McNamara tonight." He elbowed me. "I'm on Number Three, Jess—Mannigan'll care for you. I'll fix an advance on your pay and we'll get down to McNamara and play hell with the whiskey—see you at six."

Mannigan, the foreman, faced me. "So it's another bloody O'Hara? Sure to God, it would be an act of justice if they kept you bastards back home in Ireland." He gave me a pick and shovel. "Right, me boyo, strip to the waist."

Red light was flaring in the puddling-shed and the air was swirling with sulphur smoke. Here was the Pit of Acheron where an army of half-naked labourers grunted and sweated at the fire-boxes, their bodies flashing light. Fuel-carriers, furnace-rodders, and barrow-men withered and danced in the strange hue. Foremen chewed on sweat rags, peering at the pilot flame. A shouted command above the din and a furnace was tapped; the white iron streamed from the bung in a shower of sparks, flashing its brilliance at the soot-caked roof. Coughing in the smoke I stood with my pick and shovel and stared at the wonder of it.

"Right, Irish, down the chute!" and I jumped into the hearth of Furnace Six with a Pole and a Hunky. With the glowing slag

92

above us we picked and shovelled to free the chimney, bringing down fiery lumps, streaming sweat in the scorching heat while a man threw buckets of water over our sack-covered shoulders to cool us. Ten minutes of this and we were hauled out by Mannigan, and lay on the rim of the hearth while the next three carried on. Down again now, half blinded with the heat and acrid smoke, picking at the mass, ducking the sudden falls of slag that threatened to pin us. The Pole fainted in an hour. They saw him to the gates and paid him off. The bright hair of the young Hungarian working beside me was streaked with sweat and cinders, and he raised his blistered face at midday and looked at me.

"Oh, the Christ!" he said.

"You speak Irish, man?" I gasped.

"It damn kill me," he said. "Two children I have, and this work the first for a month. This man Carnegie wants to pick the slag, eh, Irish? Singer and Painter, Astor and Vanderbilt, all picking slag. You hungry?"

I shook my head, and he wiped away sweat, and spat. "Whores and bastards, these damned foremen, and I hate this bloody Pittsburgh."

"Why did you come to it, Hunky?"

He elbowed me aside, struck at the slag above him, and stood back as it poured down. "Starve to death in Hungary, work to death in Pittsburgh—what matters, Irish, just the bloody same. Three years I been here, three years I hate it. You'll see."

By late afternoon there was a band of iron around my back and my boots were filled with sweat, but still the torment went on with the foul-mouthed Mannigan reviling us from above, and all around us was the bedlam of iron-making, the thud of the drop-hammers and the clanging bells of the ladles. Up on the ladders now, hacking away, with the air swirling with heat and dust, and when the whistle went for the end of the twelve-hour shift I climbed up to the rim of the hearth with the Hunky and we lay there, gasping.

"Are you there, Jess, lad?" Shaun, shouting from the door of the puddling-shed.

I climbed upright, pulled my coat over my blistered shoulders. "You all right, Hunky?" I glanced down at him and he screwed up his hand. "One day we get a union," he said. "One day the Sons of Vulcan will change things for us."

"A union?" I asked.

"For you it do not matter," he said, and rose. "For you are Irish and you have the Mollies."

"The Mollies?"

"Are you comin' or not?" bellowed Shaun.

"Coming," I called. "Good night, Hunky."

Hank's bar was down on the waterfront, near enough to Virgin Alley for a freak, said Shaun, for more maidens changed into matrons there than in the rest of Pittsburgh, which was going some. It had escaped the Great Fire of '45, he explained, and now it stood alone in a little derelict shanty town where the workers, drained of strength, stared from sooted windows. Light and smoke hit me as we shouldered the swing doors. Up to the bar we went and Shaun hammered it for whiskey.

"Is McNamara in, Lou?"

The bald-headed gnome of a bartender just went on polishing glasses, eyeing me.

"It's me brother from Ireland," said Shaun. "Does he look like Andrew Carnegie? Sit easy, Lou," and the little man lifted his eyes at the ceiling and slid us a bottle and two glasses.

"Here's luck, Jess, let no man come between us." Shaun filled the glasses and tipped his whiskey back, but I took mine slowly, looking round the room. From a dozen little tables the whiskey was gurgling, cards flicking, money changing hands. A tall hostess slid past me on black satin legs, her upswept bosom tinkling with cheap jewellery, her buttocks swaying in her ridiculous attempt at dignity. I saw her secret wink at Shaun as he turned, bottle in hand.

"Upstairs, Jess, McNamara will be waiting."

"Look," I said, "is this fella that important? Karen will be eating her heart out."

"Important?" He groaned. "You're as green as Irish grass, Jess. The man's a power in the city for the likes of us—he can make or break you. Come on."

94

I followed him up some rickety stairs and into a tiny room. Two men were sitting at a table, both big; one was raw-boned and red-haired, the other obese, his black jowls hanging loose around his fleshy mouth. Shaun said, and I sensed his apprehension:

"Shaun O'Hara, sir. This is Jess, me brother."

"'Evening." Neither looked up from their books.

"Mr. McNamara and Jack Kehoe," whispered Shaun, and Kehoe raised his face.

I remember Kehoe's eyes to this day, for he had a squint on him like a Connemara bat in sunlight, and his face was ravaged. Gripping the edge of the table he surveyed me with cold hostility, and I returned his stare.

"Just in, lad?" McNamara had a lovely Irish brogue. Despite his flabby weight he was darkly handsome. He breathed in gasps, his black cigar drooping ash down his bulging waistcoat. Opening a little black book he flicked over the pages, then glanced at Shaun. "Did he start today?"

"Aye," I said.

"Under Mannigan, eh?" Kehoe now. "Six dollars a week?"

"Hearth cleaning," I answered, "it's worth nearer sixty," and took one in the ribs from Shaun. McNamara smiled. "Don't you like cleaning hearths, O'Hara?"

"Not much."

"Nor me, son." He bent to his book, writing. "I tried it when I started here fifteen years back, with Singer Nimick, and I damned nearly singed. But you'll come on. We're getting bigger in the Brotherhood these days, thank God, but we can't work miracles."

"What Brotherhood?"

Kehoe said, "We ask the questions here, O'Hara. Doesn't influence lie in the Brotherhood of decent men?"

"In brotherhood," I replied, "but I'm having no part of secret societies, for it's against the law of the priests," and Kehoe's face snapped up at me.

"Then what are you here for, O'Hara?"

"Wait, not so quick!" McNamara's fat hand went up. "The boy's a decent Catholic and has a right to know what he's joining." He moulded his hands before him, smiling, and his voice was beautiful. "Now, listen, son. Aren't we all sprung from the womb of old Erin? Isn't it true, secret society or not, that there's power in the mass of us and weakness in division? Isn't it right that the strength of the owners lies in their dollars and the strength of the workers in their comradeship?"

"I want no part . . ."

"Wait, O'Hara, wait—don't jump it." He smiled. "I remember when I sailed in, for instance. I was shoved into the tanneries stripping the hides off dead mules for fifty cents a day. Then I improved and went to the railroads, but when the company raked a couple of bucks out of me for their private building it was the Brotherhood got it back for me." He grunted, eased his great shining backside out of the chair, and wandered the room. "I was a big man for the Church those days, and every week saw me in the confessional. But when I raised a knife to a big Hunky foreman and got sent down the tracks it was the Brotherhood that set me up again, not the priests, for this is America. Won't you sign your name for comradeship, lad? Come Sunday you can be on your knees to the Pope."

"When I know what I'm joining," I said.

Kehoe's fists bunched up on the table, McNamara's stogie dropped its ash, and Shaun said, his face sweating, "Are you bloody daft, Jess? Don't you realise you wouldn't be in a job this minute if it wasn't for Mr. McNamara? Weren't you in a society back home?"

"Aye," I replied, staring at Kehoe.

"And didn't you rob and burn for the cause of Ireland?" asked McNamara. His voice rose and he sat again, glaring up. "Didn't the priests of Wexford take to arms in the causes of decency and spit in the faces of their oppressors, for the love of the Irish?"

"They did," I replied, "but they weren't the Molly Maguires."

"Holy God! Who's talking of the Maguires?"

"You are," I said, "or you wouldn't be talking in riddles."

Kehoe said softly, to Shaun, "So you've brought us a fighting O'Hara, is it? Best kick him back to the black peat he came from. Call in the next, sir?"

"Next," said McNamara, writing away, and Shaun gripped me,

96

swinging me to him. "Wait, sir, wait. Jess, listen. D'you realise it's a scratch and a dig for a living here unless you belong to us? For the city's hostile to the Irish nation, and if you don't sign for a union you'll finish on your hunkers. Have you thought what will become of Karen?" Hands trembling he snatched a glass from the table and filled it with whiskey, thrusting it against me. "Look, Jess, drink, for the love of God, and sign your name."

"Am I signing for the Sons of Vulcan?" I asked.

"Oh, Christ," said McNamara, "shift him."

"Because I'm not signing for the Molly Maguires—it's nothing but murderin' and thievin'," I said. "I heard it on the ship coming over."

Kehoe rose. "Get out," he whispered.

"And mind that tongue," said McNamara, still writing, "or we'll have the thing out of your head bloody and dripping."

"Och, now I know," I said. "I'm dealing with Maguires," and I went through the door with Shaun hanging on to me begging and pleading.

CHAPTER 11

Things were working up for the riot squad when I got back alone to North Canal Street that night, with the neighbours ten deep in the road and craning their necks up at our window, and Mrs. Kovaks was throwing a dead faint.

"What's happening?" I shouted, shaking her.

"It's me husband Timko," she cried. "He came home drunk five minutes back and he's up there assaulting your woman."

"It don't sound like it," said someone.

"Karen!" I cried, and dived through the kitchen and scrambled up the ladder, and I was half-way up when Timko Kovaks came down it and bundled me over the kitchen floor, and through the crowd he went and nobody saw him for hours. I shot up the ladder again, ducked a swing from Karen, and got behind the bed-rail.

"Do you want the same treatment, then?" she cried, swinging a china jug.

"What happened?" I gasped.

"A lot you care what happened! The filthy beast comes up here and tries to wrong me while you're out biting the necks off bottles with Shaun. God, men sicken me. I can smell you from here, and you're the same smell as Timko. Where have ye been till now?"

"I'm sorry, Karen."

"You're sorry! That's good! There's me pacing the room like a caged tiger and you're out oiling your gullet, and I'm bitten to death with fleas."

"Fleas?"

"Oh, Jess, I canna stand it. Look, me arm." She showed me, shuddering. "The filthy wee things have been hopping since you left. There's bugs and crawlers in this damned rat-pit to kill an army." She shuddered. "Filthy, filthy!"

98

I held her, and she was close to tears. "We will leave here," I whispered.

"How can we leave—you haven't got a job even."

"I . . . I've got a job—at the iron-works."

"You've got a job? Oh, you sweet thing. What kind of a job?"

"Hearth cleaning—six dollars a week."

"Six dollars?" She whistled. "I'd clean the hearth of hell itself for that money—could I do it with you?"

"Aye, stripped to the waist." I pushed her aside and threw myself down on her bed. "It's men's work, they have no use for women."

"Then I'm bound for the glass-works first thing in the morning," said she.

"I heard something today," I answered. "First night with the foreman or you'll never see the roof over the glass-works, it seems to be the custom."

"Poor soul," said she, "I'd be foreman in the morning."

"That's vulgar."

Hands on hips she stood above me. "Sure, it's vulgar, and Shaun's vulgar—the whole bloody city is vulgar, and the sooner you realise it the better, for you can't pick and choose in Pittsburgh."

"I'm picking and choosing right now," I said. "This dump isn't dictating to me, and I told them." Rising, I stripped off my coat, followed it with my shirt, and slopped water into the bowl.

"Who did you tell?"

"McNamara."

"Who's he when he's home?"

I ducked into the bowl, throwing the water over my head. "He's a chap in charge of the Molly Maguires—he seems to run the Irish jobs here."

"The Maguires? That's a foine institution."

"Back home it was, but it's murdering here. And I'm finished with Shaun, too."

"God help us, we're starving."

"Not yet," I said. Her fingers were cool on my back as I rubbed with the towel.

99

"Your back's red raw," she whispered. "What did that?"

I told her, pushing her aside.

"And did Shaun give you a job like that? I tell yer—I'm splitting his eye for him, and him your brother!"

"Ach, he's like the rest of 'em. The fella's addled. They sell their souls for a bloody dollar, and they call this a Christian country. Wait till you hit the streets and see the child-labour—the wee mites are skin and bone, and there's priests in black out there being a party to it."

"Do they work the children,then?"

"Twelve-hour shifts, and if they fall asleep at the mills they flog them, for Shaun told me." I paced the room, picking things up and slamming them down. "I'd give me soul to be back home in Ireland."

She sat down slowly on the bed, staring at the window. "So you'd be ducking and running for it, then?"

I ignored her. She said, rising, "Didn't you try to change things in Ireland? What you did was little enough, but at least you tried!"

"Oh, God, talk sense, woman."

"That's what I'm doing. Isn't the whole world a filthy place? Wouldn't it be dirtier still if decent men didn't try to clean it up?"

"Look," I said earnestly. "Right now we're wondering where the next meal's coming from . . ."

"And you're worrying about that while kids are being flogged?"

I groaned, turning away.

She whispered, "You're beaten easy, O'Hara, so now it's my turn. First of all, we're leaving here tonight."

"Don't be daft! D'you want to end up sleeping by the river?"

"And that's better than being eaten to death by bugs. I'm sitting here crawlin', and I've never owned a flea in me life before. Now something else. The Maguires might have frozen you, but I can earn more dollars in an hour than you can in a fortnight."

"Aye, by kicking up your legs in the taverns."

"And why not?"

"Because you're brought up decent—have you heard of these cess-pits that Shaun calls taverns? There's whiskey going down and women going up—one follows the other."

She opened large, dark eyes. "Listen, it's good clean Irish dancing I'm offering, and the first tug at me skirt brings a back-hander."

"I'm for the tanneries tomorrow and you're for the laundry." We sat together on the bed, scratching.

"The laundry, is it? Mrs. Kovaks told me they catch a woman bending quicker at the tubs than any other place on earth—that was how she collected Timko. Now wouldn't I be safer dancing in the taverns with you skinning the fiddle and watching me?"

I pondered it. "They'd never let us in."

"Who's asking? Boy, we just enter. Have you heard of Jubec's Bar? It's near the corner of Grant and Second Street, says Mrs. Kovaks, and there's more true Irish drinking there than lakes in Killarney. And they've money to burn, Jess—d'you know they're smoking dollar bills round cigars for the thrill of it, and us with four dollars to our name?"

"What about Shaun?" I asked.

"To hell with Shaun. Was he ever me favourite brother?" She knelt, gripping my hands. "Ah, Jess, I'm a noisy woman and a great trouble to you, but I've got you deep in here for the clean fella you are. I'll behave myself in the bars if you'll take me, and we'll split even on every cent we earn." She held her breast.

"Then keep off the fellas," I said, and she rose, smiling.

"Be gad, I can't promise my life-blood, but I'll do me best for you."

I nodded, sighing, and she leaped to her feet, spinning in the middle of the room, flaring her skirt to her thighs. "There now, get an eyeful—won't that draw a few dollars in Pittsburgh?"

"And a few teeth, too," I muttered.

The fiddle came sailing over and I caught it in mid-air and watched her feverish haste as she flung things into our bundles.

"Come on!" she cried, and dragged at me, and we went down the ladder. Mrs. Kovaks was standing in the room below with her hands to her face.

"Run, the pair of you!" she cried. "Me man Timko's coming back to see to the O'Haras!"

"I'm delighted to hear it, now me young brother's back," cried Karen, and flung open the door.

Timko Kovaks stood there swaying on the cobbles, fists clenched, sleeves rolled to the elbows, surveying us with bloodshot eyes. I pulled Karen aside. One in the stomach brought him double, one under the jaw brought him upright, and a swing to the ear sent him flat. Jumping over him we raced hand in hand down North Canal Street till we came to the river.

"Come on!" shouted Karen. "We'll give 'em Pittsburgh!"

Through Allegheny City we went, bundles on our backs, as usual, over the bridge and down to Ferry. Pittsburghers, waking from their exhausted sleep, were flooding like moles from their earths to the gaudy glitter of the Triangle. Doors swung open in gusts of bawdy laughter and slammed shut on whispered conspiracies: fiddles were going, organ-grinders churning out nasal music to the hopping of monkeys. Lovers passed us, oblivious to the pandemonium of the works: now a prostitute, her smudged eyes slanting at Karen, leaving a trail of sickening scent. Dray-horses stamped the rutted streets, rickety Conestoga wagons swayed by on spindly wheels. Now a trap and black mare, hooves prancing, driven by a sleek young buck dressed for woman-killing. And on either side of the Point the mighty Allegheny and Monongahela rivers flashed light at the diamond-studded glow of Coal Hill.

Now, resting, I looked at the sky. Orion was there, Venus ringed in an orb of light against the crowded gallons of the Milky Way. And a man on horseback was riding the crest of Washington Heights, his feathered headdress ragged against the stars. I nudged Karen. "Indian," I said, pointing.

"Savages? In Pittsburgh?"

"Won from the savages," I answered, "by blood," and I remembered Shaun's tales; heard again the shrieks from Smokey Island; saw the huddled English soldiers standing in blackened agony to the darts of buxom squaws; the flower of English manhood waiting in queues for Indian bonfires while the civilized French looked on. Here, I thought, within a hand of where I was sitting, the army of Braddock fell to the scalping knife; this paradise, won by a savagery unequalled in the history of men.

Karen said, "D'you remember Shaun's yarn about General Braddock burying his treasure chest? If we could find that lot we'd be buying up Pittsburgh."

"Don't believe all you're told," I said.

"Are we staying here all night, then?"

"Coming," I said, and we went over to Grant.

Light and smoke blinded us as we entered Jubec's Bar.

Here, with the coal and oil washed from its face was the cream of labouring Pittsburgh—vice on a higher scale; foremen and tally-clerks, railroad officials from whose ranks had shot up the mighty Carnegie, all crammed the long bar in raucous laughter. Sultry women stood languidly in corners weighing the wallets of solitary men. Bartenders, white-aproned and preceded by trays, glided cat-like over the floor, serving golden-haired Hungarians and their plait-eared mistresses, dark-eyed Italians and tar-brushed women, all jabbering in gushes of artificial gaiety. We entered unnoticed at first, but heads gradually turned to Karen as she stood in her scarlet, tambourine upraised. The chatter faltered and died and the door clicked behind us, as if the lid of the room had been slammed by an undertaker. I whispered:

"We can't perform here, Karen—the place is gentry."

"And who says not? The Irish are Irish, here or in Dublin, and me belly's rumbling to be heard in Allegheny." She pointed. "D'you see that sirloin on the bar and the bald-headed Negro hacking at it? I'd tangle with an army for a cut at that."

"Do you think they've got a bouncer?" I whispered.

"That's your department," said she. "Start fiddling."

I raised the fiddle and she leaped into the middle of the room.

"Hi! You can't do that here!" yelled the bartender.

"Man, we're doing it," cried Karen. "Irish, Irish, up for the reel!" and she whirled around the place tucking men under the chin and winking at the women. Now a commotion. Roars of laughter from some, others clapping the time and many protesting. But within seconds we had the Irish among them up and strutting, arms akimbo, polished shoes crossing on the boards and arming each other round in circles. But the foreign women were moving towards the door, too, skirts held aside in disdain, their obedient

103

husbands meekly following, one eye on Karen's legs and another on their wives, and the man at the bar was shrieking for the bouncer. He came within a minute. A door opened at the end of the room and he stood watching, blue-jowled and brawny. Somebody tapped me on the shoulder and I leaned down to a five-foot Italian gnome beside me.

"You see that fella, Irish boy?" he nodded towards the bouncer who was wandering up the room, hands in the pockets of his evening coat, most polite, very silky, with his white shirt front and his black hair parted in the middle and a face on him like the Rock of Gibraltar.

"I do," I said, fiddling again in a roar of applause as Karen showed her thighs.

"He is the toppa paid bouncer man in Pennsylvania," whispered the gnome confidentially. I opened wide eyes.

"You ever heard of the Killer Basardo, Irish boy?"

"For God's sake," I whispered back.

"One night he come in here and fighta this one. One hit. Finish! So you take your woman and get the hell out of here."

"I'm on me way," I said, fiddling towards the door.

"Jess!" shouted Karen. "Back here!" So I shrugged and measured the bouncer, for Karen was getting nearer the sirloin and my mouth was watering at the sight of it now. Very pleasant, this Jubec bouncer. Standing before me now he rocked on his heels, his gold teeth flashing like a jeweller's window.

"Are you enjoying yourself, Murphy?" said he.

"That I am," I said, "for there's nothing like a reel."

"I'm loving every minute," said he, "since there's a wee bit of the Irish in me, too, and there's nothing like a jig or two to set me tingling." He jerked his thumb. "And is that your woman, the bouncing bosom?"

"It's me sister," I said, proudly.

"Ach, she's a sweet thing, lad. And what part of the Old Country do you hail from, may I ask?"

"From Connemara, sir," I replied, still fiddling.

He sighed, eyes closed. "Sure, that's a fair land indeed, and now shall I tell you something? If you don't shift the wild-cat in under ten seconds I'll fetch you a swipe that will land you back there, is that understood?"

Up came Karen, banging her tambourine. "Is the big gunk pestering, Jess?"

"He's doin' more," I cried. "He's threatening violence."

"I am that," said the bouncer, and he sighted my chin and swung me one that would have taken the jaw off an Allegheny mule, but I ducked and it caught the gnome on the ear and turned up his hobnails.

Bedlam!

Off came the jackets of the Irish, up went chins, with sticks and bottles rising and falling and heads disappearing like ninepins, and there was Karen in the middle of it dancing delighted.

"Right, Murphy," said the bouncer, "you're me private property," and drew back his fist, but I had a left in his eye that put him off balance and brought down my right with the fiddle, crowning him.

"Ho!" he roared. "So it's a fight you're after, is it?" and in he came, swinging, wide open, the fool.

Out on his back was the Jubec bouncer, though it pained me to do it.

But a moment later the bar staff rushed, the bartender propelling Karen by the neck and the seat of her bustle. Through the swing doors we went, her leading, and landed in the gutter. It was raining Irish now, skirts up, shirts out, collars back to front, wiping cuts and grazes and playing hell with Jubec's and the Connemara dancers in particular.

"Quick," I shouted, dragging Karen upright.

"Go easy," she cried, "I'm dropping the supper," and she pulled out a napkin and wrapped up her sirloin and the three of us raced for the moonlit fields.

It was cold on the fairground that night under a lanterned sky, and the trains on the Pennsylvania Railroad chugged dismally in the mist of dawn. With Karen sleeping in my arms on our bundles I pulled the blanket about her, shivering. Her hands were ice-cold, her face blue in the whip of the wind, so I held her closer and remembered the warmth of the van back home, the rosy glow of the roadside fires, and the smell of Ma's cooking. With the first lights in the sky a new train-load of immigrants came in, spilled out of the depot, and wandered in pathetic, friendless groups down Morris and Clymer, beckoned by the flaring warmth of the Allegheny furnaces, and I pitied them. Disturbed by their noise, Karen woke, her eyes moving slowly over my face. In sudden strength she clasped me against her.

"Oh, Jess," she said, and wept.

There was no challenge left in her now, no fight.

"Hush, you," I whispered.

"Oh, God," she sobbed, "it's a swine of a country. It's a hell of a noise I've been making since I came here, but now I'm frightened to death. Oh, Jess, hold me."

I held her till the dawn came up red and vicious and the beat of the hammers rose as thunder from Allegheny; till the shadows of the wild hogs paled in the bushes and the stars faded into a dull, wet morning, and then I raised her.

With the bundles trailing the grass behind me I walked her, still weeping, down to the city.

We were down to forty cents and still sleeping on the fairground when Karen went into the laundry and I bumped into the Jubec Bar bouncer.

"Well, covet me soul," he whispered in the street. "Isn't it the darlin' of Connemara?"

"Never set eyes on the place," I said, for had he raised a hand I would have dropped before him.

"Then mine are deceiving me," said he. "For when a man knocks me off me spags I never forget his face. How's your savage sister?"

"Working in the laundry."

"Are you that low? Don't you realise you could be keeping her in luxury, Murphy?"

"The name's O'Hara," I replied. "What's your proposition?"

"Well! Indeed, you're a business man." He rubbed his hands together, his eyes slanting around for listeners. "Would you be keener if I told you I'm thinking in terms of fifty dollars, O'Hara?"

"I'll be keener still on a full stomach," I answered, and he steered me to the nearest tavern, where I slipped a hunk of bread in my pocket for Karen's supper.

"My name's Pat Magee," said the bouncer, "and I'm in the trade of fisticuffs—bouncing all except you in me spare time in Jubec's. But the circus is coming in to the fairground next Friday and the middle-weight champion of Pennsylvania is coming with it . . ." He glanced around at the customers, and whispered, "The man's name is Killer Basardo, and I was due to meet him over ten rounds and do a dive at his feet, d'you see? But he came into Jubec's a week last Sunday and caused a commotion and I had to bounce him, so now I'm no attraction."

"You bounced the middle-weight champion?" I asked, awed.

"For me sins, O'Hara. But I had five stone on the fella, remember, and by the look of you you're nearer his weight."

"I'll fight the devil himself for fifty dollars, Magee—hand it over."

"For pity's sake," he hissed. "This is a partnership. And you'll have to spill some blood to make it authentic, remember. Ten dollars or nothing."

"On," I said, "pay out now."

"Would you break me, O'Hara? You'll get the money when they carry you out, not before."

"I'll have starved to death by next Friday," I said, and he nodded at the sense of it, saying, "On one condition—that you lay off his chin. The thing's solid glass, for I tried it. You've got a punch in your fist like a Pittsburgh mule, and there'll be a riot if you lay him out cold, remember."

"Then I have a condition, too," I said.

"You're in no condition to stipulate, O'Hara—you're diving at Basardo's feet, for ten dollars."

"That my sister dances in Jubec's till after the fight."

Pat Magee sipped his coffee. "Well, it isn't in the contract, but I'll speak to Mr. Jubec. She's a sweet fiery creature indeed to God, and she'd double the Irish custom. Would she come as a hostess at a dollar a night?"

"Would you ravage a virgin lady, Magee?"

He rubbed his chin. "If needs be—she'd make savage entertainment, I'm thinking."

"You'd end in the knacker-yard. The knife's in her stocking," I said.

"Bless me soul, is that right? Sure, she's the first woman I've come across free of original sin since I left me ma's knee in Ireland. The place could do with a virgin—sure, we'll take her dancing."

"One thing more," I said as he paid me ten dollars. "A new fiddle, Magee—your nut broke the last one."

He grinned and dug into his pocket. "You drive a hard bargain, O'Hara—here, one-dollar-fifty. You'll have me as skinned as a new-shorn lamb. Hey, waiter! Whiskey!" He put out his hand and I slapped it. "Now we'll drink on the partnership, O'Hara and Magee."

So I went in search of Karen jingling dollars and met her coming out of her laundry with her bundle on her back.

"Are you finishing early?" I asked.

"I'm finished for good," said she. "I put in an oversuit with a dozen dress shirts, me name's mud. Have you found a job?"

I explained about Magee and Killer Basardo, but I made no mention of diving.

"Och!" she cried, "it's money for jam, Jess. Are they having a priest at the ringside to give the Killer last rites—the man'll be needing them, tangling with an O'Hara."

"And better news still," I went on. "Pat Magee's going to fix it so you dance in Jubec's."

Her mouth dropped. Her incredulity swept into joy and she leaped at me, kissing me, and I had to lever her off.

I bought a new fiddle for one-thirty-seven and we got a room on the Point in a tenement, with a Greek family below us, Poles above us, and a couple of Negroes living either side, and there we lived till the circus came on Friday, with Karen spinning her skirts in Jubec's for a dollar a night, shifting the foreigners and bringing in droves of Irish.

"Have you seen the like of it?" shrieked Karen.

"Have you got the Magee money safe?" I bawled on the edge of the crowd.

Most impressive, all this, up on the fairground with the circus coming in; a big brass band at the head of things, coloured flags waving. Redskins were there in full war paint, gun-slingers and crooks, cowboys in fringed breeches on big, sleek mares, quacks and medicine-men, fat ladies and hunger-strike skinnies, all blending with the flowing Conestoga wagons in a roar of noise. Down the street they came with a hand-springing dwarf leading them and the autumn air was split with the blasts of tubas and trombones.

"Are you there, Pat Magee?" shouted Karen. "Is that Killer Bastardo?"

"That's him," said Patrick.

"God help him," she cried. "Jess'll kill the fella."

I was having some doubts. Near six feet up, this Basardo, with ox-like shoulders on him, black curls and sideboards, and he strolled in his spangled tuxedo with feline grace, tanned and handsome.

"Are you sure that's Basardo, Pat?"

"As sure as me eye."

"And you hit him out clean, you say?"

"I did."

"With a sledge-hammer?"

"With these two hands," said he, indignant. "Mind, he'd shipped a quart or so of good rye whiskey, so you have to make allowances."

"You didn't mention that before," I said.

"And weaken your intentions, man? Am I daft? Every pugilist in the city is making for the hills, but a bargain's a bargain, so no slipping away in the crowd, O'Hara."

"Well," I said, "I've a mind to slip you one now for the lying lout you are, Magee—the man's a killer. Karen!" I shouted.

"I'm with you, Jess," she cried, coming up. "The fight's on first, so put him away quick, me honey, for I want to enjoy the circus."

"I'm seeing to you after," I murmured to Pat.

"If you're still living, O'Hara," said he. "But you can rest your mind on one thing for sure—I've got a wonderful future planned for your sister."

Light was flashing around the square ring, and the crowd, as thick as blackened corn, was swaying and sighing under the hypnotic promise of blood: now cheering in a thunder-clap as Basardo was introduced from the ring by a leather-voiced ring-master. With Patrick leading we forced a path to my corner. And as I stripped off my coat and shirt Basardo above me was doing exercises and swiping at the air in joy.

"Are you all right now, O'Hara?" asked Pat Magee.

"As right as I'll ever be," I said. "If I end in one piece I'm seeing to you after."

"You're not, fella. For the partnership of Magee and O'Hara is dissolved from this minute. D'you expect me to stay and watch me substitute slaughtered?"

"Jess," said Karen, finger in her mouth. "What's five dollars on at twenty to one?"

I swung to her. "Now listen. If you risk one cent on this fight . . ."

"Why not? The chap's a bum—I just heard a man say so."

"You hang on to that five dollars," I said fiercely. "It's the only money standing between us and the workhouse."

"Be reasonable, it's easy," she cried. "You'll be out of the ring in under ten seconds, Jess."

"More than likely," I replied, and gripped the top rope. Basardo was standing above us so she leaned through the bottom rope and tapped his size fourteen, and he stooped, grinning down at her.

"Is it true you're Killer Bastardo?" she asked him.

"I'm the Killer right enough, but you're pronouncing me name wrong, lady, I was born legitimate."

"Legitimate or not, d'you realise you're about to be slaughtered?"

"And do you realise you're the only thing round here who could do it?" he asked, and tipped her under the chin.

"You'll learn, you poor soul," she replied. "Me brother from

Ireland's got a fist on him for dropping Chicago steers, you'll learn."

"Karen, come out of it," I shouted, pulling her away.

Boos and groans now as I climbed into the ring, cheers for Basardo as he bounced about in his corner, and I saw beyond him the mountains in bright autumn colours and fringed with white clouds, and heard the music of harps. Wiping my sweating face I looked down at Karen. "Remember," I said, "hang on to that money," and the bell jangled like the toll of doom as I went out to meet Basardo.

He came at a joyful rush, grinning, but I side-stepped him and he floundered into the ropes. Taking the middle of the ring, I waited, my mind tuning in to all Hosea had taught me. Again he rushed and I propped him off with the left, clinched him well, and we waltzed.

"Will you keep your hands to yourself?" he whispered.

"All in good time," I said, and clouted him one. "Give them a run for their money," and I shoved him off and circled him, the right ready, all memories of diving forgotten. The crowd went silent as we sparred, then growled deep, as bulls nosing an empty manger. Fist back, Basardo lunged at me. I saw it coming a mile, slipped it, crossed him lightly on the jaw and he fell upon me, eyes glazed. Remembering the dive in time I forced him into a corner and held him up.

"Will you keep your shoulders out of your punches, Irish?" he gasped, recovering. "Magee's paying you to dive, not rough it."

"But if you lead with your right again I'm bound to clip you, Yank. Have you been in a ring before in your life?"

Lumbering, swinging, he came after me, and I ducked and weaved, gripped him, pulled him into a corner and let him beat a tattoo on my ribs to serve the crowd, who rose as a man, yelling. Already he was streaming sweat.

"Is it true you're the middle-weight champion?" I asked.

"You'll soon discover it," he panted, and swung one that missed by a yard.

"Then fetch me a dig in the stomach so I can drop, for I'm tired of holding you up," I said, "the people are after my blood," and he threw in a soft one and I took it in the ribs, cried out, and fell, gasping.

Up went the crowd again, out came the seconds and dragged me back to my corner.

"Did that fella hit you or was I seein' things?" demanded Karen.

I groaned, gasping, holding my middle. "Och, it's murder out there with him."

"I could have taken that punch meself and still be clouting him," said she. "Have you left your stomach back home in Ireland, O'Hara?"

"Can't you see he's a grand fighter?" I groaned, in pain.

"He couldn't skim milk," said she. "Go in and finish him."

"This round," I said.

Basardo with his blood up now, crouching like a baboon, his narrow slits of eyes weighing me up for the kill, and he came at me like Jason's bull, grunting and swinging when the bell went again, growling with fury in the clinches when I pushed him off with the left. Round and round we went, me staggering, Basardo swinging and missing by feet while the crowd roared encouragement to him and people thumped on the apron of the ring. Up came the police, wanting to cut the ropes, for pugilism was forbidden in the city, and the thugs were holding them off while I swung and ducked in the corner again with Basardo on top of me. Every time I rose I saw his glass jaw as big as a cabbage and was dying to hit it, but daren't. I'd had some easies with the boys back home on the roads of Ireland, but never anything like this. Now he was in the middle of the ring, beckoning me to fight, which is a silly thing to do to an Irishman, so I walked straight in, wheeled him, hit him left and right, and then had to dive back in to hold him up. Me in the corner again, taking his thumps on my elbows and shoulders till I wilted under the onslaught and dropped at his feet.

"That's better," he panted, and reeled away, and out came the seconds and dragged me home again.

"Ach, I'm disgusted!" hissed Karen, her nose an inch from mine. "Are you ill, for God's sake?"

"Sick to death," I said, head low.

"Oh, darlin'! Is the strength of you gone with the starving?"

"Weak as a kitten," I mumbled.

She pleaded then. "Oh, Jess, couldn't you land him a fine one before you die? I'm bleeding to death down there watching him thump a fighting O'Hara." She wept. "And now they're offering fifty to one you'll go out next round."

I closed my eyes with the shame of it and pushed her aside as the bell rang. Basardo waved to the crowd, hammered his chest, and laughed at me. "Tuck in your chin, me sweet Irish daffodil, for this is where you collect it."

I seemed to awaken, and then came anger. Clinching, I wheeled him, looking down at Karen. She was sitting in stuttering sobs, her hands over her face, and suddenly she rose to her feet, and screamed:

"A sweet Irish daffodil!" She beat on the canvas, tears streaming down her face. "And you an O'Hara! Can you imagine the belting you'd get from Hosea?"

Ho O'Hara, the champion of Ireland.

The brain goes cold, money is forgotten. There was dirt in this, a selling of honour. And with about as much fighting sense as a labouring ass Basardo waded in again, wide open, as usual, and I saw the line of his jaw clean against the sky as he coiled up for another blind swing. Stepping in, I hooked at it with the left, and it swayed away; heard him cry aloud with astonishment. A right smash to the ribs bowled him into a corner, and I heard the crowd shout as I stepped in after him with the straightening uppercut. Standing back, I hooked him solid, caught him again with the same hand as he sprawled away. Teetering, he fell, flat on his back, eyes open to the sun.

"That's for Hosea," I said, and walked away.

Into the ring they tumbled, Basardo's seconds hitting me with the stool, Karen clawing at me, men and women screaming, and the ringside gamblers trying to make off with the money. Ducking under the top rope I dragged Karen through after me, pushed off a policeman who was trying to arrest me, and leaped into the crowd.

"Wait!" screamed Karen, and ran back to the ringside.

Half the Irish in Pittsburgh were trying to hoist me on to their shoulders by the time she got back, but I fought myself free of them, grabbed her hand, and thrust a path through the cheering crowd, pulling her behind me. Across the fairground we went like things demented, raced down the alleys with the people in pursuit till we lost them on Grant. Panting, we barged through the door of Jubec's, which was empty save for Patrick Magee, who raised bleary eyes from his whiskey at the counter.

"The saints preserve us! You still alive, O'Hara?"

"No thanks to you," I gasped as we scrambled up the stairs. Locking the bedroom door we peered through slits of the curtains for a sign of pursuers, and they came at a rush past the door below, shouting for the new Irish hero. Sick at heart I threw myself down on the bed.

"Don't you realise this is somebody's bedroom?" whispered Karen.

"Ach, who cares," I retorted. "We're finished, anyway. Honour's satisfied, and there's five dollars between us and the workhouse—prepare to starve."

And Karen straightened, smiling. "You poor soul," said she. "There's big red patches on your ribs where he landed you, are you sore?"

I sat up, knowing this mood, saying, "You've still got that five dollars, haven't you?" And she shook her head.

"Karen!" I was upright now, staring down at her. Flouncing away to the window, she turned. "The O'Haras have been gamblers since the start of the race," she said. "Did you expect me to sit there and not have a flutter? And I knew what you were up to—every time you went flat you raised the odds, so I got the five dollars on at fifty to one, was that right?" She went to the bed and tossed me my coat. The pockets were jammed with rolls of dollars. I counted in a daze.

"Two hundred and fifty!" I breathed.

"And five, with the stake money back," said she. "This place reckons it's smooth, be God, but it'll have to shift some to keep up with the O'Haras. And I've just remembered something. . . . Why, the filthy beast!"

"Who?" I asked faintly.

"That fella Magee downstairs. With his own mouth he told me you was diving—you—Jess O'Hara!"

"Lord have mercy on us." I sat down again.

"Lord have mercy on Patrick Magee," she whispered, "for I'm away downstairs to see to him. The lying swine!"

So I lay back on the pillows in the deepest luxury and listened to the bottling of Patrick Magee, and she did him better than the bear from Siberia. And while he was being done the door opened and a white-haired gentleman stood there. I had never seen him, but I had heard of Mr. Jubec.

"Pray don't disturb yourself, Mr. O'Hara," he said, and smiled.

CHAPTER 12

Patrick Magee had taken to the road and I had taken his job as bouncer in Jubec's, which was poetic justice, said Karen, who danced there nightly and doubled the custom.

Autumn died on the skeleton branches of the Ohio glades and winter came, hammering the land into frosted silence. White and bleak were the mountains with towering snow-drifts on the plains, and the edges of the Allegheny River were frozen solid. But the scar that was Pittsburgh bloomed fire in the bed-sheet land, swallowed its Pittsylvania ore, digested it thunderously, and spouted it through its refining fires to the ports of the world. Blinded by the beacon of Pittsburgh's fame new shoals of immigrants poured in on the rivers and railways, and in the bitter frosts the companies cornered them, herded them into the industries, maimed or buried them, and bawled for more. The child-labour worked listlessly in the mills; peak-faced Asiatics, drained of energy, marched sullenly to work in the winter dawns. Raked from the sunny Mediterranean by the clash of dollars, the Italians sang no more in the Iron City. French, Germans, and the once rollicking Irish, bruised by the pounding of Pittsburgh's greed, sat in peaked apathy in the company shanties. Skeleton children wandered the alleys; refuse bins were scavenged, cats snatched from doorsteps by the bewildered poor. And while six shared a bed in the teeming shanty towns the taverns and hotels were flooded with a new society— the stained profiteers of a nation's misery who roistered in a river of dollars, wining and oystering in resplendent suites in a riot of spending and harlotry. Pimps and gamblers, industrialists and confidence men crammed the bars in a welter of whiskey and perversion. Fabulous parties were held, each magnate striving to outshine his competitor at the expense of his labouring poor. While opium smoke leaked its relieving dreams from the shuttered windows of the alleys, while children died of hunger, the flower of the city industry and wealth, the Carnegies, Fricks, and their ilk intrigued and schemed at their champagne parties for a bigger slice of the city's misery. And Pittsburgh blazed this beauty at the sky, its bass voice thundering the stocks and shares, at the cost of human life. Driven by greed she blundered on, emptying trouser legs, tying sleeves with string, writing for history the shame of her benefactors.

I was writing home to Ma, I remember, in my bedroom above Jubec's, when Karen came in and shut the door. I glanced up.

"Have you got a message for Ma?" I asked.

"Aye," said she. "Tell her I am loving her." She went to the window and looked out over the Monongahela where the moon was shimmering, and there was a silence in her.

"Anything wrong?" I asked, writing away.

"Dear God," she whispered, "it's bright out there, Jess. D'you recall the moons of Connemara when we rolled in with the family from Galway? Do you remember the creak of the caravans?"

"Homesick," I answered, lighting my pipe, and she turned to me.

"Are there caravans out there in the Alleghenies, d'you think? Do they rumble and whiplash like they do back home, are the bonfires red?"

"Conestogas," I said. "Girl, you've got it bad."

"Wagons? Those clumsy hooped things? Do you call those caravans? With the stinking drivers swearing to rise Satan?" She smoothed back her hair, sighing. "Ah, God! When the moon comes round and full like now there's an itch in me—I'd be the mother of the nation for just one Irish gipsy boy sitting by a fire in Derry, and smell his roasting hare."

I rose, grinning. "All right, let's have it. Is it Ireland you're after or Will Rees?"

"Did you see Shaun like you promised?"

"I was at the Kovaks yesterday again. It nearly split his mouth to speak to me, but he's never heard of a man called Rees, and he's no knowledge of his uncle's iron-works."

"They were just building the place—did he know that?"

"There's no new iron-works going up between here and the mountains—not on the little scale Will Rees was talking about. Look, the man dumped you, why bother about him?"

She closed her eyes. "Is he still in New York, d'you think?"

"He said he'd be studying there for months, remember?" I went to her. "There's more than one man in the world, you know—you've had a few in your time. If I was in skirts there's a couple of Irish lads downstairs most nights I'd be giving the eye to."

"Aye, the mauling, pawing variety—should I be interested in them?" She turned away, lips trembling. "I give myself to Will Rees, did you know that?"

"Did I know it? I've been sweating on three of us."

"And I wouldn't mind that, neither. Three times I give myself, because I loved him, and you can't be the judge of me, for you've never loved anyone in your life." She began to cry, softly, her fingers forming a cage over her mouth. Sighing, I went back to the desk, picking up the pen again.

"More fool you for giving," I said. "When you know as much about men as I do you'd be thinking twice—they're takers, Karen, not givers."

"He took gentle," she whispered. "Eh, God help me, I love that man."

I opened my mouth to lie again, but could not, for I knew this had been coming for months. Every time she danced in the bar the men were after her. Some nights she went to her room with her arms filled with flowers, with secret little cards pinned to them, but she never accepted the invitations. I rose and went to a drawer.

"It will never work, Karen," I said, "not you and Will Rees," and she spun round at me, crying:

"Will you mind your own damned business as to who I'm loving? You're nothing but a hypocrite. Every time I mention his name you spout priest lectures about him being the wrong religion, and you've not seen the roof over a church since you came to this filthy place."

I didn't reply. Opening the drawer I took out the little love-spoon Will Rees had given me. Karen took it, frowning as she turned it in her fingers.

"What's this?"

"From the Welsh boy," I said. "It's the custom they have, apparently, and it makes you his woman."

"And you kept it till now," she whispered, holding it against her. "Jess, that was a cheating thing to do. Did you send him away from the ship, too, giving no thought to me?"

"I reckoned it was best for you, Karen."

"You reckon too much," she answered softly. "When I told you in Wicklow to act like a man it didn't make you my keeper. This explains why he hasn't come back for me, so now I'm away to search for him—in New York."

"Don't be a fool. You'll starve to death in New York."

"But I'm not only going to find Will Rees," she said. "Am I likely to get recognition for me dancing in this dump, with two-bit hobos bawling for whiskey?"

"Karen," I said desperately, "I'm writing to Ma and sending four tickets—it'll be a fine state of affairs if the family arrive and you're not here to greet them."

"By whose leave? Doesn't my opinion come into it?"

"Do you want the family split up for life, then?"

She waved me down, turning. "Leave them where they are. The sweet virtue of Ireland is on them, this place will eat them alive, like us. Mike won't come, anyway—he's wedded to Ireland, and Hosea turned it down though he fought a bear for the privilege."

"We'll see," I answered, adding bitterly. "There was a time you pined for them."

"And how do you know I'm not pining still?" She thumped herself. "The ache for your own flesh and blood goes on in here, Jess, so still your tongue. Just that I wouldn't bring a dog to this cesspit."

"You've fed here," I retorted. "Jubec's was fancy enough when you were starving."

"You're right, but I'm not starving now, and that's progress. I'm away to New York in the morning, for I'm sick to death of your apron strings. Jubec's isn't good enough for me, I've got ambitions. But you'll live and die here till someone bounces you and sends you down the road like you sent Magee."

"Right," I said in sudden anger, "cut the apron strings—go north for your dancing and prove yourself a woman, but don't come back to me in trouble." Raking under the bed I pulled out my savings-box and tossed her thirty dollars. "Your share—go when you like."

She caught the roll in mid-air and pushed it down her bodice.

"And don't put it there, for it's the first place they'll find it."

Crimson anger spread to her cheeks and she closed her eyes, saying softly, "I'll tell you the truth, Jess, you're not far wrong. For you're embalmed and I'm alive. I want Will Rees, and I won't be happy till I find him."

Faintly, from the saloon below came the chatter of men, the chink of glasses, and a melodion playing a sweet song of home. I will always remember Karen standing there at the window, the moonlight sharp on her face, her eyes deep in shadow.

"Best go now, then," she said.

"All right, but for God's sake get on with it."

I turned my back as she opened the door.

"Good-bye, Jess," she said. "If . . . if I don't find him, I'll come back."

Ignoring her, I went to the window, staring out. The door closed softly.

Alone, I listened to her scuttling haste in the room next door, then heard her footsteps on the landing. Giving her time to reach the saloon below I went to the bannisters, staring down. She walked erect, swirling her cloak through the tables, oblivious of the customers and the men's faint whistles of approbation.

"Good-bye," I said.

God knows how I finished the letter home. Enclosing the four tickets I had bought for Dublin to Pittsburgh, I sealed the envelope, then counted my money. Two dollars, a few cents.

Two days later Mr. Jubec came.

He came to my room, which was unusual, for people were rarely visited by Mr. Jubec, except on pay day. Now he stood in the doorway, his pale, blue eyes watering behind his pince-nez spectacles, his small, frail hands clasped before him.

For every German who starved in Pittsburgh nine made good,

and one was Jubec. From the forced labour of a Bremen factory twenty years back he had saved enough money for the escape to America, and found himself in Pittsburgh. Beginning with a little whiskey tavern he had built up a fine business and a reputation for square dealing, and he treasured his success. That afternoon his little wisps of white hair were standing on end, giving him an elfin appearance.

"Trouble, sir?" I rose from my desk.

"Too much for you to handle, O'Hara."

"Drunks?" I pulled on my coat.

"Molly Maguires—six of them, and they are sober."

Pushing past him to the bannisters, I looked down into the saloon. The first man I saw was McNamara, sprawled in a chair with four bull-necked thugs standing behind him. Sitting alone was the big Kehoe, looking murderous. Mr. Jubec said:

"They are asking for you, O'Hara. I have seen this kind of thing before—the most brutal beatings. Please go."

I whispered, "If I run now I'll never stop running . . ."

"Mr. O'Hara, I cannot afford trouble. Please go out the back way."

I scarcely heard him, and, though I knew his advice was good, I couldn't take it. There was an intense bitterness in me now that Karen had gone and hitting out at someone seemed the only way to relieve it. And the image of Kehoe sprawling in his chair was a fascinating attraction. Whatever happened I would, at least, have the satisfaction of getting Kehoe. Pushing Mr. Jubec gently aside I went down the stairs. The six heads turned to my footsteps and I saw McNamara's nod. All rose, forming a barrier between me and the main door. McNamara smiled, took a pull on his stogie, and blew out smoke.

"All credit to you, O'Hara. They usually cut and run," he said.

"Not this one, McNamara. Have you brought enough of them? Why leave out Shaun?"

Kehoe muttered, "Fix him, sir, get it over and done with," but McNamara waved him away, and sat down heavily. He said:

"Is it right that your sister has left the city, O'Hara?"

"None of your business."

"Oh, but it is, and I'll be telling you why. For the sake of your brother we've left you alone, because you were keeping her. And we're not here for violence now, lad. Shaun's waiting down in Hank's place and he'd be pleased if you'd sign up."

"Tell my brother to go to hell. I've found my own employment."

I looked them over. Ireland had spawned some heroes, but these were cripples; bull-necked and coarse, the thugs of a city, hand-picked for beatings.

"I'm warning you, O'Hara, you're getting your last chance. Are you signing?"

"And why do you find me important?"

Kehoe said thickly, "Because you've a brother in the Society and you could know too much."

"Shall we say that we like things kept in the family?" said McNamara, smiling.

Strange that I kept seeing Karen. There was a wounding sense of rejection in her going. Not caring what happened to me I was not afraid.

"Get out," I said.

"God, we could do with you. You're a brave man, O'Hara."

Feet shifted on the floor. The hired hands edged round me in a semi-circle that pinned me against the bar counter. From the corners of my eyes I saw Mr. Jubec at the foot of the stairs, screwing his fingers, and I smiled at my thoughts. Six heavyweight thugs and I had to have Jubec. It would be some circus if Ho and Mike were here—six Molly thugs stiff on the sidewalk.

They were closing in now and I knew they would dive at any moment, so there seemed no sense in waiting for it. Kehoe was the nearest, so I ducked to confuse them, feinted at McNamara, and swung towards Kehoe, and the pain jarred to my elbow as I caught him square. He dropped, legs waving, roaring, and I stepped over him, side-stepped one thug, and hooked another on my way to McNamara, but I never reached him. Tripped from behind, I was down with two men on top of me, and we thudded and bruised at each other until a fist caught me solid. The lamps of the bar swayed over the ceiling, and I saw a mist of faces above me, mouths gaping, their fists flailing in a gathering silence. I heard a faint command.

"Stop!"

The thudding ceased. Dazed, I rolled clear instinctively, shook my head to clear it, and stared up. Mr. Jubec was standing astride me with a gun in his hand.

"Stop," he repeated. "One man against six."

Kehoe dragged himself up and swayed towards us. His hair was wild and blood was streaming from his mouth. "Out of the way, Jew, we're taking him."

For answer Mr. Jubec straightened the gun. "Not from here, sir." Rising, I took the gun, wondering which was the business end of it, and waved them into a group.

"Out," I said.

McNamara smiled, relighting his cigar. "Silly of you, O'Hara. We'll be back so soon, and there's two of you now, not one."

"Get out," whispered Jubec. "You Maguires are nothing but scum."

"As you'll discover," said McNamara, and herded the rest before him, and left.

Bolting the door I came back to Jubec.

"Thanks, sir," I said.

He did not reply. He was looking around the saloon with a strange, almost wistful smile on his lips, then turned to me.

"Now you, O'Hara. I cannot afford such trouble."

I nodded. So intense was the silence that it seemed to forbid movement. Was it years ago when Karen and I had entered this place, I wondered. The scarlet, spinning dress, the clash of her tambourine, gone?

"Did you hear me, O'Hara? I asked you to leave. I like you. I am sorry."

I turned away. "Aye, I'll collect my things, sir. Good-bye, Mr. Jubec."

I went to my room and thrust my belongings into a bundle, then opened Karen's door. Nothing in the room gave a hint of her save a faint, sweet smell of perfume.

"Good-bye," I said.

It was cold in the street and the stars were shining brilliantly. Furnace flashes were raking the sky and the city was trembling to the thudding of hammers. A German band was playing somewhere over in Allegheny, a faint requiem, as if for Mr. Jubec. I took a last look at the door of the saloon, hoisted up my bundle, and went down to the waterfront. It was raining, I remember.

CHAPTER 13

I posted the letter to Ma, then walked aimlessly, thinking of Karen, now strangely relieved that she had gone. Mist was billowing along the river, and beneath the cobweb of masts and ropes the people of the waterfront worked restlessly, despite the late hour. Coloured washing made shape through the mist, rising and dipping as wraiths walking the river, and under the hawsers came the bass grumbles of men and the piping voices of women. The mist cleared when I reached Fort Pitt and the Mother Ohio came up brilliantly, her torrents swirling under a hunting moon. I rested in a place where I had once sat with Karen, watching the wake-lights wounding the water, listening to the thumping of the paddle steamers and a trombone playing in an inn behind me; plaintive and pure, that tune, a Seneca war song I had heard before. It might have been the music but I think it was the whiskey that took me into the inn. The room was swirling with smoke, and crowded with the riff-raff of the docks. Dropping my bundle I thumped the counter.

A Negress was sitting on a high stool nearby, laughing, her head flung back, in the crude banter of three foreign sailors. I drank, watching her, for it might have been Karen sitting there; the same uproarious gaiety, the same narrowed eyes in the high bones of her face. And as I watched her the girl looked my way in a lift of blackened lashes, and smiled, accepting the appraisal in the way women have. I drank another glass, watching her intently, and the need for her skidded across the whiskey-sheeted bar between us. After the third glass she was quite beautiful, her coal-black negress face coffee-coloured. She was growing whiter every minute as the whiskey hit me. Now Eurasian, the high hem of her dress announcing her trade. As I moved to the door she winked and pulled her dress higher. In the cold air of the waterfront she was as white as me. I stood there, grinning at my thoughts, then went down to the river bank and untied my bundle. I was getting my bed down when she appeared on a rock above me.

Her teeth were dazzling white in the dim light, her cheap jewellery glinted against her tight, black coat. Strangely, the lust for her had vanished now. Ten times a night I had met her kind in Jubec's.

"Looking for a bed?" she asked, coming nearer.

"No money," I said, spreading things out.

"Who mentioned money?"

The river mist billowed between us as I glanced at her. Even in these surroundings there was a sylvan grace about her, something that clashed with the murk and stink of garbage. She said, smiling, "Anyway, the night's young, Irish boy, the money comes out after midnight."

"Not for me," I answered, and rattled my change. "I got two dollars."

"Jeez," she replied, chuckling, "then you must have shifted some. Did they pay you that for fixing Killer Basardo?"

I grinned up at her, and she said, eyes widening, "You fixed him swell—I couldn't have done it better with a full quart bottle— knew you the moment you came into the inn."

"You saw the fight?"

"Half Pittsburgh saw it, but I was special interested. I used to be Basardo's woman. He does his killing on a mattress, son—you had it easy. Where's your girl, by the way?"

I frowned up, and she said, "The red-head in the scarlet skirt. They tell me she's knocking 'em cold over in Jubec's."

"My sister." I was fishing in the bundle for an extra pair of socks. You could lose your toes in a night on the waterfront.

"She left you?"

I nodded.

"Come home with me if you like, you can call me aunty."

I could have impressed her with the truth of it, but it seemed pointless.

"I'm all right here," I said.

She shrugged. "But you won't be a couple of hours later. It's enough to chill the dead down here, never mind the living, and there's another train-load of immigrants due in. By midnight . . ."

I dropped my bundle. "Look, will you leave me alone?"

Strangely, this didn't shift her. She said, softly, her smile gone, "It's because I'm coloured, isn't it?"

"Nothing to do with it."

She drew herself up, turning. "I'm offering you a bed, mister—nobody's aiming to sleep with you. You damned whites are all the same." She wandered away.

Unaccountably, I knew a sudden and despairing loneliness. "Wait," I called, and climbed up the rock to her, and she turned. Her eyes were large and white in her clumsy face, and she smiled faintly. "Make up your mind, Irish."

I ran down the rock and gripped my bundle. "Thanks, I'd like to come," I said.

I stood in darkness as she lit the lamp in her room.

I had seen some beds in my time, but nothing like this one, brass-knobbed and quilted, with tassels on the coverlet and lace on the pillows. Some craftsman, Katie.

"Katie Virginia," she said, turning up the gas. "Reckon I never had another name. My pa was white, so they tell me, though I don't show it any. Ma was picking in the fields, and the boss-man came down—just came down and took her, and she brought forth me. You like coffee, Mr. O'Hara?"

I nodded, looking round the little room. It was pathetic in its tawdry ornaments, its bedside boxes frilled with red paper, the washing-line above the cracked wash-basin, the funereal droop of black stockings. I had often wondered about the homes of these women; if the bawdy torment of their lives brought them to squalor and dirt. Not so with Katie's. Her attic in Peebles Township was as clean as Karen's in Jubec's, and Karen was a demon for scrubbing.

"You hungry, Jess O'Hara?"

"No," I answered, walking to the window. Birmingham and Brownstown were spouting fire three stories below, turning the river into blood, and the hordes of workers were gathering for shift, thronging down the alleys as tongueless sheep.

"Some scenery," said Katie, beside me now.

"Aye, some city."

She took off her coat, looking bigger in the lamp-light, moving with a cat-like ease in her black, shining dress.

"You like my dress?"

I turned from the window. "Aye, pretty."

"Got it cheap last market-day—one-dollar-fifty." She turned on tiptoe, arms outspread. "Mostly I make my own, but you can't turn up a bargain." Bending, she drew it above her knees. "Black petticoat, too—all in. Ain't that wonderful? Most men like black on a woman, but I reckon I ought to dress in white, for you can't tell the difference between me and petticoats." She went to an oil stove and knelt, turning up the wick. Her breasts gleamed ebony above the low neck-line, and she glanced up, saw my interest, and smiled. Striking a match, she said:

"You like Pittsburgh?"

"I hate it."

"You ever been south?"

I shook my head.

"Mister, you ain't missed nothin'. Though it's supposed to be God's country. Six months ago I was south—with the Jacob family just outside Columbus." Clasping her hands before her, she sighed. "I was with the Jacobs since I was ten. They was white, Mr. O'Hara, but they was sweet." She ladled coffee into a saucepan. "They was as sweet as sweet corn, those people. No need for wars and things if all you whites acted like those Jacobs, but the son got sweet on me, and me on him, so I flew."

"You . . . you left them." I sat on the bed.

"I did. Mrs. Jacobs says to me—and she was a honey—she says, 'Katie Virginia, we're in trouble, real trouble. That damned fool Johnny of mine is finding his feet with the women. He's just mooning around the place when he ought to be out ploughing with his dad. We got a barbecue coming over at the Bentley place next Friday, an' he ain't going. He ain't going, he says, unless he's taking you, an' that means trouble, because you're black.'"

"That was her son, eh?"

She nodded. "An' he was some boy, I'm telling you." She put her

128

hands on her hips and surveyed me. "Come to think of it, he was the spit and image of you, that boy, and I fell hard. Honey, I fell so hard that I had to shift me, for I wasn't causing trouble for the likes of the Jacobs."

There was a fine simplicity about her. Interested, I said, "And then?"

"Then I came up here. First I tried the laundry, but they reckoned I might stain the sheets, or somethin'. Then I did a month in the glass-works. Boy, that was enough—I was out. If a woman's got to be the toy of heathen men she's entitled to be paid for it, I guess."

"And you manage to keep yourself?"

She shrugged. "I get by. Our Lord, He don't get rough with the harlots, for it says that in the Book. Yeh, I manage. When I left the glass-works I had fifty cents, and in six months here I've turned that into dollars. Some going, eh?"

I took the cup of coffee she offered, sipped it, and said, "Fast, Katie, down to the river—that's where your type land."

Her expression was changed when I glanced up at her. She said, softly:

"You a preacher, or somethin'?"

"You'd have been better off with the Jacobs, Johnny or not."

"If you think I'm a black whore you say so, mister."

I sighed. "I didn't say that . . ."

"You didn't say it, but boy, you're thinking it! Down to the river, eh? You sittin' there passing judgement on me!" She thumped herself. "Don't you think I'd act decent if this goddam place gave a black girl half a chance?" She pointed at the window. "D'you think I'd be street-walking for two-bit hobos like you?"

"Katie, I'm sorry . . ."

"You're sorry, eh? That's a good one! Everybody's sorry. You fellas spend six months on the breast and the rest of your lives tryin' to climb back on one, but you're always so sorry. All through the night you're weeping and whining and talking about the river, but no man I met gives a damn in the morning!"

"Katie, please . . ."

"And don't you Katie me! I'm dirty black trash, you're thinkin', and you're right, mister. But you can thank your stars that you ain't a woman in this dirty Pittsburgh—black at that—or you'd end in that bed on your back like me."

Enveloped by her fury I sat, cup in hand, watching her pace the floor, the brightness of her great, white eyes betraying her tears, and suddenly she swung round at me, gripping her hands, trembling, and whispered, "You say something, mister, don't you sit there staring at me."

I rose and went to my bundle.

She shouted after me, "If you think I'm a nigger bum you say so, O'Hara!"

Kneeling, I tied up my bundle, and she stood above me, whispering, "You ain't saying a thing, are you, but I know what you're thinking, so I'm telling you this . . ." She ran to the door and spread herself across it, glaring down. "You bloody whites are all the same. You reckon you can walk on the likes of us, but that's where you're wrong, the war's changed things and we're the top dogs now. And the time's comin' fast when they'll all be in the gutter like you while we're on the sidewalk, and we'll spit on the likes of Johnny Jacobs."

I sighed, hoisting my bundle. "It won't be before time," I said, and faced her.

She was staring at me, her mouth trembling. Some impelling magnetism was forcing me to stay when I could have flung her aside; perhaps the sadness of her fanatical anger. Then suddenly, without warning, she began to cry. I did not move when she ran to the bed, flung herself on her knees beside it, and beat it with her fists.

"Oh, Lord," she whispered, sobbing.

Being a specialist in tantrums after my life with Karen, I dropped the bundle and went to her. For a while I let her weep, then said:

"Katie, I didn't finish the coffee," and she got up, wiping her face with her hands, whispering, "And I asked you here . . . Oh, Lord above, I'm a damned bad nigger, and my white pa left me with a damned bad mouth." She held out her hands to me. "It's the dirt, Mr. O'Hara, it never comes off. It's dirty black and coloured trash and pesky nigger and darkies' skins for razor strops.

130

Oh, my God, Mr. O'Hara, you just don't know. I hate this place and its lousy two dollars a time. You just don't know the things they get up to." Rising, she fetched my cup and pressed it against me. "You finish that coffee and go from here, for I'm bad all through."

"Not likely," I replied, "I'm staying."

"You get out of here!" Her voice rose again.

"D'you think I'm sleeping on the river when I can curl up here?" I sat on the bed again. "Besides, it isn't every night when you can pick up free coffee."

She reached for the cup, hands trembling in a pathetic anxiety to please. "You want some more? I got plenty of coffee."

"Not now," I replied.

"Afterwards, then. You and me'll have half an hour together then I'll fix you a right big feed, eh?"

"I only came to sleep," I said.

She screwed at her hands, as if reviling them, saying, "Because I'm black, eh?"

I shrugged. "One pretty woman's as good as another—it all rests on cooking. They're all the same colour in the dark, you know." I gave her a grin, but she did not smile.

"What about that red-head?"

I replied, "Katie, she was some cook."

She sniffed. "Bet she couldn't boil water. You tired, then?"

I nodded, and stripped off my coat as she turned down the lamp. I undressed as she busied herself around the room as women do, seeming happy again as she hummed to herself in a minor key. I had my trousers in my hand when she turned at the window.

"You aiming to sleep, is it?"

"Aye."

"You stand a bolster down the middle, then? There'll be room for the three of us."

"That'll suit fine," I said.

"A bed's got two lying places, mind—one on and one under, take your pick."

"We'll just have the bolster," I said, and caught it in mid-air and stuffed it down the middle.

"My, Mr. O'Hara," she said, "you're some fella. I ain't never met a fella like you before, you must need feedin'. You fancy some corn-pone and pork—I got some in the larder."

"Just sleep," I said.

"Then you keep virgin pure," she said. "Don't you even look while I'm undressin'." And I got into the bed by the bolster and lay there, watching as she took the things off. Against the red glow of the window I saw her, a gyrating black shadow of fluttering hands and petticoats, until she reached nakedness, and then she stood still. So still and quiet she stood, etched into shape against the light of the window. Scarcely breathing, I watched.

"You there, Mr. O'Hara?"

"I ain't vanished, Miss Virginia," I said, taking her off, and she drew nearer, reached the bed and knelt beside me, took my hand and held it against her, whispering:

"Will you answer me something, truthful, Jess O'Hara?"

There were no ragged furnishings about her then. Instead, in my quickened breathing I saw her against leaves in a place of moonlight and dark, savage earth.

She said, "D'you think I'm beautiful like this?"

Furnace glow brightened on the window and I heard the sounds of the street: carriage wheels and iron-shod crunchings; the prancing ring of hooves as the city flooded by on the tide of its pleasures. Roll-necked bosses, I saw, a thick-lipped munching of brutal cigars and the organ-stop bosoms of their racketeer mistresses, till Katie rose at the bedside, smiling down.

"Or like this, Jess O'Hara? You reckon we're all the same in the dark—me and that red-head? For it's five dollars for a white girl and two for a nigger."

"You are beautiful," I whispered.

"Yet you ain't taking me? All you gotta do is kick out that bolster."

"No," I said.

"Because of that red-head?"

I nodded.

"Man," she breathed, "that's decent. My Johnny Jacobs said the same. 'Katie Virginia,' he said, 'I ain't messin' with any other woman until you come back to Columbus.' D'you think he'll keep that promise, Jess O'Hara?"

"Be a fool if he didn't."

"So he's in love with Katie and you're in love with that red-head. Gee, that's fine, real fine."

Strangely, I kissed her. In the bed-sheet glow of her big, round eyes I kissed her again, and she sighed, drawing away, whispering, "Don't you come nearer, Mr. O'Hara. You got a soul in a raiment of fire and some of that goodness might rub off on me. You keep those kisses for that red-head in scarlet."

She got into bed on the other side of the bolster and I lay there in the darkness and listened to her breathing and the clamour of the city below. It was clean up here with Katie Virginia.

I left her before the dawn with my bundle in one hand and the food she had given me in the other, and walked into the dismal street. The Copper Works was pinned with light in the distance.

Reaching its gates I sat down on my bundle, waiting for the dawn shift, cupped my chin in my hands and thought, about Katie.

I grinned at my thoughts. Now, in the cold light of the Pittsburgh jungle my brain was tuned to its cold reality. I rubbed my chin and grinned wider.

Missed it by inches—I'd been pretty slow.

CHAPTER 14

That winter I wandered, lost, between Homestead and Sharpsburg where the vigorous Mr. Heinz was building his food empire—a man who began with a wheelbarrow and walked his produce to the ports of the world. From McKeesport to Etna I tramped, taking job after job, losing them in brawls at the gates, and tramping again. I worked in the ship-yards, skinned mules in the tanneries, was a drain-cleaner in Reserve, a rat-catcher in Manchester, and a grave-digger in Hillsdale. I even shifted the snow from the steps of the Penitentiary, and stood outside the soup kitchen on Seventh Street till they said I was a waster, and drove me away. I blamed my bad luck on losing Karen, I blamed the Molly Maguires, saying they had posted my picture over every works gate in the city, but I knew neither was true. For this was a time when jobs were gold. With the city inundated with blacks after the Civil War new batches of immigrants were pouring in, and many were specialists. The Welsh and Staffordshire English brought with them their trade of iron. These were the specialists whom Pittsburgh welcomed, to teach her the trade of steel-making; the puddlers, ballers, and rollers; the men of the new Bessemer process who knew the colour of the pilot flame before the turn of the cauldron; the underground moles of Durham who worked with science, wedging and driving the headers and shafts, bringing out more coal a head than three rebellious Irish. And these Welsh and English sought out their fellows, giving them the jobs. Hunkies and Wops, Turks and Chinese were employed at the expense of the Irish, because they would work till they dropped, for bread. Tattered, gaunt, like a thousand other wrecks of the city, I learned that the belly is the greatest enemy of all. There is no sickness like the stomach's gnaw for food; no pain like the heady swims that cross the eyes and blind you into collisions. Then the pain subsides, the gnawing ceases. Vacantly, you wander, swaying, enwrapped in a soulless void; living, but dead. In such an agony I arrived, in February, at Girty's Run.

I remember that it was a day of perpetual rain, with the scarecrowed trees rattling in a wind from the river: that I passed a factory earlier in the day, and looked through one of its windows, seeing an endless row of benches below giant cotton looms where children were sitting in dejection. And the bully-man who had raked them from their beds that morning walked among them, stick in hand. These, I thought distantly, were the tools of a city's industry; whose misery raised the graph of profit and kicked the backside of some competitor. No word would be said of these, I thought, when the pomp and glory of Pittsburgh was written. From the pulpit and city chairs would thunder the prowess of the city industrialists who had eased their conscience with municipal gifts —giving of their loose change while children gave their lives. Later that day I met them hand in hand, these branded ones, making for the shanties and the fevered search for bread while the Carnegies jacked up profits.

Standing back I looked at the factory entrance. In huge white letters was the name—Lubinski.

Over at Girty's Run I squatted against a wall and watched the crowds go by until they were thinned by shift. Through drooping eyes I saw a strand of straw drift down from a brick-stack: so still that single strand trapped in stones, now waving in bright gyrations as it laboured for escape. And as I stared it appeared to grow bigger, as a wand of sunlight blazing in my eyes. Watching it, I dreamed, and Shaun's tale of Girty the renegade made pictures in my mind. In horror I saw a man chained to a stake, staggering in agony around an Indian bonfire, and heard the yells of the savage squaws, the delighted shrieks of children. Shivering in sleep I relived the agony of the gallant Colonel Crawford; in bitter coldness I roasted alive. Upraised hatchets I saw, and a flash of knives, and awoke, weeping from the nightmare to see a face above me. Beautiful that face, her eyes wide and full of pity.

"Eh, hush," she whispered.

I saw her in a mist at first, but the warmth in her hands was real, and I clung to her.

I said, "They chained him to the stake, and for hours he walked around the fire, and begged for death . . ."

"Aye, man. Hush, hush you . . ." She held me, kneeling.

"And then they ran in and heaped live coals on his wounds and fired their darts into his naked body, and he begged again, but they would not kill him!"

Now the hammer of feet on the flags as they lifted me. The sky was swimming, as if in tears as the rain beat down.

"Take him in here," said the girl, and they did so, and laid me down. So cool in here. I cried out for her, but she did not hear me, and when I opened my eyes again I was lying before a fire with the girl sitting beside me.

I looked around the tiny room.

A table in the middle was laid for two, the cloth was white, and the fire-light danced in redness on the faded walls. Rain was lashing at the window in squalls and the night was drowning in a roar of wind. Smoke from the chimney billowed in a down-draught, acrid in the room. I looked at the face of the girl before me. Smiling, she drew the cup from my lips though I pulled at her hands.

"Easy, man," she whispered.

She was about fifteen years old, her face pale, her nose too pert, her mouth too wide for beauty. Only her hair was beautiful, parted in the middle of her wide brow and hanging in black, shining plaits each side of her face. She said, dark eyes narrowed:

"Eh, God help us. What next, is it? Lying out there and starving with cold. Asking for it you are, man. Is it warm with you now, boy?"

Welsh. You can always tell them by the song in their voices, the lusty bawling of their men, the diminutive darkness of their women who dominated them. I looked beyond her. Above the fireplace was a stitched sampler on the wall saying, "Wales, Wales."

"You Irish, *bach?*"

"Aye," I muttered.

"Down on your luck, is it?"

Like all the Welsh she did not mince her words, but there was an honest serenity in her face that forbade pride.

"Down in the gutter," I said, and took the cup from her, and drank till it was finished, and she rose, standing above me, hands folded before her, smiling.

"There now," she said. "Good cow-steak broth do set a man up. As good as new you are."

I pulled the blanket closer about me. "Where's my clothes, woman?"

"The old things were soaking, so I took them off. Drying by the furnace they are, so you stay put in that warm blanket. Will is due back soon—just gone down to the coal yard, he has—back any minute, then he will see to you. What is your name?"

"Jess O'Hara."

She put her head on one side, listening to it. "Aye, that's pretty," she said, "though the Jess do sound like a woman. Where you from?"

"Connemara."

"Where's that, for God's sake?" She pulled up a chair and sat on the edge of it, knees wide, hands clasped in her lap, smiling her interest. Much of the boy in this one, I thought, save for the dimples.

"Ireland," I said, growing tired of her.

"Whee, there's pretty names they do have in Ireland—Jess O'Hara, Connemara, though they come just as pretty back home. Coldbrookvale and Risca, Nanty and Blaina. You warm now?"

I nodded, fighting a smile. If Katie Virginia had come after my trousers I would have fought for them, and here was a sweet fifteen who had stripped me naked and laid me in a blanket and thought no more of it than laying a table. Queer, these Welsh. I said:

"Where am I?"

"In the house of Mr. Rees, my cousin. Down at the coal yard, he is, but he . . ."

"Aye, you told me. Get my clothes now, girl, I am going."

"Going? Out into that?" She rose, pointing at the window. "Have sense, man, I wouldn't see a dog out in a night like that."

"Please get my clothes."

"*Duw*, I will not. In a Welsh house you are now, Jess O'Hara, and you do as you are told. Will is coming back soon, and then we will have supper." And she lifted her skirts and swept round to the table and laid another place. I watched her. There was a faint arrogance in her bearing, evident in the upturned chin and the glances she shot in my direction as she came in with cups and saucers. Banging down the plates she said, not looking at me:

"You alone in Pittsburgh, Jess O'Hara?"

"Aye."

"No relations, then?"

I muttered, disinterested, "I've got a sister, but she's away up in New York."

"Working up there, is she?" She was at the fire now, kneeling at a hanging-pot, stirring the stew.

"She's a dancer," and this turned her with wide eyes.

"A dancer? That's wonderful! Irish dancing, is it?"

"Just jigs and reels."

"And she earns her living at it?"

"I hope so," I answered, "I haven't heard from her since she went."

She smoothed back her hair and went on stirring. "Don't make sense," she said. "Her up in New York and you down here in Pittsburgh. Relatives should be together in a foreign country."

I was warming to her. I had taken her for a child, but she was a woman, and I said, smiling, "You try telling Karen anything that makes sense, she's got a mind of her own." And she turned from the fire, staring at me, lowering her spoon.

"Karen?" she said faintly.

I nodded.

"Karen O'Hara?" she whispered, rising. Weakly, she pointed with the spoon. "A dancer, you say?"

"That's right."

"A red-haired dancer? Come over on a ship called the *Pennsylvanian*?"

"The pair of us," I replied, "about fifteen months back."

"God 'elp us," she said, and sat down on the chair again. "*Ach-y-fi!* There's me cousin Will been searching twelve months for the Connemara dancers and they're walking in by here. Karen O'Hara!"

"Will Rees!" I exclaimed, sitting upright.

"Well! I've been having the woman for breakfast, dinner and tea. Cooked and stuffed I am, with Karen O'Hara!"

"And you're Will's cousin!" I was on my feet now, gripping the blanket for decency.

"For my sins," said she. "My name's Marged."

And in the following gabble of excitement Will Rees came in and stood in the doorway, staring down at me, his eyes widening with delighted recognition.

"Jess O'Hara!" he cried, and gripped my hands.

Into the real stew now, the three of us, with Marged ladling it out and my plate brimming with the ribs of a Pittsburgh beast, firing back answers to Will's excited questions about Karen, and I wished him to the devil, being in love myself then, with a stew-stained cousin.

"So you're starting up in business on your own?" I asked at length.

"Aye," replied Marged, "and with every cent of his savings. He could get a fine job as foreman with Carnegie or Laughlin's and he has to stoop to speculation."

"But with somebody else's money, remember," said Will. "I could be a foreman for the rest of my life in Pittsburgh, but with Lubinski behind me I could end up as an owner—the sky's the limit—look at Carnegie."

"Look at him," said Marged disdainfully. "He's like the damned rest of them—hoarding up dollars on other people's misery. And I wouldn't trust Lubinski as far as I could throw him."

"Lubinski?" I said, glancing up. Will answered:

"He's my backer. If he's not a millionaire he's precious close to it. His interests are in glass and cotton mostly, now he's going into iron."

"His interest is in money," said Marged, "and he doesn't care how he gets it. Have you been down to his mill? He rakes in his profits on the labour of children—even Carnegie can't be accused of that." She bounced things about on the table, rose and went to the fire, raking hell out of it.

Will said evenly, "Marged doesn't agree with it, as you can see. She's like all women—play safe. If I listened to her I'd spend my life on twelve-hour shifts and nothing to show for it. Listen, Jess —if this thing works out right we'll be sleeping on dollars."

"And who's interested in dollars?" Marged now, poker in hand, swinging from the fire. "If you loaded me with money I wouldn't know what to do with it!"

"All right, then," cried Will. "We owe it to industry. Have we come to America to take everything out and give nothing back? This is a fine Welsh invention and any industry is entitled to it. D'you know anything at all about the making of steel, Jess?"

I shook my head, and he went on, "The iron age is over—everybody's converting to steel-making here, and they're bringing over the Welsh specialists to run their converters. With Lubinski behind me I'm building a new furnace here, using the new Bessemer process, which is the latest. But there's more to it than that."

"Right enough," interjected Marged. "Can you tell me the difference between iron and steel? There's none. It'll be the same old stuffed shirts fighting for the profits. And will it make a mite of difference to those miserable foreigners out there?" She pointed at the window.

"It will raise their standards," said Will adamantly. "Oh, God, Jess—we have this day and night, and she won't see sense." His voice rose. "Would you be in America now, woman, if somebody hadn't invented a ship to bring you here?"

"Aye," cried Marged. "Ships to bring in those miserable immigrants so they can be sweated to death for the profits of their masters or starve on the streets when they're finished with them." She came closer. "Tell him, Jess O'Hara. Does the ordinary man get a penny out of the new inventions? You know the truth of it, Will, for you've told me. The Crawshays and their crowd sweated them back home in Merthyr, the Carnegies and Klomans sweat them here, for what? To make fat millionaires out of a few while the rest live like pigs in their shanties."

"Will you bridle your tongue, Marged? The thing's a foot longer than a serpent!"

"And it'll grow a foot longer before I'm finished, for I'll never agree to what you're doing. Now I'm away to fix Jess a bed—you can talk yourself sick on your Bessemers and Gilchrist Thomas inventions, but I'll never be a party to what you're doing."

Some fifteen-year-old. She was ten years old when she left the womb, said Will after she had gone.

I said, "I wasn't intending to stay, you know. I was only passing, Will," and he smiled, saying:

"If Marged's fixing you a bed you're here for good, whether you like it or not. She'll be putting you in the tradesmen's bunks—you're the first occupant."

"Are you offering me a job?" I whispered.

"Permanent, if you'll sign with us. I'm needing labour—the right kind—and next week I'm starting to build it up."

"Wages?"

Will shrugged. "Right, we'll come down to business. You've got no trade, have you?"

I shook my head.

"So you'll come in as rough labour—seven dollars a week, Jess—take it or leave it."

It was dark in the bunkhouse and I lay there in one of the twenty beds, watching the stars in a tear of the slates above me, thinking of Karen and my nightmare wanderings in the city. Hateful, this city, I thought, with its blown-up rich and starving beggars, and money for its god. Warm and fed for the first time in months, exhaustion swept over me in increasing waves, and I slept, awaking, it seemed, a moment later. In a shaft of sunlight Marged's face appeared joyfully over the top rung of a ladder.

"You there, Jess O'Hara?"

There was a nymph-like mischief in her now. Eyes dancing, she winked.

"Do the Irish drink tea first thing in the morning?"

I rose on an elbow. "Pepper and water back home," I replied.

"*Diawch*, man! Are you refusing tea? The stuff comes special from relatives in Swansea."

"Then it's a heathen drink, but I'll force it," and I took the cup.

141

Up over the ladder with her then, and settled in the straw beside me, swinging her bare legs over the top of the bunk, and eyeing me. She was coming a bit too close for comfort, so I shifted over.

"Will tells me he's taken you on, Jess O'Hara—that right?"

I nodded.

"Dando! That will mean I'll be feeding you." She pinched my arm. "By the look of you you'll take some fattening, boyo."

I sipped the tea, hating it, and watching her. No, she was not beautiful, but there was a winsome grace about her movements and her expressions were joyful, fleet, ever-changing.

"You got a girl back home, Jess?"

I blew at the steam. "A couple."

"Two, is it?" Mouth open, eyes wider.

"One for weekdays, one for Sundays."

"Ay, ay!" She watched me sideways. "Let's have their names, then."

"Rosa Turvey and Beth O'Shea."

"You have their names off pat but I still don't believe you."

"You can have a couple more if you like," I replied, lying back. "I always run some on the side."

"Eh, you're full of woman, is it? If that's the truth then why did you give me the eye last night?"

"Because you're in Pittsburgh and they're in Ireland."

"God help us, you must be a terror for the women, Jess O'Hara."

"I am that, and that's why I'm leaving." I got up, stretched, and shinned down the ladder, and she leaned her chin on the top rung, staring down.

"For a man who's a terror you're away pretty sharp," said she. "Who's chasing you?"

"You," I said, tightening my belt. "Because though you're not yet sixteen you're old enough for damage. If your cousin finds you here there's likely to be ructions." I slopped water into a pail. "Away out of the place while I take off me shirt."

"Your shirt, is it?" said she. "I had your trews last night."

I grinned as she came down the ladder on her heels, arms outstretched, balancing. A character, this one—girl one moment, woman the next.

"Are you bringing your dancing sister home to live with us?" she asked, squatting cross-legged while I washed.

"If I knew where she was." I groped for the towel and she tossed it at me.

"She might take Will's mind off his silly old inventions," she said. "All he can think of is making dirty old money."

"Strikes me he's got the right idea," I said, waving back into my shirt. "You have to have money if you're going to handle Pittsburgh—I know, I've had some."

This cooled her, I noticed, and she lowered her eyes, then smiled brilliantly in an instant change of mood. "Are you going into the city today, Jess?"

I went to the door. "I am. Why?"

"Because I can't go alone, says Will, and I'm fishing for an escort."

"You're brazen, girl."

"I'm Welsh," said she, "which means I'm honest, for we don't spin the words." She ran beside me, smiling up. "Do you know something? If I pinned up my hair and shortened my skirt you wouldn't know fifteen from twenty, for I'm pretty keen on the Irish, though I'm only catching one word in five."

"God save us," I whispered. "Are they all like you in Wales?"

She did not reply. Very quaint she looked standing there with her hands behind her back. Twelve months older and I might have kissed her, for the sweetness of it.

"Away outside," I said, "or we won't know Irish from Welsh."

I left her and went out into the bright sun of the compound. Turning, I saw her standing there, smiling still, with the eyes of a woman.

Very quiet, this Marged Rees, when we sat down to breakfast.

Will Rees paid me wages in advance that day, and after I had hauled in some pit timber and cleaned up the compound the shadows were falling. With the money jingling I left Girty's Run and went over the river to Jubec's. I do not know why I went that evening; perhaps it was to recapture Karen in the fierce rye whiskey or savour some Irish banter, for the humour of the Welsh is different from the Irish. Immediately I left the Rees compound I saw the man again. Twice before I had seen him that day, leaning idly against the wall where Marged had found me, watching the bunkhouse, his eyes shifting to my every movement as I worked. And I was not surprised when he followed me over the river. Lighting his stogie in the shadows of a door he watched me go up to the entrance of Jubec's.

The moment I reached the door I knew what had happened. A striped awning was nailed over the windows, the door was criss-crossed with nailed battens. Through a crack in the wood I peered within at overturned tables and splintered chairs, and the beautiful long bar was heaped with glass. Sickened, I turned, and the man was beside me.

"O'Hara?"

"You seem to know," I said.

He was tall and thin, his tanned face gaunt under his broad-rimmed hat. Taking a pull at his cigar he jerked it at the Jubec windows.

"And that's the Maguires. I know that, too," he said, and smiled. "Have you heard about old man Jubec?"

I shook my head.

He sighed. "They took a pint bottle to him and left him for dead—that was months back. And he never made an enemy in twenty years, O'Hara."

"Is he dead?"

"Oh, he's alive. The heads they grow in Bremen are even thicker than the Irish, but he hasn't much of a face, they tell me." He flung away the stogie. "Grand little chap, old Jubec, so if you're an angry man you're in good company. How's your sister?"

I moved back to get the street lights on him. "Who are you?"

He settled his buttocks against the wall and stared down the street where yellow vapours from the oil refinery were creeping up. "That would be telling, O'Hara. I'm Irish, for a start—that should be good enough. In the past I used to duck in here for a chat with Mr. Jubec, watch your sister dance—see you bouncing

144

the bums." He spat at my feet, suddenly scowling. "I liked old Jubec. He didn't deserve what McNamara handed him."

I said evenly, "Out with it, man, there's more to it than Jubec. I've seen you watching me," and he smiled and tipped back his hat.

"And risk me life, fella? Not till I know you better, for we have to till the ground, O'Hara. For all I know you'd go tearing off to McNamara, that would be unfriendly."

"If you hate the Maguires then I'm with you," I whispered.

"And how about your brother Shaun—isn't he still thick with them?"

"Haven't seen him for months—don't judge me by my brother."

His eyes moved slowly over mine, and he sighed. "Right, then, I'll chance it. Have you heard of the Pinkerton Detective Agency?" He stared at me, and grinned. "You haven't? Christ, you're a lone soul in Pennsylvania, boy. Then I'll tell you. It's anti-Union, pro-employer, and especially anti-Maguire. I'll come to the point, O'Hara. When we want a man we pay good money for the information, and last night I saw you down on your hunkers."

"Who are you after—McNamara?"

He groaned. "Get some sense. I could pull in twenty men and pick him out of Hank's Bar in ten minutes. It's not Sean McNamara I'm after, or Kehoe or the rest—it's the donkey who's wagging them." He pulled from his pocket a big roll of dollars. "I'm after the boss—the man who runs the Maguires of Pennsylvania."

"Why should I help you?"

"Because you're in trouble. Because you've crossed the Maguires, and they don't stand for that. They got Jubec quick, but they're taking their time over you, O'Hara. You rolled round this city for months, and you didn't get a job—they saw to that. You think you've got a job with the Rees people, don't you?—you have, until McNamara finds out. Then up in the air you'll go and Will Rees with you—cousin and all. And that's the way of their business. We're losing good agents and foremen every week to the bastards. They maim and shoot from ambush, they torture to intimidate. If they grow much bigger they'll have the State by the heels, Governor and all, and they'll have their finger on the pulse of this city until we cut them out. Will you help?"

"How?"

He leaned forward eagerly. "Get into them, boy—go down to Hank's and sign up with McNamara. Take the oath and swear to them. Find out all you can—their secret meetings, their plans, and report to me here once a week. The employers of this city won't forget you." He thrust the roll of notes into my hands. "This is chicken feed, O'Hara—just a start."

"And if I'm caught?"

He straightened. "Then you're on your own, and God help you."

I smiled, and pushed the money back. "Keep your bloody bribes," I said. "I've seen this city and I've seen its employers. I'd rather be a Maguire, stranger, for at least they're Irish."

"Don't you owe it to the country?" His voice rose in sudden anger.

I pushed him aside and walked away. "Find someone else to do your dirty work. I owe nothing to this damned country."

I was afraid. Even if I left Will Rees and Marged now, Mc-Namara might already have them on the list for the same treatment he gave Jubec, so I went down to the waterfront towards Hank's Bar. It was dark when I got there. The same bald-headed bartender was there, still polishing glasses, the same ungainly girl hostess with her sidelong glances. I said at the bar, "Is McNamara in?"

The bartender smiled. "Upstairs, O'Hara."

I frowned. It was almost as if he had been expecting me. A shrivelled Irish labourer barged past me with frightened eyes as I went up the stairs three at a time. Entering McNamara's room without knocking, I went up to his table. Writing away, he didn't even look up.

"So you're back, O'Hara?" His heavy face showed cynical enjoyment, and he added, "They all come back, ach, sure to God they do," and he flicked the ash off the end of his stogie and grinned up expansively as Kehoe came in by another door. "So you've realised at last that there's weakness in division and strength in comradeship, eh?"

I said quietly, "After what you did to Mr. Jubec."

"Glory be, O'Hara, we've not laid a finger on Jubec." He grinned wider.

"And you're not doing the same to Will Rees."

McNamara's expression changed. Grunting, he rose from the table. "Now, me boy, you've got me wrong—as wrong as a man can be had, I'm tellin' you. D'you think we've no respect for a fella who's making his way against odds? It's not the likes of Rees we're after, it's the fellas who profit on a working man's misery." He waved a fat hand as I opened my mouth. "Sure, we know Rees—it's the task of the Society to know who's movin' in the city, but we've nothing against the chap."

"Except that I'm working for him."

He gripped my shoulder admiringly. "Dear God, you're learning fast, O'Hara, me lad. And if you object to the title Maguires then I can tell you that it's not them you're joining—it's the Ancient Order of Hibernians, see, that's a proud title! And we're prouder still to have yer, aren't we, Kehoe?"

Kehoe sat down and opened the black book, scowling up at me. McNamara went on:

"You may be wondering at our interest in you, man, and you've a right to know it. You see, you've a brother up to his neck in our activities, and he's a mite fond of the bottle." He gave me a pen and pushed the black book before me on the desk. "He's a prattling tongue on him, has Shaun, and likely to be wagging it in his sleep, and we'd hate to see him losing it. Sign your name."

I did so.

"Now then, O'Hara, are you listening. You can call us the Brother Hibernians, you can call us the scum Molly Maguires, if you please, but you can't deny our fine intentions, which stand for the national good. You can rate us as thieves and murderers, but we're neither, unless you rank the industrialists as thieves and murderers, too, for they're cutting more throats with slow starvation than ever we do with a knife. Didn't you put a few down in Ireland, come to that, yourself?"

"I was fighting for Ireland," I said sullenly.

"And aren't we all? D'you hear that, Kehoe? He was fighting for old Ireland! Haven't the Irish fought for Ireland since Kelly's head was kicked round the cobbles of Wexford? Didn't we fight the beast Cromwell after he slaughtered the matrons of Cork? Sure, Ireland is Ireland, lad, but this is America. So you can read me the riot act from the hangings of Galway to the wreckings of Castlebar, but you'll leave me cold, for this country's a bitch to nothin' for injustices. Are you listening?" He stood beside me, and I sensed the power and dedication in him. "Has this reached your fine ears, for instance—d'you know that there's two million starving in this promised land while the Astors and Vanderbilts are rolling in gold? D'you know there's a million or so child-labourers toiling out their lives in twelve-hour shifts—that they're beating them with iron bars to keep them awake at the mills? Have you seen the children in chains for that bastard Lubinski? Have you heard the barkers going round the city at dawn—kicking them out o' their beds to skin them alive at the machines—with the city waxing fat on their hunger? Do they ever see the sun, these children? Aye, they do, O'Hara—it's the glory of God they see, for they never see the light of day when labouring for the big American man, d'you know these things?"

I watched him, unmoved, plumbing his sincerity.

"Do you know of them?" he barked at me.

I nodded.

He said, his voice low, "Right you, well it's our dream to stop it, O'Hara. You've sailed to the land of promise and jumped from the pan into the fire. For if the devil himself stalks the barren land of Connemara where a nation died, he was weaned in the cornfields of the great American South. We're not bloody fools, we're thinking men—we're up to our knees in American misery while you have its dust on your boots, O'Hara. There's as much bribery and corruption here as you'll find in the records of the English Parliament, and that's goin' some—and about as much Fourth of July liberty to cleanse the soul of the vile Lord Clare who spat on O'Connell's reforms. You'll learn, O'Hara, by God, you'll learn!" Spitting out the stogie, he wandered the room, gasping and wheezing. I said, quietly:

"And what do you hope to gain?" and it swung him, fist up, shouting:

"Control! We've lost good men fighting for it, and we'll lose a thousand more before we bring the bastards down. Perhaps I die next, Kehoe tomorrow, and you next month, but we'll each take an employer with us, and a few less workers starve. Comradeship, O'Hara—you can rape the stomach of a working man's wife and break his head with a truncheon, but that man will never give in— while he has comrades. And we are his comrades, lad—we and a million others who sweat and die for the bloody capitalists of America." He was sweating hard now, breathing in gasps. "You take this city here, O'Hara—she's big and beautiful, even in the hands of greed, but she's like a woman in silk and finery who hasn't had a bath for a year, and she'll pox you to the eyebrows, unless you cleanse her. She'll suck your blood and fling you in the gutter, unless you fight her, for she turns out her wealth for a landed class —the jumped-up financiers, not her people . . ."

"Are you a labour movement?" I interjected, and he waved me away in disgust. "Ach, don't sicken me, child—who mentioned labour? It's social justice we're after and we leave the wage-fixing to the Sons of Vulcan and their like, God help them—that's union business."

"Anti-employers, then?"

"Anti-employers, anti-judges, anti-corruption, and anti-wealth, O'Hara—from the municipal servant who sells his mate for gold to the treason of the State legislators and the Senator who can be bought for a thousand dollars. And I'll give you a joyful thought, son. The bullet that flies from the gun of a Maguire works for you and me, and the same little bullet drops clerk or foreman and lays them six feet deep, in the name of God and the Pope. Pay your tribute."

"What with?"

"Riley!" McNamara turned and bawled at the door. It opened and a man walked in. I stared, snatching at my breath. It was the man I had met outside Jubec's Bar.

"Riley," said McNamara, "he's short of membership money— give the boy some to tide him over. Congratulations, son, it's a great night for the O'Haras—sure to God you're a flower of an Irishman."

And the man Riley came over and tossed me a roll of dollars, the same roll he had offered as a bribe outside Jubec's.

"A hundred to start you. Well done, O'Hara."

"Fifty cents," snapped Kehoe from the table, "pay your fee."

"Give us credit, lad," said McNamara, "we're pretty well organised."

I paid it in a dream.

Too well organised for me.

CHAPTER 15

Spring came in glorious with flowers and the fields were decorated with yellow and gold. I lived and worked with Will Rees and Marged, and the new furnace grew higher on Lubinski's money, its red brick chimney fingering at the sky. And we, like the rest of the city builders, took our cut of the new immigrants rolling in. They came in their thousands from every corner of the world, shivering with excitement at the new life to come; tattered, gaunt from their long sea-voyages, they milled in from the railway station and the flat-boat quays with their bundles on their backs, urged on by the delighted shrieks of their spindle-legged children. And the Immigration Office channelled them into the Company shanties, slept them ten to a room in the squalid alleys, and they woke at dawn to the forced labour of steel-works or mill, oil refineries and tanneries. And we, Lubinski Inc., blundered on like the rest of Pittsburgh, becoming as disdainful of flesh and blood as the hard-bitten speculators, for the tempo of industry was rising. With the twelve-hour shift in full swing, the accident rate was rising, too. Men were trapped under white-hot tips, descended into furnaces and were evaporated, dragged from the rollers and died in screams. And at the height of the holocaust, with the Iron City flaming and thundering as something demented, Hosea and Michael arrived in Allegheny City.

I was up on the chimney scaffolding with Will and another six men when Shaun, my brother, bellowed from the ground below.

"Aloft there, Jess! They're here!"

I stared down at his pin-head face, and he cupped his hands to his mouth. "Ho and Mike—down at the railroad!"

"In the name of God," I whispered. "Did you hear that, Will? It's me two brothers come in from Ireland, d'you mind I told you I sent some tickets," and I scrambled down the ladder to Shaun. He said, panting:

"It was McNamara watching the immigrant list, as usual, for I told him more O'Haras might be comin', so he sent a note round to the Kovaks, for I was off shift."

I turned as Will jumped down beside me.

"I'm worried about bunking them," I said, "for I've got to find the men beds, can you fix it?"

"If they work as well as the rest of the O'Haras," he answered. "With Marged cooking for thirty, another couple won't break her back."

"You mean you'll take 'em on the pay-roll, Will?"

"And welcome, if they'll have it."

"God bless you for the Christian man you are," I said, and followed Shaun out of the compound, and two men never went so fast down the streets of Allegheny. We found them on the station-clearing, standing in the dusk, with Hosea bent under his bundle and his eyes rolling at the red spouts of the city. Michael was beside him, hands on hips, surveying his new, unconquered world, and between them stood Rachel Turvey, braceleted and bangled, with her black hair down her back as something stepped from a gipsy encampment.

"Hosea!"

And he turned as torn from a hypnotism, dropped the bundle, and flung out his arms to me. Here's a re-union, with O'Haras dancing in rings of joy, back-slapping and kissing and filling the air with shrieks while cold-faced officials prodded us for tickets and foreigners stared with open hostility.

"Where's Karen?" demanded Michael, and I explained in gasps.

"New York, indeed! Sure, she'll have a piece of my mind for not receiving us," said he. "D'you hear that, Ho? The woman's kicking her spags up and us travelling three thousand miles to see her."

"So you brought Rachel, Ho?" I said.

"Could I leave her behind, man? She's been me legal wife these past twelve months, and I'm hitting the pugs here flat for her and covering her with gold, isn't that right, me darling?"

And Rachel, for answer, stared around, bored.

"Is there a government here?" asked Michael.

"There is, and a fine one," shouted Shaun. "It's God's own

country you've come to, I'm telling yer." Beggars crowded round us, calling for alms, and he pushed them aside. "You can sleep in plush or sit in the gutter, just as you like, and you can't say that for Ireland." I watched Michael's eyes as he looked at the beggars.

"If your government stands for that then I'm against it," said he.

"How's Ma?" I cried.

"Ach, she's fatter than ever on horse spuds and pepper. Young Melody's a real tantrum now," said Ho. "The Beth O'Shea woman left us last summer, and Barney's moved in with Ma and the child, with Rosa between them to keep things decent, did you know?"

"It's a mating of the Celtic hordes," laughed Michael. "For Barney's mooning after Ma and there's her sleeping with her six-foot shillelagh, which she used to land on Pa, d'you remember?"

On we went, chattering and laughing, down the alleys and streets, and windows were going up and doors coming open at the new Irish invasion, with peat families cheering us and tradesmen looking down their noses at the prospect of new Irish debts.

"Did you get Joe McManus eventually, Ho?" I shouted.

"Why, didn't you know? The letter-writer was supposed to have told you, for I got him in Derry and flattened him for dead, in six."

"Is that true, Mike?"

"Aye, right and true—you're talking to the champion of Ireland, and don't forget it."

"Have you work for the big oaf, Jess?" asked Rachel, speaking for the first time. "He'll be battering his brains out over here and not a dollar to spare for a new dress. Have you beds for us, by the way?"

"We have that," said Shaun. "You'll be sleeping in a bunkhouse with another twenty labourers, d'you mind?"

"Aw, she'll like that," rumbled Hosea. On, on we went to Lubinski's, and I watched Rachel amid the chatter and laughter; noticed her glances at passing men, and I was afraid for Hosea. The stage was set for women like Rachel, I thought; the gaudy glitter of Pittsburgh would be as heady wine after the caravan wanderings of Connemara.

The foreign labour was just ending shift as we entered the

bunkhouse, and we were unpacking the bundles and shaking down beds when Marged appeared in the doorway, then rushed away despite my commands and returned with Will who carried a little barrel of ale, and with bread and cheese all round munchings and smiles were everywhere. With a curtain rigged up between us and the labourers we sat together till darkness fell, slinging tales about Wales and Ireland, with Rachel eyeing Will and Marged going dreamy at the sight of handsome Michael. But he sat aloof from the talk, eyes half closed in meditation, staring through the window at distant Pittsburgh where the night-shift was flaming the sky and the drop-hammers going like marrow-bones and cleavers.

"Is it true you're employing us?" whispered Ho.

"If you're prepared to work I can take the pair of you," said Will, "but I'm paying well under the rates, you know."

"You feed me and mine and I'll work for you free, man. I can lift three hundredweight of bricks on me back, but spare me woman labour."

"Can she help me in the kitchen?" asked Marged. "The men here eat for ten—did they ever have a square meal in their lives? I could do with a hand."

"She's big in the hands for a man's stomach," said Hosea. "Will ye work with the pretty maiden, Rachel?"

"I will if I'm not streaming buckets," said she, fluffing up her hair, "for I didn't fly here for labour."

In the awkward silence after the two of them went out, Will whispered to me:

"Is your brother Shaun of the same mind, Jess? I could use a skilled foreman."

"Sure, I'll think of it," said Shaun, overhearing, "but I'm commanding top rates, remember. Is it a Bessemer you're building, you say?"

Will nodded. "And there's a fortune in it."

"But it could also mean the road to the workhouse," answered Shaun, "for you're not the first by far. The big fellas'll be round you like bees round a jam-pot—they'll blow you sky high before they let you pour from the bung, for they don't like competition."

"With Lubinski's money behind us?"

"Lubinski's a flea compared with people like Laughlin." Shaun sighed and pulled on his stogie. "Ach, I'm well fixed as it is—I'd have to ask McNamara."

"Did McNamara birth and wean you?" I asked. "Are you dependent on him for every decision you make?"

He waved me down. "Damned near it, Jess—best ask McNamara."

"Who's he?" asked Will, shoving me.

"He's a fella who tells the stars," I said. "Shaun's superstitious."

"Right, you," said Will rising, "I'll be needing his help myself unless we get a move on. It's two o'clock in the morning and I've ten tons of bricks coming in from Millvale after breakfast." He turned to Hosea and Michael. "Will you two start with the labour gang in the morning—same rates as Jess?"

"God bless you, Mr. Rees, I'll work like a black for you," said Ho.

"Welsh and Irish," said Michael, "rags or riches," and Rachel came through the door then, and smiled. "Riches," she said, "for I'm sick of rags," and she looked at Will with unfeigned desire.

So we laboured through the summer. The women cooked and helped with the light labour, the men sweated and grunted through winter into another spring, and the new furnace called Betsy rose to the top ring capping. We shipped in bricks along the canal, dumped the puddling-shed foundations, took mule-trains to the forests, and hauled in spars for scaffolding. And in May, with the blossoms loaded pink and white down the Evergreen Grove my brother Shaun left his steel-works and the Kovaks and moved into Lubinski, Inc. by the kind permission of Mr. McNamara. A couple of days after Shaun arrived the compound gates came open and in walked Timko Kovaks, as large as life, with a three-day fungus on his chin and stinking of rye whiskey to stun a tannery mule.

"Well, God bless you," said he, swigging on his heels. "Is it me old friend Jess O'Hara I'm addressing?"

I nodded, eyeing him, for he was speaking with the tongue of his Irish mother and no hint of the foreigner in him at all. He said:

"I was just passing, O'Hara, so I popped in to see you, for I can't abide an un-Christian act. There's me woman been receiving letters for Jess O'Hara for the last twelve months or so, and her stuffin' them up the chimney because you and your sister left her without the grace of a word, d'you remember?"

"Letters?" I whispered.

"And they've risked me life to be telling of them, for me missus would be having the skin off me hide, holy God. Are they worth a dollar a time?"

"For my letters?" I exclaimed. "Hand them over!"

"And them still up the chimney. Have sense, man," said he, "for me woman's guarding them."

Out of the corner of my eye I saw Hosea striding towards us, stripped to the waist, gigantic, and said, "You're a Christian man indeed, Timko Kovaks, so will you bide here another minute and meet me big brother?"

"Another O'Hara, is it? Sure, your ma must have been doing day shifts in the beds of Connemara—there's O'Haras coming in left and right."

Ho stopped before us, hands on hips. "Who's this fat fella?" he asked.

"It's a Polish Irishman," I answered, "and his name is Timko Kovaks. His ma hailed from Ulster and his pa from Warsaw, and his wife's got some letters from Karen and is poking them up the chimney."

"Is that a fact?"

"It is," said Timko, "and it's against the law of God to come between relatives, so I'm asking a dollar a time for them, for if me missus catches me fishin' up the chimney there'll be ructions."

"To wet your whistle, is it?" I asked.

"Ach, indeed, and if you wedded a woman like mine you'd understand the need for it, sir," said Timko. "It's a dollar a week for the priest with her and not a cent for me, and me an honest hard-working man, sure it's a pity what people put up with."

"A pity indeed," said Hosea, gripping him, "for now the letters are coming down the flue and you're going up it and your missus after you for a couple of evil thiefs," and he took Timko through the gates on the end of his fist and it was the last I saw of the Kovaks.

"Holy Peter," cried Mike, "will you listen to this!" and held up a letter. "She's been dancing her feet off on the big paddle-steamers for three dollars a night, she says." And he passed the letter round, and pages of the things were flying everywhere with people reading out snatches and jumping with excitement.

"She's been playing on the halls in this one!" shouted Hosea. "T'is fifty dollars a week for her now in Philadelphia!"

"And soon she's coming down to Pittsburgh!" I cried, passing round another one.

"When?" said a voice, and we all turned to the door of the bunk-house. Will stood there, his shirt open to the waist, sleeves rolled up, his face grimed with the brick-dust.

"There's five letters from Karen!" I shouted.

"And one for you," said Mike, and rose from the bunk and gave it to him.

"From Karen?" whispered Marged beside him. "Oh, Will!"

Reaching out, Will took the letter, and I saw his trembling hands as he tore at it while we watched, expectant, and then he turned, thrusting it into his shirt, and went into the darkness while Marged stared after him.

"Is he settled on our sister, then?" asked Michael softly.

"He's daft for her," whispered Marged, hands on hips.

"I was wondering," said Michael, "for I saw the look on his face. Does he know what he's taking over?"

"She's a tongue like a lash and she's never been tamed," said Hosea. "The milk in her's for rearing tiger cubs, girl—she'll never settle enough for the marrying."

"She's not that bad," I said, "when you know how to handle her. Your Rachel was just the same, Ho, but the ring of gold has changed her—look at her now."

"Aye," muttered Michael, stretching. "Look at her."

Hosea rose. "What d'you mean by that, then?" he whispered.

Mike shrugged. "What I say." He turned to the bunk and pulled back the bed-clothes, adding, "There's us slogging ourselves day and night and the wee one there flogging herself to death in the kitchen to feed us, and there's no sight nor sound of your precious Rachel."

"She's down the city helping the Sisters of Mercy, and you know it," said Ho thickly.

"Well, if it's mercy she's showing we could do with some here," answered Mike, swinging round. He pointed at Marged. "The kid's cookin' for nigh forty men now and Rachel's never been near the hob for the last three months."

"Oh, please," whispered Marged, "do not quarrel."

"You leave my woman be," muttered Hosea. "I'll see to Rachel."

"Then you'd better get shifting, fella, or some gay young spark will be saving you the trouble," said Mike. I was quick but Hosea was quicker, elbowing me aside. Mike ducked the first one, smothered the second, ran into the third, and dropped, and Hosea stood over him. "Clean that mouth when you're talking of Rachel or I'll be cleaning it!" he shouted.

"Ho, for God's sake!" I said, dragging at him, but he shook me off. "He's been edging at my woman since the moment she set foot here!"

I nodded at Shaun and we got in between them.

"What's going on?" asked Will from the door.

"It's an Irish fight," I said. "Ho just belted Mike—it's a custom of the O'Haras, don't be bothered," and I took Hosea's arm and walked him outside. There, in the darkness, he covered his face.

"The swine," he whispered.

"Och, he meant nothing," I said. "He's a quick old tongue on him, but he'd die for you, and you know it," and Hosea lowered his hands and looked at the sky.

"I struck him for the truth of it, Jess, not for the lie. Holy God, why did I rake such a woman from Ireland?"

"You're making too much of it, Ho," I answered. "She'll settle. Isn't it true she's down nursing with the Sisters—you saw her there yourself."

"Once, but now I'm wondering who she's nursing."

"You have no proof that she's philandering," I answered sharply.

"And I have no proof she's not." He closed his eyes and wiped his sweating face. "Ach, it was a wicked thing to shift her from the caravan, for this black place has gone to her head. D'you remember the old days, Jess? Remember those Sunday mornings when

Ma took us to Mass? D'you realise we've never seen the inside of a church together since I landed here? So I went this morning. And do you know what the priest himself said for his text? He said, 'And the Lord said unto Hosea, go, take unto thee a wife of whoredoms; and the children of whoredoms: for the land committeth great whoredom, departing from the Lord.' You know, it's a queer thing indeed he should take that text."

I was empty for him, being amazed that, even with his ox-like intellect, his suspicions had not been aroused before, for Rachel dressed up in silk and finery to go down to help the fine Sisters of Mercy. I had seen her once, too—fighting a young buck in the back of a sulkie in a gale of tipsy laughter, and I knew it was the end of Rachel. She'd begin with young bucks and finish up with mule-drivers.

I said, "And you love her?"

He shut his eyes. "Life's strange indeed, lad. I've mounted some pretty ones in me time, but I've kept me vows with Rachel." He looked at the moon. "And you ferret out a woman you think will turn out ten, and she proves as dry as a desert. Ah, Jess—I'd give me ears for the sound of a son."

"She's not the only woman in Pittsburgh," I said.

"She's the only woman for me," he said, and turned as Shaun came out, saying:

"There's Mike in there wagging at his jaw, the thing won't come straight. Sure, it's ashamed you should be, Ho O'Hara," but Hosea did not answer.

Pushing past us he walked into the night.

There was a sense of power in me when Will appointed me labour foreman. A week after we poured our first steel I wandered the compound, hands in pockets amid the thudding beats of its industry. The big stack reared above me, the cooling-pits gaped below me, and all around was the miracle of the steel; stripped, sweating ballers and ladle-men, coke-shifters and roller-men, their movements quickening at the sight of me. Near the compound gates of Lubinski, Inc. I stood in the shadows and watched the waiting men; the keen, ambitious ones tense with promise, the

159

dead-beats lolling against the walls with the same vacant hopelessness in their eyes that I knew so well. Unaccountably, it was pleasing—this power and authority. If I raised a finger ten would come running, while a barked command would start them brawling at the gate and in head first, ready to kneel for a job. A year back I would have despised myself for this enjoyment of command, but now it appeared a privilege, something I had fought for and won.

"Anything going, foreman?" One saw me in the shadows and bawled from the gate.

Wandering up to them, I shook my head.

"You realise I've been waiting here for the last two days?"

"Got four kids, Irish, and they're starving."

"Hey, foreman, for God's sake!"

Outside the copper-works I had waited like this, in rain, and reached appealing hands through the bars. Outside the old Singer Nimick I had begged for food, offering free labour, and been turned away. Strange to be standing on the right side of a gate, I thought, listening to their pleadings.

"There ain't another works in Pennsylvania run like this one, guvnor. I heard you got new systems, that right?"

"I'd sure give my ears to be in there with that convertor."

They begged, flattered, and pleaded, but I did not really hear them. Safe now, well fed, I was inwardly despising them for their poverty, and the knowledge of it came with a shock. Looking past them I saw a horse and trap coming, and Marged ran up beside me, breathless.

"It's Mr. Lubinski, Jess—I saw him from the house."

I unlocked the gate, caught a man by the waist as he tried to slip inside, and flung him back. They grouped together in sullen anger, threatening, and I strode among them, shouting.

"There's no jobs here—I told you before. Out of it, all of you!" and held them, arms out, as the horse and trap came through. Lubinski had seen me before, of course, but he didn't spare me a glance. Beside him, darkly pretty in the glow of the fires, sat a woman, her ample figure bulging her lace-frilled dress. I returned her smile with a curt nod and clanged the gates after them.

I said to Marged, "Is Will expecting Lubinski?"

"Aye, he's awaiting him in the office."

"Who's the fat squaw sitting beside him?"

She smiled, dimpling. "Interested? That's Clare, his daughter."

"If I was Lubinski I wouldn't show her off."

Marged looked unusually pretty standing there in the glow; sixteen last Sunday, and I had remembered her birthday. Now some strange trick of light was turning her into a woman. Nodding back to the gates, she said, "Those men must feel low, Jess. The old man there has been waiting two days—he even sleeps there to keep his place."

"Unskilled," I said.

"Have you nothing for him?"

"Will wants skilled labour, Marged—these chaps are ten a penny."

Her eyes moved over mine. "Not even sweeping up the compound, or something?"

"You stick to cooking," I answered. "You don't sweep up a steelworks compound. If I took on every man who looked hungry I'd soon be hearing from Will."

"You stood there once, remember?"

"That's the luck of the draw, Marged. I wonder what Lubinski wants?"

She shrugged. "The same old business, I expect—return for his money. Most nights Will goes down to his hotel to report, and still he comes visiting."

"First time he's brought his daughter."

"Yes, she's just come in from New York, so I hear. Talking of New York, have you written to Karen?"

"Last night."

"Have you asked when she's coming to Pittsburgh?"

"I did, but she probably won't give a date. She'll drift in—probably rake us out of bed— Karen never knows where's she's due next minute. Where's Ho and Mike?"

"Over the river. Down Soho drinking, if I know them. Thank God they're friends again."

"Any sign of Rachel?"

"Just gone to bed."

"At this time of night? She usually comes in with the dawn," I said.

Marged wandered away, pulling her scarf closer about her head, and I followed. There was a perfume about her, a pleasing scent I had smelled before, and her eyes were dark and beautiful as she turned.

"There's a man, you know," she said.

"It wouldn't be Rachel if there wasn't a couple of them."

"Aye, but it's serious—you know how women talk. He's an agent up at the oil refinery, she says. No good talking to her, I've tried and tried."

"He'll be some agent if Hosea catches up with him. Oh, God, what a mess."

"Eh, she's a handy one from the waist down, Ho's better off without her. Oh, Jess—why are we talking about other people when we could be talking of you and me?"

There was a sweetness in her, and a hint of pleading.

"I'm still on shift, girl, would you have me come courting—away back home with you!"

"Oh, damn this dirty old steel-works," she whispered. "Nothing but cooking and sewing and no one to speak to from morning till night!"

"Would a walk in the moonlight mend ye?"

She lowered her eyes, and she swung away when I tried to raise her chin, whispering angrily, "I'm old enough to cook and mend for over forty grown men and you treat me as a child."

I grinned at her. "Then would a walk in the moonlight turn you into a woman?"

"She's a Welsh temptress," said Shaun, coming up with a ladle. "More than likely it'd turn you into a man," and he made a playful kiss at Marged who turned and ran. "Is Ho and Mike back yet, Jess?"

"No sign of 'em. Marged reckons they're tanning it up in the taverns."

Shaun frowned. "Ho's on night-shift, he'd better keep sober."

I waved him away. "Leave the man be, it'll do him good. If

you'd collected that bloody Rachel you'd be leathering it for weeks."

"Not on skip-pushing. You want eyes in your backside when you're furnace-tipping, then some." He raised his eyes to the rim of the furnace. "I've seen fellas slip in who drank nothin' but water." He turned as a breathless labourer ran up.

"Mr. O'Hara!"

"Aye?"

The man said, patting himself, "It's Mr. Rees in the manager's office, sir, he's wanting to see you."

"This time of night?" I asked.

"It's Mr. Lubinski, sir, the owner's arrived."

"You're heading for a raise," said Shaun as I left him, crossing the compound towards the lighted window.

Entering, I saw Lubinski at first, in evening dress, looking as well-bred as an Austrian count. And Clare, his daughter, was sitting at Will's desk in a sedate, fat beauty, eyes widening as I entered.

"This is Jess O'Hara," said Will, hand out, sweeping me in. "Jess, Mr. Lubinski would like to meet you."

I saw Marged standing in the door of the cottage when I left the office. Her mood was changed. Laughing, she said, "Been to meet the owner's daughter, is it? God help us, what next? You'll be climbing into high society, and walking with the nobility."

"I'd much rather walk with you," I said.

"Do you trust me that far?" said she. "I thought I was only born to feed you."

"Try me, girl."

"But Will is due back any minute."

"And he can feed himself. Come on, woman, give a break to the Irish," and she gave a whoop like an Indian and ran inside and fetched her shawl and swept it over her head.

"I've got the brand of the devil on me," I said, "and I'm mad for the women when the mood takes me, so I'm after your reputation. Are you coming or not?"

"Try holding me," she said, and put her arm round my waist.

"Ach, you're a hell of a woman for promises, Marged Rees, so now we'll see what you're made of. D'you fancy a stroll down the tanneries or a walk by the river in the moonlight."

"Since I'm a forward hussy I'll take the river," said she, taking me off. "But if you start bendin' me to yer will I'm calling me cousin, and he'll be slaughtering."

"Come," I said, seizing her hand, and we took the back path down to the broad Allegheny where the beams of the paddle-steamers were shafting yellow light on the waves, and we walked arm in arm, at first, like brother and sister, till the torment of the steel-works died.

"Eh, Jess," whispered Marged, "that's beautiful."

Away to the west the hills were rolling up in black satanic shapes in a sky of gold and blue, and to the west the great mass of Coal Hill winked myriad lights from its blackness, and the sky over Pittsburgh was beaming and flashing in redness as the cauldrons turned. There was a whisper of wind and the rustle of grass about us in that lonely place as we sat on a bank, hand in hand, the banter gone; just two people in the world then, it seemed.

"Aye," whispered Marged, "it is beautiful indeed. Can you imagine the wonder of it before men came and ravaged it, Jess?"

I did not reply, for I was entranced by her. Her dress was wide over the shoulders, and the white smoothness of her throat and breast was stained by the black droop of her shawl. Marged lowered her face as she saw me watching and lifted a hand, drawing the shawl closer about her, which was a pity, for the sweet roundness of her vanished into secrets.

"You've grown years in the last six months," I said softly.

"Will I have to be eighty before you know I'm a woman?" She smiled into my eyes. "Haven't you one single glance for me, Jess?"

"I've a couple on you this minute, girl."

She sighed, turning away. "Good grief, you O'Haras are a queer lot. They call the Welsh strange, but they don't come up to the Irish, for I can't make a whole one out of the four of you. There's Hosea mooning his life away after Rachel. He's such an elephant of a man that any minute I expect him to bring out his trunk for feeding, yet he lets her go her way and does nothing about it.

There's Shaun tied in knots with his secret societies and Michael living a hundred years back in the history of Ireland. . . ."

"And Jess?" I asked, innocent.

"Eh, Jess is a fool," she whispered, head turned away. "There's love and sweetness on his doorstep and he's dreaming his dreams of conquest and power."

"What makes you think that?"

She rose, looking over the river. "You've changed, Jess. You're like Will and the rest of them who come here. You were skin and bone when I fed you that day in Girty's Run, but at least you were pure. When Will made you labour foreman it went to your head."

"What's wrong with ambition, then?"

"So you don't deny it?" She looked down at me.

"I don't. If you'd dragged yourself round the factory gates for months you'd realise why. It's every man for himself in this black place—it's eat or be eaten."

"Eh, that's a proud thought, Jess." She smiled.

"It's all right for you," I said, "for you're a woman. You do the cooking and Will does the clawing, but somebody's got to fight or you'll both end up starving, like I did. I was hungry once, Marged, and I'm never being starved again."

She said, eyes closed, "It was the way you treated those men at the gates. God, they might have been cattle." Suddenly, without warning, she began to cry, her hands to her face.

"Marged," I said, instantly beside her, and she whispered, sobbing, "Oh, I hate this place. I hate Girty's Run and the whole damned city. It's nothing but scrubbing and cooking, and for what?" She lowered her hands and opened big, tearful eyes at me. "To make another Laughlin and Company or spew up another Carnegie."

"Don't you admire Carnegie?"

"I do not!"

"You've got to give him credit," I replied. "He started as a telegraph boy and now he's owning railroads and foundries. When his family moved in here they didn't have a dime. The way the man's going now he'll be eating Pittsburgh alive."

"She'll take some eating," Marged whispered, "and I hate ambition, Jess." She straightened. "You take Lubinski. When he first came here he was nail-making on South Side. After a while he pays other people to make the nails, building a factory to make them quicker. In the end he didn't know what a damned nail looked like, so he forgot his skinned fingers. Then he went into glass, and the money rolled in, but he never saw through a window —then into cotton, and brought in child-labour." She lowered her voice. "Lubinski doesn't see skinny kids any more, though he works his kids to the grave. Men like Carnegie and Lubinski don't eat a city, Jess, they swallow its people alive, and the way my Will's going he'll likely do the same."

"Aw, Marged," I said, "it's not as bad as that," and took her into my arms.

There was a trembling in her the moment I touched her.

"The man's got to get on," I added. "He's made that way."

"Not on Lubinski's dirty money," she said.

It could have been pity that made me kiss her, and what began in a smile grew into heat and strength. Gasping, she held me away, smiling now, her tears fled. "Oh, Jess, take me away from here! Just you and me. Let's run from this black place and build a cottage, and I will cook and clean for you and you'll come in for dinner—just you, Jess, not a damned regiment."

"Hey, hold on," I said. "Are you living with me, for I can't afford to keep you on me money."

"Just you and me, Jess, oh, kiss me again!" She clung to me.

I held her against me, listening to her gusty breathing, seeing beyond her the bright glow of the paddle-steamers heading for Sharpsburg.

"I'm still here," she whispered.

I gave her a grin. "Aye, and I know it, ye minx."

"Then kiss me again. Oh, Jess, I love you. From the first moment I saw you lying there, I loved you. . . ."

"You've years for loving yet, Marged."

Perhaps she did not hear me for she stood away, caught my hand, and sat on the bank at my feet. "Down by here, Jess, just for a minute? . . ."

"Time for home," I said.

"Please . . ."

"It's damned near midnight, the rest of them'll be worrying."

She turned away, eyes down, her hands clasped. "No need to swear."

"Look," I said desperately. "I'll walk you down here next Sunday when I come off shift, will that suit you?"

Her face became wild with excitement, and she rose. "Next Sunday, then. I'll put on my fine white dress for you, and we'll go down the Ohio glades—not within a mile of Pittsburgh, where it's good and clean. I will cut sandwiches and brew up tea and you can bring your old whiskey. Will you hold me down there and kiss me again?"

"There's no pride in you, Marged," I said, watching her.

"None, it's because I love you. Jess, love me back." Her face was pleading.

Two years more on her and I would have laid with her, and taken her. I gave my thoughts a grin. One thing or another—last time it was Katie . . .

"Why are you smiling?" she asked, lips trembling.

"Come, you vixen," I said, "back to your cousin," and hand in hand we went back to Lubinski's.

So next Sunday we walked down the Ohio glades, Marged and me; hand in hand we walked, stricken into silence by the beauty of summer after the black smoke and clanging of Lubinski's. Chewinks were singing, thrushes and bob-whites calling from the branches in the purity of that hot, summer afternoon, while behind us the jungle city whispered its song of industry. Very pretty looked Marged that day in her big, straw hat; twenty-one round the waist, she said, in a billowing crinoline with hoops to keep the boys off, she said; beautiful, too, that dress, I recall—all white and stained with deep, red flowers, and her dark hair in ringlets was over her shoulders.

Here, by the river, was the shout of summer, with the great Ohio wending peaceful through her laden banks and the plantations above her burnished green in the sun, and the bright grass cutting up swathes in the eye of the wind, all for us, Marged and Jess: this, the Indian country that had seen love before, where lips had found lips in a painted face from the savage whispers of a Delaware squaw to the harsh demands of a conquering Iroquois. And now a Welsh girl and a Connemara Irish, hand in hand in a place of ghosts. There was a dryness coming in me for Marged now, and my blood had quickened for her since that night by the dark Allegheny. A year had changed her from girl to woman, and she walked beside me now with sly glances coming from under her broad-rimmed hat, singing, now laughing at the sky, until she sat with me, and then to business.

"Let's have some more about that Rosa Turvey and the O'Shea woman now," said she, and she lay back in the grass and put her hands under her head, her eyes screwed up to the sun.

"Forget Beth O'Shea," I said. "She was really Michael's."

This sat her up. "Did Mike ever chase a woman?"

"Reckon he chased that one, but it was years back. Now he can't abide the sex—he says they're the cart-horses of the human race."

"And was Rosa Turvey a cart-horse?"

"She was some filly," I said.

"Now you're teasing. Was she your lover?"

"Would you have me blush?"

"No," said she, "I'm serious—you ever had a lover—a real lover, I mean. Not just pecks and whispers, Jess."

"Naked in a cave," I said. "That was Rosa Turvey."

"Dear me, that's romantic. Did you truly love her?"

I shrugged, lying beside her. "Suppose so."

"Was she beautiful?"

"As you," I said, "but darker. Like Rachel, she was, all eyes and bangles."

"Dark, then."

"Aye, dark—as the hand of night," I replied. "Loving that Rosa was like swimming in a jar of bumbledore honey."

"I hate her," she whispered.

"Thought you might."

"I suppose you're going back to her, is it?"

I smiled at my thoughts. "Pretty doubtful now. She said she'd be waitin' along the road to Wicklow, but if she's sitting there still she's been there some time."

"Will you singe, do you think?"

"What for?" The wind sighed in the grass as I bent over her.

"For loving that Rosa naked in a cave."

"More than likely."

"It's against the law, you know, mating out of wedlock."

"Then I know one or two who'll be frying beside me," I said.

Up she came again, smiling. "Meaning who?"

I kissed her cheek. "You fry just the same for doing it in the heart."

"You're hanging out my soul," said she, and pushed me aside and struggled up. "Don't judge others by your own ambitions, Jess O'Hara—time for eating."

"A time for sleeping and a time for waking," I said. "A time for dying and a time for loving. Is there anything there worth having?" and I helped her unwrap the cloth. "Have I got to drink tea?"

"It'll settle your nerves," said she. "Better for you than whiskey," and she suddenly closed her eyes. "Oh, Jess, am I terrible?"

"You're past redemption, woman."

"Then you're taking too much for granted," said she with a sniff. "I only walked you down here to get out of Pittsburgh. D'you expect me to come down alone?"

"I'd not hear of it, you sweet one," I whispered, and took the cup from her lips and set it on the grass. "The wickedness is mine for leading you as far as this," and I hooked my arm around her waist and drew her against me, seeking her lips.

There was a look in her eyes as something trapped, and she put her hand between our lips and lay there, trembling.

"What's wrong, Marged?"

"Whee, now I'm scared," she said.

"What's wrong with you, woman, nobody's killin' yer," I said.

Her face was patterned with sun from the branches above us, and the wind swept scurries over the silver river in the moment before I kissed her.

"We're starting too early," she said. "What about the picnic?"

169

"To the devil with eating, we can do that later."

"*Dammo di,*" said she, "let me up, for God's sake," and she pushed me away and put her hat on straight, shooting glances at me from the corners of her eyes. "If you're taking me for a scarlet woman you've another think coming, Jess O'Hara."

"Who's takin' you for scarlet?" I asked. "I'm only after kissing you, and last Sunday night you were jammed full of promises."

"Changed my mind," said she. "That was last Sunday."

I groaned. "Give me strength," I said, and lay back on the grass. "Are you telling me you walked me this distance to eat a bloody picnic—I can do that in the bunkhouse back home."

"You do that," said she, looking pert. She fluffed up her hair. "You're not eating me."

"I was only kissing you!"

"Heaving and gasping like something demented. Is it kissing or taking you are, Jess O'Hara?" She pressed her ribs. "Black and blue, I am. Like a bull in a china shop, you Irish."

"I don't know me strength, and you're getting me blood up," I said.

"Then paddle in the shallows and cool yourself down," said she. "That Rosa Turvey might settle for the rough stuff, but you're not coming savage on me, for I'm Welsh."

"Aha," I said, climbing up. "Now we're getting the truth of it— it's me business with the Turvey woman, isn't it?"

"It is," said she.

"And didn't that happen years back?"

"It did, but you're not tarring me with the same brush as Turvey —I'm not having any fella tickling up my legs."

"Didn't you damn ask for it, then, with your wriggling and hissing?"

"Next time you kiss me you keep your hands in your pockets, Jess O'Hara, remember it."

"Ach, you're daft Welsh again," I said, and left her, going down to the river. There I sat for a while, throwing in stones, watching the big trout flashing among the boulders. I did not turn immediately when Marged came and stood beside me.

"Jess," she whispered.

"Leave me be," I said. "A man don't know where he stands with the foreigners. You're beggin' and slappin' at the same damned time."

"Because you haven't yet said you love me."

"Would I be tryin' it on if I didn't love you, woman?"

She lowered her face. "Perhaps," and the sight of her brought me to my feet.

"I love you," I said, not touching her.

"Just for today?"

I sighed. "Perhaps the Irish are as daft as the Welsh," I said. "Reckon I've loved you since we met, and only just realised it."

"Will you swear on it, my precious?"

"I'll swear, and I'll prove it," I answered, and reached out for her and she ran into my arms.

Strange this Marged, no one moment, yes the next; unshocked by disarray.

"Jess, Jess!"

The dusk was silent in the clenched darkness of eyes.

"It's this damned old hooped skirt," I said.

And the river song was drowned in the stuttering breath of kisses. Didn't mean to do it, didn't even plan it. The shadows deepened into night.

"Ah, dear," I whispered, "you pretty little Welsh."

Over her head the stars were shining; the air suddenly cold, the wind making puff-adders on the silk of the river.

"Eh, my precious . . ."

And the dusk loosened her stays and spread out her skirt on the couch of darkness.

"Ach-y-fi," exclaimed Marged, "it's the last time I'm wearing that old crinoline."

"Put it back on or you'll catch your death," I said. "D'you realise you've still got your hat on?"

This put her double, giggling, holding her stomach. "Duw, what next," she spluttered. "Still, got to wear something," and she rose, looking impish, Marged the girl again, and fought her way up the dress, arms flailing. "Ah, we're wealthy people," she said, "loaded with love. Do the poor make love the same way?"

"Kings and beggars," I said, lying back on my elbows. I'd be going some, I thought, to get to the bottom of this one.

"Then put a stop to it, for it's far too good for them," she said. "Up a dando! Pick up the picnic things. Dear me, the way I'm going I'll be getting myself a name. Look at the dark! I bet Will's demented."

"You've got yourself a name," I said, "Mrs. O'Hara."

First love, last love, Marged O'Hara.

And we walked home on air to Girty's Run that night, hand in hand, with moonlight showing between us and the cobbles.

CHAPTER 16

All that summer Lubinski's grew bigger, and the orders flowed in. With Betsy, the first furnace pouring our iron we began building Sally, a furnace double the size. We took on more labour, mainly Welsh; Will bought another five acres and work began on a big refining shed. And as the Lubinski fortunes grew so grew the O'Haras. Shaun was appointed technical manager and they made me production superintendent and Michael labour foreman. The compound gates were widened to take the surge of the workers into shift, and the compound echoed to the sound of brawls as men fought for jobs like animals. Lubinski's grew as a cancer along Girty's Run, festooning waste ground with its yards and furnaces, splitting the day with its drop-hammers, lighting the night sky with its flashes. Strangely, I was sickening of it all, for it was a giant that swallowed a man's identity and everything was seconded to the graph of its profit. Life was only made tolerable by my love for Marged, but Hosea had nothing because Rachel had gone.

"Have you heard the latest?" asked Mike. "Hosea's gone after her."

"What!"

"He wasn't in the bunkhouse this morning, and I found this note on his mattress."

I closed my eyes after reading it. Michael said:

"Did you expect anything else? Rees has been using him as brute labour from the moment he came here—does he get a rake-off from the profits of that swine Lubinski?" He spat. "And Ho's not the only one—I'm sickened to death of the big black place."

"You've no cause to grumble," I said.

We were down at the gates waving in the shift.

"Depends how you look at it," said he. "Sure, I've gone up, but I'd rather scratch a beggar's arse in Ireland than roll in money in this bloody hole." He clanged shut the gates and we crossed the compound.

"Money's got its place," I said.

"Aye, sure—for some. Rees and Lubinski are rattling the stuff into the banks, and you're not far behind them." He had been drinking again, his mood aggressive.

"There's a difference between us," I answered. "I'm getting married—all you do with it is pour it down the drain. My God, Mike, you've changed some since the old days of Connemara."

"I've changed? Christ, that's good. What about you? The only fella who's kept his decency is Ho, and he's in love with a whore. D'you realise this slaughter house is perverting us all? There's Rachel lying in another fella's bed and Shaun jumping everything in skirts between here and Soho. . . ."

"And you tipping the bottle," I interjected.

He waved in disgust. "A man's entitled to oblivion." He raised his face. "Did you see those two fine chaps we took on last week. They whooped through the gates as bright-faced Irishmen—twin brothers—Derry men, d'you remember?" He thumped his chest. "Top-fillers—skilled men, and they tripped on the skip. They burned, Jess. They flared in that bloody Betsy to heat iron for Lubinski." He wiped his sweating face. "I didn't get a decent night in weeks while Ho was top-filling. Did you have a hand in that promotion?"

I shook my head.

He whispered, "Well, Ho's gone, and he's just as well out of it, but God help the man he finds with Rachel."

Betsy flared, lighting the compound to the brightness of day. I said, shielding my eyes, "So you're the next one on your way—that's what you're coming to, isn't it?"

"Och, I'd be better back in Ireland."

"All you got from Ireland was rags and hunger. Are you going back to that?"

"Better to starve to death and keep your soul," he whispered, and caught my arm, drawing me into the shadows. The whiskey was heavy on his breath. "Jess, listen. Have I your word that you'll not breathe this to a living body?"

"If it's worth hearing."

He whispered, "Have you heard of the *Erin's Hope?*"

I shook my head, and he went on, "It was back in '67. The Irishmen from the Civil War chartered an armed ship and sailed to Ireland to raise the flag of freedom—you've heard of the Fenians here?"

"Aye."

"They expected to walk into the arms of patriot Irish and raise an army to kick out England, but they walked through the doors of English jails. That was years back, but the movement isn't finished—they're planning to try again. I tell you, Jess, there's millionaires and paupers in it—all true Irish, and they'll stir up a bigger rebellion back home than Father Roche did in Wexford." He crossed himself. "So there's agents leaving every week for the old country to prepare for another invasion. Are ye with us?"

"Oh, Mike, Mike," I said. "Will you stop bleeding for Ireland? These Fenian men are dreamers, but they'll end like the fine men in the *Erin's Hope*—on a gallows. You can't free Ireland with one armed ship."

He said, "Are you Irish or American?"

"I'm as Irish as you, but . . ."

"Are ye?" He glared at me. "I was dug from the womb with an Irish shillelagh, and I've stayed that way while you've become a half-chat Pittsburgh Lubinski. There's the dear country screaming for patriots while you're pigging it out here and marryin' a Welsh woman."

"Leave Marged out of this," I said.

Pushing past me, he turned. "You've polluted your soul here and now you're polluting yer blood, Jess O'Hara, may God forgive you, but I'm still Irish—and yer sons will have a word for it. So you can tell Will Rees to stuff Lubinski."

Marged waved to me from the door of the cottage, but I did not wave back. In search of Will I went to the office, but it was empty, and Shaun ran into the place as I was coming out. He said, breathless:

"What the hell's happening—they tell me Ho's left us."

"Aye, Mike just told me."

"And Mike—what's wrong with him? He's down in the bunkhouse spitting oaths and packin'."

"He's leaving, too. What with one and the other of you I'm sick to me soul of Lubinski's. Where's Will gone, for God's sake?"

"Don't bother with him," said Shaun, "he's not important. McNamara's wanting you."

"McNamara? At this time of night?" I pushed past him. "Will you tell him to go to hell."

"Best go, Jess. You live or die by the whim of McNamara."

"If you're a bloody rabbit like you," I said, and walked away and he came after me, tugging at my arm.

"Jess, for heaven's sake get the size of the man. Your name's on the books of the Maguires and you've taken the oath of allegiance to the movement." He swung me to a stop. "Jess, I'm begging you!"

"God," I whispered, "I was a fool indeed to listen to you. What does he want?"

"Best ask McNamara."

I sighed. "Where is he?"

"Usual place."

"Right, I'll go, but this is the last time he waves and I come running. Tell Marged I won't be in for supper and make sure she knows the others have gone."

"Jess, one thing more . . ."

I turned, staring at him. His whole being threatened sudden collapse. In the red glow his face was working convulsively and he gripped his hands together, trembling.

"Tell him I'm ill," he said.

"How can you be ill, you damned idiot, when you've just delivered a message?"

"Tell him anything. Look, Jess, for God's sake cover me. An accident, that's it . . ." He was biting at his knuckles while I watched, astonished. "I . . . I know. I met you in the compound and told you, and next moment I was down under a ladle . . ."

Hands on hips I stared harder. "What's wrong with you, Shaun? Does McNamara burn you Mollies alive? Come on, out with it!"

176

He wept, drooping before me, his hands over his face.

"Straighten yourself," I said, glancing round. "In the name of the devil, where's the spunk to you?"

"Jess, will you tell him? I was down under a ladle and burned on the hands . . ."

"Why?"

His face brightened. I stepped away as he moved towards me. "Look, tell Kehoe—I'm in well with Kehoe. He'll explain it to McNamara. I'm blistered in the hands and I can't come to-morrow."

I said, evenly, "God help you, Shaun. I scare easy myself, but you're a pretty poor object for an O'Hara. Put your hands on a ladle and get yourself to bed. I'll tell McNamara, but God knows what you're up to."

I left Lubinski's and went over to Allegheny, along the waterfront and down to Hank's Bar.

The little bartender in the room downstairs was still polishing glasses. It was even the same hostess, looking older with her years of lusting pillows, her need more desperate in her jaded smile. I went past her to the bar.

"McNamara in?" I asked, and the bartender lifted his eyes at the ceiling. I took a breath and went up the stairs.

It seemed a generation since I had entered this hated room. I knocked, waiting. The bolt rasped back, the door came open, and Kehoe stood there, peering with his squint.

"Well, by the saints," he said, "it's another O'Hara," and waved me in with a bow. "D'you see this, McNamara—we're collecting industrialists," and he slapped his thigh, laughing. About twenty men were in the room, standing in groups and whispering over glasses and few looked my way. McNamara sat at his table in his usual stolid silence, his features coarsened since I had last seen him.

"You wanted to see me?" I asked, and for answer he indicated a chair in the front row. "Aye," he replied, "but later. Since you're early you can stay for the meeting. Where's Shaun?"

"I'm wanting to speak about him now," I said. "The man's had an accident . . ."

McNamara raised his face. "Ach, that's sad news, O'Hara. He'd have to get shifting to have a bad one between now and the time I saw him, the poor soul. Is it serious?"

"Blistered hands—he got on to a red-hot ladle."

"Aha, dear me, is that so? The fella's nerves are bad, d'you see, but he'll bandage. Will you take your seat now, for I'm into the ceremonies."

I sat. Kehoe was grinning at me, rubbing his chin. The men clattered among the chairs and sat in silence, their glasses empty. McNamara rose.

"Right," said he, getting up. "The oaths first. Speak your hearts, men. *The women.*"

And the men rose about me, heads bowed, hands clasped, and whispered in chorus:

"Women, the womb of the world, shall not be violated. As Irishmen we remain true to the purity of our race."

I stared about me, shocked by the sincerity of their prayer.

"Good," said McNamara. "Now the passwords. The Emperor of France and Don Carlos of Spain unite together the Pope's rights to maintain," and the men whispered.

"Will tenant rights in Ireland flourish if the people unite and the landlords subdue?"

"Fine, fine," beamed McNamara. "Said with true feeling. Now a quarrelling toast—just one—to refresh your memories—you, Kelly," and the man next to me said:

"Your temper is high."

"Reply, O'Hara," cried Kehoe with a wink. "For you're likely to get a hiding if you don't know the quarrelling toast, and you've been pretty lax over comin' to the meetings."

I put my hands on my hips and stared before me. McNamara laughed. "Tell him, Murphy," and another man rose at the end of the room, and said:

"It has good reason to be," and clattered his sticks, sitting down again.

Everybody laughed, and Murphy said, "Sure, if I'd remembered the quarrelling toast six weeks back, sir, I'd not be walking with the aid of these—they're a right set of bastards up in Philadelphia!"

The air of jollity died. McNamara sat, we all sat, watching as he flicked over pages in a book. Waving Kehoe beside him, he said, "And now to the real business of the night—the indictments and punishments. First, I name a man called Crozier."

Kehoe rose and read from a paper, "George Harold Crozier, address secret. Accused of lock-out to Irish working-men. Found guilty. Sentence, death." He raised his eyes and every man's hand went up save mine. McNamara said coldly:

"Sentence confirmed. Marbold and Shaughnessey, are you agreed on the time and place?"

"Agreed on the time and place, sir," said a man behind me. "His address is known to Marbold and me—death to the man Crozier."

"Fine, fine," said McNamara, writing in his book. "And I want a right, clean job done on the bastard, remember." Sitting back, he nodded at Kehoe, who read:

"Francis Robinson, address secret. Found guilty by Philadelphia Maguires of the rape of an Irish mill-hand. Sentence, death." He stared at the assembly.

"Death," shouted the men.

"Then I call Parfit and Herrin," said McNamara, and two men rose clumsily, one saying:

"We are agreed on the time and place, sir, and we'll make sure he goes hard for outragin' a woman, the swine, begging your pardon, sir."

For the first time I was aware that I was sitting in a court of summary justice where death was as cheap as whiskey, and men competed for the act of murder. Hunched in my seat I sat staring at McNamara while judgements were pronounced, and my mind searched the years. I remembered the agents found shot, the mine superintendents who had disappeared, the public men who had committed suicide, and McNamara's voice raked me back to the present.

"William James Branston, industrialist, address secret. Guilty of the deaths of factory employees, by starvation. Sentence, to die." He frowned up. "Confirmed?"

179

"Confirmed," said the men.

"Right. I call Ben Mulligan and Shaun O'Hara." He smiled at me.

The man Mulligan rose on my right. "I'm ready, sir, but I've been trying to find Shaun O'Hara, for I'm after making the date."

Silence, then the men muttered among themselves. I rose and said, "My brother Shaun's injured in the works, McNamara, and he'll be that way for weeks."

"Ah, yes, be God, you told me." McNamara sighed. To Kehoe he called, "Did you inform Shaun O'Hara of this duty, Jack?"

"I did, sir, and he signed for the gun this mornin'."

McNamara rose. "Has your brother still got his legs, Jess O'Hara?"

"He's well burned in the hands, he'll not handle a gun."

"Dear me, that's unfortunate, but we needn't go short of a deputy with you sitting there fine and healthy." He relit his stogie and blew out smoke rings at the ceiling. "Are you game to help Mulligan? This industrialist fella's nothin' but scum."

"I'll not do it, McNamara," I whispered.

He clapped his hands. "Mother of God, I'm delighted with you, O'Hara! It takes a brave man to stick to his principles, especially in this company. But you must have changed some. You're labour foreman at Lubinski—or you were till recently, and your firm's paying well under the union rates. And you've enough death and mutilation in that new outfit to clap the hands of the devil himself."

"I don't run Lubinski's," I said.

"The point's taken, O'Hara, and I'll not bandy words with you, for I've business to discuss with you later, and that'll be a honey. Besides, I'd prefer your brother to do his duty." Turning, he brought his fist down on the table, and whispered, "Listen, all of you. Shaun O'Hara will drop this bastard if he does it bandaged to the neck. Sit down, O'Hara."

I sat, listening in a daze. Three more men were sentenced to die that night, five to beatings and nine to threats, and rough drawings of coffins and epitaphs were handed round in laughter. And in the last mumbo-jumbo of oaths and prayers, McNamara beckoned me into a room next door. We were alone save for Kehoe standing in a corner.

"And now to the business, O'Hara." He grinned wide. "Are you getting the hang of us at last, man?"

"You're a set of bloody fanatics," I whispered.

"Ach, be reasonable, Jess—you can't get control without spilling some blood. That's big business. And I could list you a few city gentlemen whose names are up on the scroll of honour who spill more blood from their helpless workers than all the Maguires in the State of Pennsylvania, ah, to be sure. But we're not all murder, lad—get that straight. We've men in big positions in the country —some heading for the post of governors of states, and others who are a power in the land—working for us to build a common fund for the relief of the less fortunate among us—the destitute wife of the crippled man, the widows and children who rummage in the garbage bins of the fine, rich cities. D'you get me?"

I nodded, sullen.

He pointed his stogie at my face. "Right, then. We've thugs among the Maguires, and we keep those for murder, but we've good Christian men with us, too, and they are with us for the godly acts. But in the rat-race of industry you have to have money, O'Hara, for you can't be godly without it. And we have to take that money, boy, not beg it, for if you beg a dollar from a millionaire financier the swine bleeds to death."

"Get to the point," I snapped.

"Easy, O'Hara, I'm coming to it. I'm making you a present of the firm of Lubinski, and you'll cut us in on half of the profits."

I stared at him, and he crossed the room and put his arm on my shoulder. "Can you give me one good reason why Lubinski should roll in wealth while his workers are living on the verge of starving? You can't?" He wandered around me, puffing and wheezing, and I watched him, dazed. He continued, "It's a joyful employment, lad, and you ought to be grateful. You've the whole force of the movement to back you, and you'll work in the knowledge that you're dishing out social justice, for the money will go to the poor."

I said, recovering myself, "But first, I suppose, you kill Lubinski."

Kehoe laughed from his corner. "Haven't you seen the man lately? He's already on his death-bed."

"Three months, no more," said McNamara at his stogie.

"And when Lubinski dies the firm goes to his daughter," said Kehoe.

"Do you see the brutal point?" said McNamara. "If I was six feet up and with looks like you I'd consider the job myself. She's well set up and has a fine, sweet nature, they tell me."

I fought to match his coolness. "What makes you think she'd have me?"

Kehoe chuckled. "She's made no impression on the New York bucks."

"Not even with two million to back her," said McNamara. Grunting, he sank into a chair. "Be clear about this, O'Hara. You're not only dealing with steel. The Lubinski empire ranges across cotton and glass, railroads and canals. We estimate the profits at half a million a year." He smiled at his thoughts. "I'd marry me grandmother for that kind of money."

"And if I refuse?"

His face snapped up. "But you'll not refuse, lad."

I met his eyes. "Try it on Shaun," I said, "you've got the wrong O'Hara."

"You realise you do as you're told in this outfit?"

"Not this time, McNamara."

"And that you're losing the chance of a fortune."

I smiled. "Ten million a year and I wouldn't take on Clare Lubinski."

He put his hands flat on the table, his head bowed, and said, "But you'll take on the Welsh girl at twelve dollars a week, eh?"

In the silence that followed I heard my own breathing. Kehoe put his hands into his pockets and stared at the ceiling, a faint smile on his face. I whispered:

"What I do with my life is my business. Keep the Welsh girl out of this."

McNamara rose. "It's you bringing her in, son. We mean no harm to the young creature."

I was hot with fear and anger. Desperate, I measured the distance between them. McNamara first, then a dive at Kehoe. McNamara wandered past me to the window, smiling suavely. "Don't try it," he said softly, "or Kehoe will drop you." He stared out at the waterfront. "Aye, she's a sweet wee girl, that Marged Rees, but there's a thing we don't hold with, O'Hara, and that's a crossing of the blood in decent Irishmen. Can't you find yourself a young colleen?"

"That's a bloody fine one," I said sharply. "Is Clare Lubinski Irish?"

He turned, eyes widening. "Don't get me wrong. Holy Peter, man—who's talkin' of you marryin' her? It's her money we're after, not her soul." He turned to Kehoe. "We'll have to resolve this somehow, Jack. Mightn't it be a good plan to bring the Welsh girl in? We could talk the thing over like intelligent people."

He leaned against the wall, smiling over his stogie. Kehoe said:

"Shall I send Big Ryan for her, Sean? He's an eye for beauty on him and he's partial to the Welsh."

I began to tremble, and they saw it. Head bowed, I gripped myself.

"Do that," said McNamara, and Kehoe moved to the door.

"Wait," I said.

"Begad," whispered McNamara. "We can't go on waiting for ever, O'Hara, make up your mind."

I said, "She . . . she's little more than a child."

"Yes or no," said Kehoe.

"Please, McNamara."

He turned away in disgust. "Ach, raise yourself, O'Hara, I can't bear you begging! Is it the Lubinski woman, or not?"

I clenched my hands, shouting, "And you swear your oaths about respecting women?"

"Twenty-four hours," said McNamara with finality. He crossed to his desk and sat down heavily. "I can't spare more time—call in tomorrow." He began to write with an air of disassociation.

"McNamara," I said softly. "Lay a finger on that woman and I'll kill the pair of you."

He lifted his face, smiling. "God's blood, Kehoe. Everyone's after killin' us, and we're working in the name of common humanity. Listen, O'Hara. Come tomorrow. And if your answer's not yes tomorrow, I'll break you, the Rees fella, and your simpering little Welsh girl. Now get out."

"Out," said Kehoe.

The bunkhouse was in darkness when I got back to Lubinski's. In the fetid air I listened to the heavy breathing of the sleeping labourers, then went to the O'Hara bunks behind the curtain. Hosea and Michael's bed-clothes had been made up into piles, probably by Marged. Shaun was sleeping fitfully, and I stared at his sweating face, hating him.

"Jess!" Marged's whisper turned me to the door, and I went swiftly to her and took her into my arms.

"Jess, where have you been? It's nigh two o'clock?" Her eyes were wide and startled in the faint light. To escape them I pressed her harder against me.

"Man," she said, on tiptoe. "You've not even been drinking . . ." She looked past me at the empty bunks. "Oh, Jess! Are you wearying for your brothers?"

"Please, come outside . . ."

The stars were bright and the wind blew cold with a hint of rain in him, and she shivered in my arms. "I'm sorry," she murmured. "Eh, I'm so sorry . . ." She kissed my face. "Oh, you mad O'Haras —either leaving, fighting, or loving. Now come to bed." She took my hands, smiling up. "You're not sharing a bunk with that Shaun. Will is up in Sharpsburg with Lubinski, so I've fixed you a bed in the cottage."

I had a sudden burning wish for her, greater than anything before.

"Come," she whispered. "I've put myself in Will's room."

Strangely, I had never been in Marged's room before, having only known it from the kitchen below, when her feet were heavy on the boards above me. Now I sat on the edge of her bed with the moonlight streaming through the little leaded window. I do not know how long I sat there in the roar of Allegheny, my head in my hands, before I undressed. The sheets were cool, and waves of tiredness were slowly enveloping me despite my racing thoughts when the door of the room opened. I raised myself.

Marged stood there.

She was no apparition in white, like you read in books. In simple dignity she stood, smiling, with her homespun night-dress down to her feet and her hair loose on her shoulders.

"Can't you sleep, boy? You're keeping me up with your tossing and turning."

But I knew why she had come, and put out my hand to her.

"*Cariad Anwyl*," she whispered, and knelt by the bed. "Is it sad with you because you've lost your brothers?"

"Yes."

"But you still have me. Could you lose yourself in me for one brief minute?"

I had no words for her. I should have turned away, but I could not. Smoothing back her hair she smiled into my face, and her eyes had the simple lucidity of a child.

"For it's no cheap longing in me for you, Jess. Aren't I your wife in all truth?" Bending over the bed, she kissed me. "Invite your woman in, you'll sleep if you have her, and you can weep if you please."

The city whispered between us.

"Over a bit so I can come in, is it?"

The furnace flared over in the compound, the room glowed red.

"Ah, Jess," she said.

But McNamara's voice was as a rasp between us, Kehoe was smiling from the shadows.

"No kisses, then? Eh, I don't mind, my precious . . ."

Marged slept, and the moon crossed the floor. The dawn broke and the day came red and roaring over the ragged roofs of the city, and still Marged breathed beside me, but I did not sleep.

And with the morning came new hope and courage, and I held her tight against me as I kissed her into wakefulness.

"And I've been here all night? My, you O'Haras are very queer people."

CHAPTER 17

Karen came home in September.

I remember that day with joy. Leaves were blowing in crisp billows down the Sewickley lanes and the great plantations of the Ohio were waving gold in the heat, and the bright Allegheny was singing down Girty's Run.

We were singing in the cottage, too; me and Will up in his bedroom fighting our way into starched shirts while Marged was shouting we'd be late for the steamer which was bringing Karen. Done up to kill, me—in my new black suit and fawn waistcoat bought at Kaufmann's and Will in his morning coat and striped trews, shoes shining to shave in and his hair parted in the middle.

"Hurry, you two!" shouted Marged.

"Jess, give me a hand with this damned stock!"

"Marged will fix it, come on," I said, and down to the kitchen we went, and Marged was there all pink and white lace, five foot of daintiness, her hair done in plaits and tied with red ribbons. "Right," said she, "let's have a look at you," and we stood there like a pair of ninnies while she fixed Will's stock and strolled round the back of us flicking off hairs.

"Quick with you," cried Will, "the steamer's due up in the next twenty minutes."

"And I've been waiting hours! You're worse than a pair of women, I'm telling you—has there been such a dandying-up since Lincoln came to Pittsburgh?"

"You're going Irish again," I whispered, kissing her.

"Oh, Jess, do you think she'll like me?"

"If she doesn't she'll not be backward in telling you so. Are you ready, Will?"

"My trews are dropping, I've forgotten my braces," and he dashed upstairs again.

"Hoop arrah! He can follow," I cried, and seized Marged's hand, ran her through the compound, hailed a brougham, and bundled her in. Will fell in the other side and away down to the wharf we went with Marged between us under her bright red parasol.

"Don't forget Lubinski's coming before dinner," said Will.

"Tuesday! Of course!" cried Marged. "With this Karen woman coming I'm forgetting what day it is. Is he bringing his daughter this time?"

"Hope not," I said.

"Why d'you hope not? She's a sweet woman, that one, and I'm sorry for her—I'm sorry for anyone living with that Lubinski." She elbowed me. "And you want to watch her, lad."

"She's right," said Will. "She's got a wicked old eye on her."

"Why me?" I looked at him.

For some strange reason this sent them double. "Every time she comes she asks after Mr. O'Hara, and I'll wager she doesn't mean Shaun," laughed Will. "You've been leading the poor girl on, why not admit it?"

"No smoke without fire," chuckled Marged. "She's a better bet than me with two million behind her."

"The figure varies," I said. "And me heart's bleeding for her."

I was sickening of the name, Clare Lubinski. Every time her father came to Girty's Run these days he brought Clare with him, and I was absent on every excuse possible.

"It's your love requited today, old chap," said Will. "Can't duck her this time—Lubinski wants to see you."

"What for?" I demanded.

Will opened his hands at me, smiling. "Why should I know? You've done a good job as progress man, perhaps he's got something else lined up for you."

"And he can stick it."

"Easy, Jess . . ."

I fought to control myself, and failed. "I'm doing all right. I'm not having that bastard runnin' my life for me."

Will nudged me. "Do you have to swear in front of Marged?"

"Let him swear," cried she, gaily. "I could write a devil's dictionary after cooking for a regiment. And this one's as prickly as a bear these days." She turned. "Cheer yourself up, man—you're going to meet your sister. Oh, you sweet thing, I love you—is that the steamer coming round the bend, Will?"

Gay crowds were cramming the waterfront for the Governor's visit, and the river was thick with traffic—barges and schooners, their white sails flowing, paddle-steamers spouting black smoke, all shoving for room down the broad Allegheny and the air was rent with sirens and whistles. Out of the brougham we came and pushed into the crowd of laughing, chattering people. Half Pittsburgh must have been there that day; lovely women in bloomer dresses and crinolines hung on the arms of city gentlemen and children were shrieking among the clattering wheels of traps and rockaways—all the wealth and breeding of Pittsburgh, said Will, for most of the workers were on shift to keep the place clear for the Governor.

"Trust Karen to come on the same steamer as him," I said. "Are you sweating, Will?"

Fine and handsome he looked that day, still a couple of inches above me, his teeth white in his tanned face, his stock arching proudly to Marged's pin.

He answered, "I'm sweating on a man with her—I know that Karen."

"Is she like that?" asked Marged.

I grinned at him. "Button yourself up, fella—live for the day. She'd not be Karen if there isn't a couple of them somewhere, but she never mixes the breed."

"Look who's beside us," whispered Marged, elbowing.

"Who's those fellas?"

"Clay Frick and Mellon—the little chap on the right's Carnegie," answered Will.

"Can't he grow a couple of inches with all that money on him?" asked Marged.

"Eh, there's enough in those three wallets to buy half the city," muttered Will. "They reckon the little chap's income is fifty thousand a year from investments alone."

"And his workers live in his shanty houses like pigs," said Marged, "that's how he makes it. Forget him. Will somebody lift

188

me so I can see the steamer?" and I got her under the arms and hauled her up.

"She's coming!" she cried, and I put her down again. For the steamer was swinging to the tow of the river, a giant of red and gold, her bows gleaming white. People were lining its rail and cheering and a scarlet-chested band in the stern had its head in its collar blasting away on trombones and tubas.

"There she is!" I bawled. "Karen!"

"Where?" cried Marged.

"Standing by the big fella!"

"The big handsome one?" shouted Will above the sirens, and I lifted Marged again.

"The woman in white," I whispered in her ear, and lowered her again, staring.

No Karen of Connemara was this one; no gipsy dancer with bangles and brass earrings. She stood in white beauty under a big summer hat, her shoulders naked to the stretch of her fine white crinoline. Marged reached up and pulled my head down.

"Oh, Jess, who's the big man?"

"How should I know?"

"D'you think he's with her? My, she's a beauty!"

Karen looked my way and I waved my arms frantically. "Karen, Karen!"

And her face came alive. Pushing the big man aside she forced her way along the rail to get nearer me, waving and shouting soundlessly.

"You're in, man," I cried, and seized Will. "Come on!"

"Is that the Connemara dancer you're waving to, sir?" cried a voice.

"Aye, it's me sister," I cried, looking down at a youngster with a note book and pencil.

"Will you hold her for an interview for me, sir?"

"Is she famous, then?" cried Marged.

"Come on," I said, and pulled them towards the gang-plank. Cameramen were poised here, journalists at the ready, waiting for the Governor, shouting for room, but we did not heed them. At the foot of the gang-plank we were covered in joy till Karen ran down to us, arms wide, and I caught her by the waist and swung her round.

"Will!" Now he had got her. Hand in hand through the crowd they went with a porter after her with cases and me and Marged following. Quicker off the mark than I thought, this Will Rees. Tripping over cameras, being cursed by the crowd, I dragged Marged through to the shelter of the loading-bays.

Ten yards away Karen was kissing, the porter standing in drooping respect.

I whispered, "What d'you think of her?"

Marged was weeping.

"Dry up, woman," I hissed. "Why make it a funeral?"

"Never seen my Will with a woman before," she said.

I took her hand. "Ach, he's got a fine one, begad."

"You damned O'Haras." Marged looked up, smiling in tears. "She'll have him begging, like me."

I grinned. "Don't you worry yourself—he can handle her."

"Does beauty like that stick to one man?"

I scratched my head. "I couldn't guarantee it—she's every man's lover, that one, Marged, but she's nobody's woman—she won't leave him."

"Hush, they're coming over."

Perhaps she was more beautiful, because she was my sister. Now she smiled at Marged, her hands out to her.

"So this is yer girl, Jess?"

"Aye!" I was up inches.

"Have you a kiss for me, Marged?"

Which is the daft ways of women, and I caught Will's wink of joy.

Karen held her away, thumbing at me then. "For if you can stand this big oaf you can take the rest of the O'Haras. Where's Ho and Mike?"

"Tell you later, it's a long yarn," I said.

She straightened. "Sure, I'm not leaving this jetty till they arrive! Haven't they the good grace to come and meet their sister and me not seeing them in years?"

"Now hush . . ." I began.

"You're not hushing me!" She was bristling. "I travel the foreign parts for the joy of a family re-union and there's only one here." She patted Marged. "God bless you, me darling," and she smiled. "Where's Rachel? And that no-good Shaun, come to think of it."

"Are you Miss Karen O'Hara?" The boy with the note-book again, very perky.

"I am, and I'll trouble you to be away while I'm speaking to me family. D'you hear that, Will?" She pushed the lad out of it and swung to him, her eyes shining with tears. "There's me been sweating on meeting the entire family and Ho and Mike with the manners of pigs."

"Karen, we've got a carriage waiting," I said.

"It can wait! I'll be givin' that lot a piece of my mind!" Suddenly she turned, waving her parasol.

"I see what you mean," whispered Marged on tiptoe.

"She'll cool—she's a great one for the family. Karen, are you coming?"

"Stop your rushing me, Jess, I've just seen a friend." She waved the parasol higher, and a man going past smiled and pushed towards us through the jam of people. He was darkly handsome, with the finest physique I had seen on two legs, and there was a tolerant grace about him as he stood by Will and Karen gripped his shoulder.

"This is me relatives, as I was telling you, Mr. Corbett—now, stop your shovin', Jess—the fella's a friend of mine. The ugly one's me brother here, the wee girl's me sister-in-law when I marry this fine man beside me, God willing. And this is Mr. James J. Corbett, the famous boxer, Jess—well may you goggle. He's breathin' down the neck of the world champion, but I was informing him a while back of me brother in Pittsburgh who'd drop the pair of 'em and not be skinnin' a knuckle, isn't that right, Jess?"

The gentleman smiled, and bowed to Marged. I whispered, "For God's sake, Karen, do you know who you're talking to?"

"I'm talking of me big brother Hosea," she cried, "and the man's interested. Didn't he take Joe McManus in Wicklow and make bloody mince-meat out of him, for you told me so in yer letter?"

"Yes, but . . ."

She jerked her thumb at Mr. Corbett. "So I was just tellin' the man here the truth of it, is there any harm in that?" She clapped him on the shoulder. "You're a well set-up fella, sir, but if you cross the path of me brother Hosea you'd best steer clear of him."

"If it's the last thing I do, Miss O'Hara." Mr. Corbett bowed, and left, still smiling.

"Aye, and good luck to you, yer a right decent fella," she cried after him. "Look," she whispered at Marged, "would you care to meet the Governor himself, for I can fix it?"

"Karen!" shouted Will, tugging at her.

"Hey, Governor!" she yelled. She patted Marged. "The fella's part Irish, d'you see . . ."

Big hats came round at the end of the gang-plank, eye-glasses were adjusted in our direction, and Marged went double, holding her stays.

"You'll laugh on the other side of your face soon," I whispered, "this is an official reception. Will, help me get her out of it," and we got either side of Karen, steered her through the élite and into the waiting brougham, bundled Marged, still giggling, in beside her, and flung in the cases.

"Girty's Run," I cried. "Lubinski!" and wiped my sweating face.

Five minutes after we arrived the Lubinskis drove in. Will dashed to the office to receive them. Uncertain, I left Karen and Marged together and walked out into the compound. I turned to a faint whistle. Shaun was standing on the corner near the bunkhouse.

"Karen's arrived," I said, walking up to him. "Why are you skulking out here?"

"I've got a message for you, Jess." He slipped me an envelope with a furtive glance around him. "McNamara."

"God," I whispered, "what's happened to you? You're nothin' but the man's damned lackey. Have you opened this letter?"

"More'n me life's worth."

I sighed at him, wandering apart from him, and ripped the envelope. One word was written on the paper.

"Today."

I turned to Shaun. "But you know what this says, don't you?"

He nodded, head low.

"And what the Maguires are up to—you know that, too—don't you?"

"Jess, for pity's sake," he whispered, trembling.

"God, you're a miserable object of a brother," I whispered back. "You've been keeping McNamara informed, haven't you?"

He said, screwing at his hands, "I'm down to kill Branston—me and the man Mulligan. Mother of God, I canna do it . . . Oh, Jess!"

"You and your bloody Maguires," I said. "Get on with your killing, it's all you're fit for. Have you thought of the mess you've landed me in?"

"Jess, for the sake of Ma . . ."

"Aw, to hell with you," I said, and crossed the compound, for Will was waving at the door of the office. He gave me a grin and winked as I entered it.

"Good day to you, O'Hara," said Lubinski, rising.

Some man, this Lubinski; built like a string-bean, with elphin ears and a death-watch pallor.

I returned his greeting and bowed to his daughter. With her hands folded in her lap, she sat in sedate, plump beauty, her black hair clinging to her sweating face.

"Hallo, Mr. O'Hara."

Lubinski said, "I'll come to you later, sir—will you excuse Will and me while we talk some figures—Clare will entertain you."

"Marged is bringing some coffee," said Will.

I sat beside Clare Lubinski, every inch of me longing for the sight of Karen. Her shrill voice and Marged's laughter drifted over the compound to me. In the stifling silence of the room, I said, "I hear you've just come down from New York, Miss Lubinski."

"Indeed I have, Mr. O'Hara." Her voice was beautiful, with the same rich lilt as poor Katie Virginia.

"Do you like Pittsburgh, ma'am?"

She beamed, turning in her chair. "Man, I just adore this city, though I don't know a foundry from a bale of cotton. But where there's dirt there's money, like Papa says, so Ah pay tribute." As

193

shot between the eyes she sat twisting her fingers, a blush growing in her cheeks, her great bosom heaving. Couldn't imagine this one with the New York bucks, I thought.

"Do . . . do you live in New York?"

She nodded, her big, dark eyes opening confidentially. Silence again, save for the rush of the Works and Lubinski's mumbling at the desk. I said, desperately:

"Were you educated there?"

"Oh, dear no, sir. Down south, sir—Carolina, though I ain't been there lately."

"But you've still got the accent." I smiled to brighten her.

"Don't tell me you like it!"

"I do."

"My, that's wonderful! My papa reckons Ah talk like some pesky nigger, but I keep telling him—there ain't no niggers in Carolina—they're just coloured people, and under the skin they're like me an' him. And I'm right proud to speak like Carolina, it's sure a honeyed tongue." She took a breath. "You've got a right attractive voice yourself, come to that, Mr. O'Hara."

I closed my eyes with relief as Marged came in with the morning coffee. She glanced at me, softening her eyes, poured the coffee and handed the cups round as someone intent on escape, did a little Welsh curtsy, and left me to it. Lubinski was talking to Will in barks now; production graphs were being drawn in the air—which was my business, anyway, and I examined Clare while she watched her father with an adoring smile. She was, I supposed, any man's short cut to prosperity, for the man who took on Clare Lubinski would find himself loaded with a thriving iron-works, a glass-works, a cotton factory, and canal investments. The stifling size of this society daughter was the price to pay, of course, and the prospect appeared insurmountable. Like others, I was guessing her bulk in hundredweights.

"You aiming to stay here in Pittsburgh, Jess O'Hara?" She pivoted in a jangle of gold bracelets. I took it slowly, remembering McNamara, and hating myself.

"I'm ambitious, ma'am."

"And what's wrong with ambition?"

I shrugged. "Some folks reckon it shrinks a man."

"For heaven's sake, no! Don't you talk that way. It's the size of a man's ambition that makes him big or small." She was warming to me, her eyes growing large in her heavily powdered face. "You take my papa over there. He came to Pittsburgh with just nothin'. He didn't speak a word of American, but he shipped in from the Ukraine with the most unholy drive. First he starts nail-making, then spinning cotton, an' look at him now."

Aye, I thought, look at him.

She added, "It's drive that matters—there's just nothing a man can't do if he puts his mind to it—he can topple the Savage Mountains if he's got a star, yes, sir!" Embarrassed by her sudden loudness, she subsided into confusion. "My," she whispered, "just hark at me talkin'!"

"Go on," I said, "I like it."

"Well, as I was saying, ambition's everything. There just ain't a city in the world where it works better. Papa says that was true thirty years back, and Ah'm sayin' it's just as true today. If a man's got size he can't miss, Mr. O'Hara. You take a man like Clay Frick, for instance, now he's a giant. He knows that coke and steel go hand in hand, so he starts building coke ovens—he's just drippin' with dollars, they say. Or Flint and Chris Magee. Now they're smart, real smart. They've got this city in the palm of their hand. Chris builds up power, Flint makes the money, and those two, they keep piling it up."

"A political ring that's safer than a bank," I said.

"An' why not? A city like this has got to raise men like that, or she dies. She's dirty outside and smellin' inside, but she's alive and breathing because of men like Chris Magee." She smiled. "Mister, if you've got principles you'd best forget 'em. This city's a gold mine, and you just walk right in and take your cut."

"I'll remember that," I said as Lubinski walked over from the desk.

"Glad to know you're still with us, O'Hara." He drew back his lips in a click of false teeth, his grey eyes moving in his ravaged face. "Sorry to hear your two brothers have left us—good workers."

"You're still plagued with Shaun and me, sir."

195

"Shaun? Ah, yes—one of the best iron men in the city. Pity he knows nothing about making steel."

"He's an expert in the Kelly process," I said sharply.

Lubinski waved a thin hand. "Dead as a doornail—everyone's converting to Bessemer. Do you know the new method?"

"Bessemer? Only what Will's told me. Shaun doesn't approve of it."

"That's what I'm getting at—stick in the mud. It's convert or die—that's the new slogan. What Carnegie does today the city does tomorrow."

"He wasn't the first to get steel from Bessemer, sir."

Hands on hips he grinned at me. "That's open to argument, but I take your point. Are you saying I'm wrong?"

"I am. Carnegie was about fifth on the list with Bessemer, and it was making steel in Europe before Pittsburgh heard of it."

He smiled wider, gripping his cane. "One thing about you, O'Hara, you speak your mind. Do you think we ought to convert?"

Will said, "It'll cost every cent of a hundred thousand. . . ."

Clare sighed, "Whee, that's money!"

"Do you, O'Hara?" Lubinski now, still grinning.

I said, "If I'd got your millions I'd be exporting Bessemer steel years back. We've been pinching and scraping since we built the place, and you expect us to run it on a shoe-string."

"Oh, my," whispered Clare. Her father said, eyes narrowing:

"You happy here, O'Hara?"

"Not particularly."

"Why not?"

"Because you're taking everything out and ploughing nothing back." I got up, strangely elated, yet sickened by the knowledge that I was making an impression. Lubinski's dogs were expected to bark. I said, "Carnegie's right in one thing—this city's fortune is being made on steel, not glass or cotton. We're a two-bit firm, sir, when we should be a million dollars, and one day some smart gent will buy you up."

"All my eggs in one basket, son? That's not sense."

"While you're sucking six you might drop the lot."

He nodded, his face screwing up into a railway junction, and wandered the room.

Will said, "I've been trying to tell you that for the last two years, Mr. Lubinski."

"But not quite so rudely, that's why I didn't listen. O'Hara . . ." He came back to me, smiling. "You're an unskilled man, you know. You'd make a better executive than a progress man—anyone can draw pretty charts. Would you care to slip up to my office to see me?"

"If you wish."

I thought; My God, if McNamara could be here now he'd be proud of me.

"First floor—Monongahela House." He glanced at Clare, one eyebrow slightly raised, and I knew what it meant. She whispered intimately:

"Papa's got a suite there, Mr. O'Hara. You should see that office! . . ."

"Home and office combined," said Lubinski. "Tomorrow evening —say, seven o'clock?"

"I'll look forward to it, sir."

"See you tomorrow, then," said Clare, and they drifted out of the office.

I stood in the middle of the room, eyes closed, my fist in my hand. Marged clattered through the door with a tray and started throwing the coffee cups on to it. Her mouth was a little red button of hostility, her air that of a woman outraged.

"Ach, you'll like that," she said, mimicking my Irish.

"He offered me a job—what's wrong with that?" I turned away. "Anyway, you shouldn't be stooping at keyholes."

"You realise you took the wind out of poor old Will, don't you?"

"I did no such thing, I merely spoke my mind."

She gave me a look to kill as she swept past with the tray. "Yes, Mr. Lubinski, no, Mr. Lubinski, you're a tough boy, Mr. Lubinski, so I'm disagreeing . . ."

I shrugged.

"And that damned Clare—God, what a woman, what a size!"

I groaned. "Ah, now we're getting it."

"The big black spider! Another job, is it—aye, on Clare Lubinski —don't you see what they're after?"

"You tell me."

Marged paused at the door, looking down, and I went to her, kissing her face. She turned. "This means you're off, doesn't it?"

I opened my hands at her. "Look, it's another job. There's no room here for an unskilled man—I'm just a passenger."

"If you go to that office tomorrow you'll never come back."

"Marged, don't be ridiculous!"

She hesitated. "Oh, well, don't let's argue about it now. Karen's wailing for her dinner, and the damned joint's overdone." Near to tears she looked then.

Smiling, I kissed her. "I'll come over now and give you a hand."

I would have kissed her longer, drawing strength and sweetness from her, but the tray was between us. "I love you," I said.

CHAPTER 18

It was spring over Pittsylvania, the gorgeous decoration parade that even the Pittsburgh dirt could never quite obliterate, and my office in Lubinski's palatial suite in the Monongahela House was bright with flowers. In a world tainted by people like Lubinski and McNamara flowers stay undefiled; also, they helped to dilute the smell of Clare's obnoxious perfumes. Standing by the window overlooking the river I tore up McNamara's letter received that morning, but I could not tear up its threat. The letter, sent from Philadelphia, said that Lubinski was dying, and such was the confidence of McNamara that I could almost see him sitting at the death-bed. His instructions in the letter were precise; my golden opportunity to take over the firm was not to be missed, or the next thing I'd miss would be Marged. . . .

Standing there in the sunshine I clenched my hands, desperately seeking an avenue of escape. Had I not been penniless I think I would have left the office at that moment, gone to Girty's Run and taken Marged to a place of safety, but I had also to contend with Will. Marged had a mind of her own, too. There would be endless questions from the pair of them, Karen would be called in and the truth of the situation would be badgered out of me. No, I thought. The threat from McNamara was best handled alone.

Strangely, too, there was a challenge in it. Somewhere or other there must be a counter to the outrageous blackmail; handling it carefully I might even make capital out of the fantastic chain of events that had landed me in my predicament. Indeed, excitement was growing within me at the prospect of the advantages. With Clare apparently in love with me I would have access to wealth greater than my dreams. A few months of intrigue might bring me a fortune and the chance to get back to Marged with something to offer her. Standing there in sunshine, eyes closed, I was torn between love and the sudden prospect of wealth, fear of McNamara, hostility to Clare. And, with the usual disdain for unwanted affection, the effect on Clare didn't even come into it.

I was writing at my desk when Clare entered the office.

"Did you get the letter from Papa?" she asked.

"Letter?" I was instantly on guard.

She wandered towards me. "I had one from Papa. Hambro said there was one for you, too—from Philadelphia."

"Mine wasn't from your father," I said abruptly, and went on writing.

Standing before me she bowed her head. "Oh, Jess, he's ill."

"I know that. Is he worse?"

She walked about with pent agitation. "You know Papa, he don't make much of things, but I can read between the lines. He's asking for me."

She was standing before me now rather like somebody under interview, wearing the most ridiculous black dress, its frills accentuating her shapelessness.

"Then you'd better go to him, hadn't you?" I said.

"Oh, Jess, come with me!"

I sighed. "Clare, I've been to Philadelphia twice already—it's you he wants, not me. And I've got a stack of things to do here."

"Can't Mr. Hambro see to them—he always used to run things when Papa was ill."

"That's what he used to do, but I'm running things now." Mention of Hambro never failed to infuriate me. "I don't trust that one as far as I can throw him."

"He's been with my father twenty years," she snapped.

"Twenty years too long," I said sharply. "Hambro has outlived his usefulness here, it's time we made changes."

She whispered, her hand to her face, "Oh, please don't start that all over again. Look, Jess, please come with me, I hate goin' alone."

Rising, I went to the window, staring out. Sunlight was flashing on gaily-coloured barges surging up the Monongahela with the grace of swans, and the river was a maze of keel-boats and barges. A power-tug was belching along with the name *Lubinski* painted on its side, and in its wake followed a string of tiny coal-boats, their sombre black making it a funeral cortège. I turned as Clare suddenly sobbed behind me; this, the fumbling, wet avenue down which she grizzled at the slightest sign of trouble. I went to her. "Clare, Clare, you knew it had to come—he's been a sick man for years. Try to pull yourself together."

Firmness, I had found, was best for her. A single word of comfort could bring her to the tear-stained bawling of a child. Queer, I thought, how different women look in black. Marged was demure, Karen a poetry of curves and enticement. I closed my eyes as Clare sobbed against me. It was like being in the grip of some gigantic male, only the softness of her breast bringing relief in its hint of womanhood.

The door came open and Vaynor, one of the junior executives, came in. Looking awkward, he dropped a sheaf of papers, scrambled them up, and went out again.

Clare whispered, "Please, honey . . ."

I sighed, going back to the desk. "All right, I'll come with you, but I've got to go over to Girty's Run first."

"Why?"

"Because I've got business there, woman."

The tears had vanished. "You're always going to Girty's Run."

"And I'll have to keep going, won't I, since Hambro can't. If he could be trusted to handle the technical aspects I'd have an easier time. Besides, Karen's back."

"When did she get in?"

"Yesterday."

"For the wedding, this time?"

I smiled. "I doubt it. Will's having a job to pin her—she doesn't stay in one place long enough. She'll marry him when she's good and ready."

Clare tossed her head. "Then she needs to watch it, for he's some man. One day while she's touring the halls somebody else'll step in there and hook him."

I gave her a smile. "I doubt it. When do you want to leave, dear?"

"There's a train out this afternoon. I'll get Louise to pack your things. . . ."

"Right," I said, "I'll be back in an hour."

Beggars were squatting on the sidewalk as I walked up Duquesne, their thin arms stretched out to me, Italians mostly, many still wearing the grimed bandages of the maiming that caused their discharge, this, the refuse of industry. I scattered a few cents among them and hailed a cab.

"Girty's Run," I called to the driver.

Pittsburgh was beautiful on that bright, spring morning. Even the smut-layer had blown west on the wind, and the old excitement was upon me at the thought of seeing Marged. Shaun was on the gate as I entered the Works' compound, but I did not look his way. Telling the driver to wait I ran up the steps of the cottage and into the kitchen. The room was empty.

"Marged!" I called up the stairs.

Karen appeared at the back door and wandered in, her face expressionless.

"Karen, you're back!" I ran to her, seizing her hands, but she drew away and sat down slowly.

"How did you know?" she asked.

"I saw it in the Gazette. Ach, you're knocking them cold down the coast, girl."

There was a strangeness about her, an unfathomable coolness in her eyes. And she sat, severe in her tight-waisted dress, her hands clasped in her lap.

"How long are you staying?" she asked.

"For a couple of hours—I'm looking for Marged."

"Then you can spare five minutes to me. Sit you down, Jess."

I did so, smiling. "Is that all your greeting? It's nigh four months since I've seen you—aren't you pleased to have me?"

"Not this time."

"Is there anything wrong?"

"Aye," said she, "there is. Two of me brothers have gone, and no sight or sound of them—the third, out there, is goin' to the devil with his women and his secret societies, and the fourth one's losin' his soul."

I sighed at the ceiling. "Here we go again. Come on, out with it," and she rose, pacing the room, her face pale. She whispered:

"Do you realise what yesterday was? It was Marged's birthday. There's me breaking me neck to get back from Georgia and you a coupla miles away and not the grace in you to visit her. When did you call on her last?"

I said, evenly, "I come when I can. I sent her flowers—I can't be over here every damned minute—Lubinski's ill."

"And you think a bunch of those pale things make up for your presence on a day like that? The Welsh go daft on their birthdays. Come to that, did you have to leave here at all?"

"My business."

"Aye, and I'll tell you it." She leaned forward, eyes narrowed. "You're stricken with the blight of every other youngster in this black hole—you're greedy for dollars. You've got the marks of the damned grille on yer head with shovin' them into the bank, and ye're saying to hell with your friends, d'you realise that?"

I got up. "I know where you're getting all that stuff from."

She was up beside me. "And why shouldn't the girl pour out her heart? God's blood, if she can't cry to me who else can she cry to? There's her cousin up to his neck in Lubinski profits and you playing lackey to high society. Is Marged right? Is it money you're after?"

"No."

"Is it the woman, the big black one?"

"Clare's nothing to do with it."

"I'm delighted to hear it!" Her voice rose. "For the moment she is I'll have yer docked. I've met the likes of that fat porker down every street on the coast. Aw, Jess, don't you see the scheme of it? Her dad's no fool—if he could have wed her to a young buck with a fine family would he have taken on an executive who can't even add?" Hands on hips, she stared me up and down, her face disdainful. "And look at ye! You're a fine sight indeed for an O'Hara! The fella who bunked from Wicklow with a bundle and finished

203

in the Monongahela in a white tie and coat-tails. Have you looked in the glass?"

"You've not done so bad," I whispered.

"But I've got these two feet to thank for it—I've got the starvin' and the cold to bless for it. D'you think I couldn't have done it quicker if I'd taken a tumble on a bed?"

I said, "Karen, it's not like that. I haven't put a finger on Clare Lubinski."

"And you haven't put one on young Marged for months. Didn't I hear some fine tales about you marrying the child?"

"When I've got something to offer her."

"You've got it all now," she said softly, moving away. "In another six months of that Lubinski lot you'll have just nothin'. Ach! You're stacking up yer dollars and hoarding up dross."

I wandered the room. The activity in the compound was astonishing. The pig-iron was going out, the ore coming in, mules straining to the loads, whips flying. Shaun was still standing at the gate, I noticed. I said, turning:

"Where is Marged?"

"She's away up in Sharpsburg for the day. She spends her damned life cooking and scrubbing for an army—I gave me tongue to Will, so he took her. And he's worried to death, poor devil."

"What's wrong with him?"

She waved, turning. "I can't get the hang of it. T'was something about a letter on the table here—the thing was unsigned, and it didn't say much, they tell me. Just a drawing of a gun and a coffin."

The sweat sprang to my face and I turned again to the window.

"It's the third they've had this month, apparently. Will says it can't be the Union for he's paying full rates, or somethin' . . ."

"Of course it's not! The Union doesn't work like that. Why didn't he tell me this?"

"Why should he? Are you running this place, too? Don't you bother yourself with his troubles—Will can handle it. The night before last Marged found one on her bed . . ."

I swung round. "She what? . . ." I whispered.

"That's shaken you!"

204

"What d'you expect it to do? It's a threat to Marged."

"It's nothing of the sort. Will says it's meant for him—there's a few city bosses collecting them lately, it appears. Ah, rest yourself. It's a labourin' fella with a bee in his bonnet—someone near the house."

"What's Will done about it?" I was trembling.

"Nothin'." Karen smiled. "But one thing it's proved to me— you're still in love with Marged. Where are you going?"

I was at the door. "Back to the hotel."

"Yer daft hoodlum, you've only just come!"

I ran through the door and got into the waiting cab. Shaun was still at the gate. I left the cab and went to him.

"Where's that bastard McNamara," I whispered.

"Sure, he's up in Philadelphia, didn't you know?"

"When will he be back?" I gripped him by the coat. "I've called five times this past month and the man's never in."

"Am I his keeper?" He had a swanky air on him, his chin cocked up. I said:

"Right, I'll cool ye. What happened to Branston?"

Shaun's expression changed. "Shall I tell you?" I asked. "He was found in a mere with his head beaten in. . . ."

"Jess, upon me oath . . ."

"Where's McNamara? If he's still in Philadelphia he's been there months."

"In the name of Ma if I knew I'd tell yer!"

I jerked my thumb at the cottage. "Are you listening? If there's so much as a scratch on that woman's head, I'll kill ye, Shaun. As God's my judge, I'll kill me own brother."

Karen was standing at the door of the cottage, watching.

"Remember," I said. With a brief wave to Karen I jumped into the cab.

First I went to Hank's Bar, barging up the stairs and into Mc-Namara's room. It was empty. Downstairs in the bar the little round tables were stacked with chairs. There was no sign of the bartender but a door opened at the end of the room as I helped myself to the whiskey. Leaning on the counter I watched the hostess as she walked towards me; the same paste jewellery on her, the same stupid wriggle of her hips. Fluffing up her hair she stood before me.

"You wantin' someone?"

"McNamara," I said.

She poured herself a drink beside me, sighing. "Every man I meet wants McNamara. Is he so important?"

"Where is he?"

She turned. "Mister, if I don't see McNamara again it'll be a whole life too soon. . . ."

"Kehoe?"

"Who's Kehoe?" She smiled at me from under blackened lashes, her lips unmoving.

I sighed, and said, "Is this place empty now?"

"Brother, this place is a morgue."

"Then what are you doing here?"

She winked over the rim of her glass and sipped the whiskey. "Waiting for a customer. An' outside that you're getting nothing from me."

I finished the whiskey, and left her, got into the cab and went back to my office. The moment I sat down at my desk Hambro came in. His ability to time his entries made me suspicious of the keyhole, and I detested him.

"Good afternoon, Mr. O'Hara."

I nodded, picking up papers I had been studying earlier. Before his illness Lubinski had ordered a glass sell-out to Maherne Enterprises, a new and thriving company. Half the previous night I had been up, trying to understand the Agreement, stumbling over Hambro's involved, legal jargon, and I hated my inadequacy.

"Everything all right, sir?" There was a smile in Hambro's voice.

I looked at him, the power behind Lubinski. Bald, owlish in his eye-glasses, he evoked the air of the intellectually superior; he was mine, and knew it. But I scarcely heard his voice now. My brain was racing with fears for Marged.

"Perfectly all right." I signed the Agreement. "An excellent job, Hambro."

"I try to do my best, sir." He smiled with the cynicism, adding,

"Miss Lubinski tells me you're both going to see her father today. Perhaps you'll mention this business of converting Girty's Run to Bessemer?"

I glanced up. "Have sense, man, Lubinski's on his death-bed."

I was making mistakes and cursed myself as Hambro's eyebrows lifted. "Really, Mr. O'Hara, I didn't realise it—I don't think Miss Lubinski does, you know. Did the letter you received from Philadelphia? . . ."

"That . . . that was a personal letter; nothing to do with Mr. Lubinski."

"I see." Hambro wandered about. "A very lovely city—I didn't know you had connections there." He paused. "You see . . ."

"You were saying . . ." I interjected.

"Ah, yes. Bessemer—you still intend to go through with it?"

"Certainly—it is what the Chairman wants, isn't it?"

"But does he realise the cost? Do you know the cost, Mr. O'Hara?"

"Not till you show me the estimate."

He had the astonishing ability to produce things like a rabbit from a hat. Now he laid a file before me. "A hundred and eighty thousand dollars, sir."

I was appalled, and said, "Well done—less than I expected. Does this include the cost of the patent?"

"Naturally."

"Who owns the American patent?"

"Mr. Holley, sir. Vaynor will arrange that side of it."

"Is Holley capable?"

Hambro sighed at the ceiling. "He built the works at Troy. He also built the Harrisburg Bessemer which is ten times the size of Girty's Run. Not that I am interested in the technical aspect, sir, for I am not a technician." His eyes added that I wasn't either. "But as financial advisor I am bound to tell Mr. Lubinski . . ."

"Miss Lubinski," I said. "Face the facts, Hambro. At this very moment her father's probably dead. I've seen him lately—you haven't."

"And she agrees that the future lies in steel? The capital of this firm came from cotton."

I began to write. "You're out of date, Hambro—you're like the rest of them—dazzled by a ten per cent profit. The future of Lubinski's lies in steel."

"You realise we haven't got the technicians, don't you?"

"The Welsh are the technicians and Mr. Rees is Welsh—he'll pull in droves of them."

"You are very fond of the Rees couple, aren't you, Mr. O'Hara."

I looked up, lowering my pen. "What the devil are you talking about?"

His watery eyes showed a hint of a smile. "When I'm dealing with a cost like this I don't mince words. Personalities are involved in this stupid speculation."

"You're right. I own fifteen per cent of the shares." I tapped my pocket. "And I've already got Mr. Lubinski's signature to the conversion."

"It would have saved my time had you told me that. May I see it?"

"You may not. The sooner you understand that you're not running this firm the easier it'll be for both of us—now get on with it."

"You will regret this, Mr. O'Hara."

"Do as you're told and leave the regrets to me."

It was rather like a play being enacted, I thought. Soon the door would open and the woman in the case appear to make some dramatic announcement, the finale to the first act of the Lubinski drama. Hambro and I were staring at each other, I remember, and to my astonishment the door opened and Clare stood there clutching a telegram. She was shaking. Tears were on her face.

"Oh, Jess," she whispered, "my papa's dead," and ran into my arms.

I held her. Over her shoulder I saw the Lubinski power-tug with another cortège of coal-boats behind it, nearly out of sight, its black smoke drifting across the river.

CHAPTER 19

Marged and I were drifting. Whenever I went to Girty's Run she was either away on some pretext or another or treated me with the dispassionate reserve in which the Welsh are expert when it comes to unwanted visitors. By summer I was writing to her, by autumn she was not replying. Lonely, bitter, I turned more and more to my interest in the firm, yet I was strangely determined, despite her rejection of me, that the works at Girty's Run should grow as Will had planned it. For the trend everywhere was in steel and no sensible business man could afford to ignore it.

Big names were mushrooming in the city—men like Henry Clay Frick who, surviving the Panic of '73 which had ruined his partner, was turning out coke at nearly five dollars a ton. Nine years later, with over a thousand ovens and three thousand acres of land, he had the key to steel-making in his fist. Carnegie, too, was growing to a giant. Ejecting one competitor after another, intriguing with the vision of a clairvoyant, he was acquiring business after business, his ambitions canalised into the ownership of the whole of Pittsburgh steel-making. Wage demands, strikes, and union protests from the Sons of Vulcan came and went, while Carnegie, the little white-haired Scotch devil who had started with nothing was sending his steel rails to the ports of the world. From the moment he and his brother acquired an interest in the Kloman Twenty-ninth Street mill, their fortunes grew to staggering proportions. From his control of the Edgar Thomson Works leaped the great success of Bessemer in America. Heads rolled, one suicide followed another; a man who was rich one day was a pauper the next, and I watched Carnegie's rise to power with admiration, priding myself that I, as he, realised early the potential of steel in a city that was hanging like a leech on to iron. One by one the smaller concerns were swallowed in the vortex of the combines. Tentative offers for a sell-out were made to us that autumn, but I refused, with growing pride.

Girty's Run was going over to Bessemer if I broke Lubinski in doing it. Of course, had any minor technician asked me to explain the beautiful Bessemer converter—the English invention that made Pittsburgh's fortune—I would not have been able to do so. Such technical facts, I had found, were not necessary to the speculator, who needs but money, courage, and the ability to select advisors. And I had one hand-made in Will Rees.

The flatteries that come with success are pleasing, I found; there was a sense of power in sitting behind Lubinski's big, mahogany desk with a bell under my fingers that would bring people running—a long cry, I reflected, from the early days in the city when I worked on hearth-cleaning with a blistered Hunky. Another year passed. I sold out the canal investments despite Hambro's entreaties. I would have got rid of the cotton mill, too, had it not been for Clare's objections. I would have got rid of Clare, had it not been for her control of the stock. Eighteen months after I took over the firm's leadership with the twenty per cent granted me by Lubinski's will, I visited the Citizens' National Bank to check my account. A sharp-nosed clerk behind the grille announced with secret admiration that it stood at forty-two thousand dollars, an amount equalled by McNamara, though he banked elsewhere; it was a poor repayment for the loss of Marged.

"Come in," I called.

Will entered my office, looking handsome and completely at ease, and I admired the man. He had the ability to divorce his social life from business, which diluted a little of the embarrassment.

"You sent for me, Mr. O'Hara?" It sounded ridiculous, but I did not smile. The gap was too wide between us now, better this way, perhaps. I nodded, turning away. "Drink, Will?"

"Too early, sir." He opened his hand-case and brought out papers, studying them with an artificial interest. I sat down at the desk.

"How's Marged?"

He glanced up, surprised. "Fine, fine—she was in bed all last week with a fever so we had the doctor in—he leeched her, she's better now."

I was relieved. The very sight of him brought her memories flooding back.

"No more threatening letters?" I asked.

"Threatening letters?"

"Last time I was over—when Karen was there . . ."

He smiled. "Oh, no, that's all stopped. You know what it is—you only want one of them with a sense of injustice. Mixed labour, that's the trouble. You know I'm running down on them now and bringing in Welsh?"

"Can't beat them. How's the conversion going?"

He put down the brief-case, his face lighting up. "Wonderfully, if you're talking of progress. We're half-way up with Betsy now—that'll take another four months, and we're a fortnight ahead of schedule. The engineers are working on a bonus and penalty clause so I expect they'll finish on time. When Betsy pours steel we'll start on the second phase—Sally."

"And Sally's iron output is being maintained?"

"About forty-two tons a day, sir."

I grinned at him. "No need for titles, Will."

He shrugged. "Just as you wish."

"What's your labour force these days?"

"Two hundred and eighty—about sixty per cent Welsh."

"No Irish?"

He raised his face. "Not if I can help it, nor English."

"It's an American firm, Will, don't make it a Welsh oasis. Sixty per cent of your people, the rest open to foreigners—keep it that way."

"If you wish, sir."

I had an intense and almost ungovernable desire to laugh. Life was strange, I reflected. A few years ago I was a bare-footed immigrant walking the planks of a coffin-ship with a well-fed technician. Will had the world at his feet in those days, I had nothing. Now he still had the brains but I gave the orders.

"Is that all, Mr. O'Hara?"

"Not quite. Tell me, how's Karen?"

"Still away touring. She was home last month for a couple of days."

"A job to pin her, isn't it?" I gave him a smile and he returned it faintly. "She's had ants in her shoes from the day she was born—give her the rope, Will, one day she'll settle. No news of Hosea and Michael?"

He shook his head. I drank, my elbows on the desk, watching him, saying:

"You must be sick to death of these damned O'Haras."

He buttoned the hand-case and rose. "I'd better be going, sir. Is that all?"

"Good gracious, no! I asked you to come for a particular reason. Every letter that comes into this place talks Bessemer. Every meeting I attend goes right over my head, for I don't know a damn thing about it. Tell me how it works."

"You don't know?"

"Not the technicalities—that's what you're paid for."

He sat down again, saying softly, "It is really very simple, and very beautiful. Crude, molten iron is poured into the converter. Powerful air jets are forced up through the boiling mass. Little happens at first, save a few sparks, but the mass becomes hotter till a temperature of four thousand degrees Fahrenheit brings a dull, red glow. The glow becomes brighter as the imprisoned silicon begins to separate from the pig-iron, and this further increases the heat. The air-pressure increases. A battle ensues as the boiling mass tries to rid itself of the carbon atoms . . ." Excitement grew in his face and his hands moved before him. "An erupting volcano is a bigger turmoil, Mr. O'Hara, but the ferocity is just the same. For the iron can be heard moaning, and the moan grows into a shriek as the carbon is dragged loose from the boiling iron. A light begins to burn in the converter—God, you should see that light—building up in brilliance. And still the air jets spurt in until a pillar of incandescent flame shoots into the sky. This is the victory, sir. The carbon has vanished into gas. The molten steel in the Bessemer is as pure as water."

I sat entranced. "Wonderful, exciting," I whispered, and he lowered his hands, his expression suddenly changed.

"Aye, it's exciting, O'Hara, for it means your ruination."

He rose and approached the desk, staring down at me. I sat back, smiling.

"Why?"

"Because we're a two-bit firm compared with people like Carnegie and Laughlin."

"Didn't you advocate conversion once. I seem to remember . . ."

He waved me down and turned away in disgust. "That was two years back. We're too small and we're too late, O'Hara. You're diving down paradise and playing the big man, but you'll never get away with it—the big combines will eat you alive. Didn't Hambro warn you against conversion?"

"Who the hell's Hambro—the man's a bloody clerk."

"And where do you think the advice came from?" He thumped his chest. "From me. You didn't trouble to check with me, did you?" He reached for his hat. "You're so damned high and mighty with other people's money that you couldn't even visit the works, or were you too ashamed?"

"Don't let your dislikes interfere with your business, Will."

He leaned towards me. "Listen, O'Hara. Before I got a penny backing from Lubinski I built the furnace arch at Girty's Run—aye, and you helped me from there—remember? Now you're determined to tear everything down."

"I'm trying to build you up, you fool!" I rose, shouting. "You're as bad as Hambro, you won't take a chance. It's convert or die. A year from now the profits . . ."

"Profits," he breathed. "All you can think of is bloody profits! Where do human beings come into this? There's one thing money can't buy, O'Hara, and that's forgiveness."

"Now we're on another subject."

"Aye," he answered, "you're right. You damned O'Haras—I'm sick to death of the lot of you. You're either round our necks or stabbing us in the back—we never know where we are from one minute to another."

"You'd better go," I said.

He went to the door, gripped the handle, and turned to me. "I might have to work for you but I'm not your lackey, O'Hara.

Next time you want me you come to Girty's Run, like Lubinski did." He waved at the room. "For it stinks in here, and I'm not being run by a man who pimps for his money."

"Get out," I whispered.

After he had gone I put my hands over my face. "Get out," I said.

I rang for Hambro but Vaynor came in.

He was a brown-haired youth, handsome in a lanky way, hand-picked by Lubinski from one of the best, poor families in the State. Born of lesser parents he would have been called a fool, for his sole virtue was charm. Such individuals, I had discovered, were carried as surplus baggage in the industrial freight car, la-belled gentility. I tolerated Vaynor because of his hostility to Hambro and his apparent devotion to Clare. In this direction he had been doing very well, it seemed, until Lubinski brought me on the scene.

"You rang, sir?"

"I rang for Mr. Hambro."

Vaynor gripped his hands. "He . . . he's at the meeting of the Iron Trades Federation, sir—second Thursday in the month—re-member?"

"Yes, yes, of course. Give him a message, Vaynor. Tell him to speed up the conversion of Sally."

His eyes narrowed with veiled amusement. "Delightful thought, sir."

"Don't be a fool, Vaynor." I glanced up sharply.

"Of course not, sir." To attention, straight-faced, he stood. "It's as a result of your meeting with Mr. Rees, I assume."

"Assume nothing, Vaynor. Just tell him—also that I want him to make the necessary financial arrangements for the second phase of the conversion."

"Certainly, sir." He wavered, shifting from one foot to the other. Glancing up again, I said, "All right, all right, I'll see that the money's there."

"Thank you, sir—is that all?"

214

His presence, his tom-foolery after Will's visit was infuriating me. "It is," I replied. "No—wait—have you got the tickets?"

This stunned him, and it was Vaynor's trouble. A chance question like this evoked in him total surprise. Raising a limp hand he wiped back his untidy brown hair.

I said, "The tickets, you fool—for the Maherne Reception—weren't they comin' by special messenger?"

"Ah, yes, sir. Miss Lubinski's got them." He beamed with success.

"Right, get out."

When he had gone I went to the window and looked down on to the street. Almost immediately I saw Marged among the swirling crowds, looking beautiful in a white, cotton dress. And as I watched Will crossed the road to her. As they walked down the sidewalk she suddenly looked back at the hotel windows. I drew back into the room. Such was her grace and loveliness that it seemed impossible that I had ever possessed her, and the trembling within me was doused into limpness as the door opened behind me. Clare was standing there, her great eyes appealing in her pathetic anxiety to please. Nothing in Lubinski's was so intolerable to me as this dog-like devotion. Going to the desk I poured another whiskey.

"Oh, honey," she said, "don't start so early, you know it just ruins your stomach."

I drained the glass. "Are you ready?"

"I've been ready this past hour. You like my new dress?" Arms out, she turned on tiptoe.

Its white satin accentuated her obesity; the bustle, the enormous bow, and the absurdly low neckline were ridiculous.

"Charming." I turned away.

"You think so? I'm so glad. White, you see—your favourite colour. Had it made specially in Kaufmann's. Have you seen that building? My, they're going places. Cost me a fortune—hundred and twenty."

I remembered an attic in Peebles Township and a sylph-like Katie Virginia in a one-dollar-fifty. I said:

"Clare, I've got to talk to you."

"You just go on talkin', honey."

"Clare, I'm very short of money."

She smiled. "Is that all? Ah thought it was something serious. Well, you ain't alone, sweetie—d'you know what I heard yesterday? Even Abe Lincoln's wife was short of money after that fine man passed on—selling her furniture to pay her way—ain't that a national scandal?"

"Clare, please . . ."

She looked over her shoulder. "How much?" and she asked it like Papa Lubinski.

"Two hundred thousand."

"Whee, jakes! What for?"

"Look—you remember your father decided to convert the ironworks to Bessemer? . . ."

"What's that, darlin'?" She was fussing about the room like a great, white seal, smoothing herself and swirling out her dress.

"The conversion of Girty's Run to a steel-making concern, you know very well what I'm talking . . ."

"Does Mr. Hambro agree?"

"To hell with Hambro—am I running this firm or not?"

She played with a bow. "Papa always told me to lean on Mr. Hambro. 'You lean as hard as you like on Hambro' said he, 'everything that man touches turns to big, silver dollars.' What's all the hurry about makin' steel, honey—ain't we doing all right with iron?"

Her stupid endearments, her southern drawl were sickening. I said, "Forget about Hambro—he doesn't know a roller from a ladle—am I getting the money, or not?"

Her arms came out to me and I actually stepped away. "Jess, keep your shirt on. Can't we discuss this like grown-up people?"

"You've been talking to Hambro, haven't you!"

"Why, sure, ain't I entitled to? He's my financial advisor. You got twenty per cent on Papa's will, honey—that's big money. What you done with it?"

I sighed. "Clare, listen, for God's sake. I get twenty per cent of the earnings of the firm—I've got no capital at all to play with."

"Boy, you sure ain't playing with mine."

"Then for heaven's sake how do you expect me to expand?"

"Who wants to expand, sweetie? Ain't we doin' fine?" She patted her stomach. "Look what expanding's done for me. Jeez, would I give two hundred thousand to lose six inches of that."

"Oh, my God," I breathed, and turned away, but she was after me instantly, her arms reaching out.

"Now, now, man, don't you fret. I guess we'll get around to it one way or another. Now you pop upstairs and change, for if there's one thing little Abe Maherne can't abide it's folks comin' late for his Receptions."

"You . . . you'll give me the money?"

She sighed. "Jess, I'm my father's creature, and us Lubinskis don't part easy with cents, never mind dollars." She turned me to face her. "So two hundred thousand of those pretty little things are likely to cost you somethin'."

The smile died on her mouth. She whispered, "Jess, kiss me . . . just once?"

There was a sincerity, a sweetness in her eyes I had never seen before. In her stumbling, obese loneliness she was an object of pity. I kissed her, and she said, twisting at her dress, "My, at two hundred thousand a time those things come real expensive."

"Don't say that, Clare."

She looked away. "You reckon my papa ever had plans for us, Jess? Other than you just runnin' the firm, I mean? I guess he did, for he passed over a dozen bright experts just to get you by my side . . ." She did not weep this time. "And you hit me right here, straight from the start, d'you know that? You never thought of me that way?"

I shook my head, and she whispered, "That's a real pity. Didn't think you did, somehow, but I loved you from the minute you walked into that office in Girty's Run. You walked into that office with a face like ice, and stood there in the dirt you brought from the furnaces, but I loved you. Guess my pa saw the look on my face . . ."

I said, "And Vaynor?"

She smiled. "I could fetch in Vaynors at ten dollars a time." Drawing nearer, she took my hand. "Look, Ah'm no beauty, leastways, not outside, but my God, Jess, I think real clean for you. I'm just fat and rich. Eh, my! You could search the whole world over and not find a love like mine. Do I ever bother you?"

"No, Clare."

She walked slowly to the window, head bowed. "Then I don't bother you because I'm loving you. You stop to think of that sometimes. I got over two million dollars now, and I got nothin', not since Papa died—and Ah'd change the whole damned lot to get some loving back, but those Hambro dollars don't buy love." She turned, smiling. "I ain't asking for your bed, but remember, I got you around me from mornin' to night, and this love keeps growin', Jess. Ah kick the old thing round me, but it keeps growing and growing, so you remember something—I may be fat and ugly, but I'm still a woman. An' the yearning comes fierce for you inside me, ah, Jess, this yearning comes fierce."

"Clare," I said earnestly, "it's the wrong religion . . ."

She lifted her face. "The way I see it that ain't the cause. The religion's the same for that little Welsh girl, ain't it? The way I see you look at her one time, there weren't much Pope in that." She walked about, holding herself, and I was overwhelmed with a pity for her greater than before. Now, reaching me, she leaned her head against me, her eyes closed.

"Jess, you hold me . . ."

I held her, and she said, "Don't you feel nothin' for me at all?"

"Clare, Clare, I'm very fond of you."

"That's the kind of love a man gives to a dog. Eh, fella, you just don't know. You just wink your eye an' a woman comes running, so you don't know the pain in me."

I held her, hating myself.

"Jess, you listening?"

I nodded.

"Tell me something true. D'you just hang round here 'cause of my money?"

Marged first, then Will, now Clare. I screwed up my hand when I thought of McNamara, and she took the fist and held it, saying, "Tell me truly, best for me to know."

"Yes," I said, and she glanced up.

"But the funny thing about it you don't give a damn for money. I've watched you. Oh, sure, you'll skin me alive for your damned conversions, I know. You'll beg for my stocks for this and that, but I ain't down a cent—I know, 'cause Hambro told me. You got the golden touch yourself, he says—you just pile up money, and all you're takin' is your twenty-odd per cent . . ."

"That's all I'm entitled to," I said.

"But you don't spend a dime—I know that, too . . ."

Somehow I had to put a stop to her. I said, "Clare, please, it's getting late."

"Oh, to hell with Maherne and his damned Reception!"

Vaynor tapped the door, opened it, and said, "Mr. O'Hara, the brougham is waiting . . ."

"All right, all right!"

Clare sighed, nodding at the door. "Now, if I had that fella I'd be bleeding to death. Oh, Jess, why do you stay here—what are you after?"

I heard her in a dream. Until this moment I had not realised the extent of the crime. Perhaps I didn't swindle her, or even try to, but I was enjoying her wealth and her power. It had all started with McNamara's blackmail—I had hated every minute in the place once, but now I was enjoying it, and the knowledge came with waves of increasing shock. Going to the desk I poured another whiskey, staring before me. Clare said softly, "That won't help you. Man or woman, you've got to know yourself some time. Some time or other you gotta get a straight look, and . . ."

"Be quiet."

You could go downtown and buy a suit and not miss the money. You could toss up a dollar and not wait for the change, or alter the living standards of a hundred men by scribbling your name on a piece of paper. Clare said:

"So it's my money."

I nodded.

"Only that?"

"Yes."

She whispered, "I'll say one thing, at least you're honest," and I swung round upon her, shouting, "Did I trap you or you trap me? Did I barge into your life or did your father fix it?"

She ignored the outburst. "Jess, have you got a woman around?" I shook my head and gulped at the whiskey.

"Thank God for that. Are you listening, for I'm telling you something free. This ain't news, Jess, for I'm used to it. All my life folks have been after something I've got, I never had a single thing given free, so I'm used to paying for the pleasures of life. And right now I'm paying for love. I got two million dollars, and you can have the lot, but don't you leave me for another woman, or I'll kill myself."

"Clare, please . . ."

"I'm tellin' you. I mean it."

The door opened. I listened to the noises of the foyer below, the raucous laughter of men, the clash of glasses. The door closed, bringing silence.

For a long time I sat there staring at the whiskey, then rose, opening the door.

"Vaynor!"

Hambro came, suspiciously near, as usual. I said:

"Tell Miss Lubinski that I won't be going to the Maherne Reception."

CHAPTER 20

I walked that night in a demented Pittsburgh.

The rebellious spirit of '77 had caught fresh fire in the city's House of Labour, and mob law was rife again. Sullen strike pickets marched the streets; strikers stood on street corners and belligerent union leaders harangued them with upraised fists. Companies of the Pittsburgh militia, backing the strikers' cause, squatted on the sidewalks flicking cards. In the seething discontent of wage cuts the workers were once again attacking the Pittsburgh system of oysters for the owners and bread for the poor. Looms ground to a halt, furnaces were being blown out, the doors of factories locked and barred. Bosses had been attacked, agents and Pinkerton men savaged, and it was unsafe on the streets. Gangs of men and women roamed the alleys, and the dregs of the city, penned till such an outbreak by hunger and poverty, spewed out of the shanties with their banners and threats.

On my way to see McNamara I leaned against a wall and watched the mob go by, seeing its emaciated faces, its drink-ridden cheeks. Establishments and creeds, I thought, were combined against the poor, for gain. From executive suite to the gilded bishop in church, the lust for power and wealth was the same, it seemed. Financier broke financier and women thieved in beds. And this mob was the same, I thought, in its howls for fair shares. Every man there was a potential Carnegie who had tasted the cake and bolted the lot. Rich or poor, not one differed from the other. Head bowed, I walked in the shadows, aware that, by devious processes of rottenness I had acquired more wealth than had been owned by Homer, Scipio, Raphael, and Dante. A fresh rush of men howled by, placards waving in the light of flares. Any man there, I thought, given the chance, would end up being a millionaire pig, his greed sustained in the race of the tiger, the greed inherent in the human breast.

I went up Ferry and Duquesne and along the waterfront to Hank's Bar. A light was burning in McNamara's room, though the saloon below was empty. I climbed the stairs and knocked at the door.

"Who's there?"

"O'Hara."

The bolt rattled and the door swung back. McNamara was there alone.

"Well, O'Hara, I'm glad to see you!"

Not the same McNamara, this one. His hair was grey at the temples, the loose flesh was hanging on the pins of his cheeks, and his shoulders were bowed. He smiled, rubbing his hands in business-like joy. "Will you sit you down, me son!"

"You've been away a long time," I said.

He sat facing me. "Ach, I'm a busy man, you know. There's trials and tribulations calling me from north to south, but I've had you in mind—did you get me letters?"

I nodded. "Where's Kehoe?"

"Didn't you hear? A Pinkerton fella got among us—passed himself off as a Maguire, as God's me judge. And he made a few rifts in the pattern of us for a time, and Kehoe, the fool, had a big mouth on him. Sure, they hanged him for dead, God rest him." He crossed himself.

"Where's Shaun?"

"Your brother? Now why should I be knowing that? The last time I saw him was two days back when I sent him on a mission to the east. He's a fool of a man, that one, but he's a broth of a Maguire these days, for the fella never flinches. D'you know, Jess —it's an amazing thing. With the sword of the patriot in his hand a coward is the best when it comes to duty. Congratulations on your own success, come to that. The way you're going these days you'll have the big industrialists lookin' over their shoulders."

I watched him. The door to the adjoining room behind him was open. Kehoe might be dead, but McNamara was never alone. I said:

"I'll come to the point. I'm getting out, McNamara."

"You're what?"

"I've had enough of it, I'm going back to Ireland."

222

He got up. "You're leaving a crock of gold and you sitting on top of it?"

I nodded.

"Are you in yer right senses, O'Hara? Is it drinking you've been?"

I said, evenly, "I've made you over a hundred thousand dollars. If you're giving it to the social causes you spout, I can see no sign of it."

"And there's me travelling the breadth of the land dishing out the money . . ."

"Don't lie. The misery's on your doorstep. There's not a soul in this place who has seen a cent of it."

He smiled. "But you're making no mention of the fortune you've set up for yourself, O'Hara—have you dished that out to the starving poor?"

"You can have every dollar," I said. "I'm leaving for Ireland."

He smiled wider, hands clasped on the desk. "Forgive the bluntness, son, but you're doing no such thing. Wouldn't I be twice the fool you take me for if I slit the throat of the golden goose—God alive, you're the biggest money-spinner the Society have ever had on their books."

I rose. "Try stopping me."

"Would I do that when I can throw you to the Authorities? Ach, get some sense to you, O'Hara. Your name's on the books with your signature against it, and the Pinkerton detectives would be stretching your neck at the sight of it—Kehoe himself is the living proof of it, poor devil." He waved me away. "Now sit yourself down, son. You've got a fine fighting spirit for a man in irons, but you're chained to me, and that's an end to it. Now tell me what's troublin' you—is it a woman?"

I shook my head, glancing at the door behind him, for a shadow moved in the light.

"Then it can't be your family. There's yer sister Karen the rage of the halls, your brother Shaun striking blows for old Ireland, and your large brother Hosea laying them cold from coast to coast . . ."

"Hosea?" I sat down.

"Don't you read the bloody papers? They've never seen the likes of him since Daniel Mendoza. I have a hundred on him every time he fights."

I forgot McNamara for a moment, closing my eyes with pride. He went on, "Didn't you know? He's got the big John L. himself giving him an eye." Lighting a stogie, he gasped out smoke. "And Michael, yer middle brother—have you heard of his fine progress?"

"Mike? . . ." I was upright in the chair.

"He's working with the Fenians on another *Erin's Hope*—travelling the country rousing up the patriots. Och!" He opened his arms to me. "The O'Haras are cuttin' their names on the tapestry of this country—would you sell them all down the river for a whim?"

I did not reply. I was thinking with joy of Hosea and Michael.

"I'm waitin', son—have you one good reason for stopping them in their tracks?"

"You swine."

"For if I slip your name to the Pinkerton detectives you'll raise such a dust that you'll blind the family, and you'd be a slob of a man to sink to that." He peered. "What's ailing you?"

"Nothing you'd understand." I got up.

"God's blood, fella! Is the calf love still on ye?" He followed me to the door. "If it's the Welsh woman over at Girty's I can settle your mind on her, too. It's race to race the whole world over—wasn't I telling ye? She's walking out with a young Silurian, and there's talk about them marrying, even."

"You know everything, don't you."

He grinned, pointing with his stogie. "When the knowledge concerns you, O'Hara, and I'll tell ye why. You're full carat gold, man, and rare with diamonds, and if you send me to the grave I'll still be wooing ye. Ah, me son!" He clapped a hand on my shoulder. "I'd rather plunder you than the city treasurer, for I own you body and soul. A wink brings you runnin' and a frown sets you trembling. For I can raise or stamp on you O'Haras. I can wed you to your Welsh kid or bury the pair of you, and God, you know it."

I said, softly, "And one day you'll make a mistake, won't you, McNamara?"

He clapped his hands and shouted with laughter. "Mark, Mary, and Joseph! That's what I like about you, O'Hara—you're a fighting cock of a fella, you are."

"One day," I said.

His expression changed. "Right, then, we'll sign on that, me son. But if ever that day comes you'll be kicking on the rope beside me, remember it. Now get back to Lubinski's—while you're biding here gassing you're losing money for the pair of us—good night to you."

It was cold in the street, and I closed my eyes as I thought of Marged. Some time ago Clare had mentioned that she had seen her downtown with a handsome young escort on her arm, but I had not believed her. The thought of my loss brought emptiness. I had sold myself to keep her safe, to no avail.

A dead man was lying across the sidewalk down Duquesne; another crumpled in a grotesque attitude of death, and blood was streaming from a doorway. And I leaped beside him for shelter in the shadows as a new mob came screaming up the waterfront, its bawdy placards and animal arms waving in its torch-light flares. Aproned women milled past me, hair flying, screaming fresh courage into their men. Children, wide-eyed with fear, ran in droves beside them; cripples, beggars of the pavements, flooded past, and I watched, unmoved by their stumps and rags. Penned by their smell and animal roar I crouched, revolted; they were not worth saving. When they had gone I came from the shadows, crossed the Triangle, and went down Smithfield. The Monongahela was bright in moonlight. Aimlessly, not knowing why, I wandered down Water Street.

I remembered Katie Virginia when I heard the trumpet. It was playing the same plaintive Seneca war song I had heard before. Following the music I came to the tavern where I had first seen Katie, and pushed the swing doors. All heads swung to my top hat and cloak, but I did not worry. Most top hats and cloaks were under beds that night and I realised the danger, uncaring, knowing only a stony emptiness within me now that Marged had gone.

Sitting on a high stool I looked round the room. Nothing had changed, and I was glad—the same broad benches, the same customers—bright-haired Slavs and jerseyed seamen, and white-bosomed harlots weaving among them. Leaning on the counter I listened to the trumpet. An Indian in feathers and full war-paint was playing it—a Delaware by his looks, broad-chested and tanned, with the high-boned cheeks of a noble race.

"Whiskey, sir?"

I nodded and the bartender slid a bottle towards me. Filling a glass, I drank. Strange, I thought, that the stool where Katie had sat was empty, for it seemed only months since I had seen her there. A big Scotch-Irish was sitting beside me, telling a bawdy joke in the uproar of chatter and music. Half listening, I drank, watching the door. Soon, I thought, the door will come open and Katie will stand there.

"Looking for someone?"

I glanced at her. She was as dark as Rachel, and might have been beautiful under the heavy rouge and powder. She winked at the whiskey and I pushed the bottle towards her.

"Help yourself."

She did so, smiling secretly over the rim of her glass. "I bet it's a woman. Won't I do?"

I shook my head, aware, with sudden shock, that the whiskey was getting me. Uncaring, I drank again, closing my eyes to the pulsating waves of oblivion.

The girl said, "Do I know her, mister?"

"Katie."

She put the tip of one finger into her scarlet mouth and stared at the ceiling.

I said, "She used to live in Peebles. I've just been up there but they've pulled down the tenement."

"Katie Marsden?" There was a sudden purity in the girl's face, her eyes serene with human interest.

"Katie Virginia."

"Mister, she's black." The harlot's face returned.

I lifted my glass, sighing. "Coloured," I said, "American."

"My! The company you fellas keep. There's me as free as air

226

and you chasing niggers. You jist find out where that Katie lives."

I gave her ten dollars and she pushed it down the front of her dress, and said, "Wood Street—next door to the shoe warehouse. D'you always get what you want so easy?"

"Aye," I answered, "money buys anything."

"Is that so." She looked me up and down. "You've got another think coming, mister. It'll cost you fifty for a ride with Katie but strange to relate you can't buy me."

I gave her a grin, drained my glass, and went out into the night.

When I got to Wood Street I began to wonder who was doing better in Pittsburgh—Katie Virginia, or me.

"Why, Mr. O'Hara!" She caught my hand and drew me into the ornate little room, shut the door and leaned against it, eyes shining with unfeigned pride. "Well, I'm blessed! I never seen such a dandying in my whole life. Five years back you walk out of my attic in rags, now you come back here dressed in peacock feathers."

"That's Pittsburgh, Katie—you've not done so bad."

"Jeez, in that frock coat you look like five hundred thousand."

"Getting on that way," I said, sitting down.

"My, that's money, real money. I'm knocking up to five, but it ain't no comparison. More'n likely you've got dozens of fellas working for you but I've only one fella working for me. Coffee?"

"Just like last time," I said, and looked around the room. Carpeted, papered, it was adorned with artificial flowers in huge vases, the bulging, stuffed arm-chairs lending an appearance of inflated wealth. Katie was at the kerosene stove; she turned, looking as young and graceful as before.

"But it ain't like last time, is it?" she said. "Man, I'm kept—I'm respectable. The way I'm goin' I'll be in the *Godey's Lady Book* —there ain't no limit to the rise of my ambition."

"Who is he?" I asked.

"Would you have a wife in here bustin' my head? I ain't telling that, but I'll tell you something else . . ." She poured the coffee. "The days are past when I give out free beds to bums, for I've learned something." She poured out two cups and sat beside me. "After you left that night I lay there thinkin' till morning. 'Katie,'

227

I said, 'if you go on giving free coffee and benefit beds you ain't going any place, for this big city rips and tears.'" She smiled, eyes narrowed, the brown pupils strangely dilated. "You know something? You feed a bun to this pig of a city and you'll be losing your fingers." She sipped her coffee and I watched the gleam of her eyes. "So I just lay thinking after you'd gone, and next day I'm thinking the same. I reckoned that if you cage yourself with a city tiger you got to grow claws same as him, or you ain't surviving. You gotta grow claws real sharp, Jess O'Hara, or you'll finish up in shreds . . ." She sighed. "I was a mighty big fool those days. I brought in men and women off that waterfront, and I shared my all with those folks, like I shared with you." She smiled white at me. "I had 'em all colours, you know—black white and yellow— they was all the same to Katie, 'cause I'd been hungry, too, and I couldn't bear the sight of a dog sleepin' in the mud of the river, but then I got wise, for nobody shared with me. D'you know that, Jess O'Hara—no single man or woman gave me more than a thanks, and sometimes they ran through my wallet. One fella raked me out—left me flat—hadn't got a dime." Anger grew in her face. "I hadn't got a single dime between me an' salvation, the bastard—he had my bed, wallet, and me, all in one, an' he never even asked me, and when I'm doing the paying I like asking."

"White man?" I said, and she grinned, eyes dancing.

"He was a big buck Negro, an' blacker 'an me." She sighed deep. "Jess O'Hara—Mr. O'Hara if you're a customer—there ain't no difference in the colour o' the skin. The human race is a big rogue elephant, an' you don't stroke that fella, you don't feed him, you don't bed him, except he pays, real big." She stood up, smiling down, the curves of her fine body accentuated by her tight, silver dress. "And the moment Katie realised that she starts living. D'you know something? I even charge for social visits, for time means money. If they come to weep I charge just the same, for I've got no time for mother-confessing. Now, are you staying or going 'cause I've got a visitor."

"You've changed, Lord, how you've changed," I whispered.

She went to the door. "You're right, and the path I'm takin' don't lead to the river."

"Quicker, Katie, you can't live without friendship."

She bent to me. "Yes, man, I've changed to wisdom, and you've changed, too, but you don't realise it, so there's more God in me than you. You're wearing those fancy clothes an' you're hitting it high, O'Hara, but somebody somewhere is paying for you real big. I'm not a fool—I can read, an' I've read about you, so don't you set yourself high to me. If you're up and dandying then somebody's starving, somebody's weeping, and somebody's dying, and you don't care any more, do you?" She shook her head and opened the door. "You don't care no more than me, and that's how it should be when you're living in a jungle."

"I haven't finished my coffee," I said.

"Then you do so quick and get out of here. You stay and have me and pay, or get, like a customer, for you didn't want me when I was low. I starved for six months after I saw you. The Union was busting things up, and the men had no money. So I just laid in that attic and starved, O'Hara, while you had a job up at Girty's Run, and feeding. An' you didn't come near me. Man, I got so skinny I was scared to turn over lest I disjointed, and you never come—nobody come." Her face screwed up in sudden anger. "Of all the goddam, useless bums I've helped, not one come near me, man or woman, and I was sick and ill and crawling." She pointed to the window. "That city out there is ripping itself to pieces in the name of greed, an' I don't care—mister, I just don't care what happens to the whole damned human race, for there ain't no manhood, womanhood, nor God—there's only one fella, and that's this Katie."

I got up.

"Good-bye," I said.

"Good-bye, Mr. O'Hara. And when you leave here you start knowing yourself, like me. You got nails and teeth to tear with, and boy, you're using them, like me. But there's a difference between us. When you leave here you peep into a shanty. You'll see fighting and quarrelling, and hunger—that's all you're giving to your creature kind, like all these big city fellas. But there's a lot more honour in me, for I'm giving ease—fifty dollars of ease for this little body."

She shut the door.

"Good-bye," I said.

Marged, Will, Karen, and now Katie. I was suddenly, intensely lonely, and with it came defiance. Hands in my pockets, shoulders hunched, I wandered down to Bluff again, seeking to lose myself in darkness—anywhere, I thought, but the corn-sweet honeying words of Clare and the opulence of the Monongahela House. I grinned at my thoughts. Prostitution took many forms. Katie Virginia was conducting it in Wood Street for fifty dollars a time. I was doing it in an executive suite, for two million, with no other hardship than putting up with Clare Lubinski facing me at breakfast, and, unlike Katie, I was giving nothing.

The moon was shimmering on a flat, calm Monongahela. Squatting on a rock, I watched, and listened to the riots.

" 'Evening," said a voice.

I peered down to the edge of the river. A boy was sitting there, apparently oblivious of the pandemonium, which is the way of fishermen. I climbed over the rock and stood beside him.

"Caught anything?"

He was about ten years old, his clothes ragged, and there was a sort of pinched beauty in his face as his expressionless eyes drifted over me. Most urchins scuttled at my approach in the city, but not this one. Leaning over he pulled a flat stone nearer his, and jerked his thumb at it. Obediently, I sat.

"Caught nothing," he said. "Been here hours, they must be on strike."

So we sat in the holy bond of silence, the brotherhood of fishermen, and stared at the float. Suddenly, he turned. "You ever fished through ice?"

I knew the joy of being accepted as an equal.

"No, sir," I said.

He considered this. "You should try it some time." Frowning across the river, he added, "There's a pond behind the Passionist monastery with trout in as long as your arm, you know—you want to flog that pond one winter."

"Thanks for the tip," I said.

He wiped his nose with the back of his hand and sniffed, turning. Again those great eyes. "D'you know Jay Kenny?"

I shook my head.

Sighing in a reverent memory, he said, "Some man. He's a Wop, see, but he don't let folks know that—real name's Kenillo. He's a friend of mine. Gee! He can pull those big trout out with his fingers—you seen that done?"

"No." I was back in the reeds of Connemara again with a cold, wet captive wriggling in my fingers and the sound of Karen's voice whispering over the mere. I said, "What is your name?"

"Tom McGrath."

"That's Irish."

The eyes narrowed slightly. "American," he said.

"Where do you live?"

"Up in a tenement on the Point—with Ma Kelly. She calls herself Irish but she's really a Hunky. I got no parents, see, so she feeds me."

"Do you work?"

"Lubinski's—cotton mill. You got the time, mister?"

I closed my eyes. "Nearly midnight."

"Midnight!" He reeled in his line with frantic haste. "Gee, I gotta get back. I ain't been home yet, an' old Kelly's a bitch if I'm late—she fans my breeches with three feet o' rawhide." He rose, breaking down his rod. "You know Creeky Pipe?"

"No," I said.

"You know Lubinski's?"

I nodded.

"That's where Jay Kenny lives—up a pipe. He don't trust folks, so he lives alone. But any time you want to fish that monastery pond you just go down there and mention my name—he'll teach you. He's some fella, I'm telling you."

"Thanks," I said. "Do you really have to go now?"

"Gee, I'm late."

"Are you often here, then?"

His hands paused on the rod and he lifted his face. "Most nights. You come when you like, you're welcome." He scrambled up the rock and stood there, smiling down at me, clutching the rod against him.

"Gee," he said.

I stood there, watching till he was out of sight, running down the waterfront until he was lost in the darkness.

The riots were spreading. Distantly came the boom of a cannon. Flames were leaping in the city, and I heard the murmur of the mobs. Thinking of Marged, I walked slowly back to the Mononga-hela. Guards were on the door, the foyer was empty. Tiptoeing to my room to avoid meeting Clare, I locked the door and sat on the bed.

There, on my knee, I wrote a love-letter to Marged. Two months later she had not replied.

CHAPTER 21

And six months after that Marged became engaged to her young Welshman, a foreman at Girty's Run, and I no longer cared.

I heard of the event on the anniversary of the Maherne Reception. Clare was excited, I remember, running from room to room, begging me to hurry, while Hambro, with his ice-cold vision, was explaining to me the importance of Abe Maherne in slow, thoughtful phrases.

"A merger would be ideal," he said.

"Perhaps, but do you have to raise all this now?" I asked. "In half an hour I'm away to the Reception."

"I've been trying to raise the point for weeks, Mr. O'Hara, and now I insist that you listen. I happen to know that Maherne is very impressed with you and you don't meet people like him twice a week. He's extremely powerful. More—he's always ready to talk business, even on these occasions."

I smiled. "More than likely he'll throw me out. Remember the glass sale? Ever since he collected it the damned stuff has been sliding."

Hambro sighed. "But that is exactly the point, sir. I hear the city talk—the old man's intrigued. You beat him, and that's important."

I said, "Face it, Hambro—you beat him, not me."

He opened his hands. "We all have our roles in the world of finance, Mr. O'Hara. The power and glory comes to the figureheads. You have the looks and the personality, I have the brains. It is a combination that has succeeded down the pages of history."

"You're waxing poetic," I said, "come to the point."

"A merger with Maherne, that is the point. We have steel, he owns oil . . ."

"And you're after oil, is that it?"

Hambro sat down and polished his spectacles. "Twenty years from now oil will dominate industry—take my word for it."

"Twenty years from now you're likely to be dead, Hambro—you're over sixty now."

"Which shows the measure of my loyalty. I am thinking solely of Lubinski's."

"I bet," I said, and wandered about, glass in hand.

Hambro said, "He also has a daughter."

"Who—Maherne?"

"A very beautiful woman."

"What the devil has that to do with it?"

"On Maherne's death she inherits nearly twenty million." He adjusted his spectacles with meticulous care, and peered at me.

"Poor little devil," I said. "Does she know we're after her?"

"Frankly, I think she'd be delighted. She saw your photograph in the Gazette, apparently—she was most impressed. A talking point in the family, I suppose. Few people take half a million off Abe Maherne without some admiration being accorded."

"You're like another fella I know," I answered. "Is there anything that happens that isn't your business?" I went to the window, staring out at the street. "Anyway, I don't like Maherne's methods."

"Admirable," said Hambro, looking at his fingers. "He draws two million a year from his tenements alone."

"From people stupefied by misery." I turned. "And it's not progressive. Landlordism is the last refuge of the landed class—I learned that back home in Ireland."

"During the war he made ten million on boots alone."

"And most of those dropped off," I said.

"Precisely what they were intended to do," said Hambro.

I turned. "You know," I said, "I might be tainted, but you're a dirty little devil, Hambro."

He smiled. "Coming from you that's a compliment, Mr. O'Hara. But in this game there's no room for inhibitions. I'm sharply aware, you see, that this firm is going down. In the last two years we have merely maintained our profit, not increased it. There was a time, you see, when Miss Lubinski would do exactly as I advised her, but not now. She has control of the bulk of the capital. When it comes to parting with a dollar these days she's as tight as a kettle drum. A situation that could be reversed, of course, by one simple word."

"Marriage," I said.

He rose. "There's enough humanity left in me to revolt at the word, but you'll have to do something, sir. The young Welsh girl has found a husband, I understand. I would hate to see you left on the shelf."

I gave him a grin. "Marriage to Maherne's daughter, eh?"

"Irish extraction, with the body of a Helen. And charming, too—highly intelligent, they tell me. And Maherne, apparently, has a liking for the Irish." His eyes went dreamy. "God knows why."

The door opened. Clare's head appeared done up in curlers. "Get moving, honey—ready in an hour," she called, and shut the door.

Hambro said, "You'll have to do something soon, Mr. O'Hara, for you are in trouble."

I turned from the window.

"You're in trouble because you lack capital and I have lost control of it. Miss Lubinski will take my advice when it comes to a merger, but she will not part with her money, and you are going to need it, unless you are prepared to see Lubinski's die."

"Let it die," I said. "I'm knocking a hundred thousand."

"Two hundred thousand or Lubinski's dies—and your friends over in Girty's Run will die with it—not, of course, that you mind."

Slowly, I sat down at my desk. "What are you talking about?"

"Bessemer," he said. "Didn't I warn you?"

"What about Bessemer?"

Hambro sighed. "Yesterday, while you were out, your friend Mr. Rees called. He was very distressed. Apparently, the firm who is doing the conversion to steel has run out of some essential parts. These parts are not covered by the British patent. They are the invention of Captain Jones . . ."

"And he won't part with his patent?"

"Something like that. As you know, I understand little of these technical things."

"All right, all right—get back to Will Rees. What has he done about it?"

235

"He has blown the Betsy furnace and started the second phase of the conversion on Sally."

I got up. "The damned fool," I said. "Doesn't he know that we can't afford a total stoppage?"

"He had no option, sir. We have been using an integral part of a process for which we do not own the patent—to continue using it would be begging for legal action. It's quite simple, of course— Girty's Run is getting too important and the big boys are after it. The squeeze is on."

I walked about, my fist in my hand. "The damned swines," I breathed.

"It's a very wicked world," said Hambro, "but you can't say I didn't warn you. Now we have a perfectly good steel-works that won't produce anything."

I swung round, shouting, "Why doesn't Rees invoke the Penalty clause? Doesn't he read his contracts? Doesn't he know we can tan these contractors for a thousand dollars a day?"

"My dear chap," replied Hambro, "that wouldn't stand up in court. The essential parts required are quite outside the conditions of contract. Further, you can never enforce damages for delay unless you've got a bonus clause, and the contract lacks one. To say nothing about the possibility of the official arbitrator being bribed when we land in court." He sighed at the ceiling. "I know, Mr. O'Hara—I've bribed them—they are notoriously poor, bless them."

I paced the room. This was frightening. It meant a total discharge of labour, too, and the Union wouldn't like it. McNamara wouldn't like it. This, I thought, was the result of living hand to mouth in industry. A man like Maherne would invite someone to lunch, sign a cheque, and pour himself a whiskey. Hambro murmured:

"You mentioned just now that you had nearly a hundred thousand dollars, Mr. O'Hara. Not that this is enough to cover the contingency, but are you sure of the amount?"

I looked at him, and he said, "You must forgive me, you see, but I have taken the trouble to check your account—ways and means, Mr. O'Hara. Actually, your credit stands at about eighty thousand—you will need double that amount to save your friends, I fear."

"You little swine, Hambro."

"Not at all. Frankly, if I had my way I'd sell out steel and buy oil, but this is purely a personal preference."

I fought to keep calm, for Hambro was watching me. Sitting back in his chair now, he watched, his eyes narrowed behind the thick glasses. Something else was coming—another stage in the industrial blackmail.

"Go on," I said.

He shrugged. "You have made a big mistake, sir. You have allowed a personal emotion—the love of the Welsh girl—to enter into your calculations. This must never be so, for this sort of thing ends in financial suicide." He tapped his pocket. "In here I have a contract for the Jones' patent. Actually, I paid twenty thousand for it last week—wheels within wheels, you know. You can still save your friends from ending on the streets, but its purchase will cost you double the amount you possess. So don't you think a merger with Maherne is quite a possibility?"

"My God, Hambro," I whispered, "I give you credit."

"I try to do my best, sir—in the interest of the firm, you understand."

"It's filthy, and you know it."

And he said, looking at nothing, "We are all a little tainted, Mr. O'Hara. It is a jungle law, you know, a sort of tigerish race run by tigers—forgive the sentiment. You were pure when you entered it, now you are impure, as I. Negotiations such as this have one target —total victory. The suicide rate is high, as you know. And total victory in the world of finance means that the loser sells his wife's possessions when defeated—nothing less." He shrugged. "Naturally, as a man of the Church I denounce it—I am very religious, you know. But as a financial expert I applaud it, for it is most terribly exciting." He brought out the contract and tossed it before me. "You are very fortunate, really, for you have an option. This contract sits solidly on your affection for the Rees family. By your decision to agree to a merger with Maherne—and this, naturally, means working through his daughter—you can save your friends.

If you do not agree then the Bessemer conversion will never be completed, and this will break them."

I said, "And suppose I have means of raising the money for this patent?"

"Delighted," said Hambro. "Then I will be a hundred and sixty thousand dollars better off." He smiled. "And if you had access to an even larger amount I'd be pleased to act as your financial advisor."

I nodded, watching him. "And Clare Lubinski, whom you have sworn to serve?"

"The size of the amount might stretch my loyalty, Mr. O'Hara."

"You've got no honour, you've got no soul, Hambro."

"But I give to the poor, Mr. O'Hara—my passport to heaven. And I will not die rich, I assure you—bigger men than me are employing this method more and more in Pittsburgh."

"You really believe that, don't you?"

"With all my heart. Don't you?"

"Have a look at this," I said, and picked up his contract and tore it into pieces. He watched, smiling thinly, and whispered:

"Poor little Welsh girl, poor Will Rees."

"Now get out, you crooked little swine."

Hambro shrugged, went to the door, opened it, and even bowed. "It's a mutual admiration, sir. I'm glad we're still friends. Ah, Belle Maherne—such a beautiful name. Yes, it's a wise decision, and she'll make you a lovely wife. I'll have another copy of the contract made while you're at the Reception."

"Get out," I whispered.

In order to arrive at Maherne's beautiful house on Fifth Avenue one had to possess certain qualifications, for even the graves up there were laid out in income groups; the trees, according to Marged, being labelled *Pedigree Dogs Only*. But to be invited to one of the famous Receptions you had to be a millionaire, married to one, or even sleeping with one, said Marged once—an eminence I couldn't claim since Clare and I had separate rooms. Now, sitting in plump sedateness beside me in the carriage, she said:

"Oh, but little Abe ain't landed, honey, oh, dear no. He's self-

238

made. D'you know he's got interests in cotton and oil, railroads and glass and a dozen other things—if that little monkey touched steel it'd turn to gold."

The carriage swayed on, the horses' hooves clattering in metallic rhythm on the dusty road. Bored, I lay back on the cushions. Clare was wasting her breath, for I had traced the graph of Maherne's meteoric rise to power and envied him the wizardry. Clare said, "And now, I hear, he's buying up newspapers."

I murmured reply. This was a newspaper that had recently investigated him—for his methods, like most of America's men of big business, did not stand scrutiny. Everything in his path he destroyed. He evaded tax by personal perjury; called in the State militia to suppress his factory riots, an effective method for a man who had his hand on governors. He had a mansion in Cincinnati and another in Baltimore. Romantically, and to please his countless concubines, he also had a castle in Spain. An ardent believer in the inviolability of property under rent, he was ruthless, a rogue, and knew it.

Through the window of the brougham I watched the night-shift crowds thronging along the streets in dejection, the men in tattered apathy, the women, shawled and pale, their faces slanted against the driving rain. Children went by in clusters for the mills, their movements slow, their eyes expressionless, but none brought me pity, for I saw no individual face, I remember. Compassion, I believe, has no undying limit. It is as expendable as a thread that weaves a garment. For in the maelstrom of the fight for personal gain the heart pulsates at a different speed. Even the vision is distorted by the shrinking retina in the eye of conscience, pity is bleached under the glitter of wealth. So I watched them pass, remembering Katie. She was right, I thought. Scruples had no place in this world of Maherne and Hambro, McNamara and Lubinski. It was a fight to the death where the strongest survived and the weakest wept.

"You still breathing, honey?"

Clare now, poking me secretly, giggling. I instantly despised her as the one obstruction standing between me and success, and her nearness, her touch brought revulsion. She said:

239

"You'll wake up when you meet young Belle Maherne." There was a hint of bitterness in her words. I replied absently:

"I didn't know he had a daughter."

"Honey, he's got six, but only one official—that's Belle. They say he tried and tried for a son, but his poor wife fetched out Belle, and died on him. When Abe passes on Belle collects his millions." She poked me again. "Don't that make your hair curl?"

I did not reply. The gap that had been growing between us was too wide to cross; the knowledge that there could be nothing between us save friendship was bringing her to petulance and cynicism. Only her money could save the works at Girty's Run, and she would not part with it. A vision of Marged rose before me then with astonishing clarity, and I closed my eyes. If Clare would not help I would go elsewhere.

In the gigantic ball-room the tables were laden with flowers and hundreds of guests were chattering in groups under the brilliant light of chandeliers. We entered and I was staggered by the opulence. For here was the wealth of a thriving city, the sylvan grace of its daughters, the dowagers of a past generation with their flattering escorts.

"Here he comes," whispered Clare, and I straightened as Abe Maherne came towards us. Bald-headed, bent, rather like a hairless spider he threaded a path through the guests with Belle, his daughter, on his arm, and I took a deep breath. For this was Karen's loveliness, in blonde. Full six inches taller than her father she walked in elegance, flashing with jewels, her long, white gown skin-tight over her handsome body. Clare introduced us in halting phrases, and I took Belle's hand, seeing a hint of mockery in her eyes as she glanced at Clare.

"Good evening, Mr. O'Hara."

Maherne put his arm around Clare's shoulders, eyeing me. "Well, I'll give you this—you sure know how to pick 'em." He raised his voice above the orchestra. "And it ain't all personality, is it, O'Hara?" Playfully, he put a fist in my ribs. "D'you know somethin', Belle? I paid this young fella a cool half million for his damned Lubinski glass and the stuff's still sliding. Every time I come to this damned city I've got shareholders breathing down my neck."

"One up to the O'Haras," said Belle, smiling.

"Two up to my Mr. Hambro, actually, honey," said Clare.

"Hambro or O'Hara, I'm skinning somebody alive," said Maherne. "When I find a man who can put one over on me I reckon to incorporate him." He took my hand. "How's cotton, young fella?"

"Slow," I said, and gave him a grin to test his nerve. "There's been too much about it in the papers lately."

"Jess!" whispered Clare.

"Let him be." Maherne shouted with laughter. "I like a young stripling to speak his mind. But did you see my reply, O'Hara?"

"I read it in the newspaper—the one you bought up, remember?" This was neat. He had discharged its editor and dismantled its machines.

"But I told 'em—that's the point, O'Hara—I told 'em!"

"Please," whispered Belle.

He waved her down. "Aw, shucks! You make me weep. Didn't I tell 'em, O'Hara? Don't you reckon ten dollars a week is a living wage, son?"

"I've managed on less."

"And so have I. I was scratching a beggar's backside when I first hit America, so I know what it costs to live. They were giving me all that stuff about killing two kids in ten—what the hell! Ain't I keeping the other eight alive?"

Belle said, "Daddy, please, do you have to talk business?"

"Honey, I don't have to, but I am." He jerked his thumb at her. "Would she be having such a damned good time if I wasn't in business? You take a jump, girl—O'Hara's got the size of it." He levelled a finger and peered up at me. "And I'm telling you this free, son—you're young—you ain't even started to live. You give them working-class slobs a single inch and the whole damned mob'll come snarling all over you." He thumped his hand. "Man, they need watching. They got the Sons of Vulcan and the Knights of Labour, and . . ."

"Hey, Abe!" cried Clare, "where's your manners? I'm hungry."

He stopped, grinning amiably. "D'you hear that? All they think of is stomachs and dresses." Turning, he slapped Clare on the rump. "Away with ye then and fill the thing, for one the size of yours needs comfortin'. Hey, waiter! See to this lady."

I took Clare's arm, smiling down at him. "There was Irish in that, sir."

He mimicked my accent. "Could I be anything else but Irish with a beauty like this on me arm, O'Hara? And well may you stare at it. Me mother came from Iowa and me pa from Derry . . ."

I was aware only of Belle's eyes, one brow slightly raised as if in excuse for his patent vulgarity. I smiled.

"Oh, come," whispered Clare, and tugged at my arm.

"We'll be seeing you later," said Belle.

Clare was into the oysters by midnight, sliding them in with greedy relish. I joined her at the table, being unable to dance.

"Ain't you eating, honey?" she shouted.

"I'm not hungry."

She pushed people aside and joined me. "Well, what do you think of Belle?"

"As you said, she's very beautiful."

She peered, stooping. "Man, you're real affected—but don't get too affected—she's Abe's, and he don't like folks nibbling at his property deals. Have a cigar."

I took it absently, lit it, and stood watching the guests, aware immediately of an acrid tang in the smoke of it. I found it was wrapped up in a hundred-dollar bill. Fascinated, I watched the bill scorch, first with an inborn disgust, then with a sudden, authentic thrill. Clare shouted beside me:

"If you live to be ninety you'll never smoke a hundred dollars again—ain't that little Abe just wonderful?" She swung round. "Why, Mr. Vaynor!"

Instantly, I turned. Vaynor was standing there with his usual limp humility, as a child waiting to be thrashed. Instantly, I turned my back upon him.

"Darling, what's wrong?"

"Who invited him?"

"Why, Abe, of course. Ain't you pleased to see him?"

"When I accept an invitation I don't expect to mix with my employees."

The guests surged about us, thronging in for the dancing. Clare said, "But Mr. Vaynor isn't an ordinary employee, Jess—he comes from the best family stock in Pennsylvania."

"And I pay his wages. Who invited him?"

"Darlin'," said Clare earnestly, "I just don't care, for this ain't my party."

"May I dance with Miss Lubinski, sir?" asked Vaynor.

"Honey," said Clare, "you dance with whom you like," and took his arm. "Mr. O'Hara ain't my keeper, you know."

I walked away. It was hot in the room, and I was sweating. From the hall I watched Clare in Vaynor's arms. She was a little drunk, I noticed, her hair untidy. Standing alone I wondered if, by starving her of love, I had forced her into his arms. At least she was happy, I reflected, living for a moment under the spell of his fine manners, paying as usual. It was cool in the hall. Holding the charred hundred-dollar bill in my hand, I stared at it. Two sessions with Katie, I thought. Two months of food for a family of ten. It was a damnable waste. I looked round the hall, seeing the deep-piled Oriental carpets, the Renaissance chair, and the tapestries of exotic colours. Corot and Meissonier, in gilded frames, competed for pride of place on the ornate walls. It was a scene of staggering wealth, a gormandizing comparable with a Roman spectacle for gluttony and grandeur, and I envied Maherne his gigantic success. Hambro was right, I thought. That I should have to beg to Clare for capital seemed suddenly degrading, when the key to success lay in Belle Maherne. I looked at the hundred-dollar bill. Less than half was burned, it was still legal tender. I tore the remainder slowly into pieces, dropped them, and ground them into the carpet. Entering the ball-room slowly I took a side aisle that was free of dancers, saw Belle in the grip of a bearded dwarf, and gave a smile of understanding. She smiled back, shrugging her helplessness. Hands in pockets, with feigned loneliness, I wandered into the terraced garden.

It was a night of full moon and Pittsburgh was beautiful under the stars. Leaning on a balcony overlooking fountains I watched the red glow of a distant furnace—probably the Twenty-ninth Street mill making Carnegie steel. The music ended behind me, and I waited, tensed, aware, as always, that I possessed no great attraction for women.

"You look lonely, Mr. O'Hara."

Even her voice was beautiful. Turning, I saw Belle standing against the light of the windows, almost wraith-like in her white gown, as if waiting to fade at the first human touch.

"I'm getting some air, Miss Maherne."

She smiled, leaning on the balcony beside me. "Miss Lubinski seems to be enjoying herself, but aren't you neglecting her?"

"Miss Lubinski has suitors," I said. "I'm part of her executive. They can also dance, which is more than I can."

"Don't the Irish dance? I thought it was a national habit."

"Not quadrilles and minuets. Jigs and reels and a raising of the blood." I paused. "You're missing some pretty good escorts yourself, come to that."

"Old men or boys, Mr. O'Hara." She took a deep breath and looked at the sky. "But mostly boys. You know, life's queer. When a woman's middle-aged she's attracted by youth, when she's young she seeks maturity. I suppose they mean well, these young bucks, but how they bore me."

"That's the privilege of youth, Belle. It has nothing to do with maturity. Can't you snap your fingers and take who you like?"

"Belle," she repeated, head on one side. "The way you say it sounds very pretty."

"Must be the lilt. You're a bit Irish, too, I hear. We like the things that are ours, you know. Have you never been to Ireland?"

She did not reply but wandered down the steps leading to the garden, and I followed her with a backward glance. Now, in an arbour of roses she stopped, picked a rose, and held it against her.

"You are no more beautiful," I said, and got a winsome, fleeting smile. She wandered on. The music behind us faded to a whisper. Pausing, she looked towards Coal Hill with its sparkling lights.

"Do you like Pittsburgh, Mr. O'Hara?"

"Beautiful city."

"They tell me you've done well here."

"Not so well as your father—he'll take some catching."

She smiled wistfully. "He's a strange man—a great admirer of yours, you know. The people who occasionally beat him are his firmest friends, only the weak are his enemies."

"That's a business approach. But you must be very proud of him."

She looked hard at me. "Sick, Mr. O'Hara, sick to death of him."

"You can't mean that."

"Don't I? You try living with him." She sighed. "Oh, people get things so wrong. It's not all fun and games being the daughter of Abe Maherne. It's . . . a surfeit of wealth, for one thing, and such a damned disgrace . . ."

"Disgrace?"

She shrugged her emptiness. "Well, I suppose many women would give their souls for a tenth of what I have, but they can have it. Depends on the woman, I suppose, and the measure of hatred she can stand." She sat on a garden seat and I sat beside her. Softly, she added, "It's completely artificial, you know, and we're so utterly friendless. You can't have love in this world if you put people to death for money."

I said, "I know somebody else like you."

She smiled. "The way you say it . . . it must be a woman."

I nodded. "But she had nothing when she aired that view."

"And I have my cake and want to eat it?"

"Something like that."

She smiled, turning to me. "At least you're honest."

"Not very. If you go deeper you'll find I'm just like your father."

"Was she pretty?" she asked.

"Welsh." A wind moved the roses and the night was scented. "I suppose you couldn't call her beautiful."

"But you loved her?"

"If you want the truth of it, I still do. Why didn't I marry her? Don't ask me—I had the chance. Life has a habit of parting people."

245

"I'm so sorry, Jess."

It was the way she said my name that turned me to her. There was a sweetness and simplicity in her that I had not expected. She said, smiling:

"Now, if you were my father you'd incorporate her. I don't know what stopped you having her but nothing ever stops him."

"She's engaged now."

"He must be an Eastern potentate, the way you speak of her."

"An iron-works foreman over at Girty's Run—twenty dollars a week."

She rose. "It sounds to me she's well worth having."

"And you? Don't tell me you're on the shelf."

She smiled down at me. "Ah, no," she answered softly, "don't examine me. I don't part so easily with secrets."

"Never been in love?"

"At least ten times, but they're never in love with me. It's all part of the purgatory—being Belle Mahcrnc. Oh, yes, they come in scores, but they haven't got a heart between them. Surprised?"

"Not really, I've met 'em."

She stood back, examining me with sustained interest. "But you are not deceiving. Self-made? Looks probable." She narrowed her eyes, and the pupils were pin-points of light in the redness of the furnace-glow, the tip of her tongue touching her teeth, impish. I straightened.

"Go on, say it."

"But I'm bound to. Anybody's bound to if she's interested. Clare?"

I said, "We share the same table, that's as far as it goes."

"I believe you. Oh, dear—poor Clare. But don't look so glum— she doesn't miss much, you know. It's one thing to be fat but another to be starving, and there's always young Vaynor, though he mightn't last a week." She glanced over her shoulder. "Shouldn't we go back now?"

"If you promise to see me again."

"Oh, dear, that's very tricky. You see, Daddy's going off to Baltimore tomorrow for a week. The most fantastic property deals are involved, syndicate swallowing syndicate and Dad swallowing the lot. . . ." She lowered her voice, looking down. "Actually she's Eurasian, two years younger than me. Horrible, isn't it."

"Perhaps, when it's your father."

She raised her face. "Strange. You understand, don't you? Other people think it's so damned clever of him when I think it's disgusting."

I said, "I'd like to meet you, Belle. When?"

She pouted prettily. "There won't be an opportunity, I'm afraid, least of all next Tuesday, the day of the Fair. Daddy will be in Baltimore and not a servant in the house." She fluttered an eye.

"Next Tuesday, then?"

"Ah, Jess O'Hara!" Raked from the secrets and beauty, I swung to meet Maherne. He came down the terrace steps three at a time. "So that's where you both are!" He smiled expansively. "The hostess and guest of honour playing ducks and drakes with the time-table. Most people are leaving." He screwed up an eye. "Can you spare me a precious moment, O'Hara, or are your brains with women?"

I hardly heard him, for the spell was not yet broken. Belle was running against light, taking her enchantment. Maherne grunted, threw up his coat-tails, and sat down heavily. He said, "You're a cheeky young devil, you know. You sell me sliding stock, laugh in my face at my own reception, and pinch my daughter. What makes you think you're so damned good?"

"Get to the point," I answered.

"Hambro suggests a merger. He wrote me this morning."

I stared down at him. "Hambro has no authority . . ."

"Aw, come off your high horse, O'Hara. You're the best thing that's struck the city since Frick, and you know it. And with Hambro behind you you'll be rocking a few of 'em—the man's a genius. How much can you raise?"

I smiled at him. "Too much for you, Maherne."

"I don't believe it."

"Take it or leave it. I was about to say that Hambro has no business suggesting anything—I'm running Lubinski's, not him."

I could scarcely see him, for the moon was fading, but I knew he was watching me. He said softly, "Public stock or private backing?"

247

"Both."

"That's knocking ten million, then."

"More," I said.

He laughed softly. "Brother, you produce it, I'll match it. I've got a damned good mind to call your bluff."

"Sorry, Maherne, you're not big enough."

"Who is?"

"I won't name him. There's a world of difference between us, Maherne. But any man who can get a yield of six thousand tons a month talks my ambitions."

"The Edgar Thomson works, eh?"

I smiled. "The same old combination, Frick and Carnegie. You stick to real estate and rents, sir, I'm aiming higher." I looked around. "Coming back?"

He stood up. "Not yet, son. Steel or real estate, I go for anything. If you can get that kind of backing I want to be in it. What's your idea?"

"Look, you wouldn't be interested."

"If I'm not, I'll tell you." He was aggressive now, his chin thrust out.

I sighed. "Oil-fired furnaces."

He peered at me, coming closer. "Man, you're addled—you're years too early."

"I'm years too late," I said.

He rubbed his face, deep in thought. "That'd knock out coke. I suppose you realise I'm collecting oil?"

"You'd come too high, sir—I know others. I'm not bothered, the patent's covered. But that's not the only thing. There's a new process—Welsh invention—we're trying it out at Girty's Run. By using the useless phosphoric ore as a lining we're getting a higher-grade steel. With the railroads coming on there should be millions in it."

He said, "I don't trust you, O'Hara. First you reject an offer, now you're going courting."

"Just whetting your appetite, Maherne—you won't be in it. And when you reply you can tell that to Hambro. Pick your men better, sir, you'll likely go wrong. Hambro's all right, but he's got his limitations, like all of us." I looked at him.

He said, "How much?"

"Five hundred thousand."

He actually spat. "I thought you were talking money!"

"For a ten per cent holding."

"Double it—twenty for a million."

"Fifteen for a million," I said.

"Split, O'Hara. Seventeen and a half."

"And a merger," I said, "with access to further capital."

"You damned loon!" He shouted now. "When I mentioned merger just now you hit it in me teeth!"

"Daddy!" called Belle from the balcony, "people are going."

Maherne was grinning. "I could do with you, O'Hara, you're a cool bit of Irish—will Clare approve of it?"

"Who's Clare?" I walked away, and he followed. "While I think of it—do you mind me visiting Belle while you're in Baltimore?"

"Why, sure—she can cool 'em—real quick, I'm telling ye."

I stopped him. "And a controlling interest, Maherne. I'm not taking you in for nothing."

He chewed on his cigar. "I'll consider it. I'm breaking new ground, you know—not in my line. Get out a contract—see what it looks like on paper." He gripped my arm. "You fiddled me once, O'Hara—do it twice and I'll break you, remember it."

"See you next week," I answered, "you'll feel better after Baltimore."

CHAPTER 22

Clare was sleeping it off.

It was nearly midday when I went to the room. She was lying half-dressed on the bed in the vulgar disarray of the roll-into-bed drunk; stockings draped the coverlet, stays and petticoats littered the carpet, shoes had been kicked off. On a table by the bed stood an empty whiskey decanter and two glasses. Going to my office I rang for Hambro and Vaynor came in.

Had he stood there in pyjamas with Clare in his arms he could not have looked more guilty, and I suppressed a smile.

"Sit down," I said, and Vaynor sat.

He sat in the low arm-chair beside me, his head on a level with my elbow. I had learned this psychology from Lubinski, whose office chair was set on a dais, while the arm-chair for the interviewed had its legs sawn off. As the hair of a serf was worn bobbed on the order of the baron, so Vaynor sat on the floor, so to speak, and it induced in him an abject servility. Now he sweated it out while I went on writing.

"You like this job, Vaynor?" I asked at length.

"Charmed, sir, charmed," said he.

"And you wish to keep it?"

"Most decidedly, sir—dreadfully cut up at the thought of losing it, sir."

"I'd be equally disturbed at the thought of losing you, Vaynor."

He turned an appealing face to mine, and I went on writing. His lank humility, excessive education, reddish hair and pimples induced in me a horror, and an intense desire to humiliate further. Also, the fact that Clare apparently found him attractive brought a strange and moving jealousy. I said:

"You have a mother and sister to support, I understand."

"Yes, sir."

"You are their sole means of livelihood?"

"Yes, sir."

I turned in my seat, facing him, "And yet you would endanger that livelihood by carrying on a disgusting intimacy with Miss Lubinski?"

His eyes widened. "Heaven forbid, sir!"

"Forbid what, Vaynor?"

The colour rushed from his face. Sweat sprang to his forehead and he closed his eyes and wiped it into his hair. "I have done nothing of the sort, sir, upon my oath . . ."

"Don't lie."

He screwed at his hands and lowered his head. "How . . . how did you know, Mr. O'Hara?"

"I didn't, Vaynor—you've just told me."

"Oh, God," he said, staring at nothing.

I got up. "Which goes to prove that you lack two essential qualities necessary to a successful executive—morality, control under fire . . . to say nothing of honour." I turned back to my desk. "With these shortcomings I fear I cannot continue to employ you."

"Mr. O'Hara!" He rose slowly, hands clenched before him.

"Draw your wages from the cashier and get out," I said, and went on writing.

But he did not go. Staring, trembling, he hovered about me as some wilful ghost, incoherent sounds coming from his throat.

"Get out," I said, "and while you're about it send in Hambro."

"Sir, I beg you . . ."

I rose, shouting. "Get out!"

As a man broken on the wheel, he went slowly to the door and opened it.

"Come back and sit down," I said.

He obeyed in a trance, and I despised him. Still writing, I added, "At least you've admitted it, which is more than I expected, though I expected more from one of the best families in the State. There's really nothing much in this business of breeding, is there, Vaynor?"

He looked at me.

"Is there, Vaynor?"

"No, sir."

"That's much better, let's dispel one myth at least. Are you in love with Miss Lubinski?"

He shook his head at the floor.

"What was it, then—a sort of sacrifice on the altar of womanhood?"

He did not reply. "Answer me," I said. "Even you'll admit it's a sacrifice."

"Just . . . just sorry for her, sir."

"Did your pity extend to personal enjoyment?"

This raised his head, his eyes were suddenly unflinching. "Not your kind of enjoyment, Mr. O'Hara."

"Well done. I deserved that. You've got better manners than I gave you credit for. But you're very poor, Vaynor. People in a workhouse can't afford sweets, you know, so don't be too glib with that tongue. How much do I pay you?"

"Twenty-eight dollars a week."

"Do you spend all of that?"

"I send home twenty to my mother and sister."

"So you can't afford the frills of life."

"Neither can they."

"Keep to the point, I am not discussing your relatives. But you occasionally receive money from Miss Lubinski, don't you?"

"Not for what you think, Mr. O'Hara."

"I didn't suggest it—she helps you, doesn't she?"

"Miss Lubinski is very generous."

"Are you in love with her?"

"No, sir." He added, "You've already asked me that, sir."

"Would you be prepared to marry her, Vaynor?"

He closed his eyes and looked away.

"Can't you answer that?"

"I'd rather not discuss Miss Lubinski. Anyway, the choice is hers, not mine."

"You'd be surprised, Vaynor." I got up and walked around the room. The activity on the Monongahela was incredible—a forest of masts shining as needles in brilliant sunlight. Vaynor was watching me, I sensed it, so I took my time.

I said, "Your prospects would be improved considerably if you did marry her, you know. The combination of wealth and breeding can produce the most staggering results. One of the tragedies of this generation is the sharp division between industrialism and gentility, and this is sad. After all, people are people."

He did not reply.

"Your mother and sister, for instance, their lot would improve."

"Please do not discuss them, sir."

"To say nothing of Miss Lubinski's. If you possess the least compassion, Vaynor, you must know that she is extremely lonely."

He got up, trembling. "May . . . may I have a whiskey, sir?"

"Help yourself."

He poured from the decanter, slanted the whiskey in the glass, staring down, and said, "Then I'll go, sir . . ."

"Oh, no you don't—not till you hear me out."

"Before you buy me as you buy everything else, Mr. O'Hara."

I sat down on a corner of the desk. "Three hundred a week."

His eyes widened with incredulity and he gulped the whiskey.

"Nice round figure, isn't it, Vaynor."

"Three hundred . . . What for?"

"Ten times your wages—for the next six months. All expenses paid, too, if you like, then a ten-thousand-dollar settlement on the day of the wedding."

"My God," he whispered, and sat down slowly.

"After all," I added, "it's the least you can do, considering you've betrayed her."

"But she might not . . . I mean . . ."

"She will, never fear. I know Clare."

He drained his glass, staring at me, then rose and wandered the room.

"What do you get out of this, Mr. O'Hara?"

I shrugged, smiling. "Peace of mind."

For the first time his face showed hostility. "Oh, no, I'll never believe that, Mr. O'Hara—there's bound to be a dollar mixed up somewhere in this business." He slapped down the glass. "Supposing I refuse?"

"But you won't, Vaynor, will you?"

"Supposing," he whispered.

I laughed. "Look, don't play games for you haven't the least intention of refusing, have you? Up to now you've played it safe because I was around, but now the coast is clear. Woo and wed the lady, Vaynor, you've got nothing at all to lose."

"My decency."

"That's already gone, and so has Clare's."

He said, going to the window, "I happen to care for her, but you wouldn't understand that. A tumble on a bed is one thing, marriage is another. Perhaps I couldn't stick her. The very thought of it would make my father sick." He turned. "He may be dead, O'Hara, but to me he's still alive. He never did a dirty thing in his life but die for this damned country. And what for?" His voice rose. "For God's sake, what for?"

"I'm sorry about your father," I said softly.

"Don't you mention his name, O'Hara, for you're not worthy to—neither am I, for giving this filthy business a thought."

I sighed. "It's up to you. I'll give you till tomorrow midday—think it over."

"I've thought it over—I'll do it, if she'll have me."

"Well done."

"For two hundred on account—now."

I counted the notes and put them on the table. Snatching them up he stuffed them into his pocket. "And you know why I'm doing it, don't you?"

"Not my business, Vaynor. We all do things for one reason or another." I opened the door. "Now tell Hambro I'd like to speak to him."

Hambro came in, smiling suavely. "Congratulations, sir, I hear you made it."

I glanced up from the desk. "How the devil did you know that?"

"This letter from Maherne—came by special messenger. Apparently the old man's on his way to Baltimore."

I took the letter and read it, smiling.

"He's breaking his neck—what did you offer him?" he asked.

"A merger with Maherne Enterprises for us. In return he gets seventeen and a half per cent for a deposit of a million—and we have access to more capital. Hook, line, and sinker, Hambro—he went mad for it. He takes care of his own companies and we run the subsidiary."

"What are we producing?"

"The oil-fired furnace—Rees's prototype."

Hambro said, "But the thing isn't working yet—don't you know that?" He flung out his hands. "It'll be over twenty years before the idea's marketable."

"But Maherne doesn't know that—he's completely untechnical. We can always fall back on the Gilchrist Thomas invention."

"But Carnegie holds the patent."

"Let him sue—if he ever discovers it."

"If he ever discovers it he'll sue right enough—he paid over a quarter of a million to that young genius."

"When you're riding it high you take a chance—the big thing is the merger. We'll have money to play with. Now how much will this essential part of the Bessemer cost me?"

"What I paid for it, sir—twenty thousand dollars."

I took the contract from him, signed it, and wrote him a cheque. "I give you full marks, Hambro. In this game, apparently, one strangles one's sister."

"And mother," said Hambro, "but you're getting the hang of it." He sat down, made a cage of his fingers, and peered over the top of them. "Now what about Clare?"

"What about her?"

"Presumably you won't be needing her now."

"Not now, Hambro—just her capital."

"She's likely to become discontented, you know. After all, she's extremely fond of you to say the least of it . . ."

"But she's guided by you—she's agreed to the merger, hasn't she."

"Yes, but . . ."

"Right, forget her—leave Clare to me. Get out the merger contract as soon as you can—I want it ready for Maherne when he returns from Baltimore—scour the city for capital. I promised him two million."

255

"Two million! Don't be a fool, sir—I can't get backing worth that kind of money."

I smiled. "Of course not, but I had to promise something. You don't beg from the likes of Maherne, Hambro—you impress him."

"And if I can't get anywhere near the figure?"

I went to the door. "You'll probably not raise one million, Hambro, but I have a way of improving it a bit. He'll sign us in, don't worry."

Hambro was shaken, and the sight pleased me. For the first time since I had joined Lubinski's his equanimity vanished. His hands were trembling. He said, gripping my desk, "And if he doesn't? We're likely to end in the State penitentiary—do you realise that? It's nothing else but stock-pushing."

"A ride on a tiger, Hambro—you taught me, remember. Where's your nerve, man? The stakes have no limits when you dice with the devil. Come on, cheer up—ten to one in hundreds I marry Belle Maherne."

Hambro straightened, and smiled. "That, of course, is very different."

I dined alone in the Monongahela House, accepting the bowing subservience of the waiters as my due. Mellon, the banker, sitting nearby, seemed to receive a lesser service, which seemed fair. At the table once occupied by President Lincoln I drank champagne, thinking of Will Rees and Girty's Run. Unaccountably I knew a sense of fulfilment at the touch of Hambro's contract in my pocket.

Marged, at least, was saved.

Pittsburgh was still bright with sunlight as I went out into the street.

CHAPTER 23

I sent a card to the Maherne residence on the following Tuesday morning and received a prompt reply. Belle would receive me for dinner at eight o'clock, and I remembered with sudden joy that this was Fair day. A long cry, I thought, as I set out from the Monongahela House, from that sunlit day when I had dropped Killer Basardo. Clare was nowhere to be found in the hotel, neither was Vaynor, an excellent sign, so I walked down Duquesne in the sunshine with a clear mind that afternoon.

"Jess!"

A group of tattered men were standing outside a factory and one hobbled towards me on sticks. His clothes were in rags, his legs grotesquely twisted. I had often wondered what had happened to Patrick Magee after I had taken his job as bouncer in Jubec's. Now he was beside me, his thin hands shaking with excitement, his eyes bright in his cavernous face.

"Jess O'Hara—don't you know me? Pat Magee!"

I closed my eyes. One of the factory maimed, this, one of the countless tragedies of Pittsburgh; mutilated for profit, now left to beg. He stepped away, looking me up and down with pride. "Ach, you're a fine fella indeed, O'Hara. I've been readin' about ye in the Gazette. Sure, it takes the true-blood Irish to show them the way in this fine city. How are ye?"

"Hallo, Pat," I said.

He screwed up his face. "Hallo, Pat, is it? Is that all you've got to say to me? There's me been boastin' to me friends about the great man Jess O'Hara, and you stand there scarcely knowin' me."

"Do you think I could forget?"

"Och, I'll never forget the right you served me, but you'd kill me if you landed on me now, indeed to God, you would. D'you see these two legs of mine?"

"Where did you catch it?"

"At Edgar Thomson's—the place is a bloody abattoir—I was feeding into the machines and got mixed up with the rollers—that was years back."

"I'm sorry, I didn't know," I said.

"An' I wasn't telling ye, O'Hara, for I'm not after charity." He grinned, the skin stretching tight over his pin-bone cheeks. "But it was only the other day I was talking of ye, Jess—it was your brothers Mike and Hosea working over in Homestead."

"They're together—in Homestead?"

"Aye, it's them getting a belly-ful of this Carnegie fella instead of me, and they're welcome, for the devil pays not a penny-piece pension for the men he mutilates."

"Are . . . are they well?" Magee's tattered friends were crowding about me and I was desperately anxious to be away, but I had to have news of Hosea and Michael.

"They're well enough, though they've no great guns blazin' for you, if you know what I mean. There's yer big brother Hosea goin' great hoots for the championship till he meets up with the great James J. Corbett—didn't you hear?"

I shook my head.

"And Hosea, the fool, gets cut to pieces. I saw the fight meself, God forgive me. The fella who matched your great lumberin' oaf with an artist like Corbett will be standing shiverin' before the hand of St. Peter, and me bearing witness. Ach, it was terrible, terrible."

"Was Ho hurt?" I whispered.

"Hurt? The man was crucified. There was Corbett himself beggin' them to stop it and your brother swinging and bellowing like a baited bear. Didn't you hear of this? The poor devil's cuttin' paper dolls, an' there's a great thickness in the head with him, but there's no blame to Corbett, the man's a gentleman fighter if ever there was one."

"Oh, God," I whispered. "Where are they now, do you say?"

"In a shanty in Homestead, the pair of 'em. There's Mike working in the steel-yard and Hosea does the cookin', he's fit for nothin' else. And your fine sister Karen visits them when she's in the city but not a penny piece they'll take from her, the thick heathen."

The men pressed closer about me, their thin faces and bright eyes peering.

"I'll . . . I'll go to them," I said softly.

"If you're a wise man you'll do no such thing, O'Hara. They've little left to 'em save pride, and they're keeping that. But have you a mother back in Connemara?"

I nodded.

"Then you owe it to her fair name to raise your big brother, Jess. For while you're dandying yerself up with the finest in Pittsburgh you're leaving him to the mercy of Andrew Carnegie, and see what happened to me." He looked into the sun. "Hasn't Hosea got a woman somewhere or other?"

"Rachel, his wife."

"He's callin' and callin' for her. His eyes are gone and he's blind and stumbling. Couldn't you link him with his woman and send him back home?"

"Blind?" I stared at him.

"These last ten months or more, didn't you know?"

Blind.

I pushed past him, filled with a sudden and freezing anger. Hosea blind, and I did not know.

"Haven't you a buck for me, Jess?" Magee again, tugging at my sleeve, but I shook him off. Somehow I had to find Rachel.

"For the sake of the old days, Jess O'Hara?"

Automatically, I pulled out my wallet and thrust money into his hands.

"The saints be praised for ye!" he cried. " 'Tis nigh fifty dollars. D'you see this, fellas? Fifty dollars!"

Governments, financial houses were all the same, I thought bitterly. In one hand they wave the banners of progress, in the other a fist for their dismembered patriots. I walked on in sunshine, seeing the strand of home again, hearing Hosea's voice piercing the thunder of the surf. I reached the Fairground without really knowing it.

"Hi!"

On the edge of the Fair day crowd, in the blast of its trombones

259

and its blaze of colour, I came face to face with Tommy McGrath.

"Hi," I replied, mimicking, for his eyes were narrowed with suppressed excitement. In stammering delight, he said:

"Gee! You seen the elephants, mister?"

"In this crowd? I can't get near enough."

"Jay Kenny did—he had a ride on one—you remember Jay Kenny, my pal?"

I scratched my chin, thinking, and he said, almost violently, "You gotta remember him—he's the one who's takin' you fishing. Boy! He just took a ride on that elephant—he up and mounted that thing and rode him—you try mounting an Indian elephant—an' he don't even pay, you know."

"Some fella," I said in wonder, and brought out a dollar. "Would you like a ride on an elephant, Tom?" but strangely, he pushed my hand away.

"Aw, it's only five cents, and I'm scared of elephants. You staying for a while, mister?"

"Well, I'll have to be going soon."

"But the fair's only just started. There's boxers coming, you know—Johnny Hutch and the Barbados Kid . . ." I heard a brass band and Karen's shrieks of joy.

"Yes, son . . . but I've got things to do," I said.

"But you've only just come—gee, you grown-ups are queer. You comin' fishing soon? We've been waiting years. Jay got a two-pound fish out of the Passionist pond last Friday—we spend a heap o' time looking for you, and you don't come."

There was a hint of admonishment in his voice; this, for me, was his charm—I was being treated as an equal. He said, "Why not tomorrow?"

"I'll see. Tom, are you still living with that old woman?"

"Oh, no, she died."

"Where are you living now, then?"

"Up Creeky Pipe, with Jay."

"Where's that?"

He gestured impatience. "I told you once. You go up Bluff till you get near the copper-works. Do you know where that is?"

"Yes, sir," I said.

"Up near the Works—anyone'll tell you. Gee, just look at those horses . . ."

"And you're still working at Lubinski's?"

He nodded, disinterested, and I knew I was taking up valuable time. "Mister, I gotta go."

I knelt. "I'll try to come soon, Tom—look, won't you take this dollar?"

He stared at it, rubbing his hands down his ragged trousers.

"Jiminy, a dollar!"

"Fifty cents for Jay," I said. "Go now, Tommy, you're missing the fair."

He snatched the money. "Thanks," he said, and ran, flinging a grin at me over his shoulder. On the edge of the crowd he turned and cupped his hands to his mouth. "Don't you forget now—Creeky Pipe—we'll be waiting."

The loneliness was suddenly intolerable after he had gone. I walked the streets of a deserted city, my spirits alternating between despair for Hosea and a carnal excitement when I thought of Belle Maherne. I knew I would make love to her. It was a long time since I had possessed a woman, and the expectation brought a sense of inadequacy tinged with a suffocating joy. On the corner of Fifth and Liberty I took off my cloak and stood there, watching the river. When I turned I saw the poster. In waves of increasing surprise, I stared at it.

THE CONNEMARA DANCER

BENEFIT

Supported by the famous Royal
Troupe, the rage of New York

KAREN O'HARA

OPERA HOUSE

I do not know how long I stood there staring at the poster. Karen was dancing in New York, and the knowledge of her success brought me to a pitch of almost demented joy. I wanted to fling off my clothes and dance in the street. An aged man passed me dolefully and I gripped him and swung him to face me.

"Look, fella! Karen O'Hara—my sister—dancing in New York."

He stared at me with pouched eyes, then at the poster. There appeared to be some doubt in him so I shook him. "It's me sister— the New York dancer."

"Sure, mister, sure." With an apprehensive, backward look he pulled himself free of me and mingled with the crowd, but I did not care. The one magic name in my life was Karen. Almost without knowing it, it was for her I schemed, seeking her acclamation, and the thought of her banished all loneliness. Rocking back on my heels I read the poster again and again, savouring every letter, every gum-ridge on its new, white surface, and then came pride, fierce and puffing up. God, I thought, these O'Haras are shifting. This success of mine was no cheap coincidence. Hosea, near to blindness, had faced the artist of the ring, James J. Corbett. Karen was at last a famous dancer: Michael, even yet, might prove an Irish liberator comparable only with the revered O'Connell. Aye, Ma indeed had reason to be proud. Exultant, almost faint with emotion, I went through the streets and ran up the steps of the Monongahela House two at a time, and into the foyer.

There, with a glass of whiskey before me I sat, nursing this new family joy. It brought a strange withdrawal from the social whirl about me—the elegant, chattering women, the impressive rush of messengers. Content in this new, secret world of Karen's success I considered the jabbering mass about me as something obscene, and I sat hunched up, staring at them; the bright-haired young bucks with their fanciful airs, the growls and commands of the black-jowled magnates. Even the women looked alike, entering with a false, fastidious grace and artificial smiles. Carnegie and Frick came in with some high-powered associates, and I returned Frick's bow with a nod. Glass in hand, I watched them engage in deep conversation, like anarchists crouching over a bomb, and I smiled as I guessed the subject. Strikes. I had never had a strike with any of my labour, but the mutterings among Carnegie's men years back at the Edgar Thomson works had grown into a shut-down at his Beaver Falls mill. Rather than face a trial of strength with the

Amalgamated Association, he had ordered a sell-out to the Wire Trust. His book, *Triumphant Democracy*, expounded the equality of men and glorified the toiler, but to me it was a mess of hypocrisy, for in his heart he hated and feared organised labour. Now there were grumblings at Homestead and Braddock. I smiled, staring at my whiskey. All men of destiny, it seemed, had troubles, but a two-faced attitude, quicker than any other, always came home to the roost.

"Jess!"

I glanced up, disbelieving my eyes, for Michael was standing beside me.

"For heaven's sake," I whispered, getting up.

The Monongahela House was no place for dowdies, and Michael was dowdy now. He wore no tie. His ragged coat hung limply about his thin body, his shoes were broken and mud-stained, his face pale, his hair dishevelled.

"Aren't you pleased to see me, Jess?"

I glanced about me. The conversation had chattered to a whisper. I said:

"Sure, I'm pleased to see you, man. What d'you want?"

"I've got to talk to you." His eyes were shining brilliantly from his gaunt face. "Do we have to talk here?" And he added, to himself, "To think a man could sink so low, with this damned riff-raff."

"Look, you say your piece and go," I whispered back.

His hands went out to me. "Will you not come out to a decent tavern, Jess—I can't bloody breathe in here." His voice rose and it stopped all conversation. A waiter was hovering near so I waved him away.

"Come upstairs," I said, and picked up my cloak.

Michael looked slowly round the office, his eyes disdainful. "Do you call this a home, for God's sake—sure, it looks more like the halls of the harlots."

The same old Michael. I gave him a smile as I went to the decanter.

"Drink?"

He shook his head. "I've taken a holy pledge against the vile stuff."

"Then I will." I filled a glass. "Now then, what have you come for?"

He said earnestly, sinking down on to the edge of a chair, "I had to see you. God knows, if I could have ducked it, I'd not be here . . ."

"Wait," I interjected. "If you've come about money we can discuss that later. Will you tell me at once what's happened to Hosea?"

"Haven't you heard?"

"I heard today. Is it true he's blind?"

"He's not so blind he can't eat his dinner, so save your pity. Ach, he's stumbling in the midst of his almighty hammerings, but he'll be mending. But he'd mend that much sooner if I could stitch a tail on Rachel. Have you seen or heard of her?"

"Not a sign." I drank, watching him.

"The fella's raving for her, the damned big oaf. But I haven't come to discuss her." He clasped his hands and leaned towards me. "Jess, listen. D'you remember the idea of a second *Erin's Hope?*"

"Nothing's come of it, eh? What did I tell you?"

He grimaced. "And you were right, for once. I've been tramping the roads and riding the rods for years in raking up decent people, but the soul of Ireland must have died with the men of the Civil War, and ideals died with it. Then one day I met Hosea, and he was needful of me, after his thumpings, for he was standing there seeing six of me and not a breath of the porter on him. And the blood was still caked on his face from the murderin' fists of the Yankee pugilists, so in the name of pity I took him in."

"Where?"

"Homestead—I had him in Duquesne for a time—nursing the fella. For his eyes were near gone, d'you understand, with the cuts and humps, and he'd weep and smile and sing—at the same time, poor divil. And at night when the shift was over he'd be there on his knees by the bed, though he prayed to no God, but only prayed to Rachel."

"The poor soul," I said.

He thumbed his chest. "The poor soul was me, fella. For I had to work to keep him and feed him like a child, though he's better now. We took to the road for a bit and then came back to Pittsburgh, and landed in Braddock with Carnegie. And a week or so back I called at Girty's Run and saw the sweet Marged woman, and she told me you were living with the Lubinski woman in style, is that true?"

"That is what she thinks," I said. "Not true."

He rose, his eyes shining with the old lust to fight. "She didn't say you were sleeping with the clown, but livin' with her. For God's sake, Jess, are you loving that big black spider, or loving her money?"

I put down my glass. "Look, Mike, if that's all you've come to say you can get out of here."

"Sure, I will," he said, "after I've had me say, not before. You mentioned money. Will you give me some?"

"I will. How much do you need?"

"Can you better a thousand dollars?"

"You're coming heavy," I said. "Will Ho eat that much?"

"It's not for Hosea. Do you think I'd be coming begging to feed a body? I've lost most things, but not my pride, but I'm giving you a chance to regain some of yours." He came nearer. "Jess, listen—have you seen this cess-pit Carnegie calls Homestead? It's a place of pits and holes, and a crucifying labour for the poor devils who live in it, working their twelve-hour day in the heat and smoke of it. There's this fella Carnegie spouting fine words about the nobility of labour, but he's drawing his fat profits while the people of the town are sinking into graves."

I was interested. "Go on," I said.

"It's a brutalised people, Jess. I'm working in the furnaces, and I drink two buckets of water every twelve-hour shift, and at the end of the day the sweat is filling me boots, and there's blisters on me back the size of prunes, so I can't stick me shirt on it. Sure, it's nothing to see the fellas fainting off in the red-hot slag, and resting for a bit before going back into it. And there's shouts and screams left and right with the scalds and accidents with the hammers . . ."

"But he pays you well?"

"Ach, sure, he pays. The top-rate fellas collect ten dollars a day, though I get four, but that's poor consolation for a blast of molten iron in the face or chewing on a sweat rag for a coupla hours while they pull your legs from between the rollers. Have you visited the place? It's Dante's inferno and Beelzebub's combined, with the white heat blazing from its gaping holes. Sure, we thought we were hard-pressed on the bogs of Ireland, and I'm made for labour, as you know. But it's a crime on the body of mankind the fella's committing, an' he's getting away with murder every day. And d'you know something more? While that fella Carnegie saying that good honest labour is a higher calling than an English peerage, his Pinkerton men are working among us day and night to list off the fellas who are grumbling about the conditions."

"Police conditions." I sipped my whiskey, smiling. "So you're fighting another cause now, eh?"

He set his fist into his hand. "If there's an ideal worth fighting for you can pledge me life to it, so I'm working big with the Knights of Labour . . ."

"The Union? That's dangerous."

"Aye? With the rate we're going it's dangerous to Carnegie, for we're sick to death of the twelve-hour day and working for peanuts while he's hoarding millions. It's the rise of the common man against a private tyranny, Jess. It's the guts of the workers awaking to snatch at their share!" He was shouting now. Smiling, I sat on the edge of the desk and watched him. "And we'll bring the edifice of greed and hypocrisy tumbling till it ends on its knees before God."

"Carnegie on his knees, you mean, isn't that the target?"

"The whole bloody lot on their knees, Jess—Carnegie and Frick, for Frick's doin' little better with his Connellsville coke; Laughlin and Jones, Oliver and Phipps and a score of others. Jess, will ye help us?"

"How?"

266

"With money. For you're risen in the boots of the common man —didn't you fight with Ho and me once in the name of common justice?"

I smiled again. "You're forgetting one thing, Mike—I'm an employer."

"And your name stands fair in Girty's Run, in steel."

"But I'm still an employer. Times have changed, Mike—we're on the other side of the fence. I'd be cutting my own throat if I supported the unions."

There was a long silence, then he said, his face pale, "So you'll not help us?"

"I will not, Mike—not a cent."

A whisper now. "Then in the name of Ma will you answer me one question. Isn't she the proof of the living bond between us— didn't she bring us out on the same scream?" He paused. "Are you off yer head?"

"I'm saner than you, and you know it."

He waved at the room. "Your brains are warped. D'you call this muck-heap living sane? Was there an O'Hara born who sold his loins to the highest bidder?"

"A thousand dollars would have bought you, you swine—so hold your tongue."

"I'm bridling it." He was breathing heavily, his fists clenched. "You were never up to clipping it in the past, so I shouldn't try it now, by God. D'you realise you're no better than a tavern tart— hawking the thing round for the almighty dollar. Boy, I should have known better than waste me time on ye, the only thing you're shy of is perfume."

I gripped my hands, cursing myself for even listening to him, and then a blind anger flared. As he turned away I leaped, hooking him clumsily, knocking him over the desk, and as he staggered upright I caught him with the other hand, sending him flying. Trembling, I stood over him. Michael sat up slowly, feeling his chin, grinning stupidly up at me.

"That was a fine brotherly swipe," he said.

"Get going," I whispered.

"Indeed I'll not, for the moment I'm on me feet you'll fetch me another one—I know ye." He winked. "It's the best news so far, Jess, for I thought you were dead."

I had cut his mouth, and was ashamed. The blood trickled down his jaw, staining his ragged shirt. Fed, strong, he would have killed me, and I knew it. With shaking hands I poured another whiskey and took it to the window. The Monongahela below was splashed with moonlight. Derricks and cranes were raking in the stars. "Mike, please go," I said hoarsely, and heard him get up.

"Not till I've got to the bottom of you, Jess. The world's not daft, remember. There's a reason for it when a fine man like you gets the fever of money, after his fine record in Ireland."

The city looked beautiful in moonlight, the sky stained with fire.

Michael said, desperately, "You're a fair employer of labour in steel, but do you realise you've got child-workers in rags in your mill? What would Ma say?"

I turned from the window. "Mike, it's late, and I'm tired."

"You're tired—that's a damned good one. Holy saints—if you want to know what tiredness is you should slip down to Water Street and peep at that cotton factory, for I've just come past it. The wee fellas are dropping to sleep at the looms and there's only a kick in the backside keeping them awake—you've got a foreman walking the floor with a fist on him for stunning mules, and he's using it."

I sighed. "Mike, you're wasting your time."

He stared at me, whispering, "Holy Mother of God. You don't care, do you?"

"No—does that satisfy you?"

He put the palms of his hands against his coat and wiped them down, his eyes growing wide. Faintly, from the foyer below, came the clash of glasses and the shrill voices of women.

"God help ye, Jess."

I opened the door. "What happens now? Do you want some money to help keep Hosea?"

But he was still staring. "Even your voice has changed . . ."

I opened my wallet. "Look, here's a couple of hundred."

Slowly, he backed away from me, as if dazed.

"Good-bye, Mike. Won't you take this money?"

He did not reply. There, by the door, I listened to his footsteps thumping down the stairs.

I changed quickly, cursing Michael for delaying me. It was nearly eight o'clock when I hailed a buggy for Fifth Avenue, and went to dine with Belle.

Belle might have been waiting behind the door of the big house on Fifth Avenue, such was the speed with which she answered my knock.

"No butler?" I asked.

"No servants." She smiled brilliantly, adding secretly, "Fun, isn't it—got rid of the lot of them, it's Fair day."

"And your father?" I handed her my hat and cloak.

"Safe as a house in Baltimore."

I gave her a smile and followed her into the big reception room. "You might be taking a risk, Belle—you may not know what you've landed."

"And I don't care." She turned to me. "Do you think I'm cheap?"

"Why should I? What's wrong with a tryst in an empty house?"

"Clare would kill me if she knew," she said at nothing.

"I doubt it." I sat down beside her on a sofa. "If my hunch is right she's in the middle of killing Vaynor—no sight or sound of the pair of them for the past two days."

"That should suit you. Where do you think they've gone?"

I took the whiskey she offered. "Carolina, without a doubt—everything seems to happen to Clare in the deep, green South." I raised the glass. "Give you a toast, Belle—Clare and Vaynor."

She smiled, eyes narrowed over the rim of her glass. "Belle and O'Hara," she said.

"Would your father approve?"

"My father would love it. Think of your qualifications—Connemara Irish, business instincts, trade connections; young enough for marriage, big enough to justify incorporation."

"You're cynical."

"No, just realistic." She rose and wandered about, and I shifted uneasily.

"We're covering ground too quickly," I said. "You don't come into it from that point of view—we're already merging."

"Yes, so he mentioned."

"Which means that I've come here to see you, Belle—nothing more."

This brought her back on the sofa beside me. "Do you mean that, Jess? Tell me, it's terribly important."

"Snap your fingers once and I'll get my hat and go. Don't tell me that your father uses you in his business deals."

She said, "Drink that up and I'll get you another."

"Belle, answer me."

She shrugged. "No, he doesn't need me, but I thought you did."

"Oh, for God's sake!"

"I'm . . . sorry."

I got up. "A damned fine start to a joyful evening, isn't it?"

She said, at nothing, "I said I was sorry. You don't live my life, so you can only guess at it. Ten times out of ten I've shown them the door." She raised her face. "And now, for the first time I've found somebody attractive."

"You've had some bad experiences," I said.

"Belle Maherne and ten per cent of the stock. I'm sorry, but I couldn't bear it to happen again."

I said, taking her hand, "And it won't. Look, there's a smell of perfume and cold marble in here, this place is a morgue. Shall we go out?"

"And blaze our names in every paper in Pittsburgh?" Her eyes were suddenly appealing. "Let's stay, Jess—just the two of us."

I looked around the enormous room. "I can't get used to the size of it, nor can you, if you think of it. I detest spaciousness—give me a caravan."

"You've lived in a caravan?"

"Born and raised in one—Gipsy O'Haras for six generations, and I'm damned proud of it."

"And you should be—oh, Jess, tell me about it!"

I had a sudden desire to tell her about Karen, but I did not. Drama was not quite the thing among the socialites, but progress from nothing was always deeply admired. So I told her about the roads of Ireland, the lusty freedom of the encampments, the pegs and cans, and the excitement and admiration grew in her face.

"And you started from that?"

I told her about the bear fight in Wicklow, but I fought the bear. I crossed the Atlantic in the *Pennsylvanian*, but not with Karen. I bounced Pat Magee and worked at Girty's Run, and I told of my start with Lubinski.

"From nothing! You must be proud."

"Reckon I've been lucky."

I was disturbed, and badly wanted a drink. The plans I had made for a scene fiercely romantic were dissolving into pictorial fantasy, a useless spate of words that diverted me into the old, loved emotions of home. And here was an individual, separate, something apart, that must be possessed by calculation, not dreams. Even her total interest in my lies built the barrier higher. Belle said softly, her eyes shining in the candlelight:

"One day you will take me along the road to home and show me the bay of Kilkieran."

I chuckled. "You'd be bored with it in a week."

"Jess, take me one day—anywhere away from talk in millions."

"If you give me another drink," I said, and got up, helping myself.

The gurgle of the decanter was an echo in the uncanny silence of the great house. Beyond the door was the ball-room, like a mausoleum, its floor a mirror of light. The room seemed blanketed by an enveloping silence. Steamed dry of words I sat by Belle again; sitting outside myself, it seemed, watching the ineptitude of Jess O'Hara. I smiled at her. She was sitting with her hands folded in her lap, the blackness of her dress deep in shadow, her profile etched clear against the spluttering candles, awaiting my will with a sort of bowed docility. I drained my glass, looking at the decanter. In there, perhaps, lay the key to the kiss, a commanding love-making that would transport us from this macabre silence into passion and beauty. I said, to save myself, "Forgive me, Belle, I'm neglecting you," and got up and refilled my glass. "It's like slamming the door on the present when I think of the joy of those years in Ireland."

"And were there no nights of gipsy love-making?"

I rubbed my chin, grinning. "None that would stand repeating."

"Tell me, Jess. I'm such a terrible romantic," she whispered.

I turned to her. "There were women."

"Vixens of women, dark-haired, flamboyant, and . . ."

"But none like you," I said.

The whiskey was helping now, heating up the years of ease and dissipation. Taking her hand, I drew her against me, instantly aware of her need for me. And the sudden gust of our breathing banished the silence as I kissed her again.

"Jess, please . . ."

I felt her trembling. The flickering candles cast deep shadows in her face, and her hair was beautiful in the wavering light. She said, head turned away, "We have only met twice. How can you love me?"

"But you love me."

She nodded against me. "Ridiculous, isn't it?"

"Then snatch at the joy while you can," I whispered. "This costs nothing, and you can dream all your life." I kissed her. "Oh, Belle, I want you."

"As you dream—for the Welsh girl?"

"The moment we kissed she was forgotten. Belle, Belle . . ." I held her away.

She rose beside me, smiling down. "Jess, not here . . ."

I caught her hands and drew her down again, but she fought herself free in a sudden flurry of laughter. There was a purity in her, and she was incredibly beautiful. Standing away she smoothed her dress. "Not here—not in this room. You see, my father meets his friends here, and . . ."

"I see," I answered softly.

"I . . . I'll call you. But, oh, Jess, only if you really want me. I couldn't bear it, if you . . ."

"I'll wait, Belle. If you don't call, I'll understand."

I watched her go to the door. For a moment she stood there, looking at me, suddenly matured by a subtle, transfiguring trick of candlelight.

"For you," she said, and left me.

In restless agitation I paced the room, listening to the creaks of the house. The least movement, even the rubbing of fingers seemed to violate its hostile emptiness, and I knew a sudden and overwhelming pity for Belle. With it came an urge to escape: to run through the hall, sweep my hat and cloak off the peg, and go through the front door into the night, and cleanness. The seduction of Clare, achieved without love-making, seemed different. It had entailed no promises or kisses, and Clare, a monstrosity, enlisted no pity in her obesity. Belle was different. She was younger and wilting for affection. To ensnare her for wealth seemed suddenly obscene, to fulfil her taste for love savoured of defilement.

I was in the hall when she called me, and I turned.

The broad, ornate staircase faced me, its black and white marble and embellishments gleaming dully along its crimson carpets. And at the top, clad in white, stood Belle.

"Jess!" she called again and her whisper echoed.

Honour faded in the first touch of her, repentance was flooded out in the heat of possession.

"Say you love me, just once?"

"I love you," I said.

CHAPTER 24

I married Belle Maherne in the spring, a quick courting, even for the city's standards. Abe Maherne, delighted by the merger of business and family relations, rushed down from New York, organised one of the most splendid weddings ever seen in Pittsburgh, and rushed back again. For months before the wedding I had put up with petulant silences or emotional outbursts from Clare, but Vaynor blunted the edge of her grief during my courtship of Belle. Vaynor, indeed, worked like a Trojan. He even managed to take her South a week before the wedding, and I was deeply indebted to him. And in this new glory of marriage to Belle, Hosea, Michael, even Karen were forgotten. Envied by every bachelor in the State, in the top crust of the social whirl, I was standing on the brink of enormous wealth.

There was a nip of cold in the air, I remember, on the night I walked out of the big house on Fifth Avenue to take stock of my new position. Hambro was at some meeting or other, Belle had visited a ladies' circle whose charter was the feeding of Pittsburgh's destitute. The city was beautiful that night, I recall. A dull, rosy glow hung over the rivers; the iron-works down Second Avenue and Duquesne were competing in their flashes at the sky. Quite aimlessly, I wandered down Smithfield and Diamond Alley and listened to the sounds of people: the bawled greetings of drunks, the sobbing of children, and the whispers of doorstep lovers. Standing there within the beating heart of the city I loved I gathered relief from a sudden loneliness. A group of Scotch-Irish passed me, quarrelling their way to the night shift, and I envied them the coarse banter of their manhood. Yet there was a joyful recompense for the loss of such comradeship, I reflected—I was carrying in my wallet over five hundred dollars—more than such men might save in their lives; this was life—profit and loss, but my world was preferable to theirs.

The cotton operatives were spilling out of the waterfront factories. Standing in the shadows I watched them, and remembered,
with a shock, that one of the factories was mine; that I had seen
this factory only once before—on the day I was starving in Pittsburgh. Above the main door was the name *Lubinski*, soon to be
brushed out, I reflected, for the name *Maherne*. Pushing my way
through the people, I went nearer. And I found myself peering
through the same window through which I had looked before,
years back. The children were sitting at the looms—presumably
the children Michael had referred to. True, a few of the younger
ones were drooping—natural enough, after a twelve-hour shift, but
most looked quite happy; some even laughing and chattering to
each other, their hands enmeshed in cotton, their fingers working
deftly over the shuttles. I was suddenly angry. It was agitation
that cleaved the goodwill essential to employer and employee. It
was the tub-thumpers like Michael who raised the temper of decent people and turned them into mobs. These children, in their
labour, were happy, and it was amazing to me that Michael could
not see them with the same unbiased perception as mine. Some,
in fact, were slacking, I noticed, and this raised a vital point in my
mind. It was something Lubinski had taken up quite seriously with
me before he died, but I had been too busy to do anything about
it. Now I watched, getting the proof of it. With only one bully-man
patrolling, the children in the east wing of the mill worked slower
when he was in the west wing. Some, watching his position, actually stopped, their hands in their laps. Lubinski had suggested
the employment of another overseer, but now I considered this
debatable. I counted the children—fifty-three: scarcely enough to
warrant it. A rise in tempo from over a hundred children might
be worth the extra outlay, and this could be obtained only by an
extension to the building. I turned away, deciding to take this up
with Hambro in the morning, for he was excellent when it came
to the economics of hours, tempo, and production. Then, suddenly, I remembered Tom McGrath, and scanned the faces of
the children, but I did not see him; most were girls, anyway, their
fingers nimbler with cotton.

Two or three young mothers were waiting outside the factory gate, their shawls scragged tight over their heads, and I pushed past them. One, at a glance, was Irish: the usual blue eyes and black hair. And she lifted her face to mine with a gesture that lent her nobility, and clutched a sleeping child closer against her. A toddler beside her was gripping her skirts, staring up, his grimed face tear-stained, and I pitied them. This was the tragedy of Pittsburgh, I thought; not the individual poverty, but the mass. One well-meaning man could do nothing about it.

"Good night," I said softly, giving the woman a bow.

She did not reply but held the baby away from her, and spat.

It was forgivable; the deep-seated hostility between rich and poor. She was spitting at Pittsburgh, not at me. Sighing, I walked on, losing myself in the sparkling beauty of the Monongahela River.

It was a night of full moon and shafts of light struck through the smoke-layer, emblazoning the crazy forest of the waterfront, and the city looked beautiful against its patchwork stars. I passed well-loved places in that solitary walk—first, the rock where I had met Katie Virginia on the night I shared her bed: the bank where I had lain with Karen, freezing in the wind of the river; the muddy strand where Tom McGrath went fishing. I stood there, lighting a cigar, seized with a sudden nostalgia for the past. Those were the years of poverty and degradation, of rebuff and swipe, yet they now seemed so strangely joyful. No furious shareholders harassed me then, no fall in the stock-market panicked me into decision; no Hambros and McNamaras pestered my days, and no women stole my nights. Staring at the river I calculated that I was now worth something like half a million dollars, with a strike-potential at twenty millions, for Belle was no tight-fisted Clare Lubinski, and neither was her father. Maherne thought big and acted big. In the five months since my marriage to Belle he had granted me greater and greater power. He was ageing fast. Soon he would hand me both reins of his financial empire, and with Hambro's genius behind me, provided I could contain it, I would have men like Carnegie looking sideways. I frowned as I remembered McNamara, who was lying too quiet these days to be healthy. He must have read of my marriage to Belle, he must have realised the new advantages. The press, I remembered, were giving little publicity to the dying Maguires; a brief account of the hanging of a couple, nothing more. McNamara might even be dead, I thought, like Kehoe. The possibility brought me a rush of joy, until I remembered Clare. Vaynor, however, was doing quite well with her, said Hambro. I offered a prayer that he might earn his ten thousand dollars, and marry her.

In this happy soliloquy of wealth and ambition, I wandered up Wood Street to the big house on Fifth.

Belle had not returned. I put my hat and cloak on a stand in the hall, went through to the vinery, and helped myself to a whiskey. Hambro appeared in the doorway behind me.

"Drink that, you'll need it, O'Hara," he said.

I turned. "Will you have one?"

He gave me the rare smile he reserved for special occasions. "If I do it will be the third in an hour. Maherne's dead." He went to the decanter and began to help himself, still smiling.

"Good God," I whispered, and slowly sat down. "When?"

"Came through on the telegraph soon after you left tonight. I've been trying to contact your wife—where is she?"

"But how . . . how did it happen?"

"They found him dead in New York—in the East River. Three bullets in him."

I stared at him, uncomprehending. "Murder?"

Hambro sipped his whiskey. "Three bullets—he'd hardly manage that himself." Glass in hand, he wandered about. "You know, O'Hara, you are the luckiest man alive. Every damned thing you touch turns gold—and they talk about me." His voice rose, and I could see he had been drinking. "But I have to engineer it—I have to scheme and plan and sweat for results. With you . . ." he snapped his fingers, ". . . it just happens."

I rose. "The way you're talking you must think I did it."

He actually laughed. "Good heavens, no—you don't even have to be brutal. There must be arch-angels working for you. Have no

277

fear, you have the perfect alibi—not that you need one—tucked up in bed with his beautiful daughter. God, when it comes to biscuits you take the plums."

I ignored him. "Poor little Abe," I said at nothing.

Hambro's face snapped up. "And didn't he deserve it? He had more enemies than the mother of Nero. For God's sake don't pity him—I couldn't bear it. You can't make millions without killing people, and you know it. What happened to Maherne can happen to any of us."

"A joyful thought."

He smiled wider. I had never seen Hambro in this mood. "It's the penalty of extreme wealth, O'Hara. And New York shanty-town boys are not very particular—it's amazing what they get up to when they can't pay the rent." He took off his spectacles and sighted me through them. "Nurture your inheritance, O'Hara, but take great care."

"I'm not a dollar better off, you fool, and you know it."

"You're not, but your wife is. If she cuts you in on half you're worth ten million—there's a nice little thought when you take her to bed."

"Don't be disgusting."

"And don't you be such a damned hypocrite," he replied.

I did not reply. Hambro was beginning to disturb me. While I was with Clare his attitude had been one of servility; during the merger with Maherne, which was little else but fraud achieved with Hambro's usual artistry, he had assumed an air of equality measurable with his genius. Now he was almost commanding. Knowing the size of his ambitions, I decided to handle him with care.

"Listen," I said. The front door had opened and Belle entered the hall, humming breathlessly. I heard her go up the stairs and close the door of her room.

Hambro said, "Now you can tell her—that's your job. It's one thing I don't intend doing for you. Now for your next piece of news. God, it just piles on and on . . . Clare's married."

"Married . . . how d'you know?"

278

"Vaynor cornered her. He called here this afternoon, so said the butler. Apparently Clare stayed outside in the carriage. They've just returned from a honeymoon in Carolina."

"When did that happen?"

"Search me, I didn't marry them."

"What did Vaynor want?"

"No doubt he's after his money—wasn't it ten thousand?"

"The mercenary little devil—he's got two millions in his pocket with Clare."

"Ah, no," answered Hambro, "that's all part of the corruption. You said marry her, not live with her. He'll grab his ten thousand and be head-first through the window."

"Well, well . . ." I said softly, "good old Vaynor."

Hambro opened the door. "Good old O'Hara, you mean—give me a call when something goes wrong."

I drank another whiskey, braced myself, and went up the stairs to Belle's room, knocked, and entered. She turned at the dressing-table, a hair-brush upraised, smiling beautifully. A strange trick of the lamp was casting a shadow over her bright hair, staining it into blackness. It could have been Marged sitting there, but the vision faded as I neared her.

"Hallo, darling, I thought you were still out," she said, and went on brushing. "Josie usually does this but I'm trying a new style. One of the women at the Meeting for the Destitute . . ." Her hands paused as she saw me in the mirror, and her smile faded. Slowly, she turned. "Jess, what's wrong?"

Women cry best alone. I told her, and left her.

The following weeks are stamped into my mind. Belle had never professed an overwhelming love for her father, yet his brutal death changed her from gaiety into moroseness, and her morbid brooding cast gloom on the household. She dressed in black, she used every possible excuse to stay in her room. No cajoling, no command could rake her from her sense of loss, and I could not understand it. She accepted my love-making, she listened to my plans for stock-buying and -selling with the same, feigned interest. At dinner, with the snow-flakes falling heavily down the leaded windows of the dining-room, we sat at either end of the long, polished table with Hambro between us, and I cursed his high-flown financial jargon that stifled all domestic conversation. Quite still, she sat, eyes downcast, as a stranger in her own house, and I pitied her. And week after week the enquiries into her father's death went on; each ring at the door another visit from the Pinkerton detectives that opened up the wound of her grief. And Hambro sat through it all with the complacent smile of a man filled with success. At his suggestion, I learned afterwards, not mine, Belle had transferred all interest in Maherne Enterprises, administrative and financial, to my name. She did not question any action, big or small. She had taken no part in her father's business organisation, she showed no interest now. She attended no social functions, nor did she entertain. As if her spirit had died with her father's in the mud of the East River, she sat, beautiful still, smiling still, and did not speak unless to make reply. And then, after Christmas, with the city steaming with rumours about the next O'Hara moves in big business, with the name Maherne Enterprises appearing in every other edition of the financial press, she awakened, it seemed. I was in my room, I remember, dressing to go out with Hambro, when the door opened and she appeared.

"Jess . . ."

I was fighting with my collar and bow, something she usually did for me, cursing the coming dinner where I was guest of honour, cursing the boredom of the dreary procedure and Hambro in particular. I turned from the glass.

"Why, Belle!"

She was dressed in black, as usual, and looking drab. It is sad how grief can age. First the shadows in the face appear, then the lined eyes; the youthful movements slur, the step grows heavy. As if with the weight of twenty years, she stood, pale but smiling.

"Jess, I must talk to you."

"Why, of course." I took her hand and drew her into the room, closing the door. Almost immediately somebody knocked, and I opened it again. Maherne's ancient English butler was hovering outside on the landing, also Belle's little French maid. She whispered, "Oh, please, sir, Mrs. O'Hara is ill . . ."

"I know, Josie—I won't be going out tonight."

"She ought to see the doctor, sir."

"Yes, of course—you run along, I'll take care of her." To the butler I said, "What do you want?"

The butler's likeness to Abe Maherne was astonishing; hand-picked, said Hambro; a sort of stop-butt to the gunman's bullet. Born within sound of Bow Bells was his claim, and it was my intention to get him back to them as soon as possible, for he was Hambro's ears and eyes. Now he said:

"Mr. Hambro's compliments, sir, the carriage is waiting."

"Tell him I'm not coming," I whispered back.

"But sir . . ."

"You tell Hambro to go to hell and go there with him." I shut the door.

Coming back to Belle I knelt before her chair.

"Now then, my dear, what is it?"

She raised her head. Her eyes, I noticed, were large and bright in the shadows of her face, and the garish gas-light intensified their brilliance. Her cheeks were white, her lips colourless. She looked, that evening, suddenly and intensely ill, and I could not understand it.

"Oh, Jess, hold me . . ."

I held her, overwhelmed with pity for her, and I knew a jagged thrust of conscience. What I had thought were the ravages of grief were translated into fear. She was ill, she had been ill for months, and I had been too engrossed with Hambro and the business to try to understand it. But it was only pity. Eyes closed against her face, I hated myself because I did not love her.

"Darling, have you been to the doctor again?" I asked.

She shook her head.

I said, desperately, "Look, for heaven's sake, why won't you have him here? There's no need to go running to him, Belle."

"My illness doesn't need a doctor, Jess." She took my hand and held it against her lips. "Please . . . take me away from here—anywhere."

"A holiday? Of course . . ."

Her voice rose and she put her hands into her hair, "For good. Oh, Jess, you say you love me. If you do, then take me away. Give it all up. Throw away every damned dollar."

"What are you saying?" I gripped her hands. "The business is here, Belle. I can't just leave it to Hambro. Your father . . ."

"That damned little Hambro," she whispered between her teeth.

I got up. "You may think that but there's not another like him. Don't you understand that he has taken over where your father left off?"

"My God, he certainly has."

"Face it, Belle—I do. I've got limitations. The firm's employing hundreds of people, and we owe it to them. There's thousands of stockholders all over the country dependent on Hambro, we owe him a lot."

She raised her face. "We owe him so much that he's swallowing the pair of us. Oh, Jess, don't be a fool—can't you see what he's up to? He's taking the firm over. He's so indispensable now that the whole thing would crack. Yes, I'm just a woman and I'm not supposed to know anything, but I'm an expert when it comes to the big financial house. I'm an expert because I've been breathing this damned money and intrigue since I was as high as my father's knee—I've known nothing else. You think I'm grieving for my father, don't you, then listen to this. Since I can remember I've hated my father and everything he stood for, and I hate him now. I've seen him tear men to pieces—not for a million but for a thousand dollars. I've seen him chat and drink with a man and swear to that man his bond of friendship, and while he was doing it that man was financially dead. He was dead because my father had bought him up—had coerced his stockholders and bought his way into his board-room. And the man didn't know it." She closed her eyes, trembling.

"Belle, please, you're upsetting yourself."

She whispered, "I suppose I'm dead, but don't accept it. Oh, God, you die every day in this business if you happen to be born decent, like my mother. You never met my mother, but it killed her, too." She looked at the lamp and tears were on her face. "You say that people are dependent on you." She sighed deeply. "You're right, they are. But not the people you are thinking about—not the money-grubbers who sit in their club arm-chairs in idleness, and rake in your profits—they can take care of themselves, unless Hambro outwits them." She pushed me aside and rose unsteadily. "There are thousands of others you haven't mentioned. Have you seen your New York tenements? Have you seen the misery and squalor in them, the dirt? There's thousands starving to pay our rents, there's children going hungry, and dying in the name of Jess O'Hara—you've owned these places and you haven't been near them. There was a child killed in the old Lubinski factory last month—fell in the looms, and you don't even know it."

"My God, I'll see to that agent," I whispered.

"And God will see to you, Jess, unless you put a stop to it." She wrung her hands. "When I married you I thought I was marrying somebody decent. I thought you would take a minor place in the firm, and I could start to live. Now I know differently. You came to me for the same dirty reason that brought all the rest of them—for money and power, not love. Oh, what a fool I was. It was staring me in the face, and I couldn't see it. You've used me as you used Clare Lubinski."

"Belle, that's not true, and you know it."

"Right," she whispered, "then prove the truth of it." She was trembling more, verging on hysteria. "Since we've lived here together you've shown me lip-service, not love. You've kissed me when you wanted something and loved me when you needed me. I've given you everything on Hambro's advice, and now I know why he gave that advice—to get more power. Now listen, Jess. It's me or the firm. Sell out—every cent—the city will jump at it. Take me away from this terrible house."

"For pity's sake, woman, it isn't as easy as that."

"Sell out—we'll give the damned money away. God knows there's people begging for charity." She suddenly clung to me. "Oh, Jess, I beg you. I love you, love you. Remember you told me about the caravans? Oh, I could live in one with you—for you . . ."

"You stupid little fool," I shouted. "The thing's too big, don't you realise that? You're talking about charity—don't you see I'd be ruining hundreds of people?"

She went limp in my arms. Drooping before me she put her hands over her face.

"And yourself," she whispered, and I turned away from her.

"Yes, myself, too—can't you see what you're asking me to do? There's a difference between us—you've never been hungry. I have, and I'm not being hungry again. I'm a name in this city now. I was rich before I met you, and I'm not slinging it all up on a silly woman's whim."

There was a strange quiet in her, and she smiled. "Ah, well, that's that. Funny, when you think of it. I married you to escape my father. He's dead now, but I'm married to him all over again."

"Now we're getting the truth of it, so stop accusing me." I glared at her.

When she reached the door, I said, "Belle, you're ill. You must see the doctor."

"There's no doctor can cure what is wrong with me, Jess." She turned, the door open. "Money, power. It kills even those who possess it, sometimes much quicker than those who don't. You know, come to think of it, I prefer my father. He was so brash about it, and very honest. But it's nauseating when greed is mixed with hypocrisy."

She closed the door softly and I stood there, my pity for her mingling with hatred; a hatred that enveloped them all—Hambro, Maherne, even Belle.

The door opened. Hambro stood there. He said, quietly yet commandingly:

"Come, there's still time, we mustn't keep them waiting."

CHAPTER 25

Hambro said, "It's a very sad thought. There's big trouble coming for poor Mr. Carnegie," and he folded his copy of the *Gazette* with the meticulous care he took with all documents.

I shut my book. "I shouldn't lose sleep over it, Carnegie can handle it."

Hambro said at the ceiling, "But it's strange, you know. Here we have a city where vice is protected. We've got rings within rings, the Common and Select Councils riddled with rogues. We're paying double the cost for our city contracts. We've got bawdy houses rented to official agents who charge the dear ladies stifling amounts, and pay a mere pittance back to the landlord. All this we accept and put up with, yet a decent employer like Carnegie is victimised."

"Speak for yourself," I replied, "it's a matter of opinion."

"You don't agree with me?"

"No, he's not being victimised—he's just getting what he deserves. One thing I've learned in business; you're either an employer or employee, you can't be both. Carnegie's getting what he's asked for over years—resentment from his workers. You can't run with the hare and the hounds."

"There's going to be trouble in Homestead, and I blame the Union," said Hambro.

"As usual," I answered. "Everybody blames the Union; it saves them the trouble of examining the problems too deeply. I'm against organised labour as much as any other employer, but I've also been a worker, and that's why we don't get strikes."

"You don't get strikes because you pay them over the odds, O'Hara."

"Least line of resistance. Do you blame me? I'm not big enough to break the Union. If Carnegie thinks he is let him try."

Hambro chuckled. "He doesn't break anybody—he leaves that to Frick."

"Then good luck to Clay Frick, for at least he's honest. At the first sign of trouble Little Andy will be over the sea to Scotland—his usual duck and dive."

The garden gate creaked, and I glanced up. Belle was going out, looking thin and pale in the bright spring sunlight. It seemed impossible that, in so short a time, she could have changed from a beautiful woman into a social-worker drag. She was giving away vast sums of money anonymously, she was working herself to the bone for half a dozen different charities; it was a new dogma that possessed her existence, a paradox of all she had enjoyed: either a mental illness, I thought, or an attempt to highlight my supposed deficiencies. From this new state of mind sprang moods of either deep depression or a scintillating joy—one never knew how to take her. One day she would greet me as a long-lost friend, next day she would pass me on the stairs without a word. Frankly, I was sick of her. I rose and watched her walking down the avenue, her shabby black coat held tightly about her, rather like a shanty Irish labourer going on shift. Hambro said:

"All discussion of the wage question in Homestead is strictly forbidden, they say the Advisory Council have notices up to this effect in Homestead. I give them credit, they're pretty well organised—four thousand men involved, you know, a damned sight more with the women and children."

I said, turning from the window, "You seem concerned with Carnegie's problems. How would you handle it?"

"Go in with troops."

"You can't use troops unless you've got a riot."

"Give him three months—he'll have his riot."

"And how can we make capital from that? Come on, Hambro, you're cooking up something."

He said, looking at his fingers, "Sell up everything and buy up in steel."

"With the shares at current price?"

"If Carnegie blows up the shares will drop. But we'd have to sell

286

out now—property, oil, glass, everything. We'd have to rake in every cent, even personal accounts, the loose change in our pockets."

I looked at him. He never failed to astonish me. Had he been sitting on ten tons of gold it would never be enough. I said, "Hambro, tell me, how much are you worth?"

"Good Lord, what next?" He eyed me.

"Three million, four? You're probably better laced than me. If you started bulk spending now you'd never get through it before you're boxed in cedar and brass handles, so when are you calling a halt?"

"Never, O'Hara."

"But in heaven's name why? If we tried this new idea we'd panic the city, and more than likely we'd lose the lot. Now tell me, why?"

He did not reply but just sat there, a smile on his thin lips.

"Look, I'm interested," I said. "Would you do it for the thrill of it—only that?"

"The thrill is secondary." He rose and polished his spectacles.

"Even Maherne would have boggled at this new idea, and he was tough enough," I said. "It's a three-to-one chance, and you know it."

"And a three-to-one profit, make no mistake, O'Hara. I'm watching Homestead and Braddock. I've been spending time there lately, too. It could be the biggest thing that ever happened to Pittsburgh. But you asked me just now why I was considering this speculation. Frankly, I don't know. It's amazing, but I simply don't." He shrugged. "Opium, I suppose, has much the same effect; a sort of delirium of the brain. But shall I tell you one thing? I may not know why I'm going to do it if the shares index looks right, but I certainly intend to."

"By all means," I replied. "You can do what you like with your own money, so the best of luck."

"So you don't agree to the idea?"

"I certainly don't."

"Oh, dear," said Hambro, "that's a very great pity," and he smiled his thinnest smile at me, turned, and went out.

I remember that I glanced at the clock the moment Hambro was gone, wondering vaguely what time Belle might return, for I was always worried about her going out alone. It was nearly midday.

At exactly midday the telephone bell rang. Idly, I lifted the receiver.

"O'Hara," I said.

"Might I speak to Mr. Jess O'Hara?" asked a voice.

"Speaking," I replied, and my body went cold. Instantly I recognised the voice.

McNamara.

"Well, well—is that me old friend Jess? Listen, son, me heart's bleeding to have to bother ye, for I know you're a busy man . . ."

I whispered, "How dare you telephone me here."

"Fella, I'm doing it. Gracious God, are ye not happy to hear me? You see, I was thinking of a trip up Fifth Avenue for a sight of ye, for I've not been seeing you for months, and I'm missing ye . . ."

"Get off this line, McNamara!"

"All in good time, lad, but have the great goodness to hear me out. D'you think we might meet tonight for a jug together—at the usual place, or will you receive me in yer wife's fine mansion?"

"Wait," I said, and stood there, my eyes closed, trying to collect myself. The seconds ticked by from the clock above me.

"Are ye vanished, Jess?"

"No, I'm still here."

"Shall we say eight o'clock? There's big things in store for ye, lad, and I'm near dying to spill them—will you be there?"

I heard myself say, "Yes, eight o'clock, at the usual place."

"Man, thank God for ye, I'll look forward to that. Good-bye now."

I put down the receiver, feeling physically sick. For more than two years I had nurtured the dream that McNamara was either dead or in hiding, and now he was back in my life as a threat.

Going into the hall I took my hat and cloak, standing there for a moment in its forbidding, mortuary chill, listening to its silence. I went into the ball-room, where I had first met Belle. It was repulsive still in its flamboyant show of wealth: the enormous, bulging champagne-coloured furniture, huge Corinthian columns, and gilded metopes. Turretted, domed above its six great chandeliers, it stood, for me, as a monument to the lavish mind of a dead Maherne, and regarded me as a stranger. I knew an urgent need for escape from its very enormity, and turned. But I paused at the door when I heard footsteps.

Hambro came through the french windows at the end of the ball-room, and stood there, his size diminished by distance to a three-foot goblin.

"Was that the telephone?" he called.

I said, with an effort, "Yes, I took it—a personal call."

"Are you going out?"

"Yes. If you see Belle tell her I'll be late."

He actually bowed, something he had not done in years.

"Good-bye," he said.

I do not know what took me to Girty's Run that day: nostalgia, perhaps; a wish to bring back the past, and Marged. I walked slowly through the crowded city streets to the Point. The Allegheny lay flat calm and hazed in brilliant sunlight, a scene of astonishing activity. Barges and paddle-steamers, prows foaming, swept to the Ohio like hunting-packs. Sirens hooted, gaudy funnels belched smoke below the serene, green beauty of Washington Heights. I watched, tortured with a sense of an impending disaster. Pittsburgh, in its race for lavish wealth and thrusting progress was slowly, inexorably turning its screw of defeat. I felt enmeshed, in her toils; she who projected the exiles of the world to power and banished them to poverty on a whim. And there came to me that day a need to once more enjoy her smiling hospitality. Turning, I went down to Penn, and to the Duquesne Club for lunch, in search of her gaudy impropriety. Here was the seat of the great names of the city; men like Schoyer, Campbell Herron, Phipps, and Oliver. Here had dined the great Ulysses Grant. Here was planned, over vintage wines, the business transactions that arrowed to the world. I sat alone, despite the friendly nods, the raised eyebrows of invitation; I was determined to be alone and taste to the full the spoils of success, if for the last time. I watched, with dying interest, the animated conversations of the table guests; men whose power helped to build a bank-clearing index of nearly two thousand millions; men who accepted me.

At three o'clock, with the tables thinning, I left, without paying the bill, as usual. Waiters bowed, the door was held open; friends and acquaintances waved farewell. But nothing could obliterate my growing sense of defeat.

A German band was playing on a corner, I remember, a sweet, sad requiem I had heard once before in Pittsburgh—on the night McNamara had lost me my job in Jubec's.

It was nearly six o'clock when I reached Girty's Run. It was bellowing steel. Betsy and Sally were flaring at the sky and their smoke clouds were billowing down the streets of Allegheny. It was years since I had been on this side of the river, and the growth of the steel-works, which I owned, astonished me. Men were still waiting in pathetic groups around the compound gates, lounging in grotesque attitudes of boredom and defeat or gripping the bars with the lust for work, and I joined them, knowing again that sinking sense of rejection. One or two of the men watched me, but did not speak, and I was glad, for I was suddenly, intolerably lonely. Through the drifting smoke I saw the little cottage, the lace-frilled window of the room where I had slept with Marged; still the same bunkhouse, I noticed, where she had brought me morning tea, and I smiled, despite my sadness; that vile morning tea, a habit of the English. Mule-trains were coming in from the canal, coke and ore, pig and finished steel, and the compound was lit with furnace flashes. I waited, watching, but did not see her. The gate foreman approached with keys, unlocked the gates, and swung them wide.

"Back, come on, back out of it!" His accent was Welsh.

Obediently, I stood against the wall with the rest of the deadbeats, then turned as a mare and trap came in. Instantly, I knew terror. The black mare stopped, hooves clattering on the cobbles, neck arched to the bridle. And in the moment before she surged to the gate I heard Marged cry:

"Jess!"

Through the throng of men I raised my face. She was sitting in the trap as if transfixed, her eyes wide and startled. Not beautiful, for she had never been beautiful, yet the sudden shock of my presence brought to her a new and pale loveliness, in her maturity. I gripped my hands at the sight of her. Slowly, she rose in the trap.

"Wait!" she called to the driver, and fumbled with the door. "Jess, Jess!"

But I was away. Head down through the clustered men, I was away from the sight of her, into the thronged streets of Allegheny.

A city clock was striking eight when I reached what was left of Hank's Bar. The building was derelict, the door creaked on broken hinges as I entered the saloon. The counter was wrecked and showered with glass, the remains of splintered chairs and tables littered the floor. It was a scene of vandalism; desolate in its wreckage, deserted. But a light was shining under the door on the landing, the hated McNamara room. The stairs creaked as I climbed them.

"Well! May the holy saints be praised, it's Jess O'Hara."

McNamara rose from his table as I entered. He was changed. The years had ravaged him, at my expense. He was unshaven, the fleshy jowls of his cheeks black with growth. But the stogie still jutted from his thick lips at a cocky angle and he was light on the feet for a man laden with obesity. He opened wide arms to me. Quickly, I stepped away.

"Say your piece and I'll go," I said.

"Is that yer greeting? And years dividing us without setting eyes on each other? Ah, God!" He shook his head in mock depression. "It's a hostile meeting you're giving me, an' it's not worthy of ye, Jess. Must you spit in the face of the only living soul who has helped ye climb?"

"What do you want?" I sat down, watching him.

"For the love of God, listen to it! What do I want? Must you tune every thought in your head to a fatted calf? There's me sitting here trembling for the sight of ye . . ."

I said, quickly, "Waste your words, then. I'm giving you five minutes and not a second more. What do you want of me?"

He sat down heavily, grinning at me. "Five minutes, or none. In the name of common decency may I inquire about yer sweet wife?"

I lit a cigarette, watching him through the smoke.

"I can't, eh?" He sighed. "Ach, that's a pity, for the sigh of a grieving woman is the wail of the world, and me heart bleeds for her, the sweet thing. 'Twas a fearful thing about her father, ye know. It strips me to ribbons to think o' that fella sinking to hell in the mud of the East River, an' no chance at all of floating, with the holes in him."

I scarcely heard his words. I was wondering if anyone was in the room behind him, for the place was grave-silent and echoing. It was unlike McNamara to see me without a guard. He said:

"D'you know who done him?"

"No."

He rubbed his bristled chin, squinting at the window. "One thing's certain—he'll be brewing up tea for the devil himself on the white-hot coals of hell. Would it be the New York shanty boys, d'you think—they're no great shakes, you know, when it comes to landlords—they're hotter than Irish Maguires."

I glanced up instantly. "What makes you suspect them?"

"Och, I was only wonderin' in case you had a line on it. Have you seen your fair brother Shaun lately, for instance?"

"What's he to do with it?"

There was a silence and he smiled benignly, shaking his head. "You know, wee Jess, I'm a terrible fella when it cames to breaking sad news to relations. I remember when poor Ma Mulligan lost her son in the cause. I was a stumbling tongue of words for her, and . . ."

"What's happened to Shaun?"

He crossed himself and bowed his head. "God ease the shaft in ye, my son. I'm here to inform ye that the poor boy's dead."

I closed my eyes, fighting down a strange, leaping emotion; not of loss, but pity. I heard myself say, "How?"

"Dear God, you must be worthy of him, for he died as a patriot. When the last trumpet sounds for the power and the glory . . ."

"Answer me, you damned fool. How?"

He raised his head, smiling. "Indeed, you'll be proud of him. He was doing wee Abe Maherne."

292

I rose from the chair. "Abe Maherne!"

"Rest ye in peace, lad, he didn't suffer. It was a man from Derry and your brother Shaun—the pair of them set off to New York to settle the landlord—according to the oath of the Mollies, you understand? . . ." He tapped the black book under his hand. "But there was fight in the little bastard, for all the wee size of him, and Shaun, you know, was never great shakes with a gun. It took Shaun six chambers to catch little Abe with three of 'em, and the fella comes back and takes Shaun between the eyes. Didn't know what hit him, said the man from Derry. May God have mercy on his unstained soul."

I asked softly, "Does anyone else know about this?"

McNamara grunted, rising from his chair. "Not a living soul, so rest yourself. But it's a tragic state of affairs, come to think of it. There's yer poor wife flooding buckets for the death of her old man, an' you lying beside her in the bed grieving for the brother who knocked him off." He sighed deep. "Ach, life's strange, but I'd have it no different."

Through the rasp of his words I had been listening for a sound in the room behind him, but the silence tingled. The key was in the door but the lock was unturned. It was a calculated risk, I thought. Possibly he was getting too sure of himself and his power over me. This could be my only chance to settle him for good. I knew I was going to kill him; no horror attended the thought. It was McNamara, or me. A month from now I would be blackmailed out of existence.

I stared at the floor in assumed grief. "Thank you for telling me, McNamara," I said flatly.

"Me son, it's no trouble." He opened his hands in a gesture of suppliance. "Sure to God, if I could bring your loved one back to life I'd breathe the breath from me livin' body."

Between the creak of his footsteps on the boards, I listened.

"My mother will break her heart," I said.

"The angels be with her, he was a fine and valiant son."

I moved towards the entrance to the room. "Are you still getting your money regular, Sean?"

"By the Grail!" He slapped his thigh. "You're using me name

293

at last, Jess! The wheel has turned its circle. I'm a terrible enemy, but I'm a wonderful friend. And you're full worthy of that friendship, Jess, the money comes in regular."

"There's more where that came from," I said, and opened the door.

He said, behind me, "But don't be going for a minute, lad. You see . . ."

I spun, back-handing him. And as he staggered I was upon him, seeing the rise of his chin. Steadying my hands, I hooked it with all my strength, but it took him high on the cheek, driving him backwards. He was a big man, and I enjoyed him. Crying aloud with exultant joy I was after him, smashing blow after blow into his face and body. Flattened against the wall, he slowly wilted and I followed him to the floor with both fists, and stood over him.

"Right, that's enough, O'Hara," said a voice, and I swung round to the door of the adjoining room.

My face slack with amazement, I stared at the little man with the gun in his hand.

"Hambro," I whispered.

Hambro came nearer, waving me away from McNamara. He said, smiling, "One must be fair, O'Hara, you were entitled to that. But that was your turn, and now it is mine." He actually kicked at McNamara. "Get up, you fool," he said.

Trembling, I watched Hambro's gun, still disbelieving my eyes. McNamara rolled on all fours and staggered up. His eye was cut, his mouth streaming blood.

"Now, you Connemara swine," he breathed, "I'm flogging the livin' daylights out of ye . . ."

"Leave him alone." Hambro's voice was flat calm. "If he'd had any guts he'd have done that years back. Right, sit down, O'Hara."

"What are you doing here, Hambro?"

"Sit down!" His finger tightened on the trigger. I sat, and there was no sound but McNamara's laboured breathing. Hambro smiled, leaning against the wall. He said, "Yes, now it's my turn, O'Hara. How many years have we been together? God, it seems a lifetime. Yes, Mr. O'Hara, no, Mr. O'Hara. The best years of my life in subservience to you, you damned swine. I've got the brains, but you've got the looks, eh? I do the desk-work and you do the beds. . . . Financier, tycoon, eh? Of all the stupid clod-hopping idiots I've had to work with you take the prize. . . ."

McNamara whispered, "Pull that trigger and finish him, sir."

"Heaven forbid, Sean, there's better ways of killing. How much have I put into your bank, O'Hara? Two million, three? . . . And every dollar I earned despite your stupidity. By God, those years have taken some enduring."

"I know a better combination," I said. "Hambro and the Maguires."

"But you've learned it too late, O'Hara. How much in the bank?"

I turned away. "You flatter me, Hambro. I doubt if I can rake up half a million cash."

"Private account, stocks, bonds? Your wife's settlement—placed on my advice? The bit you collected from Clare Lubinski? Don't bother to add up. I've saved you the trouble."

"As usual, Hambro, you did it once before, remember?"

"But this time I'm having every cent," he said.

"I can't think how," I replied.

McNamara said, "Then I'll tell you. Your name's on the books —a Molly Maguire. There's an oath of death to Maherne in here —signed by your fine brother Shaun, and the man from Derry."

"Your wife wouldn't like it, you know," said Hambro. "A copy of this would send her straight to the police."

"I doubt it. She probably wouldn't believe it."

"Then a copy to the Pinkertons, they'd just love it. They're scouring the states for the last Maguires."

"That means the three of us," I said, but it was bluff, and they knew it.

McNamara laughed, and Hambro said, "Don't count me in, I've written no oaths—neither has Sean, come to that. Apart from the Derry man, whose name is also here," and he tapped the black book, "you could be the last Maguire living. Brother to the one who killed Abe Maherne." He smiled. "You're finished, O'Hara."

"So what happens now?"

McNamara grinned, picked up the book, and went out. I heard him descend the stairs. The door of the saloon closed. Hambro deliberately emptied the bullets from the revolver and laid them in a pile on the desk beside him while I stared with incredulity. "What happens? Just this. This is real financier gambling—the thrill of the risk, O'Hara. We are alone. With one hand you could kill me, but you will not, and I'll tell you why. McNamara holds the capital now, not me. Killing me would merely add to the danger of your predicament, and you will not do that—there would be absolutely no point in it."

"But it would give me the greatest satisfaction."

"Perhaps, but you'd hang, wouldn't you? At the moment you are only faced with prison. Besides, I need not send a letter to the Pinkertons."

"Providing I make my assets over to you," I said.

He nodded. "Every cent, as I said before. You see, it must be a total victory, it is a matter of principle. You have lost, I've won."

"You must have a proverb for that somewhere, Hambro."

He nodded. "I have, but it always escapes me." He fished about for his note-book, brought it out, and read, "Financiers are to financiers what a tiger is to a tiger. Both are savage, both prey on the weak, and are pitiless."

I raised a smile. "You have the lot—and the skirt off his wife."

He did not appear to hear me. I think I realised, as I sat there watching, that he was not really sane. I knew a sudden desire to laugh at the incongruous situation in which I had landed myself. Yet, strangely, I was relieved that the game, at last, was finished. I said:

"Just one more thing. What about Belle?"

He glanced up. "Your wife?" Taking off his spectacles he polished them vigorously. "Not a hair from her head, not a dollar out of her bank."

"Will you swear to that, Hambro?"

"If you wish, but it wouldn't be worth a lot, you know—you'll just have to trust me. You see, the Company Ownership clause is so difficult to bend in law—even with the help of the most efficient lawyers."

"Thank God for that," I answered. "Now what do you want me to sign?"

He patted his breast pocket. "I have the document here. But, oh, dear . . ." he stared around the room in distaste. ". . . not in these squalid surroundings. We'll draw it up properly when we get back to the house." He peered at me with undisguised admiration. "You know, O'Hara, I may hate you but I do envy you that dignity—never, never lose it, it is a valuable asset. You see, it is no use grovelling when one is so utterly trapped."

"I agree," I said, "don't forget the gun."

"Ah, no, that was kind of you." He actually bowed as he opened the door, a habit of Hambro's when he was well on top, I remembered.

We walked home together down deserted streets. He mentioned that the river looked beautiful in moonlight.

CHAPTER 26

Josie, Belle's little French maid, said that her mistress had taken the night train to New York, and might not come back. She told me this in tears, and the shock of Belle's rejection of me at least saved me the embarrassment of a last good-bye. I signed Hambro's document with a flourish. We did not trouble to discuss actual amounts, nor did I examine the papers in detail, so I never knew my total wealth. Hambro's argument was simple; he contended that everything I possessed belonged to Hambro, which wasn't far from the truth. He left me, I remember, with the money in my wallet—about twenty cents short of a hundred and sixty dollars, and he even pondered over that. Strangely, I was happy for the first time in years. Overnight I had descended from riches to poverty, and was content with the situation, which was ludicrous after the long years of intrigue when I had haggled over cents. But that night, in the wide bed which Belle and I used to share, I slept my best sleep for months—a peaceful, dreamless sleep unattended by stock-market apparitions; unsullied by involved projects and transactions. In brilliant sunshine I awoke next morning refreshed and happy. I washed, shaved, and had breakfast, astonishing Maherne's butler with the size of my appetite. Suitably dressed for taking the road, I sat at the long refractory table while Maherne's butler hovered about me as his murdered ghost.

"Where's Mr. Hambro?" I asked, munching toast.

"Mr. Hambro is still asleep, sir. Shall I call him again?"

"No, leave him—he's doing less damage where he is." I took a letter for Belle out of my pocket and put it on the table. "By the way, I'm going away and might not be back for a bit—see Mrs. O'Hara gets this immediately she comes home from New York."

"Certainly, sir. On a business trip, sir?"

"Sort of. This letter explains it."

"What about your mail, sir?"

"Give it to Mr. Hambro, he'll handle it."

I walked out of the dining-room without a backward look.

But standing outside on the sidewalk with my suitcase in my hand, I paused in the jamming rush of people to look once more on the house of Abe Maherne. I knew no sense of loss and no retribution. I felt neither hostility nor hatred; just a vast relief that, at last, the tigerish race for power was over. And the tranquillity that possessed me then was more than recompense for the loss; it was a purifying that swept away the inner, nagging conscience, and made me cleaner. My only regret was Belle, though I had never loved her. The curtains of Hambro's bedroom were still closed, I noticed, as I went down an avenue glittering with sunlight.

I don't know what took me down Water Street to Bluff, perhaps it was a long-remembered wish to keep my promise to Tommy McGrath, and now, in this new freedom, I had found an opportunity. It was a Sunday. Church bells were pealing faintly from the city centre and the air was perfumed with spring. The moored barges on the river were awaking to a bright, forgiving morning and among the dipping lines of coloured washing the sailors were shouting and clanging themselves into activity.

"Creeky Pipe?" I shouted from the bank, and he answered me, stripped to the waist, his razor delicately poised.

"About six boats down, sir."

I found it; a huge, concrete pipe jutting from the foreshore, and went slowly to the entrance. A boy of about seventeen was kneeling before a boiling-pot. He had the lanky gauntness of the undernourished, yet there was a dignity, almost arrogance in the way he rose to face me, his large eyes narrowed in the high bones of his cheeks.

"Good morning," I said.

"'Morning." He tossed the remaining sticks onto his fire, and straightened.

I said, "I'm looking for Tom McGrath."

His clothes were ragged, his boots mud-stained. Jay Kenny? I wondered. He did not reply. Perhaps he had not heard me, so I came nearer.

"Tommy McGrath," I said. "I'm a friend of his. Would you be Jay?"

He nodded, watching me.

"Jay Kenny?"

"I'm Jay Kenny. If you're looking for Tom you're wastin' your time, mister—Tommy McGrath is dead."

I just stared at him, and he said, nodding up the river. "Killed in the Lubinski factory about two years back—fell in the loom."

The wind buffeted between us, and it was cold. I closed my eyes. When I opened them he was bending to the fire again, his gaze steady on my face. Wiping back his bright hair, he said, "Reckon you'd be knowing that since you own that bloody Lubinski's."

"I'm sorry," I whispered, lowering my suitcase.

"You're sorry—that's a good one. What about him?" He turned his back and said, over his shoulder, "You were swell, according to Tommy. He was just a kid, and he talked and talked about you —always the same yarn, about the three of us goin' fishing. Mister, he just jacked up his ideas about you. Every morning coat he saw fetched him out o' here shouting. That kid waited years for you, and you never come." He slopped water into a bucket and stripped off his shirt. Gripping the edge of the bucket he said, "You and me've got nothin' in common, mister. He pointed you out in the street once—you was going up Liberty in a cab with a lady." He ducked his head into the bucket and came up streaming water. Wiping his eyes, he added, "I knew you were Lubinski's, but I never let on; it seemed such a pity—lettin' down a kid. Why am I telling you this? Because you can't do me no harm. After Tommy stopped it I left your Lubinski's—got myself a job over in Girty's Run."

"Look," I whispered, coming closer to him, "if there's anything I can do . . ."

He gave me a sudden, boyish grin. "You're late, ain't you? Jeez, you're late. If you'd come before you could have done something for Tommy. You killed him, mister—if you'd have knifed that kid you couldn't have done it better. Six years we lived in this dirty old pipe, six years we worked for you, but not any more.

300

Christ, we'll give you fellas something when we get goin' in the unions."

"Jay . . ."

His eyes held hatred, and he said softly, "You want to do something, you said?"

Hands clenched, I nodded, and he rummaged in his pockets and gripped something in his hand. "Then you can," he said. "See this dollar?" He held it up before my face. "This was the only money on him when they pulled him clear, an' I took it out of his breeches. D'you see it?" He spun it up and caught it. "I'll give you somethin' to remember him by, Mr. Bloody O'Hara. You know what he said? 'You bust this dollar and you bust your luck, Jay, so I ain't ever busting it. That swell gent gave it to me, an' he's different. Maybe he's got three legs, or somethin', that man, him being a Swell, but he's different.' Gawd! I could have told him, but I didn't. Sometimes we were hungry, but he'd never bust this dollar." He spun it up again and it landed at my feet. "Now you get out of here and take your bloody dollar."

He wept.

Bending, I picked it out of the mud and stood there watching him, but he did not speak again. Face averted, he went on building the fire.

"Jay," I said.

On his knees now, he glared up. "You get outta here before I start lacing."

I climbed up the river-bank to the road. The waterfront, I remember, was almost deserted, but a Salvation Army band was playing in a beautiful, moving harmony from somewhere in Marie Place, and I listened to the tune, "There Are No Flies on Jesus." I stood there till they moved off, thinking of Tommy. Later, I went up Forbes and into a tavern, seeking the oblivion of whiskey. Tipsy, I ate there, and came out in the afternoon. Unaware of direction I wandered down to the Point, and stood there amid the shattered tenements and the dust of the demolitions, watching Mount Washington and the creeping cars ascending the incline. As one entranced I stood there in the grip of sadness, unable to un-

ravel my bemused thoughts, hearing the voice of Tommy Mc-
Grath, seeing his face. When the sun was setting I wandered again.

Dusk was falling when I reached the Alvin, and I saw once again
a magic name.

In the wreathing waves of whiskey, I saw it, and shook my head,
disbelieving my eyes.

Karen O'Hara.

I stared at the walls around me, and wherever I looked I saw
her name on the posters, as if this part of the Iron City had be-
decked itself to her rising glory. The entrance to the theatre was
clustered with people; the foyer, and beyond, was filled with chattering people. And even as I stood there in utter disbelief, the
lights suddenly grew as a beacon and blazed out her name. Karen
O'Hara. In the shadows, I waited, watching. Within an hour the
activity was complete. Cabs and buggies were thronging the
theatre entrance, ladies and gentlemen in evening dress were
jammed in the bright doorway. Through the fumes of drink came
realisation, and with it came joy. Karen was dancing in Pittsburgh.
Gripping my money in one hand and the suitcase in the other I
swayed across the street and pushed through the people to the
ticket-box.

"Good evening, Mr. O'Hara." A pale-faced youth smiled behind
the grille.

"Eh?" I stared at him.

"Only rear stalls and boxes left, sir."

"Give me a box," I muttered.

"Fifteen dollars, sir. Guests with you tonight, sir?"

I paid him, not replying, and shouldered my way upstairs with
growing excitement, for now, alone, I could savour to the full
Karen's triumph. For a long time I sat in the box, staring in pride
at the stalls below, for the theatre was filling. And then, to my
astonishment, I saw Clare and Vaynor, looking as wan as a man
recently leeched. A rising whisper of protest was coming from the
aisles as attendants searched vainly for seats, and I saw Clare
angrily point up at the boxes and I drew back into my seat. My
excitement grew as the whiskey cleared and I gripped the arms of

302

the chair. All the wealth and dignity of the city were arriving to pay tribute to Karen, my sister. Somebody whispered:

"Excuse me, sir."

I cooled his ingratiation with a hostile stare. "Yes?"

"Have your guests arrived, sir?"

"I have no guests."

He wiped his moustache with trembling fingers. "I . . . I am the manager, sir. We are very short of seats. If you have no guests, I am wondering . . ."

"Go to the devil," I said.

"It is only one lady, sir." He stood away, his hand out.

Beside him, framed in the droop of the red entrance curtains, stood Marged.

No Marged of Girty's Run, this one; elegantly dressed, with her hair beautifully styled, she stood there, smiling. I rose, narrowing my eyes for a clearer vision, cursing the whiskey.

"Please come in," I said.

The same old Marged with the same old self-composure. We sat as strangers with two seats between us, eyes fixed on the stalls below. Marged said quietly, not turning:

"I've just won a dollar. Will said you wouldn't let me in."

"Will?" His name was a ghost in the mist of the years. "Where . . . where is he?"

"Back-stage with Karen." She smiled beautifully. Her maturity had brought her loveliness; her dress and jewellery lent her enchantment. "You know they're married, of course."

"Married?" I stared at her.

"Last month."

"Why didn't somebody tell me?"

"Were you interested, Jess?"

"Interested? I'm her brother. Why didn't you write to me?"

She inclined her head. "Hush, don't shout. Karen handles her own business—you know that as well as anybody."

"Didn't she want me to know, then?"

"Look—don't start on me—I'm not a mad O'Hara. Karen makes her own decisions, like the rest of you."

"Well, my God," I whispered. Furious, I closed my eyes as the curtain rose to a strident blare of brass and drums. A troupe of dancers ran on to the stage in a splash of colour, handsprings, and cartwheels, the men's white tuxedoes flashing with spangles, the skirts of the girls flowing to the waist, and Marged moved, sitting beside me. She whispered, "Oh, Jess, I'm so sorry."

I did not reply, for the pain of it was turning deep in me. True, I had drifted away from the family, but nothing could excuse this utter shut-out. The dancers were whirling in a circle on the stage, and I saw them in a blur of light, cursing both Marged and my neat-whiskey tears. Although I sat with an averted face, I sensed her nearness.

"Please don't be unhappy," she said. "I'm sure she didn't want to hurt you. It's . . . well, it is just that you've made your own way. You've seemed content . . ."

"She's a bitch. She knew how I'd feel about that."

"Please don't call her that."

"She's my sister, I call her what I damned well like."

"Lord," she said, "you don't change, do you?" She touched my arm. "Jess, how's your wife?"

"She's another one—she's changed." I turned to her. "We all change, Marged, that's life. You included—Karen, Will, Mike, and Hosea; if things stood still there'd be something wrong with the business of living. Every life has a different direction."

"Hosea's took a sad one, have you heard?"

I could have told her of a sadder one—Shaun's—but I did not. I said, "Yes, I've heard. I'm . . . going to Homestead to see him and Mike."

"Not before time, is it? When he's not asking for Rachel he's asking for Jess. He thought a lot of you, you know."

I was wishing her to the devil. I had come up here to be alone, and she was sending shaft after shaft into me, and I was powerless to resent it, because she was Marged. I did not see the dancers now, despite my staring attention. I could have struck her and kissed her, all in a moment.

"They say you're very rich," she whispered, "but I wonder if you think it's worth it."

I wanted to laugh; thought of an ironical reply, and stifled it, for the music was rising to a crescendo, the dancers were spinning on the stage. The curtain closed to a shout of applause, and the theatre grew expectant, silent.

The conductor's baton came down and the orchestra sang out our old Connemara dances. Slowly, the curtains went aside. Karen was standing there, motionless, her hands upstretched to her tambourine, the same scarlet skirt she wore in Jubec's draping her fine body. With her red hair flowing to her waist, she slowly turned on tiptoe, and the sight of her brought an upsurge of the greatest emotion in me. It was as if the laden years had been rolled aside. In her effortless, spinning grace I was back on Galway Quay with the pennies rolling in, for I knew her every gesture and gyration by heart. And my fingers moved as they changed the tune; tunes that transported me to a Wicklow sky and the bows of the *Pennsylvanian*. I played for her in Bantry and along the cobbles of Dublin, and down the streets of Clare; in Kerry market-place and in a swaying caravan I played for her, until I could bear it no longer, and rose.

"Jess."

"Ach, I'm away, I can't stick it." I was outside the box when Marged gripped my arm.

"Where are you going?" she asked.

"I'm waiting back-stage to see her when she's finished."

"Oh, please, don't do that."

"And why not? Haven't I the right to see my own sister?"

"Oh, you damned fool!" Marged stood before me, face flushed. With trembling lips, she said, "Can't you see she wants nothing to do with you?"

"Wee jakes, we might have drifted some, but I'll never believe that."

She said bitterly, "When you've sobered up you'll see what I mean. Jess, not tonight, I beg you."

"D'you think I'm not used to the length of her tongue? I've been collecting it for as long as I can remember."

"Oh, God," she whispered, screwing at her fingers.

"If you think you'll save me a hammering you can come down with me."

With astonishing rapidity her expression changed to joy, and she took my hand. "I fancy a drink, Jess, will you buy me one—there's an inn across the street. . . ."

"And we'll all have a drink—the four of us."

"You know you're drunk, don't you?"

I was sliding between despair and joy, and knew it. Good sense told me that I should take her for a drink, but I had to see Karen. From the theatre came a rising clamour of applause and a roll of drums. "Quick," I shouted, and seized Marged's arm, but she pulled herself away.

"If you go down there you'll go alone," she said.

I ran down the stairs, round the building and through the door leading back-stage. I saw a flash glimpse of Karen going through a door and Will following her, looking fine and handsome in evening dress. Going to the door, elbowing stage-hands aside, I knocked and opened it, and faced Will. The astonishment of his face changed slowly to fear, and he said huskily:

"Jess, not now . . ."

"What are you talking about—I'm after seeing Karen."

"You're drunk and you know it. Come back tomorrow."

I moved and so did he, guarding me. I said, "Are you her keeper, then? You'll do your dictating to me when she says so, and not before," and I reached out and pushed him aside. He tried to grip me, but I slung him off, and we stood there sparring like cats, glaring.

"Let him in, Will."

Karen appeared in an adjoining door.

"Ah, Karen," I whispered.

The room was heavy with a scent of flowers as I went in slowly. And the sight of her standing there in her simple, gipsy dress brought back the old nostalgic memories, from the quarrels of the footboard to the Connemara stars.

"Right, you've seen me, now get out," she said.

"Steady, Karen," commanded Will.

"Steady, me eye. If this fella wants it, by God, he'll have it."

"Mother of God, aren't you pleased to see me, woman?"

Hands clenched, she approached me, whispering, "Have you kept brothels, Jess O'Hara? Have you had your kids on tread-mills to earn your dirty money?"

"Karen, for pity's sake," said Will, and she turned on him, eyes flashing.

"If you can't stick it you can damned well leave. This is an Irish fight." She swung back to me. "Have you drawn the bones from the backs of the gentle heathen and pounded the faces of Christian Irish for your loot? Eh?" She was shouting now. "Because from what I hear of ye between here and New York you've done all those things . . ."

"What are you talking about?" I shouted back. "Who's been poisoning your mind—this fella?" I pointed at Will. "Is it a crime for a man to be a success? Do you wipe mud in the face of a man because he piles up riches?"

"It's the way you get the money," she breathed. "You've wheedled and schemed and bedded for your wealth, an' you know it. You've sold your soul for the fine fancy graces and spat in the face of God." She stooped before me with tigerish fury, her face white. "You jumped that fat Lubinski woman to start you and slung her off for Belle Maherne." She pointed to the window. "There's sweet Irish begging for food out there while you've been buried in a hoard of money. It's the rents of harlots you've been living on, d'you realise that? Have ye seen those New York shanties and tenements?"

"You've not done so bad," I whispered.

"Aye—on these two spags, and I told you so before. Holy Mother. I'd rather throw me arms round a decent man in the stink of a tanning-yard than see you stand there with your guts tied fancy and the light of hell on your face. D'you know your mother's dead?"

I raised my face.

"You don't, do you? Do you care? Do you know your brother's blind and ravin' and asking for you?"

Will said, desperately, "Karen, Karen, you're back on in two min-

307

utes," but she swept him aside. "Listen, Jess Lubinski, Jess Maherne, whatever you call yourself, I disown you. I disowned you
years back when the sweet Michael told me of yer tricks, so now
get to hell from here before I have ye shifted."

"Karen . . ."

"Come on, get out," said Will, and gripped my arms. The door
opened and slammed behind me. In the rushed activity of back-
stage, the waves, the whispered commands, I stood there and listened to her sobbing. I waited, in despair, sober at last, and the
door opened and Karen came out.

"Karen!"

She walked past me and Will paused, his hand on my shoulder.
"Oh, you fool, did you have to come then? I sent Marged up to
you—what the hell was she doing allowing you down here?"

I did not reply. He whispered, "Look, I'll talk to her—I'll do
what I can. Come over to Girty's Run tomorrow. Marged will be
there, and . . ."

He said more, but I did not hear him. I went through the wings
to the door.

The lilt of the dances were still in my head as I sat down at a
table in the tavern across the street. The place was crowded, but I
wasn't aware of it. I was looking at the whiskey, savouring its smell,
its threatening slant in the glass. I had the fourth glass to my lips
when Marged came in, staring about her.

"Jess," she said, sitting down beside me.

"And what do you want?"

She said, head lowered, "Will has just told me."

"Aye, Will tells everyone. I know where she got it from."

"Don't say that, you know it's not true."

"Doesn't matter now. Have a drink?"

She held herself, looking furtively around her. "Oh, dear, I can't
leave you like this!"

"Why not? Everybody else has. Hey, waiter! Bring another glass."

I thought she was going to cry when she said, "Oh, Jess, don't
slide . . ."

"Who's sliding? On a single family row? That's the Irish—we die for each other, but you wouldn't understand that, being Welsh." The waiter brought the glass and I filled it. "Here—cheer yourself up, you're making too much of it."

"I don't want it." She reached out quickly and took it from my hand. "And you don't want it either, you've had enough." She stared around the room again. "Oh, God, what shall I do?"

I patted a belch and grinned apology. "Nothing, Marged, just nothing. Nobody ever does anything. Life just goes on. What's all the fuss, anyway?"

"Please go home to your wife."

"Go home? Good Lord, you're miles out. Go home—to what?" She said, evenly, "Something's happened, hasn't it?"

I opened my hands to her. "Load me with pity, my dear. No home, no business, no wife—that's what you want to hear, isn't it?"

"Belle?"

I shrugged. "God knows. Right now she's in New York, and if she's wise she'll stay there, poor soul."

"She's left you?"

"I don't think she was ever with me."

"Oh, Jess, you're so friendless!"

I smiled. "You sound as if you mean that. Am I that important?"

"You are, to me."

I drank again. "Don't you pity me, Marged, I've got scores of friends. I've got Hambro and Tommy McGrath, Vaynor and Clare and Katie Virginia—she's coloured, but she's a damned good friend—did I ever tell you about Katie?"

She lowered her head. "I don't want to know about her. Look, I must go." She rose. "They'll be waiting for me. Jess, come back to the theatre with me."

"Not on your life!"

"Then tomorrow? Karen will feel different tomorrow. Will's going to talk to her, and . . ."

"You tell Will to go to hell."

But she did not go. She stood before me, her eyes filling with tears, and said, "What are you going to do, then?"

309

I raised my face. "That's my business. I can't remember when you were concerned about me before."

"I'm more concerned now because something's happened, hasn't it? You'll just drift now, because you're broke."

"Broke? Me? Don't be daft, woman—I'm lousy with money." I rose unsteadily. "My name's good in this city. I can walk right into a bank . . ."

"No doubt. But this will tide you over until one opens." Before I knew it she had an envelope in my pocket. I gripped it, glaring at her, torn between anger and love, humbled by her kindness. I whispered, "How did you know?"

"You can't keep anything from me, Jess, I know you backwards."

I looked away. "You're a damned good one," I said softly.

"Don't you know why?"

I saw her against a bar of chattering faces, upraised glasses, and smoke.

She whispered, "Because I love you. They say you're worthless, and they're probably right, but I can't help it." She opened her hands. "Silly, isn't it, I've always loved you."

She turned without a good-bye, and I followed her to the door of the inn. A brougham was standing on the other side of the street and I watched her get into it catching a glimpse of Will's shirt-front as she opened the door. Leaning there, I tore open the envelope Marged had given me. There was a cheque inside for a thousand dollars, and I read the note she had pinned to it.

'Half from me and half from Karen, to help you take care of poor Hosea.'

Remembering Hosea put me back on the whiskey. Ever since I had met Pat Magee the thought of Hosea was a pester; a nagging sense of duty that could not be denied. And somehow, somewhere I had to find Rachel. It would be useless to go to Homestead without Rachel. But first I had to find myself. I drank, staring into my glass, and the roar of the tavern beat about me unheard. It was a challenge that came quite suddenly. It brought no remorse, no yearning for a cleansing act of expiation, for I was already clean, now that I was free of the hated McNamara. And so, at midnight, with the customers drifting out, I picked up my suitcase and went into the street. It had been raining; the puddles reflected the gas-lamps and the pale, misted moon. I walked towards Soho and the deepest dives of the city.

All that month I searched Pittsburgh for Rachel. From Sharpsburg to McKeesport, Beaver Falls to Uniontown I wandered, calling at inns, enquiring of wagon-trains, and digging deeper and deeper in the slush of the slums. All next April I tramped the roads, sheltering in wayside ditches against the silver rods of rain. I chopped logs for a housewife in Nanty Glo and laboured in the spring fields outside Grafton, seeking the comradeship of the road where a woman might hide the shame of her existence. And then, with the blossoms of May showering the trees of Buckhannon, I came to a mansion by night, a place where I had sheltered before.

The big house stood in its decaying plantations, defaced by neglect and the pillaging swarms. Here, in the faded splendour of the hall had settled the riff-raff of the road; the bone-lazy drunks and prostitutes, and the degenerates that Pittsburgh's destitution offered. I entered the place silently, stepping over sprawled bodies, and stood at the foot of the smashed staircase listening to snores, the bass whispers of men, the bawdy giggles of women. Finding a corner I unrolled my bundle.

"You jist in?"

I turned to the voice. "Shift over," I said.

A tug at my sleeve. "Reckon I know you—haven't we met some place?"

Kneeling, I peered at him. He was raw-boned and big, with a beard on his chest like an Irish shovel, and his red-rimmed eyes were blinking in his ravaged face. "Never seen you in me life," I said. I had walked twenty miles that day, and I was weary and sick of the thought of Rachel Turvey. In the morning I was going to Homestead. I flung myself down on the blanket. The bum came up on an elbow, peering at me through the moonlight.

"Where you from?"

"Pittsburgh," I replied, "go to sleep."

"You ever worked in iron?" He drew closer. "Singer, Nimick?

Carnegie, even?" Silence, and then he snapped his fingers. "Got yer! Lubinski's." He crowed triumphantly. "You were labour foreman."

"You've got a good memory, that was a lifetime back."

"Sure, I've gotta good memory, bud—you shut me out, remember?"

"I'm likely to remember that, aren't I?"

He spat. "Now they've shut you out—serves you right." I expected trouble, but strangely, he was grinning. "Three days you signed me on for, then you booted me. Mister, I starved, d'you realise that? Furnace-tipping—Jeez, you should try it some time." He shook his head in deep memory. "Jeez . . ."

Through the open entrance the fields were white under the moon. Owls were screeching from the undergrowth, crickets cheeping under the boards. He said:

"Then I tried Homestead, but that was worse. I sweated to fill my boots, mister. If ever those Carnegie foremen land in heaven then I'm going left, for hell." He turned back to me. "What brought you down, pal?"

"Money," I said.

"Money? You was lucky. Drink and women got me, mostly women. Man, I just have to have a woman to make me tick, and I've covered more beds in the State than you've had dinners." He chuckled. "And I'm still at it—fifty-eight come Sunday, and I'm a better performer than a mating stag."

"That'll fix you quick. Good night," I said.

"An' Ah'm dyin' fine. There ain't nothing like skirts to drop a man, you know. Anything between sixteen and sixty, gee, they're wonderful. You gotta woman?"

"Had enough of them to last me a lifetime." I thumped my coat into a pillow, and turned away from him.

"Is that so? You ever got jammed on one? Marriage, I mean. Not me. The institute of marriage is a threat to the human race, like I tell 'em. You sleep with a woman—okay. You make it legal and you're handing 'em a club. Mister, you put a club in the claws of an animal and next thing you know you're just beaten to death." He sighed. "But they're wonderful—I'm telling yer. You get cream-puff dolls and tough dolls, some in fancy breeches and some in rags, but they all got something we ain't got, mister, and a flash o' that pride and glory can sink an empire. I read history, you know, an' I can tell you this. You get a smooth, white knee turnin' in a bed and you've got a hook in an Emperor's eye. Next thing you got is ten thousand corpses, all for one goddam knee. Did I say me name was Joe?"

"Look, for God's sake . . ."

His hand was out. "Joe Huckley, sure glad to know you. You want a woman?"

"No, go to sleep!"

"I got one upstairs you can have for a dollar—she's an Irish bitch but she can cook for a savage. Belly O! You know, stranger —she don't ask for anything now except protection. An' that doll don't reckon she's got protection unless I skin a knuckle on her once a week. If old Napoleon had skinned a couple on Josephine things might've turned out different."

I rose on an elbow. "Listen, if you don't shut your face and leave me in peace I'm skinning a couple on you . . ."

"All right, all right, keep your shirt on. Just thought you might be interested, you knowing her, an' all that."

He was sitting hunched up, sucking at his pipe, his jaws champing steadily, his eyes bright points of moonlight in his sunken face.

"I know her? What are you talking about?"

"Reckon you should do, mister—I first met her at Lubinski's. Saw you talkin' to her—Rachel O'Hara." He waved me away. "Aw, I know'd you the second you come in here."

"Where is she?" I threw aside the blanket.

"My, you're real keen, ain't yer—two dollars."

I had him by the wrist, twisting and his eyes opened wide with pain

"Where is she?"

"Upstairs. She's sick." He snatched at the money. "Hauled her in here three days back—that's the trouble with women on the road, they don't stand up to the winters, an' she's been sick all winter." I rose slowly, staring beyond him, and he said, "But she's real sweet with cookin'—I give her that. I ain't never met a woman in my whole life who can turn those hard-rock rabbits into spring chicken like my Rachel . . ."

I pushed him aside and went up the stairs.

Alone, on the landing, Rachel was sleeping.

The house seemed empty save for us next morning, for the sunny dawn had shouted new life into the ragged sleepers and one by one they had taken to the road. Opening my eyes to sunlight I listened to the bird-song of the tangled garden, and rose by a window. With Rachel still breathing softly below me I looked over a brilliant, sun-lit land. In twos and threes the hobos were crunching down the gravelled forecourt and across the dead plantations where a century of labour was being strangled by convolvulus creeper, yet it was beautiful still. Coloured flowers bordered the paths and the park-land beyond was covered with snowy trillium, the two-week purity that dies with a cloud on the sun. Somewhere in the brightness of the morning a meadow-lark was singing, his voice insistent and clear, and I knew a sudden and intense happiness. Rachel, at my feet, groaned in sleep, and turned her face from the brightness. Her face was stained with mud, her ragged dress was pinned tight across her thin shoulders.

"Rachel." I knelt, whispering, and took her hand.

No Rachel of Connemara, this one, yet her beauty was still un-tainted, her face in deep repose. The years had caught her up, thumping her from youth into premature middle-age; fed, washed, she would still be young, I thought, still more beautiful to a near-blind Hosea.

"Rachel!"

Her eyes opened. Recognition dawned, mingled with disbelief, and she sat up slowly, staring.

"Holy Mother of God," she whispered, and crossed herself. "Jess O'Hara. Is it ghosts I'm seeing?" She clambered up. "Where's Joe?"

"Gone," I said.

"Gone, to hell! D'you realise he'll belt the wits out of the pair of us if he finds us together? What are ye doing here, in the name of Jesus?"

"On the road, like you."

"And Joe Huckley's gone, you say? Has he just walked out without the grace of a word and left me to fend?"

"He's gone, and I've come for you, Rachel."

"The hell you have! I'd rather be with Joe." Her eyes moved over me. "But what's happened to ye, man? Where's your dandy clothes? Yer brogues are ruined entirely and you're no better a sample than me."

"Will you come back with me, Rachel—to Hosea?"

"To Hosea? Sure, I'll get a bigger hammering off him than Joe Huckley. Will you explain this? Are you after me death? You were high and mighty in the old days—did you have even a spit for the Turveys then?"

"Rachel, Hosea's asking for you."

"Then he can go on bloody askin'. For between the pair of ye I've fallen on evil times, an' it stands to your account, O'Hara. If it wasn't for yer dirty Americay ticket I'd be alive and kicking today, working the road to Dublin with the cans and pegs, and wearing proper brogues instead of bidin' here bare-footed, and dead."

"Blame me, but do not blame Hosea."

She eyed me, hostile. "Did ye say the big fella's asking after me?" I nodded.

"Is it true, now? For I'll have the skin from ye if you're lying. Why would he be askin' for me when he's got the pick of the women roaring at the ringside?"

"Those days are over, he's blind."

She drew the dress closer about her. "Blind, d'you say?"

"Nearly blind, according to Mike, who's with him. And from the day you left he's never stopped wanting you."

"Blind, is it?" She turned and looked out of the window and I saw, for the first time, the ravages of Joe Huckley, and his kind, for the lines were deep in her face in that pitiless light, her cheeks sunken, their shadows deep. She whispered, thumping the sill with her fist, "The lumberin' oaf! Was I not forever telling him? Have you ever seen the likes of that one for going in leading with his head? Ach, the fool! Didn't I warn him? He could never duck a

315

left, you know. He'd be standing up there taking 'em and spittin' back oaths . . ."

"Rachel, are you coming, for I'm away now."

She turned back to me. "Blind?" Her eyes came bright, and she raised her hands to her face, her fingers tracing down her cheeks. "Would he be seeing me plain, Jess O'Hara?"

"Doubtful."

"In a mist, would it be, do you think?"

"He'd not be seeing you like that," I said, "but as in the old days, more than likely."

"My, that's good," she replied, and turned back to the window. "For I'd be back to him, like as not, with him needin' me. But I'm not needin' him, do you understand?"

"Of course not."

"For I still wear his ring of gold, do you see?" She held up her hand. "Ah, dear, dear! Do you know this, O'Hara? It's a roasting sun coming up today. It was the same roasting sun that rose in Pittsburgh on the day I left him, the big fool. It was all brawn and no brains to the fella, so I left him, but I've been weeping since, you know." She narrowed her eyes. "And you'll tell no man that, Jess O'Hara."

I nodded.

Silence. Birds sang. The wind moved and it was perfumed with spring, and Rachel made a fist of her hand and bowed her head, and said, "Ah, Alannah, ah, me sweet Hosea. The ache within you must have been worse than the hungering for the fancy, worthless bitch ye took to your bed." She wept suddenly. "Barrin' the priests you haven't an equal in the land of Connemara, but I'll never love ye, not as long as I live."

"But you'll come, Rachel?"

She straightened, the pride back, and wiped her face with her hands. "It's a long haul to Pittsburgh, O'Hara, and me spags are troubling me—do you see them cut and bleeding on the stones?"

"I have money, I will buy you shoes."

"Would you be meddling with me in the nights, and me not willing? For I'm sick to me heart with men."

"Just back to Hosea," I said.

She brightened. "And a new dress for this one, is it?"

"A fine new dress, and pretty."

"Why, that's good. Indeed to God, it's a venturesome morning, and I'm obliged to you, O'Hara. With new brogues on me feet and a fine tasselled dress for wearing I'll be as good as new. Could I have me hair washed and combed, do you think?"

"You can have it all—for Hosea."

She tied the girdle at her waist. "Then to hell with Joe Huckley and the likes of him," said she. "It's a wonderful life, d'you know—one never believes what's happening from minute to minute. Have you me bundle?"

"I have it here."

She clasped her hands. "God bless ye for the Christian thing you are, Jess. That's fine, fine. Just lead me across the top of the brae to meet the Big O'Hara."

CHAPTER 27

Homestead

Homestead was sleeping. The moon was flashing on the roofs of its company houses and the mist of the river sent its wraithy fingers down the narrow streets. But the big Bessemers were spurting flame and smoke and an acrid cloud-layer hung over the town. In the thunder of Carnegie's works we walked, Rachel and me, with our suitcase and bundle, and did not speak. Curled up and well washed, was Rachel; new brown dress on, high-buttoned boots, with her waist pulled well in and her hair flowing free, the harlot in her fled before the wrath of her blind Hosea. From Brown Bridge we went down Amity and along the line to Martha Street, knocking at doors, asking in the alleys, until we came to a house. I knocked. And the creak of the floor within told me of the coming of Hosea. Fumbling with the key now, the lock grated, the door swung back, and he stood there.

And his eyes, sightless as marble, stared over my head at the flare of the distant furnaces. Great he looked standing there in his ragged shirt, and bearded, with the red light sweeping over his face. He smiled, and I put out my hand and stayed Rachel.

"Have you no tongue, whoever you are?"

"Hosea," I said, and gripped his arm, and his smile faded into astonishment. His blind eyes opened wide and he cried in joy:

"Jess, Jess!" And reached for me.

"Hey, easy, you'll kill me with your hugs," I shouted, and fought him off, leading him back to the tiny kitchen where he thundered and stamped with child-like excitement. Gripping me, one hand waving, he steered me into a chair, and I sat to please him while he knelt on one knee before me. "Have you come to work with us again, man? Are ye fit for the furnaces? There's Mike been tellin' me what a tremendous power you are in the city."

"Och, I'm solid gold," I cried, pushing him off.

"Can I feel on you, son, for I've lost the touch of yer face," he said, and his fingers traced over my cheeks; neck, hair, and throat he touched, nodding and smiling, and he whispered, "Dear God, you've fattened some since the old days, boy. There's a fine power in ye now, not skin and bone." A train thundered past to Munhall Station, carrying ore, for I knew the beat of it, and he shouted, "Is it true you've been travelling the ports of the world and no time to visit us?"

"Aye, Hosea, no time to come."

"And us biding here sweating out our guts for the wee Scotch divil, while you've been knocking it up with the gentry, getting orders. In England, even?"

I closed my eyes. "Aye, in England, too," I said.

"And what would ye be doing in that damned place. Sure, Mike had no explanation for it. London, was it, in the wealth of the world?"

"Two years," I said, thinking of Michael.

"And how did ye find our Ma back home, then?"

I cursed Michael and his lies. There was no shame greater than sitting there following the lies. I said, "She's as well as can be, Ho, and sends her love. And Melody, too, for she's a fine young woman now and thinking of the fellas. Did Mike also tell ye that Beth O'Shea's left them and that Ma and Melody are on the road with Barney and Rosa, selling the cans between Wicklow . . ."

But he was not listening, so I stopped, watching him, and the silence grew against the beat of distant hammers. Slowly, he rose, staring towards Rachel, and I saw his eyes wide under the humps and cuts of the ring, staring. He said:

"But we're not alone, Jess, I can hear another's breathin' . . ."

Another train rumbled by, and we stood there, the three of us, and only Rachel was smiling. Unafraid, she stood by the door, hands clasped before her.

"Hosea," she said.

His lips moved, making no sound.

"It's Rachel, your woman, Ho," I whispered, and beckoned her to him.

And he wept.

319

I went to the little window above the sink and stood there, seeing their reflection in the glass. As still as black stone they were in each other's arms against the blaze of the lamp, and they did not speak. For many minutes I watched the moon staining silver on the clouds above the Monongahela, hearing nothing but Hosea's sobbing and Rachel's whispers, and presently I left them, unnoticed, and went into the street. It was cold. The Bessemers were flaring, the night trembling to the drop of hammers and the whine of mills, in this, Carnegie's empire. Hunger and prosperity went hand in hand amid this razoring scream of metal. The slush-pools of the pitted road glinted yellow and red, the desecrated town lay sooted and black in shadows, its eyes glinting red like an animal coiled for the spring. On the corner of Dickson and Eighth I stood in the wind of the river, seeing the chimneys stark black one minute, narrowing my eyes next minute to sudden gushes of sunset as the cauldrons turned. Thunder from the rail-yards now, the shunting of engines, the clanking of trucks, but the town still slept in its whispered threats, and I remembered Hambro, and smiled. Strange this town, I thought, that spoke from its sleep.

But when it burst into wakefulness at the end of the night shift, I hurried to Martha Street and waited in the grey, cold dawn, to trap a man from the yards. Shivering, I waited there, and he came, whistling, his cap at a jaunty angle, his face black with coal. Just him and me in Martha Street, Homestead, in soot, when it should have been in the wind off the sea back home in Connemara. Mike stopped his whistling when he saw me, and his arms came down, the barrier growing around him in steel. He pushed back his cap and eyed me.

"So you've troubled yourself at last, is it?"

"Mike . . ."

"Were you invited here, for I don't bloody remember it. Are you short of hard cash. Down to your last million or so, is it?"

"Mike, for God's sake." I pulled at him, and he drew away, whispering:

"Time was I needed you, but not now, Jess. There's hatred in me, because of Hosea, so tuck in your chin, don't tempt me." He pushed me away and walked swiftly to his door, going inside without a backward look. I followed, leaning against the railings, waiting. Gates were grinding open to the men coming off shift, lamps brightening in kitchens, and I heard the scurrying of women and the homely clank of pots and pans. The street awakened, and the door behind me came open with a bang. Michael stood there with a towel in his hand.

He said, "Will you tell me what's happening? I was away to the bed but there's fellas sleepin' in it, and women's things on the floor and stockings on the rail of it."

I gave him a grin.

"The fella's got a woman in there, believe it or not," said Michael. "Do you think he's as blind as he's making out?"

"Rachel," I said.

"D'you think I don't know, ye nit. He's never been abed with anyone since Rachel. It's a virgin house no more, man, and I think I'll be needing company. Do you fancy some breakfast?"

I nodded, going past him but he gripped my coat and pushed me against the wall.

"Are you with yourself at last, Jess?"

I did not answer.

"Jess, did you hear me? Have you found ye damned soul? It looks mighty like it, since you brought him Rachel."

"Not yet," I said.

"You're honest at last, man. And I can't name a town in the world where you've a better chance of finding it than here. Inside with you, you look worn to death." He slammed the door. "That should shift 'em. If she's got any conscience at all the bride'll be up and cooking. I've never had much time for her or you, but right now I'm blessing the pair of ye. Ho! Rachel! Your brothers are back home." He pushed me before him into the kitchen.

Michael said, "The root of the trouble is the reduction of the wage-scale. Carnegie's knocking us down three dollars a Bessemer billet, and the Union isn't wearing it."

I replied, "Is that all the fuss is over? Doesn't the Union know that the world price of steel is dropping, and it's a question of supply and demand?"

"Are you talking as an employer still?" Michael raised his eyes.

"I'm talking sense," I said. "Can you call a man an employer when he's working the same shift as you and not complaining?"

"Aye, fair's fair," said Hosea, and rose and felt his way to the sink to dry up the supper dishes with Rachel. Every night it was the same now; wage-scale arguments and talk of the Pinkerton detectives that Carnegie was sending in in droves. Processions were marching the streets, Union agitators tub-thumping on street corners, and the Carnegie steel town was becoming a closed barracks, with pickets out on every highway checking on strangers. Hosea said:

"Did you hear the Association have hanged Clay Frick and Mr. Potter in effigy? They tell me it was a fine sight indeed to see a Chairman and Superintendent dangling by the neck last night, and when a fella hauls in to cut them down he got a soaking with water." He chuckled.

"And I was aiming the hose," added Michael. "I'm against hanging in effigy. If I had my way we'd be stringing them up in the flesh. D'you mind these Carnegie and Frick chaps, Jess—there's you spouting the employer's angle about the price of world steel dropping, but shall I tell ye this? The wage-cuts are handed to the workers when the world price drops, but there's nothin' coming to the workers when the world price raises, and that's the rub. And there's children hungry in this bloody Homestead while the Carnegies are wallowing in gold. I heard some talk today that two hundred million wouldn't buy them."

"That's a scandal," said Rachel softly.

"And how would you handle him, woman?" Hosea now.

"Ach, it's men's business," said she from the sink.

"And women's too," said Michael. "Whenever there's a riot on the go you can bet it starts with the women, for they're the belly side of life. And one gave a hammering to a Pinkerton detective man only this morning, did you hear?"

"If they land in here they'll collect more than a hammering," said Ho, "blind though I am."

"Sure, one came yesterday," said Rachel.

"The devil he did!"

"Ach, he did. You two were on shift and Ho diggin' the garden, and he comes to the step with fine airs about him, wearing stained clothes as straight from the furnaces and a greasy cloth cap, and him never seeing a furnace in his life, for his hands were softer than mine."

"What did he want?"

"He wanted to know if me men were in the Amalgamated Association, for he said he was, you see. So I told him I had an eighteen-stone one in the garden who was eating Pinkertons for breakfast, and should I call him, and it shifted him quicker than Beelzebub with his tail alight."

"Do you call that decent, Jess, spying on the women?" asked Michael.

I did not reply. I was watching the state of Homestead with growing anger and fear. With the usual sweet unreason of the toilers the men would not go half a yard to meet the demands of Carnegie and Frick, and neither would these two budge a single inch, but I was more disdainful of Andrew Carnegie. He was using Clay Frick to wield the club against the Union and following his usual dodge of simpering the glory of the sweating workers; sitting in his Coworth Park in England sending cables denouncing the attitude of the labour union when he could have been in Homestead settling the trouble himself. And trouble was coming right enough. The workers were heating it up, for they wanted the show-down to come in summer since they knew the horrors of a mid-winter strike, and some said that was what the Carnegies were fishing for, since the men broke more easily.

We were into June now, and I was working with Michael on the big ten-foot plate mill, and had got my Union card with Michael's help. It was a red-hot horror of labour, the first month nearly killing me, with men going out feet first, worse than anything I had known at Girty's Run. It was a mutilating place, this Homestead, with cripples and blind on the streets, some begging, and the amount of compensation Carnegie paid was less than nothing. I was thinking of this now when Michael said:

"It's more wanting more the whole bloody time. Do you remember John O'Hugh you met on the big Carrie? His father collected it under a skip about fifteen months back—as Irish as us, the O'Hughs, you know. The old man collected it in the legs and feet, and left a hand under the wheels. He used to walk the streets here —do you recall him, Ho?—he was a waddling, bandy dwarf of a man when he used to be six feet up, and proud. And the kids used to mimic him and whistle 'Johnny Half-a-man' after him in the street, to make him mad. Was his home in Bantry, Ho?"

"Aye, Bantry," muttered Ho.

"So the Union gave him a grant from the funds to send him back to Ireland to die, for he was pining for the smell of the place. Right, he went, and when he got to Bantry he sent his son a letter. He told that he met Andy Carnegie on the boat in the Atlantic—Carnegie was off for a holiday in his bloody Castle Skibo. 'Do you remember me, Mr. Carnegie?' asked John. 'I do not,' said Carnegie. 'With three thousand sweating for ye in Homestead you're not likely to, of course,' said John, large as life. 'But to sadden your heart I'm being sent home to die without a penny compensation from the firm of Carnegie, and me only half a man now when I used to be six feet up. Has your heart turned to stone, Mr. Carnegie?' "

"What happened?" I asked.

"I'll tell ye," said Michael, getting up. "Carnegie turned on his heel and left John O'Hugh standing at the rail—the dividing spot between the two classes, ye understand—an' that's all he collected in the way of compensation. Can't you see the standard of it, Jess—can you wonder why there's trouble comin' in Homestead?"

The Pinkerton men were on the streets, disguised as workers in the bars and taverns, picking up the whispers of the Union, writing up the rumours and sending the evidence back to Carnegie. As the days turned into weeks and we hit midsummer Homestead was changing into an armed camp. Led by O'Donnell, the Union held a fruitless meeting with the management towards the end of June, and by the end of the month every furnace in Homestead had been blown out and not a wheel turning in the town. Pinkerton men were captured and beaten brutally, every entrance to Homestead was sealed by the strikers. Carnegie called upon the

324

sheriff of Allegheny County for protection, to save his property from destruction, and the sheriff came down with deputies and were hustled out of the town, their proclamations against unlawful acts torn down. Michael said:

"And now they're handing out arms."

I nodded. "More fool O'Donnell, this will be the end of the Union."

"Do we just sit down on our backsides and whine, then?"

It was a brilliant summer day, I remember, and we were sitting above the river, which was calm and hazed with heat. Nothing stirred. The fields around Homewood and Point Breeze were decorated with flowers, and the sky was filled with bird-song. Joyful in the clear sky they nicked and dived, freed at last from furnace-smoke. But the smoke-layer hung heavy over Pittsburgh, and I sat there watching it, thinking of Marged. I had hoped, desperately, that I could gain my rightful place in the family by this return to work; that one day Karen might come to Homestead, bringing Marged. For all ambition had left me now, sweated out, it seemed, in the heat of the mill and open-hearth. And with this new state had come a peace of mind I had not enjoyed in years. Belle was forgotten, Hambro was slipping into the recesses of my mind; all the frenzied worries, all the greeds had been smoothed out of my life by the unending labour of Homestead. There was a quietude, a peace here that I had unconsciously sought for years. It was as if I had transported my body back to Ireland, such was the simplicity of this kitchen living; me and Mike on night shift, mostly; coming home at dawn to Rachel's cooking; sitting with Hosea, smoking a pipe, listening to his tales of the Yankee pugilists. Rachel, her face reposed, would darn and stitch under the lamp or stir the pots on the hob, for supper. And sometimes Mike and me, with Hosea between us, would walk the river in the cold, clear moonlights or slip down to a tavern and hammer it for porter. Church on Sundays, too; kneeling there with Rachel, feeling clean at last in the dust-mote silence of a revived belief, and Ho on the other side of her, eyes open to his eternal darkness. Aye, it was good. And I resented the coming explosion of Homestead that would shatter this new and peaceful existence.

325

Michael said, chewing on a straw, "If they think we'll weaken they're mistaken. Violence will be met with violence, killing with death. For this is the rise of the common people against the greed of the likes of Carnegie and Frick, Schwab, Potter, and the rest of 'em. And for all your peaceful arguments you can't deny it."

"He'll bring in the Military," I said.

"Let him."

"He'll bring the whole force of the State against us, and the Governor won't rest till he has us flat and begging. For if he allows the Union to dictate to Carnegie then the workers will grow stronger and the employers weaker, and that would be a threat to the whole system of rich and poor."

Michael glanced at me. "God, you've changed your tune some since the old days." The sun was on his face, and he was smiling.

"And I'm a better man than you for it, except for one thing. I had to lose everything before I made the change. No man changes, Mike, not when he's loaded with possessions, but there's a marvellous tranquillity when he's relieved of them."

All was splendour and brilliance sitting there with Michael; an enchantment that snatched at breath, and I traced the pattern of my life with an intense and growing shame; that I had exchanged such free and noble beauty for the transient enjoyment of misbegotten wealth. It called for some great and sacrificing act of expiation, nothing short of death. Marged's face I saw on that shimmering day, the laughing eyes of Tom McGrath, and the hopeless tears of Jay; Clare's voice whispered in the lull of Michael's words, Belle rose clear in beauty.

Michael whispered, "You'll be making up your mind soon, I hope, for you're either with us or against us."

I said, "It's not all taking with this Carnegie fella, Mike, so be fair. He's spent his money on schools for you, he gives to the big Trusts to educate his workers."

"To mend his conscience, but does he give the children bread?"

"For all I know."

"Then I can relieve your mind on it, he doesn't. And his gifts are public ones to garner a national tribute; money he has earned like the rest of them—at the expense of human lives and a crushing poverty. They're charging much more for a passport to heaven. But it's not the man Carnegie we're after, nor his brother, it's the things they represent. The Lubinskis, Mahernes, the Hambros you tell of, aye, and the O'Haras, and that's important to me." He rose, looking fine and handsome still, eyes narrowed to the sun. "So if you won't fight to wash the family clean, then Ho and me will be doin' it for you."

"Don't go," I said, "I'm coming."

That night, with the rest of them abed and the hob-nailed boots of armed strikers echoing up and down Martha Street, I wrote a letter to Marged.

CHAPTER 28

I lay sweating on the pillow, listening to the sounds of the night; the grumbling of Homestead's guards on street corners, the rattle of arms-drilling from the Works, and the dull engine-thuds of the strikers' little steamer *Edna*, which was patrolling the river against a Carnegie night attack. Alone in the bed I shared with Michael, I watched the sleeping faces of Rachel and Hosea; as corpses, those faces, so still and white, and their hands were clasped on the blanket. Michael was up at a meeting of the Advisory Committee of the strikers with their leader, Hugh O'Donnell; in the vanguard of trouble, as usual, and I feared for Rachel and Hosea, for all heads would roll under Michael's roof, if we were defeated. And there came to me the temptation to wake them and spirit them out of the house and down to the river; to seize a boat and ferry them to Girty's Run, and safety, but I knew the idea useless. Every yard of the river was covered by workers' rifles. Presently I could stand it no longer, and rose, dressed quietly, and went out into the street. Standing in shadows I watched the pickets pass; most of them armed with staves, but many with guns. Reaching the river bank I sat there in darkness. Behind me the town lay black and dead, rushing into life with each fair face of the moon, before sinking again into squat shapes of darkness. I began to walk aimlessly, suddenly consumed with a yearning for Marged greater than anything I had known before. Torn between sense of duty and love, I wandered up-river towards Pittsburgh, till I came to Brown Bridge. There, beyond the outpost picket, I sat again, watching the river and the *Edna* clanked past me towards the city. Death was in the wind. I had smelled this death on the Connemara roads when the famine people clustered along the reaches of the strand. In the Maumturk Pass when we had raided the grain carts, I had smelled it. It was unmistakable, this tang in the night, a smell that comes in the nostrils of the pegged savage before the raking horn,

328

and scream. For maybe an hour I sat there by the fence that surrounded Homestead, freezing into the darkness as the pickets came up on their farthermost patrol. They passed within feet of me, then turned back to the bridge. Next came the *Edna*, engines silent as the flow took her; now heading for Lock No. I, three miles below the town. Somewhere across the river on Squirrel Hill a clock chimed dolefully. Wondering if Michael was back, I got up, turning. And in the moment before I set my face to Homestead I saw a light coming down the Monongahela from Pittsburgh, and gripped the fence, watching. The light came nearer. Squat shapes of barges came from the mist, towed by a steamer. Nearer, nearer they came, and I heard the chugging of an engine. And even as I cupped my hands to my mouth and yelled the warning of an attack the *Edna* turned down-river. Lights flashed at her masthead and her siren shrieked. With astonishing speed the town lit up. Windows were blazing light as curtains were pulled aside, street lights went on and men and women came running from doors with lighted flares. As if uncoiling its threat, the beleaguered town unleashed into the night. I heard the shrill voices of women, the barked commands of men, and Homestead spilled into the streets. Pell-mell they came, men, women, children, shouting threats and waving arms and pitch-flares, down to the river bank in fury. Every steam-whistle in the town was blowing, alarms were banged on gongs from every street corner. Rifles stuttered fire from the windows, men flung themselves into the mud of the river bank and opened broadsides into the on-coming barges. Running now, I watched the Pinkerton men on the barges firing back from the shelter of the gunwales, and the night was alight with shafts of fire. Down the river went the steamer *Little Bill*, her skipper crouched over the wheel, towing the Pinkertons, Carnegie's hired militia, behind her. And the crowd followed them along the bank. Under Brown Bridge they went in a spray of bullets; now slipping into the dead-water of the far bank to escape the fusillade, on, on to the Carnegie Works where the strikers were waiting behind windows and stock-piles. Fresh broadsides rang out as the barges reached the pumping station, past the fence that surrounded beleaguered Homestead.

I arrived at the fence with the rest of the crowd, suddenly inspired by their rioting anger, and tore at the staves that barred the path. Men and women were slipping through the palings now, disdainful of cover as the Pinkerton bullets whined among them. But the fence delayed us, and the barges grounded on the Homestead bank. Out spilled the Pinkerton detectives, firing on the run, till fresh volleys from the stock-piles forced them back to the cover of the barges. The firing ceased. Gripping tufts of grass I laid flat, peering. The first faint flushes of dawn were rising in the sky. Whispers were flung round in the waiting crowd. Watching too, they laid behind their hastily constructed barricades, and the night was still.

"Jess!"

I turned as Michael squirmed up beside me. He was grinning, his hair standing on end, his face blackened with smoke.

"Doesn't it take you back to the old days?" he whispered. "We're giving them hell, eh? What d'you think of the Carnegie fella now?"

"Clay Frick's in charge," I replied, "not Carnegie."

"Don't you believe it, the orders are coming from Rannoch on the other side of the Atlantic—Frick's only obeyin' 'em."

"Carnegie or Frick, I'm with you now," I whispered. "What happens next?"

"Look," said Michael, and pointed.

A man had come ashore from the barge nearest the shore. Quite still he stood, an easy target to the strikers' guns, and a voice nearby shouted:

"No firing, anybody!"

"That's O'Donnell," shouted Michael, and rose.

"Are you there, O'Hara?" shouted O'Donnell.

"Here," shouted Michael, and hauled me up. "Your chance to make history, Jess, lad, we're parleying with Carnegie men— come on!"

With the man O'Donnell leading we went down the river bank to the watchmen. They had been joined by Pinkerton men now, and they stood in a sullen group as we came up. I looked at O'Donnell, the strikers' leader. Irish, by his voice, his face square and strong in the dawn light. Hands on hips, he went towards the Pinkertons.

"You come with enough noise," said O'Donnell, "is there nobody here with a tongue, then?"

"Surrender the Works," said a watchman.

Mutters and laughs from the men of Homestead as they pressed about us, and O'Donnell cried, "'Faith, it's not as easy as that, man, for before you enter here you'll be trampling over the bodies of three thousand working-men."

"So be it," replied the watchman, "we'll take it by force." He raised his arms to the Homesteaders. "This is the property of Mr. Carnegie, and we are sent in a lawful duty to protect it, so you'll let us ashore or take the consequences."

"Is Carnegie himself aboard, did you say?" cried Michael.

Roars and cheers from the rioters at this, with the women dancing in circles on the river bank and children killing themselves with laughter.

"Or Clay Frick and Potter? Is Mr. Leishman comin' with a gun?"

Hoots of disdain from the crowd, then silence, and O'Donnell said, his voice low, "We're sick to death of the name Carnegie, but the smell of the Pinkertons sticks in the throat. So get back to Pittsburgh where you came from, watchmen, or we'll blow you out of the water!"

The strikers pressed about them, rifle bolts clattered, women took a fresh grip on their clubs and knives. Sullenly, the Pinkertons trooped back into the barges. O'Donnell watched them, smiling, and turned. I gripped his arm.

"And if you get rid of these fellas you're only buying time," I said. "The next ones here will be the State militia, d'you realise it?"

"Who are you when you're home?" said he, and Michael came nearer.

"It's me brother, Hugh—didn't I mention Jess O'Hara, me brother?"

"God help us," muttered O'Donnell. "This is a rise of the labour union—do you have to bring in a failed industrialist, Mike?"

"He came from the people and he's back with the people," whispered Michael.

331

"And I've seen both sides of the fence," I said. "You're only buying time, O'Donnell, and you know it. I've worked with these fellas, and you haven't. After the Pinkertons you'll get the State military, and if you boot them out you'll get more Government troops—in the end you'll get monitors on the river and Government cannon against you. They'll never give up, O'Donnell, and you know it, for the rise of the Unions is death to the industrialists. State, Church, and the power of America are against you, all save God."

He rocked back on his heels, eyeing me, smiling. "You've a fine tongue on you, O'Hara, you ought to be on the barges."

"I tell ye, he's with us, Hugh," said Michael, his fist up.

"Aye? Then let him prove it." O'Donnell added softly, "Now you listen, O'Hara. This is the fight of the common man against the dirt that comes with industrialism. And it's not the outcome of this fight that matters, or the death of me, or you, or the women and kids of Homestead. For we are but hundreds when there will soon be millions. D'you know there's hunger here? D'you know this is the show-down between capital and labour and that a flag of blood will be waving here unless the Union stands? And it stands or falls by us, O'Hara, by the grace and courage of the people at large. Perhaps we'll go down. Perhaps he'll send in troops and blow us off the face of the earth, but you'll never kill Homestead. For the spirit of this town will strengthen the union of decent men and women against the likes of the Fricks and Carnegies for generations to come."

"You'll need the martyrdom of the town to do that," I said.

"And we accept that, too." He was shouting now, and turned to the barges, cupping his hands to his mouth. "So away back to Pittsburgh and tell them we're ready for them. Tell 'em we'll raise such a storm that it'll sweep to the ends of America. Now get off the river, before we shift you."

But the barges did not move. Squat and still, devoid of life, they sat in the river, with port-holes going back from time to time to see what we were up to. And with the coming of morning the people of Homestead worked as beavers, building the barricades higher

332

between the barges and Carnegie's Works. New cases of rifles and
ammunition came in from Pittsburgh. On the opposite side of
the river the strikers brought up a cannon. Aproned housewives
worked, the children laboured, running from one firing position to
another with cartridge cases. The old men worked in organised
gangs, for the Advisory Committee had divided the fighting force
of Homestead into three divisions, each with a military com-
mander and eight captains from the trusted lodges of the Union.
Even the Slavs and Hungarians, eight hundred strong, were under
the command of captains, with interpreters for liaison. Scores of
armed row-boats were on the opposite bank of the Monongahela,
snipers were moving behind windows of the Works. I watched it
all, and smiled as I thought of Hambro again. More than one Pittsburgh industrialist was watching this trial of strength of the Union
against Carnegie, waiting as vultures to fly in for pickings. Andrew
Carnegie, I thought, the friend of the toiler; the penniless lad from
Scotland, now the giant of American industry—safe in Scotland—
was planning an attack on American freedom, besieging a town
with the thoroughness of a Hannibal, conducting his war against
women and children, his bluff now called; vicious to the end for
the sake of principle, and dollars.

The sun was rising in the mid-summer sky, the river steamed
into a day of heat, and all was silent in Homestead. Locked in silence, Homestead watched the barges, rifles sighted, waiting. And
before midday the gang-plank of the nearest barge went down.
Out poured the Pinkertons into a roar of fire from the barricades.
Plumes of water rose about them as they ran, throwing themselves
flat in the mud, returning the fire. But the fusillade quickened,
and they panicked. Retreating, they scrambled back to the barges
and into the cover of the bulwarks, firing through port-holes now,
while the bullets of the defenders rattled on the hulls. Men were
crying from the cabins as the fire got among them; some dropped
on the sun-baked decks, arms flailing in agony till they were
snatched below by their comrades. A woman had been hit in the
barricades, her thin screams echoing over the river. Volley after
volley of fire swept the river; staccato flashes of gunfire winked

along the port-holes of the barges. Trapped, the Pinkerton men lay stewing in the rising heat till the roar of the cannon from the far bank shattered them into silence. I watched, sick at heart. Timber from the two barges sailed lazily into the clear morning air.

And Michael, reloading beside me, suddenly turned.

"Rachel!" he cried.

I leaped up. In a whine of bullets she was coming down to the barricades, leading Hosea. Tripping, stumbling, he came, shouting my name, and I ran to him, twisted Rachel down behind cover, and kicked Hosea's legs from under him, bringing him flat behind the beams.

"You damned fool!" shouted Michael. "Did you have to bring him, woman?"

Sitting behind the barricade she tied back her hair. "Then you try keeping him, for a change—he's like a raging bull up there in the bedroom."

"Would you keep me from a decent fight, Jess?" cried Hosea. "Besides, it's safer here for Rachel. There's a bullet through the front window and another down the hall. Ach, it's like old times— are we winning?"

I did not reply, for I was watching the barges. Hosea said, "Is it true the *Little Bill* has steamed up to Pittsburgh with the Pinkerton dead and wounded?"

"And left those fellas to rot," said Michael, nodding at the barges.

"She's been taking a raking all the way up, did you hear?" gasped Hosea. "There's rumours of dead men on the *Little Bill* herself. God, the way Homestead's doin' 'em they'll be sending in the Harrisburg troops, same as they did for the '77 riots. D'you think that, Jess?"

"Look," I said, pointing.

"My God," whispered Michael, "I bet they curse Carnegie."

The face of the river was stained black with oil that was swirling down upon the three hundred Pinkertons. And from upstream a burning raft was launched. Leaping with fire, the raft came down and the oil ignited with a roar. Down, it came, nearer, nearer, a wall of fire that threatened to engulf the barges and I heard the imprisoned men shrieking with fear. Rifle muzzles disappeared, port-holes were slammed shut as the flames leaped high above the gunwales. I closed my eyes to the cries from the cabins, but opened them to a fresh volley from the far bank. The hatches of the decks had been thrown open and the Pinkerton guards began to pour out, choking with smoke. Splinters flew from the deck-rails as the bullets raked them, a man fell, clutching at a wound, and the flames billowed above him. The rest went flat, squirming in the blinding smoke for the safety of the cabins, and still the burning oil came down under a blazing sun.

"Can ye smell them frying?" asked Rachel, dancing beside me.

"Get down, you bitch," I shouted, pulling at her, for the sickness was rising in me.

"Isn't this what they asked for?" said Michael.

Rockets, fired from the river, were exploding in balls of fire in the oil and fresh flames billowed and ran, preceded by billowing smoke. Shouts and cries were coming from the barges, screams of victory came from the bank behind me. I looked over my shoulder, seeing women and children dancing with joy. In horror, I stared at them, and then back to the river, knowing an utter relief as the wind changed and took the flames clear of the barges, and the sight was accompanied by howls of derision and disappointment. Smouldering, the barges hissed in the water, an oven for the three hundred human beings within.

Michael shouted, nudging me, "What the hell's wrong, Jess, can't you stomach it?"

"This is butchery, not fighting."

"And didn't those bastards start it, then?"

"Not them," I said. "You should be burning the men who sent them, not the watchmen."

His face showed disgust. "Ach, to hell with you. Look, a white flag!"

I stared over the barricade. A man had appeared on the decks of the second barge, running up a white flag to the mast-head, and the cries of anger behind me changed to cheers as he staggered and fell in a hail of rifle-fire. Buttocks arching, he flailed around the hot deck, and the next volley stilled him. So still he lay, arms outflung, his face turned to the sky, and the white flag slipped down from the mast-head and covered him as a shroud. Now men were racing from the Works to the river bank, disdaining the desultory fire from the barges. There, close to where we were lying, they broke open boxes of stick-dynamite. Laughing, gesticulating at the crowds behind them, they bent to the business of tapering fuses; lit them, and threw. The Monongahela shuddered to the blinding explosion. A hatch door blew up, exposing the jammed bodies of the trapped Pinkertons, and immediately shore-fire raked the hole, searching for victims. Another bomb sailed over, landing on the roof of the barge. Smoking, it lay there and the attackers held their breath. A blaze of fire and boards shot up, followed by a man's hat making strange gyrations in sunlight. Fresh waves of men came marching to the river bank, from the Edgar Thomson Works at Braddock; strikers from Pittsburgh, even, rallying to the cry to destroy Carnegie. And the barge farthest from the shore, in which were crammed the desperate Pinkertons rocked and bucked to the impact of the bombs. And at midday, with the sun high, three men scrambled from the cabins to the prow of the barge to rescue wounded comrades. This was the signal for the most brutal firing. Two more men dropped; others darted out to rescue them in a hail of bullets, and the Pinkertons retreated into their stifling coffin. Lying there in the heat of the sun, I looked at Rachel. Her face was moving with excitement, her eyes were alive with the lust to kill. I looked at Michael. Gone was the Michael I knew. He was gripping the top of the barricade, his hair awry, teeth bared as an animal; now screaming at the sky as the bombs descended on men impotent to defend themselves, men outnumbered by fifteen to one. The bile rose in my throat and I swallowed it down. Animals, I thought, all animals; from the lowest intelligence in Amity Homestead to the highest Superintendent of Works; Carnegie, Frick and Potter, O'Donnell, and Michael O'Hara; Rachel, aye, even Hosea, who was grinning, and Jess O'Hara—all animals, with the pitiless claws of animals, in the jungle of Homestead. Hambro was right.

I rose, unseen, for the people of the town were crowding down to the river bank now for the final attack that would kill three hundred men; men who had lain for a day in the packed holds of a barge; who had suffered the torments of fire and bullets and explosions; men as trapped as the British soldiers who, over a hundred years before, had suffered this same torture in this same place, in the searing fire and the shrieks of men uncivilised. In the space of hours, before my eyes, the veil between civilisation and barbarity had been torn aside. Over a hundred years of progress had taught us nothing, I thought; we were back where we had started, to the inhumanity of the Redskin.

Suddenly the firing ceased, the dynamite explosions reverberated into silence. Standing near the Works below the mass of the people of Homestead, I looked again towards the river. A white flag was waving, the Pinkerton men streaming down the gang-plank of the barge. Many were wounded and being half-carried by comrades, many were spent, staggering on to the bank. And they were herded as cattle, these men, bare-headed, in single file, to run the gauntlet of blows and insults. On either side of the path to the mill and the public road beyond, the men, women, and children of Carnegie's town gathered, a snake of screaming, infuriated people that reached for a mile. And the watchmen walked, ran, or crawled this mile to a rain of blows from sticks and cudgels, musket-butts and stones. Beaten nearly senseless, they ran the same gauntlet of the Indians. They were flung on to all fours and kicked along, they were jabbed at and prodded and lashed with sticks. Bruised, bleeding, some weeping, many walking proudly, they were shrieked at by women and spat at by children. Streaming blood, they were battered by the fists of men and booted by crones; some hobbled, guarding their broken limbs, begging mercy, and there was none, their pleas urging their torturers to even greater fury. One, I remember, walked erect, as a soldier marching, bare to the waist, accepting the lashes and cuts with disdain. Hands on hips he walked, bleeding, defiant, the one pure human in Amity Homestead. And when the last man staggered into the gauntlet the crowd closed in behind them, sticks coming down, fists raised. I watched, sickened, listening to the animals.

The river bank was empty. Alone, I looked down at the river

and the burning barges, for the workers had first looted them, then fired them, and for me their funeral pyre was a testament to the bestiality of the day. I walked slowly down to the edge of the river, stepping across the discarded arms of battle, the broken barricades where blood-stained bandages were fluttering. There, I listened to the fiery crackle of burning timber, the sounds of summer, and the distant cries of the prisoners. The Pinkerton dead were lying on the bank as men asleep in sunshine, their faces covered against the vicious rays of the sun. Soon, I thought, they will come and bury these men, and they will be no more, save in the hearts of sobbing wives and children. But I envied them their peace, these nameless ones now freed of the battle of life.

Sitting on the grass, chin cupped in my hand, I stared towards Pittsburgh. Still billowing smoke, this mighty one, still snatching at the last minutes of the day shift, to draw the last line on the day's graph of profit. Financier would still break financier there, as Hambro had broken me, I thought. The McNamaras would still scheme the downfall of some unfortunate, blackmail would follow blackmail, the strong wax fat, the weakest crucified. How sad, I suddenly thought, that Christ should die for these most greedy, aimless ones. And the realisation that my fine ideas of self-cleansing had come to nothing brought me to empty bitterness. I rose, wandering the bank, kicking at things, and found myself standing again above the Pinkerton dead. Staring down at them, examining their grotesque attitudes of dying, I knew utter and complete defeat. Dusk was falling as I walked towards Pittsburgh, and I was thinking of Marged. The one substantial human in this world was Marged.

I walked towards Pittsburgh, under Brown Bridge, and came to the Homestead boundary fence. Here the strikers' attack boats were lying beached and I dragged one into the shallows, climbed into it, and began to row towards the city, one eye open for roving pickets. Rowing steadily through the gathering darkness I began to wonder what would happen to Hosea, Mike, and Rachel. Soon, I knew, the National Guard would come and sweep Amity Homestead into a town of tears. No plea of the brutality of men like Frick and Carnegie would save those who had opposed them, for

Homestead had revelled in its own brutalities, and deserved no pity.

The river wind was cool on my sweating body when I stripped off my shirt and rowed faster. Homestead was dying into the shadows behind me, and I heard, distantly, the crying of the captured Pinkertons and the howling of their tormentors. Workers and masters alike, I thought; their brutality shocks, their hypocrisy sickens. And Carnegie, the friend of the toiler of Homestead, was three thousand miles away in Scotland, fishing.

CHAPTER 29

I put the boat ashore at Peebles Township and walked up the river to Bluff, stopping for a moment in every well-known place; the rock where Karen and I had slept some fourteen years before; the bank where I had seen Tom McGrath, the pipe where Jay Kenny lived, the tavern where I had first met Katie. In the blinding light of its windows I stood, listening for a trumpet, but heard instead the sweet, sad song of a melodeon. It was playing a song of home, but I did not weep. Up Water Street and Duquesne I went, looking at the people, the white-faced wanderers going on shift, the eager faces of the merry-makers. Brilliant was the Allegheny with her swaying masts and spars, with lights winking from Coal Hill, and the great Ohio sweeping along in glory. Hoof-beat and the iron ring of wheels, the crack of whips, the thin voices of Italian beggars crying for alms. Still the same old Pittsburgh, I thought, unchanging, unchangeable; bountiful and miserly, caring and uncaring. A Negro drunk now, white teeth blazing in his face, arms outspread, roaring a song at the sky; now a black-robed priest hugged in his visions of the all-saving Christ, neglectful of children wandering off shift. I leaned against a wall, and watched. Then I went to Jubec's, I don't know why, and found it vanished. Not a trace of Jubec's in the big office block, the place where Karen had danced. In the coming moonlight I walked to Hank's Bar. Demolition contractors were working here, and the building was sliced as with a gigantic razor. And the razor had cut through McNamara's room, exposing the faded wall-paper, and the door I remembered so well, but I knew no hatred; I knew only peace, standing there in the dream of Pittsburgh, and the dream took me on to Fifth, and Maherne. There, on the sidewalk facing the great house, I leaned against the railings and watched the windows, looking for a sight of Hambro. But I saw, instead, the image of Maherne, his butler, standing under the chandeliers with his old servility. The beard was inches long on my chin these days, and I rubbed it, grinning with ironic joy. For the man sitting at table was McNamara, not Hambro. In regal grace he sat, his chins bulging over his white napkin, shovelling it in like a feudal baron. Triumphant, with the vulgar ostentation of city success, he drank and fed, snapping at the food as a dog snapping at flies, and I pitied Hambro. Far better death than to be loaded with McNamara. I could have cheered him. I could have knocked and waited and pushed past the butler and presented myself as a life-long friend, but I did not, for the wheel of my life was completing its circle; the last degrees were closing with such remorseless certainty that I could not delay them, if only to discover what lay after.

Girty's Run.

It was suddenly imperative that I should once more see Lubinski's monument. Still smiling, I went back to Duquesne and crossed the bridge into Allegheny and walked down to Girty's Run.

This time I did not go to the gate, for I was fearful of being seen, despite my longing for a sight of Marged. Still the frightening activity of steel, the clanging, the smoke, the Bessemer roar. I thought I saw Shaun at the gate, poor, condemned Shaun, and sighed. I thought I saw Will, but I did not. But I knew a certain pride standing there in the darkness, enveloped by the giant that I had schemed to build. Presently, hands in my pockets, I wandered away.

There was a church I knew. Until this moment I had forgotten its existence; a place where Marged and I had once entered, when there was spring and love in Pittsburgh. It was Catholic, I think, but I had never been sure. We had gone there one bright, sunlit evening, I remember, hand in hand, and wandered up the aisle in the cold silence, our footsteps reverberating on the flags. And now, through the thunder of Lubinski's, between the siren-shrieks of the waterfront, I heard its tolling bell. Plaintive, thin were the chimes, making the night into Sunday. And the sound of the chimes ripped back the darkness into that bright, April day.

Pretty, that April Marged; big straw hat shining yellow on her shoulders, bright, flowered dress sweeping out in crinoline, and black was her hair.

Damned old Lubinski's!

Rotten old Lubinski's . . . I heard her voice again and again.

I smiled now, remembering the sweetness; remembered, too, that day on the Ohio, when we made love; when the blushing prim slaps she gave, the eye-closed whispers of rejection turned in quick heat to an abandoned giving to Jess O'Hara, who took, and gave back nothing. Only this, so strangely . . . only the vision of Marged brought sadness, and repentance.

Up a dando, she said. Whee, look at the time! Poor old Will must be having a fit with his leg up. Whee! Oh, Jess . . . Jess!

I walked on in the darkness, clenching my hands.

"Good-bye," I said, and turned once more to the blaze of Girty's Run.

You silly, *bloody* fool, Jess O'Hara.

On the sidewalk opposite the little Catholic church, I counted my money. Forty-one dollars, fifty-two cents. Down to the Emigration first thing in the morning; train to Philadelphia, then ship to Liverpool; across the Irish Sea, and into Galway, down the road to Rossaveal, and up to Connemara, me. No damned point in staying. Off with the fancy accents, I thought, on again with the rollicking Irish. Welsh girl, Irish girl, Marged Rees or Rosa Turvey —or the like of her, cutting up the peat for a cottage by the sea. And I knew not the slightest hint of self-pity, or grief, save for Marged.

Eyes closed in that grief, I stood facing the church.

The people were coming out, in twos and threes, the matrons with dignity, stark black in their worshipping; frock coats and big buttons on the men; bulging men with well-creased waistcoats, skinny men, sallow in the face, in misery for their invisible Lord, when they should have been dancing in the streets for the glory and humour of Him. Top hats coming off now, Good evening, Mrs. Kroyshny, Good night, Mr. Mulligan. Bowed good nights and curtsied greetings—all the fussy, clustering fellowship of the after-service joy, the washed-clean sense of purity that only Church can bring, and all its sincerity. They jabbered, they laughed in common gaiety, and I envied them. One boat after another, missed, always missed . . . Lubinski, Maherne, Hambro, and McNamara . . . and I could have had this, sharing it with Marged.

I watched.

The street was emptying. Against the misted stars of the city sky the lych-gate beckoned. There was no all-saving grace in me as I went through it and up the flagged path to the church door, no heaven-bred yearning for a cleansing. It was simply that I had remembered this place and now sought its friendly image of a well-beloved, as one recaptures time in touch and smell, or the taste of a vintage cup. Incense was heavy in the cold air, a ball of mist around every lighted candle, a halo wreathing about the golden altar, where Christ hung dying. Wonderful, I thought, how Marged had wept that bright, spring day, seeing it in sunlight.

I went in slowly, oppressed by the tombstone silence. Catholic, of course.

Presbyterian, Protestant, Congregational and Baptist, Catholic, too—all the same to Marged. I smiled, listening to her echoing whispers, and was no longer quite alone.

What you talking about, boy? Any church will do. You'll find no peace in those dirty old taverns. Catholic, is it? Eh, Jess, there's damned stupid! You can talk to your God in a back pew of chapel or go on your knees with a beggar Jew. Same old God, mind, same little Jesus . . .

A rustle of silk as she slid along the bench.

Your church, remember, and time you remembered it. Down by here, Jess, show some humility . . .

It was suddenly important that I should find the right pew, to sit where I sat that day with Marged. Fifth row down? I wandered, searching for something with new desperation, strangely remembering the Pinkerton dead, and the blood-soaked ground of Amity Homestead, and why this should return to me I never understood. A knot in the oak, was it? A shake, a wane, or merely a cut of a careless adze?

It was a knot in the bench; a little mouse-and-tail knot I had seen on that day when I had knelt in this place with Marged. But

343

I did not kneel now. Sitting there, I thought of her, staring at the knot so polished and brown by the hands of Pittsburgh's generations. For the first time in years I was complete, in the lost company of Marged. I stiffened to footsteps a moment later.

A door creaked open and slammed shut in the pin-drop silence. Heels hammered the stone flags with the urgency of Homestead musket-fire, and my conjured visions fled. Seeking obscurity, I sat motionless, head bowed, but the footsteps came closer. I raised my face as they reached the altar rail. With patriarchal dignity an aged priest was standing there, smiling over the crimson sea between us.

"Good evening." As Irish as a Dublin cobble, that voice, and I was glad.

I nodded back.

He said, "Will you be staying long, son, for I'm after closing the church."

Rising, I answered, "No, Father, I'm away just now."

He came nearer, his hair flowing white over the shoulders of his sad-black cassock. "There's no reason for hurryin', you know —that's the trouble with the world—it's always running somewhere, and there's no rest for any of us save in the house of God."

"I was going, anyway."

He came around the benches towards me, and I felt trapped. The chasm was too wide between us for leaping, my shame too strong. He whispered, smiling:

"Might ye be needin' me, son?"

I shook my head and he turned, waving towards the Cross. "Or Him, then? Man alive, you don't come into an empty church unless you're needing something. There's people come in here for weeping, repentance, shame, or joy. Which would it be, son? The confessional, for instance?"

"For shame," I answered, "but I'm not wanting the confessional."

He hunched himself, spreading out his hands. "Then I'll not be pushing ye, for you know your business better than me. God bless you, anyway," and he raised his head, staring past me down the aisle. "Ach, would you believe it? There's more folks wandering

344

the place this night than sitting in at the service. Are you wanting me, young woman?"

I turned at the bench.

In the dim light I saw her, and knew no heated trembling of excitement, no surprise. It was as if I had looked for her, and found her; that she had been standing waiting there through years of time, carved from the visions into reality.

"Marged," I said, and took my bundle against me and went down the aisle to meet her. The shadows were deep under her eyes in the strange light, her shawl pulled tight over her head and her face was shining with rain.

"So you came again, Jess?"

I did not reply. It was enough to be standing beside her in this sweet and sudden calm. She whispered:

"The end of the road, is it?" and smiled.

"Aye."

The metal-tipped boots of the priest clattered between us. One by one the candles went out.

"You're wet," I said, smoothing her coat.

"To the skin," she said, "like a duck in a thunderstorm. And you with no coat at all? Stupid! Are you coming?"

"Yes." I opened the door, and the night drizzled at us, the downspouts flowing and splashing, and the bright cobbles of the road were flying in drowning sheets to the river.

"It was Will who saw you," she said.

"Will?"

"He was up in the bedroom window, making ready for the night train north, and he saw you, so I followed."

"Ah, yes."

"And I knew you were bound for here. You don't mind me saying that it's not before time, do you?"

"You said that once before."

The tears flooded to her eyes then, and she smiled. Wisps of her hair were prematurely turning grey, I saw, against the black scrag of her shawl.

"My God," she said softly, "I've waited long. And if they asked

345

me why on the Bible itself I'd never know the reason. Where are you going now?"

"Back home."

"And where's home? Pittsburgh, Wales? I never know."

"Ireland," I said.

She sighed. "Then Ireland it is. One place is as good as another, I suppose, when you're living in sin." She looked at the leaden sky. "Twelve years out of my life, Jess, oh, what a waste of loving."

"You're wanting to come with me?"

"I'm telling you I'm coming. If I'd told you instead of begged you these twelve years back your life and mine might have been different, so I'm taking a hand. Damned old Lubinski and Belle Maherne, rotten old money!" She shot me a look to kill.

"That's better," I said. "But what about Will?"

"Don't you bother, he can manage. Two women in one kitchen now, you know." She spread part of her shawl over my shoulders and stepped out into the rain. "Karen O'Hara might be a gift from heaven to you, but she's a devil to live with, bless her."

We walked on in the rain, and did not speak.

"Where's Karen now?" I asked as we neared the Works.

"Up in New York. Will's away up there to meet her."

"So the house is empty?"

She smiled. "Would it be the first time?"

So I sat by the same fire where I had sat before while Marged busied herself about the kitchen, and felt at rest, at last; such was the sweet peace after the maddened race of the years. Presently the rain stopped and I went into the compound. A mist was billowing down the face of the river, the mast-head lights were dimmed. But Coal Hill was ablaze with windows, and the glare of furnace and glass-works heaved red and vicious against the smoky sky. Somewhere a clock tolled midnight through the thunder of Allegheny. I closed my eyes.

Clare would be sleeping by now, I thought; Vaynor beside her still, perhaps, smothering his conscience in his dreams of grandeur. Belle, far away, might be thinking of Jess O'Hara, the one she loved, not the one she hated. Rachel, Ho, and Mike would be under the roof of Homestead, gripped in the spell of O'Donnell's fight for power—the tools of a newer, vicious ideology. Hambro would be wandering his ice-cold world of shares and holdings, Mc-Namara triumphant in his patent vulgarity, swallowing the profits. And the ghosts of others were about me now. Did the wraith of Tom McGrath wander the river in his lust for fishes and decent men? Did the ghost of Pat Magee still beg in my despising, for he, surely, was not living. And Katie Virginia in her ornate house? The pet poodle of a big city dog, when she could have been loving with Johnny in Virginia. Shaun I remembered next, and bowed my head.

Dreams, all dreams.

Here, in this pulsing, straggling sea of concrete and bricks set in the Land of the Fork, others had dreamed, and found that their dreams had come to nothing. Land of the Whiskey Rebellion and the Pontiac wars; of Moravian missionaries and Simeon Ecuyer; here, in this place of water had rested the ambitions and greeds of a hundred races from German frau to Indian squaw, and their loves.

How small the race of Jess O'Hara.

Light swept the path from the door behind me, and I heard the clatter of pans and the tinkle of cups.

"Ready, Jess. You coming?"

"Aye, coming," I said, and closed the door.

347

E9